THE ENGINE HOUSE

A DCI EVAN WARLOW CRIME THRILLER

RHYS DYLAN

WYRMWOOD
BOOKS

COPYRIGHT

ISBN 978-1-915185-01-3
eBook ISBN 978-1-915185-00-6

Published by Wyrmwood Books.
An imprint of Wyrmwood Media.

EXCLUSIVE OFFER

Please look out for the link near the end of the book for your chance to sign up to the no-spam guaranteed VIP Reader's Club and receive a FREE DCI Warlow novella as well as news of upcoming releases.

Or you can go direct to my website: https://rhysdylan.com and sign up now.

Remember, you can unsubscribe at any time and I promise won't send you any spam. Ever.

OTHER DCI WARLOW NOVELS

CAUTION DEATH AT WORK
ICE COLD MALICE
SUFFER THE DEAD
GRAVELY CONCERNED
A MARK OF IMPERFECTION
BURNT ECHO
A BODY OF WATER

CHAPTER ONE

COLIN TOMLIN GLANCED at the sky before pulling back three layers of sleeves to look at his watch. Bad weather was coming in, and they were only halfway to their destination. At five minutes past one in the afternoon, he began packing the flasks and Tupperware away and turned to his wife, Julia. 'I think we'd better get a move on.'

The Tomlins were examples of those hardy people who, like every other resident of the western side of Britain, did not need newspaper headlines to tell them it had been the wettest month in one of the wettest winters ever. All they needed to do was look out of their southwest-facing living room window. Day after day through December and January, the citizens of Penzance, Barnstaple, St David's and Aberystwyth awoke to the noise of battering winds and slashing rain driven in from the Atlantic via the Irish sea. Drab dawns brought soggy confirmation as one anticyclone followed another, as if an elemental beast stalked the coast. And someone's bright idea of giving the storms innocuous names like Brendan, Ciara and Dennis only added insult to injury.

Occasionally, the beast rested. When it did, the watery

sun lit up flooded fields, drowned vehicles and submerged homes ruined by filthy water that spilled from swollen rivers roiling with power. During respites, the cowed citizens needed little excuse to escape confinement: exactly what Colin and Julia Tomlin were doing on the Pembrokeshire coast this late winter day.

They'd got up, greeted the sun – for once – and decided there and then. Both in their early sixties, and both fit, the urge to do a 'proper walk' made Julia get the ham and mustard sandwiches done while Colin dusted off boots and backpacks. They were in the car and off by eight thirty. Poppit to Newport was a rugged, remote stretch of the coastal path; a good thirteen miles at least. But with the height of the cliffs, the constant up-and-downs equated to a hike up Snowdon. They'd walked this stretch in summer twice over the years but hadn't done a good ramble since Christmas.

They'd taken two cars, Colin following Julia's Renault to Newport, where she'd parked in the beach car park before joining him in their tiny SEAT for the run up to Poppit Sands. The Poppit Rocket, the bus linking the two locations, didn't run every day in summer, let alone in winter, and given the parlous state of the weather, Colin hadn't wanted to take the risk. So they used the old trick of leaving one car at the start and one at the end of the walk.

They'd made excellent time, too, and stopped for lunch about halfway along, their backs to the rocks in the lee of the brisk onshore breeze. Julia had given Jasper, their five-year-old Cockapoo, a handful of biscuits but kept him on the leash. The Tomlins had read too many stories of boisterous dogs, caught up in the frenzy of a seagull chase, going over the edge.

Colin noticed the low clouds building to the west over the last half hour. He expected more rain by nightfall but what he didn't want was a sea mist. Not with less than four hours of daylight left and six miles to go. The Tomlins had met no one that morning, apart from two walkers ahead of them who'd taken the only other way off the path to Moyl-grove. Now, with the afternoon ahead, only the cliffs lay before them.

'Got everything?' Colin looked over at Julia.

'Yes. Want a fruit bar?' She unwrapped a date and apricot rectangle she'd made herself.

'Later.' Colin waved away the offer and arched a stiff back before grabbing Jasper's lead and setting off. 'Careful up here,' he called over his shoulder. 'There's a good size runoff.'

A great deal of rain was finding its way to the sea through channels in the sodden earth that had been bone dry the last time they'd walked this stretch. Not so today.

'Did I read somewhere that there's only a fixed amount of water on the planet and it all gets recycled through rain and evaporation?' Julia splashed through a puddle.

'Knew those Geography A-Level notes of Dan's would come in handy one day.'

'Is that why you won't let me throw them away?'

'Someone might want them. Grandchildren—'

Julia puffed out her cheeks. 'Don't make me laugh. No one will be reading from textbooks by the time we see any grandchildren. It'll all be downloads straight into your brain via laser by then.'

Colin smiled but didn't turn around. Julia's grasp of the sciences had never been her strong point. Like a lot of couples, it was one of many differences that both separated them and made them paradoxically compatible. But when it came to family, they were of one accord, though Colin would never admit it.

'It'll happen. Jordan seems a nice girl.'

'How can you tell underneath all that makeup?'

Colin's smile turned into a snort. Mothers and their sons. Girlfriend discussions were always thin-ice territory.

He stepped gingerly over a gushing rivulet.

'If that's true – about the water, I mean – someone needs to tell the Management it's okay to send it somewhere else. We've had more than our share this year, thank you very much.'

'Tell them yourself,' replied Julia. 'We're as close to Head Office as it's possible to get here.'

Colin didn't answer. He paused and looked up into the vastness of sky, water and land all around him. The Irish Sea stood before them, leading out and down into the vast Atlantic to the south and the cold treacherous expanse of the North Sea in the other direction. If you jumped into a boat and missed Ireland, that was it for a long, long way.

Julia had a pithy knack of summing things up. A sharp, sardonic edge that cut through when miffed. A state which talk about Daniel and Jordan always seemed to trigger. But she was right about the landscape. If ever there was a place where the lines of spiritual communication might be open, it was probably here, on the very edge of solid ground where it gave in to the ocean. Colin let it envelop him, this sense of weather and space; let it remind him of how small he was in the grand scheme of things. A visceral antidote to the minor irritations of life.

Perhaps that was why, for a fraction of a second before they heard the roar, when the ground beneath his feet trembled and he threw out a hand to grab a rock for support, Colin wondered if someone or something had been listening. A fleeting thought drowned out by a rumble, growing louder, pierced by the crack of enormous stones colliding, and the splash of something huge and heavy hitting the water below.

A shuddering bolt of fear shot through him. 'What

was—' His words froze when he turned to see Julia pointing behind her towards the path.

There, fifteen yards from where they'd sat and had lunch, the cliff had fractured. Earth and rocks were still tumbling down, rolling over the raw surface of the new face. Where the track had been, a bare concavity of rock and soil arced back towards the field behind. Colin mentally filled in the blanks. Nature's weapons of attrition, the wind and rain, had eroded the soft ground and stolen into rocky fissures over millennia. The recent unprecedented rainfall must have tipped the precarious balance enough to send a hefty slab of Pembrokeshire sliding off into the hungry sea.

'Lucky we moved when we did,' he murmured.

Intrigued, Jasper jerked forward, the lead slipping from Colin's grasp. Yelping, the dog bolted back towards where the trail was now a gaping maw hanging over the frothing sea two hundred feet below.

'Jasper, come *here!*' Julia roared.

Colin lunged after the dog, who, upon hearing the terror in the recall command, stopped five yards away from where the path now ended. But Jasper didn't turn around. Instead, he put his nose up, sensing something in the air like he did when an abandoned sandwich or an apple core tossed beside the path piqued his food-obsessed interest. Even when his master got to him and tensed the lead, Jasper didn't move back.

'Come here, you silly boy.' Colin reeled the dog in. 'Come away.'

Jasper whined.

'What is it? Seagulls?'

Only then did Colin's gaze follow the dog's nose towards what had triggered the response; at what poked up out of the rocks not ten yards from where he and Jasper stood. He couldn't quite make out what the long pale shapes and scraps of material were. When he realised, when his brain finally put the shapes together, he blurted out an uncontrolled grunt.

'Colin? What is it?'

'There.' Colin bit back the bile that threatened. 'Jutting out of the rock below us.'

'*Oh my God*,' Julia whispered, as her eyes focused in.

But the thought that occurred to Colin then, the one that burrowed to the surface amongst a nauseating slew of others jostling for position, was that God had long ago abandoned this place. No entity with any compassion could have sanctioned what he and his wife were seeing on this sharp winter's day on the western edge of Wales.

There, reaching up out of the rock at a forty-five-degree angle, were two entwined corpses, both with their arms raised in supplication to the sky.

CHAPTER TWO

Evan Warlow and his black lab, Cadi, are almost home.

They're on a bend in a lane that winds for forty yards before it opens out into a wide clearing in front of a small stone cottage. The standing is occupied by a van bearing the name of Davies and Clough, Building and Roofing Contractors. Bryn Davies is on the roof, putting the finishing touches to the neat oak-framed extension Warlow has added to the rear. Somewhere to sit of an evening with a beer and a good book, to kick back and look out over the fields and reed beds of the estuary stretching to the coast.

He's even set up a little writing table for when he scribbles one of those stories he's been meaning to get down. Once the extension is done – and the boys are nearly finished – there'll be no more excuses.

And isn't the cliché 'Write what you know'? But unless he wants to titillate with gory descriptions of fly-blown corpses – of which he's seen his fair share – or enthral people with the details of slow and steady police work in a memoir, he'll need to use his imagination. Get the grey matter in gear. After all, he has time, and he is still relatively young.

Relatively. Glorious word, relatively. Lots of leeway in a word like that. Because he is young as retirees go. Very much so when compared with some old uniformed plods. But not when compared with the fresh-faced lot coming in from university with their Criminology Degrees and Psychology Diplomas.

Not that any of that matters now.

The tiniest of moths flutters in his gut at the prospect of another step into the great unknown. He bats the thought away and crunches over the gravel to his front door, Cadi panting at his side.

'Cup of tea?' Warlow shouts into the ether.

Bryn Davies stops hammering and looks up and then down. 'Never say no to a cup of tea, Evan.'

'What about Alwyn?'

A disembodied voice from around the back of the house shouts back, 'Coffee for me, please.'

'I suppose you expect a biscuit, too?'

Alwyn's head pops up over the roof edge. Only the middle third of his face is visible, the top encased in a woolly hat, the lower covered by a curly beard. His neck is broader than his head and is exactly the width you need to play in the front row for a local rugby club. Within the curls of facial hair is a broad smile. 'Wouldn't say no, Mr W.'

Warlow grunts and shakes his head. 'You two are costing me a fortune in digestives.'

'You'll miss us when we're gone.' Bryn, too, wears a tight cap, but his trademark thick glasses sit above the hollow cheeks of a thirty-a-day smoker. 'Not many visitors dropping in on the off chance here, I reckon.'

'That's the plan.' Warlow slides the key into the lock. 'And just as well, because I doubt there'll be any bloody tea or instant coffee left.'

Alwyn barks out a laugh.

It's warm inside, courtesy of the log-burner's efficiency. He'd stacked it up before Cadi's walk, and the open plan kitchen/dining/living room never gets cold once the fire is lit.

Bequeathed to Warlow when he was a teenager, the house was his Uncle Gron's old place, bought originally as a shepherd's cottage with prospects. It was a bolt hole near the coast where the family could go fishing or to the beach. A place to retire to, maybe, even if Gron was only thirty and retirement was a mere blip on the horizon when he bought it.

But he passed away before that homely dream came to fruition.

Warlow remembers seeing it for the first time, when his uncle proudly announced his purchase. Gron had envisioned an idyllic hideaway, but Warlow had seen an unimpressive pile of rocks and the remains of a doorway. There'd not been one intact wall. More a cairn than a building. He'd laughed, and Gron had laughed twice as loud; something he did a lot of, until the fates conspired to eat all the joy out of him.

The neighbouring farmer thinks the place might be medieval. It's marked on maps as far back as the fourteenth century.

Ffau'r Blaidd. The Wolf's Lair.

For nigh on forty years, the cottage had sat as a derelict, crumbling wreck until Warlow found the means and the time to restore it to a habitable state. And for restoration, read 'rebuild from the foundations up'. But with walls a foot thick, once he got a roof on and waterproofed the place, it surprised Warlow how cosy it could be.

Cosy.

Warlow snorts. 'Cosy' is not a word he thought would apply to anything connected to him. He'd be googling best buys for pipe and bloody slippers next. And until recently, he'd spent his retirement in the tiny rented caravan parked onsite to let him get on with the majority of the renovation donkey work himself.

That caravan was as far removed from cosy as Nevern was from Timbuktu.

He'd watched dozens of those self-build programmes over the years, wondering how difficult it could be. He'd found out the hard way. But part of him knew it would be strenuous and all-consuming, and that had formed much of the attraction. A little mental and physical game he played with himself, and a good thing to focus on; to keep his mind off the anxieties that came with leaving the force and the job he'd done. The job where he'd been liked and well respected. The job he had been good at for almost thirty years.

But he'll never be investigating anything ever again. Apart from the droppings in the wood store, which he still can't decide are mouse or rat.

The caravan has gone, and he and Cadi have been in the cottage now for three months. Three dark, damp months, but spring will follow winter. And with it, opportunities for some more exploring. Just him and Cadi, with all the time in the world to do it in.

Well … almost. No one had all the time in the world, unless you lived in the Tardis. And thanks to the scratch card of life with its pot-luck windows of biology, genetics and disease, some had a lot less than others. *Tempus fugit*, as they say. Or, as one of his old sergeants nearing retirement preferred, tempus you-git.

Soon, Warlow is going to wake up with no more plumbing, or chasing wiring, or pointing – none of which he thought he would ever do but which he's secretly enjoyed – left to do. There might be some gardening, but even that is low maintenance stuff. He is not a vegetable grower sort of bloke.

But it's winter now. Too wet and miserable to go out. Sixteen hours of darkness. Eight hours of daylight. And even that is nothing to write home about because often it's too gloomy to see the ink.

What then, Evan, eh? What then?

Join a choir? Start a blog? Take a dance class?

He pushes away the question with a mental toe, like he might do to something distasteful dumped on the garden path; knowing it's unpleasant but preferring not to inspect it too closely in case it leaves a smelly daub.

By way of a distraction, he switches the radio to the local news as he stirs sugar into the mugs.

The third item is all about walkers finding a body on the coastal path.

A sudden, hollow twisting in his guts puts paid to the stirring. Alwyn's coffee and Bryn's tea grow cold on the countertop as Warlow cocks an ear to listen and dares to wonder.

––––––

IT HAPPENS. Heart attacks, strokes, falls. People can drop dead anywhere, and the coastal path is better than any gym as an aerobic stress test.

But the report on the local news is sketchy. No mention of whether the police suspect or rule out 'foul play' – that catchall phrase that says everything and nothing. It doesn't sound as if the news desk has corralled the hapless walkers who made the 'harrowing discovery' yet for anything juicy. Given the time of year and location, it's unlikely many other hikers would have been on the path for eyewitness accounts. And by now the police will have cordoned off the entire area.

Warlow wonders where the finding was made. It's a long path. 870 miles bordering the whole of the country's coastline. He hasn't walked it all, but he knows bits in the south around the Gower and Vale of Glamorgan, and parts of the north around the Llŷn Peninsula. But the trail around the coasts of the three south-west counties from Amroth to Aberystwyth he knows very well. That's his patch. He walks some of it every week because although the location never changes, it's different every time. The sky, the sea and the weather make up the palette of an ever-changing land and seascape that calls to him. Out there, where there are few people and no distractions, it's possible to find solace and angst in equal measure.

He thinks again of the dead body scenario. An inexperienced rambler in worn footwear who trips and cracks a skull, perhaps? Or a naïve enthusiast who underestimates the path's fitness requirements and gets a coronary for his trouble. Or one of the already lost who go for a walk and have no intention of coming back. Who bring a month's worth of prescription pills in their back packs and find the strength to swallow the lot with a tot or two of brandy on the solitude of the path. At the right time of year you could buy a good fourteen hours or more alone as you drifted into oblivion in the cool Atlantic breeze.

Lights out for the pill-taker and screw the poor buggers left behind to pick up the pieces.

The path can seduce them all with its siren call, but she's an unforgiving mistress.

And whether accident, natural or deliberate, he empathises on all counts. Warlow has had the odd tumble, been breathless on some of the more up and down sections, and he's had his moments of contemplation, too. Moments he's been glad that Cadi has been with him because if not for her …

He lets the thought dwindle, latches on to another. The

radio report had said body, singular. More than one, and there'd be no need to consider the 'foul play' epithet. 'Bodies' was a game changer. And that's partly why Warlow has picked up on it. Why it's blipped on his radar. Even after all these years.

Cadi is sitting in the kitchen, looking at him. He's read that some owners struggle to make eye contact with their dogs. He has no such trouble with Cadi who reads his expressions like a mood board.

'You want a chew, girl?'

Her ears prick, and she tilts her head.

Warlow goes to a cupboard under the sink and pulls out an old half litre yoghurt pot with a lid. He throws Cadi a twist of pizzle she plucks easily out of the air before trotting off to her basket.

Once, more years ago than he cares to remember, he'd spent a lot of time searching the path for some missing hikers. They'd been looking for lost people at first – at least that was the line they toed with the press – but in truth, after the hours turned to days, they were searching for bodies.

It was simple maths.

Once the golden hours following a missing person's report passed, a sad and distressing misper rule applied across the board. The longer people remain missing, the less chance there ever is of finding them alive. Especially a middle-aged couple with no money worries, family to care for, fit and well and enemy free.

He'd been the SIO, coordinating the investigation into the Pickerings' disappearance. A couple whose mysterious vanishing remained an unsolved mystery and an unanswered blot in the Warlow copybook. He knows in his heart that they are dead. But he, like their relatives, is yet to find closure.

Alwyn's hammering has stopped. There's a knock on

the door. It's Bryn Davies and behind him the van is idling, and the afternoon has descended into gloom.

'Right, we'll be off. Back tomorrow for the scaffolding.'

'I was making you tea.' Warlow glances back towards the kitchen.

'We thought you'd forgotten.'

Alwyn calls from the van. 'Don't worry about it, Mr W. Bryn reckons you must have had an afternoon nap. That's what retired people do, isn't it?'

'Oy, I haven't paid the bill yet.' Warlow feigns umbrage and Alwyn's big broad face breaks into a grin.

Bryn hands over two dirt-smudged mugs from their morning cuppas. 'Take no notice, Evan.'

'I got distracted.' Warlow accepts the mugs with genuine regret. 'Extra biscuits tomorrow.'

He waits in the doorway while the Davies and Clough van trundles away. In its wake there is silence. He lets it embrace him, looking out into the growing dusk. Over to the left of the small patch of lawn there's a bed of Sedums with brown stalks getting flattened and slimy by last month's rain. Nothing much is growing but he won't trim them yet. If there's frost, they'll look interesting. Like miniature snow topped trees.

By the time he turns back into the cottage, the Sedums are forgotten.

Perhaps he should ring someone. 'Get the skinny' on the body on the path, as they'd say on one of the too many cop shows he watches on Now TV … He pauses there, thinking it through. He knows he won't. Too needy. The retiree poking his nose in where it's not wanted. He remembers how defensive you could get about your own cases. The way they became part of you and you of them.

No, I won't, he decides. This isn't his fight anymore. He gave up the right to that when he took retirement at fifty much to everyone's surprise and many people's dismay. Warlow is still bemused and genuinely touched by the responses to his leaving. Not his bosses; the Superintendents in two of the forces' BCUs who tried to cajole him into staying with hints of promotion down the line. It was more the secretaries and ancillary staff and colleagues and uniforms, some of whom shed actual tears, who'd wished him well and said they'd miss him.

But he'd made his mind up, and there was no deviating from that.

They could have offered him double his salary, and the answer would still have been no.

When they asked why, he trotted out the usual plausible lies. He had other things he wanted to do, there was more to life, he wanted to enjoy it while he was still young. Blah-de-sodding-blah. Top of the list was renovating the cottage. Warlow was happy to couch it in those terms because no one, least of all his colleagues, needed to know the real reason. The one that arrived gift wrapped in the form of a hospital appointment two and half years ago.

Has it really been that long? Of course it bloody well has. Yet he can remember the moment down to the day, the hour, even the minute.

He'd donated blood as he had a dozen times before. A week later he got a call out of the blue. Something had shown up in the screening tests and they wanted him to see the haematologist for a chat and more tests. He felt fine other than a bit of tiredness. But being knackered on the job when something big was up was the norm. And he was in the middle of a murder enquiry by then. They'd fished a body out of a lake near the sewage works in Pwll, a coastal village near Llanelli, only to find that someone had strangled it before throwing it in. Long hours, terrible food, the usual. You put up with it knowing that eventually, when the adrenaline faded, you'd kip like the dead. Sleep deprivation was par for the course.

But he'd gone to the appointment and met Dr Emmerson, the haematologist. She must have been in her thirties to have got where she was but looked no older than fourteen in DCI Warlow's eyes. She explained the situation with an expression that implied a wisdom beyond her years. An expression that comes with the responsibility of knowing that what you say changes people's lives in a second.

Warlow hoped he exuded a little of that vibe during his career. When he had to tell people the worst kind of news. But even though he'd been there and had T-shirts in every colour and shade, he still wasn't prepared for being on the receiving end.

You never are.

CHAPTER THREE

DETECTIVE INSPECTOR JESS ALLANBY sits in Superintendent Sion Buchannan's office, waiting while the superior officer reads his computer screen. She's typed up a report of the day's activities and inputted it into the records system. It's this report Buchannan scans on the HOLMES system.

'Only the one item of ID?' he asks.

'In an inside pocket of a fleece. A bus pass. There's some water damage, but it's plastic coated and the name is still legible.'

He flicks his gaze to Jess. 'What state are the bodies in? Badly decomposed?'

She nods. 'There's clothing, skin and hair but nothing left of the features. Dental records and DNA are in the pipeline.'

Buchannan sits back, staring at a point on the ceiling. He's a big man. Broad and tall. From the healed damage to his ears, he looks like he might have once been a second-row forward. He has pale Celtic colouring, thinning red hair and freckles. His nickname is the Buccaneer. Allanby doesn't know why and isn't about to ask from where in his long career it originated. But it doesn't surprise her. He's a stark contrast to Allanby who isn't much bigger than five foot seven in heels and whose ears have nothing but stud earrings in their lobes.

Neither does she have Celtic colouring. Allanby's dark hair and grey eyes come via Italian genes from a Tuscan grandmother, even if Manchester is what forged her. A city of reds and blues. Where wearing the wrong colour in the wrong pub can invite stares if not violence. Where rivalry is a way of life.

But this is Wales. Her new home. They play with a different shaped ball here. In the eight months since joining the Dyfed-Powys force, she's made herself learn more about rugby, given that it's almost a religion. Investing in the culture she's rationalised it as. Under-standing the mood music. The buzz on six nations Mondays when the national team win. The long moody silences when they lose.

'The press has already decided.' Buchannan arches back in his chair.

'I've never known them to let little details like certainty get in their way.' Jess offers a weary smile.

'Disinterment?'

Jess nods. 'There's an archaeologist onsite. Trying to preserve the scene is proving a challenge.'

Buchannan narrows his eyes. 'We can't wait for that.'

'No, sir.'

Decision made, Buchannan sits forward. 'You lead for now. Deputy SIO. Get the ball rolling.'

Jess feels the tingle dance around the small of her back. She wants to smile. Wants to make a fist and punch the air. But she realises it's not the time, nor the place. Buchannan wouldn't look kindly on any triumphalism here. Still, it's a milestone worth celebrating. Chief Investigating Officer in a murder doesn't do the CV any harm. If the case escalates, is classed as a category A major investigation, someone else will assume the senior role. Buchannan himself in all probability. But for now, she is it.

Nothing huge has come her way since arriving eight months ago. But she has a place on the SIO Hydra course in twelve months' time. The other DIs and DCIs are all knee deep in ongoing operations. Dyfed-Powys desperately needs more accredited SIOs. And Jess requires as much experience in big stuff as possible. If she passes the course national accreditation will follow. So a case like this is one she intends grasping with both hands.

'We're on it, sir.'

'Make yourself familiar with the Pickering misper file. But so's you know, I'm about to make a phone call that may prove helpful. Even a game changer.'

'I'm intrigued.' Jess's neat eyebrows arch.

The Buccaneer rubs his chin with a big forefinger. 'No point going into details until I've done it. It might come to nothing, but it also could mean some collaboration on your part.'

Jess shrugs. 'I'm all for that.'

She stands. The Buccaneer doesn't. It's a relief. He's six-four and his office isn't designed for two people, let alone two and a half.

'Good. I'm counting on you, Jess. This is going to be messy,' adds Buchannan.

Outside, Jess shuts the door, takes two steps and makes a fist. In the corridor, a younger, smaller woman leans against the wall in wait. She pushes off as Jess approaches.

'Well?'

Jess opts for mock formality. 'Well, Detective Sergeant Richards, we need to set up an Incident Room.'

Both women smile. It isn't a victory. Not yet. It's merely the response to a welcome spurt of adrenaline. It's been a long day. They've both done shifts in front of screens in the stale air of the office and Jess has had the pleasure of a long trip out to the windblown coast.

Enough to tire anyone. But they're not tired anymore.

They're energised by the thought of hunting a killer.

———

THE BODY on the path has now become bodies.

Warlow watches the 6pm news that night with heightened interest, though the story remains frustratingly devoid of detail. There has been no public confirmation of who the bodies are. But speculation is growing. He re-lives on screen archive footage of a police line hunting through fields. The footage is generic, not from the Pickering case. It's depressing to think that he's probably the only person in the country who knows that. Who even cares?

His phone buzzes. He picks up. It's his youngest son, Tomos.

'Hi, Dad.'

'Hey, Tom.' His son is a doctor on an ENT rotation in North Thames, at Northwick Park. It's a busy job but usually Tom rings at weekends and this out of the blue call triggers a mild parental pang. 'Everything alright?'

'I read the newsfeed on my phone about these walkers finding bodies on the path.'

'It's gone national, has it?'

'Yeah. Is this tied up with your case?'

Your case.

'I don't know. Too early to speculate.'

'So no one's contacted you about it?' There's concern as well as interest in Tom's voice.

'Hah. Not yet. I doubt they'll be beating a path to my door. I'm an ex-police officer, don't forget.'

'Sure, but the press …'

Warlow has thought little about the press and Tom's

warning comes as an unwelcome reminder. He's right, of course. Like hyenas around an isolated member of the herd, the press might begin to circle. He considers himself pretty much off the grid, but they will no doubt try to find him.

'It'll be no comment from me.'

'You're curious, though, aren't you?'

'If it turns out these are the missing couple from seven years ago, then yes, I'm curious.'

'So weird though. I mean, if it is them how did they get inside a cave? This would make a great book, Dad.'

Warlow snorts. He'd give short shrift to anyone else suggesting this, but family gets special dispensation. And Tom has always been the encouraging one. Alun, his eldest, the one keenest to fly the nest at the earliest opportunity and ensconced in a mining consortium in sunny Perth in Western Australia, thinks he's mad to retire early and worries that he'll get bored. He's told neither of them the real reason he left. That's a conversation he hasn't yet prepared for. 'It's intriguing, I admit.'

'Aren't you tempted to ring a colleague and find out?'

That's an easy one. 'Nah. It'll be enough of a circus as it is. The last thing they want is another clown hassling them.'

'A clown with lots of experience, though.'

'I've hung up my red nose, Tom.' Warlow finds the blandishments uncomfortable and so he switches conversational direction. 'How's Northwick Park? Did I tell you I spent some time in Harrow on a case when I was in the Met? Nothing to do with the school. Nasty stabbing. Mind you it was twenty odd years ago.'

Tom launches in to how his week has been. There's a lot of jargon that Warlow doesn't understand, but he doesn't stop his youngest. He's proud of both his sons and Tom was never pushed into medicine. But he was always interested, right from the age of ten when he got his first toy stethoscope. Talk drifts to sport and rugby. Tom's given up playing. Medicine and shifts do not lend themselves to serious training. And without training it's easy to get hurt. Swimming and gym are the new fix.

'Your mother okay?' Warlow asks, as he always does. There's nothing wistful in this, he's only being polite and letting Tom know he still cares. The subtext of the question is that he hopes her drinking is under control.

'She's alright,' Tom says with an inflection that suggests she barely is.

Warlow hasn't talked to Denise for almost three years. The marriage was over two years before that.

They split as amicably as two people who have fallen out of love can, dividing the spoils of the house sale and his pension pot. The cottage in Pembrokeshire was his long before the marriage, so that was never in the mix. Warlow is glad of that because he didn't want to bicker over anything. Not his style. And there was enough in the pot for him to get on with the renovations.

Now with Denise it's exchanged texts only. Family stuff, celebrating something the boys have achieved, news about a friend or relative. All polite, emotionless words with no intimacy. Which is what their marriage had become by the end. They both prefer it this way. Amicable but estranged. Though, when Jeez Denise gets enough vodka on board, the amicable tends to take a back seat. Tom reassures him and the conversation drifts to the cottage and repairs. Safe ground and a path that meanders to a natural close.

But the call gives Warlow food for thought. If the press do contact him, he is going to give them nothing. He has Bernice Meech's number – Dyfed-Powys's press officer – stuck on the notice board next to the fridge. Above her name he's written 'Rottweiler'.

He takes a sip of Primitivo. On weekends he'll have a

couple of IPAs with a Balti or some fish and chips. But in the week, it's wine or maybe a G and T. And not every night either. He turns back to the TV and finds a documentary about open air pools in Hampstead and wonders how anyone would enjoy swimming in brown water where ducks and geese swim. He's read somewhere that geese defecate up to a hundred times a day. He notices now that not many of the swimmers put their heads under the water and tries to imagine how they'd respond if one happened to get an accidental mouthful. It was worth watching just for that. When his phone goes again, this time signalling a WhatsApp message, he assumes it's a follow up from Tom.

But it isn't. It's from Sion Buchannan of all people.

SB: Findings on the coastal path. You okay to talk?

He texts back:

WARLOW: Yes

A minute later, his phone rings.

CHAPTER FOUR

WARLOW answers and it's the Buccaneer's deep baritone on the line.

'Evan, thanks for taking my call.'

'No problem, Sion.' There would have been a 'sir' before, but no more. It's first names now.

'You well?'

'I am.'

'Good. That's great.' Said with feeling. The Buccaneer is one of the good guys. Warlow has a lot of time for him. 'I suspect you know why I'm calling.'

'The Pickerings?'

'Yes. We're awaiting confirmation but there is ID on one body. The husband's bus pass.'

The corroboration squeezes a sigh out of Warlow. 'Shit.'

'It's what you suspected though, am I right?'

'Maybe but … thanks for letting me know.'

'Pleasure. But I won't lie to you. This is not purely a courtesy call.'

Warlow waits. Buchannan is a straight arrow. He'll find his target quickly enough.

'We're stretched pretty thinly, Evan. Did you meet Jess Allanby?'

'No.'

'Ah. I didn't think you'd overlapped. She's smart. A transfer from Greater Manchester. Beat the opposition for the Inspector job hands down. This will be her first big one with us. We'll wait for the post-mortem, but my money is on it being a bad one. Yours too, isn't it?'

Another pause before Warlow agrees. 'If I was a betting man, then yes.'

Niceties over, Buchannan goes straight for the jugular. 'I'm ringing to ask if you'll come back on board for this.'

Warlow snorts. 'I don't think so, Sion.'

'Hear me out. You're what, sixteen months since finishing?'

'Eighteen.'

'There are at least half a dozen forces who would take you as you are.'

It's a compliment of sorts but Warlow brushes it off. 'You, of all people, know why I can't.' And it's true, of all his ex-colleagues in Dyfed-Powys, Sion Buchannan is the one person whom Warlow has confided in. One of a handful he'll still talk to or meet up and have a coffee with to chew over police cud.

'No, I don't know why you can't. You say you're well so I know you're bloody thumb-twiddling in that cottage of yours. I'm not asking you to slog it out full time. I'm talking about consulting. You know this case better than anybody. Jess is whip smart, but it'll save her an enormous amount of time to have you helping. Name your hours.'

'What's wrong with Caldwell?'

Warlow instantly regrets he's asked, even if a not so small part of him is hoping that the superintendent will say something along the lines of – *apart from him being an unmitigated little turd you mean?* It's petty of him. What Buchannan actually says is, 'Nothing. But he and all the experienced boys are up to their necks.'

'You know I'd help out like a shot normally–'

'I do.'

Warlow resents having to explain, but he does anyway. 'Then you know why I can't. I was walking on eggshells at the end. Nothing's changed.'

'I appreciate your awareness and responsibility, Evan. But this will be even less hands on than before. Besides, I've done some homework, too. And the risk to others–'

'Is minimal but not impossible,' Warlow finishes the sentence for him.

Buchannan sighs. 'I wouldn't be asking if I wasn't sure it was the right thing to do.'

'For who?'

'For the Pickerings.' The Buccaneer's words are a gut punch.

'I've got to think about this.'

'That usually means no.'

'I've still got to think about it.'

'At least let Jess come and talk to you.'

They both know that Warlow has no right to say no. Such a refusal constitutes a failure to cooperate in an investigation. Helping the police with their enquiries doesn't always involve likely perpetrators.

Buchannan twists the knife. 'Some bastard killed those two poor people on that path, Evan. Killed them and hid them. Now the gods have opened the trap door for us to look inside.'

He's right. The cold flame inside Warlow flickers. He douses it with a bucket of humour. 'Christ, Sion. Have you been reading books again?'

Buchannan snorts. 'I've missed that dazzling wit.'

'You need to get out more.'

'That'll be the two of us, then.' Buchannan lets the jibe

hover. When he gets no comeback, he tries conciliation. 'You'll like Jess Allanby. And she'll bring along your number one fan, Catrin Richards.'

'I'm not succumbing to bribery. I made myself a promise.'

'Sleep on it.'

After the call, Warlow stands and stares without seeing at the phone and then back up at the TV, his mind flitting between his inner thoughts and what his eyes perceive. On screen it's January and someone has to smash the ice on Hampstead pond before they can swim. Warlow makes the silent, ironic observation that they're making a better job of it than the Buccaneer could in his phone call. But that's not fair and he knows it. There have been other calls in the last twelve months. Other invitations to reconsider his retirement. Recruitment is down. Funding low across all forces. At least Buchannan didn't ask him to work with Caldwell.

His resentment runs deep. Deeper, for his own dark reasons, than anyone including Buchannan will ever know. Mel Lewis, a detective sergeant whom Warlow worked with for almost fifteen years, called Caldwell a treasure. And then qualified it with delicious contempt by adding: 'As in should be buried on a desert island somewhere and forgotten.'

He smiles, but it soon fades.

The flame flickers.

Much of his reluctance has to do with a strong desire never to be in the same room as Caldwell ever again.

Sleep on it, the Buccaneer had said. Good luck with that.

———

HE DOES SLEEP ON IT. Badly.

At 7am the next morning, Warlow checks the weather and sees no rain due until the evening. He throws eggs and tomatoes into a pan and scrambles them with cheese for breakfast, drinks two coffees and by nine he's in his Jeep with Cadi, heading up the coast. He parks at a spot halfway between the seaside towns of Aberporth and Cardigan.

The beach at Mwnt and its isolated whitewashed church is a tourist honeypot in summer. He knows all about the failed Flemish invasion in 1155 on that shore. A date once celebrated on the first Sunday in January as 'Sul Coch Y Mwnt'. The literal translation being 'The Red Sunday of Mwnt', but of course the more accepted words are 'Bloody Sunday'. It's ironic that the sea lapping the shore is Irish yet there was a Bloody Sunday here long before Dublin's or Derry's.

West is Cardigan Island and it's that direction Warlow takes with the dog. He needs to blow away some cobwebs. But Buchannan's call haunts him more than he thought it ever would. Today he's one of a handful of walkers. But he and Cadi are the only ones taking a path above the beach that leads to the Chough Walk out along the cliffs.

Chough. It's an odd word referring to a red billed member of the crow family. Rare apparently. But birds are not his thing. Unless they're stuffed with sage and onion and served with roast potatoes and gravy. He likes them well enough.

Few people walk here because the signs clearly warn that there is no access further along the clifftops. Much to the chagrin of the tourist board, the official path takes an inland detour thanks to an ongoing dispute between a landowner and the local council.

But, though it's closed off, the path is still there. It's wild and dangerous. There's a drop of 100 feet to the craggy rocks below and Cadi stays on the lead, though Warlow doubts she would go near the edge.

Half a mile along the land curves inwards where the path cuts in and the precipice edge is sheer, with the shore below invisible because of an overhang. Man and dog ignore the NO ACCESS TO PATH signs and head up a bank towards a gate in the fence.

The path, now on his right, tracks down towards a ravine. Warlow unties the rough rope securing the gate, slides open a bolt and steps into a field that once contained cattle judging by the deep hoof prints he has to negotiate. This time of year there are no livestock and he follows the fence around to the top corner where he stops. The field stretches on and down towards the ravine. As it narrows and the land rises, two buildings nestle in the cleft between, one on each side of the divide. The one nearest to him, on his side of the steep inlet, has a garden and fencing and a few outbuildings. He counts three donkeys in a paddock and a dozen hens clucking around a coop.

The building on the far side is a ruin. Unoccupied for decades, it's an industrial relic.

Warlow takes it all in. He knows both buildings well. The nearest started life as lime workers' residence and retains the name Limehouse Cottage. The farthest, the Engine House, once functioned to transport stone and lime up and down the ravine from a perilous quayside.

He doesn't know who owns Limehouse Cottage now, but it was the Pickerings' home when they disappeared. Yet, even as he ponders this, a woman emerges from the rear of the house and looks in his direction. She's young, mid-thirties he estimates, slim, dressed in wellingtons and a padded jacket, blonde hair under a beanie hat. She looks like someone who might care for, or at least about, donkeys. On impulse, Warlow raises a hand in greeting. The woman reciprocates, but they are too far apart to speak, even by shouting. After a moment, she turns and walks towards the paddock, glancing back as she does so.

She's nervous, he thinks. But then, living out here you had every right to be. Especially if you were mad enough to do so alone.

And, as if in answer to his concerns, another figure emerges in a waxed jacket, jeans and wellingtons. This time it's a male. Tall, dark-haired, scarf around the lower part of his mouth. He doesn't notice Warlow. Instead, he disappears into an outhouse.

Warlow has been in that outhouse. He's been in every room of that cottage more than once. During the search for the missing couple, he led the team that had literally picked over the Pickerings' abode. In fact, picking over the Pickerings had become an annoying alliteration that, once thought of, remained as a caustic reminder of how slim those pickings had been. How futile the police's efforts turned out to be in uncovering what had happened.

And here he is once again. Staring down at the property that has no right in these days of conservation and preservation to occupy such a unique and idyllic position. Had it not been developed and occupied by two reclusive sisters – one a writer, the other a painter – after the Second World War, it would have remained, like the Engine House, an abandoned ruin. Planning permission for renovation would never have been obtained in this day and age. Accessible only by farm track, the old stone building sits in a cleft on a sharply sloping coast, both it and the Engine House barely seeing the sun in the depths of winter. Yet sheltered in their northern exposure from the gales and rain that howl in from the Atlantic to the south and west.

Cadi sits at Warlow's side. She is a patient dog, but he senses that she might wonder why they've stopped at this lonely spot. If she could ask him, he'd struggle to come up with an appropriate answer. He remembers his words of dismissal to Tom last night and allows himself a hypocritical smile.

You're not kidding anyone, Warlow.

He's here because … because he wants to remind himself of the scene. Wants to know if someone else is living in the Pickerings' place. It stayed empty for months after they went missing, and then he'd heard it had been rented out as holiday accommodation. But, judging from the sacks of building materials in the yard, someone is intent on making changes.

It takes seven years from being last seen alive before relatives can ask the courts for a grant of probate. It's been nearly seven and a half since the Pickerings went missing.

Cadi whines gently. She's getting bored.

On the other side of the ravine there is no sign of activity. The Engine House remains derelict.

Warlow retraces his steps to the fence and back down to the cliff edge. The path goes on to a wooden bridge spanning the narrowest part of the divide. It's partially collapsed and not safe, though the stream is navigable with care. He's below the cottage now, and the swollen stream rushes by beneath the broken platform of the bridge. He crosses and climbs up the slope and looks back. The top corner of the Pickering property is just visible. From here, there is evidence of ongoing construction.

Warlow reads an apology for the path's disruption from Natural Resources Wales on a weatherproofed notice stuck to a post. The deserted path runs on for two miles and, behind him, the craggy headland of Pen Yr Hwbyn cuts off the view to Mwnt. He's sees no choughs but there are gulls wheeling and bugling above him. Yet he's seen what he came to see and there is no reason for him to be further along the path than where he is now. But he's drawn to these places and so he stands with the dog at his side, looking out over the grey expanse of sea at its incessant motion. As if a restless serpent roams beneath it. He considers the solitude that walkers sometimes seek. Considers how easy it is to underestimate the weather, the terrain, the imagination.

He'd considered all of those things when he investigated the Pickerings' disappearance.

But, as with seven and something years before, there are no answers in the air, on the ground or in the waters here.

Cadi's ears prick up and she turns, drawn by something only her canine senses register from the direction of the ravine. An animal of some sort? Warlow wonders. He puts his hand on the dog's head.

'What is it, girl? Rabbits? Cwningod?' He defaults to the Welsh, which is often how he'll speak to the dog. She doesn't respond, ducks away, refusing the reassurance of his touch.

How easy it would be to believe that she was sensing something else.

He snorts, ridiculing his train of thought. This isn't the first time she's acted this way on their walks. But only ever on the path, and only ever when they've been totally alone. If he was a nervous man, he might maintain that she was seeing, or hearing, or sensing something that he could not. Wales was a place steeped in legend, this coast especially. There were scattered remains of Iron Age settlements everywhere. And below there were caves and disused lead, silver and zinc mines. If ever there was fodder for an overblown imagination, it was here.

But Warlow prefers to deal with what he can see and hear and touch himself. And though Cadi remains slightly skittish on their way back to the car, they encounter nothing and no one. But, unusually, the dog sits and looks through the back window of the car until they crest a rise and the beach and church disappear from view.

CHAPTER FIVE

At lunchtime, Bryn Davies knocks on Warlow's door and peers through the kitchen window. Cadi's tail goes into overdrive and dog and builder greet each other as long-lost friends, even though it's been only an hour since he arrived, and the dog greeted him with equal enthusiasm.

'Right, that's about it,' says Bryn. 'We'll bugger off. Any problems, give me a bell.'

Warlow follows him around to the front of the house. Alwyn is in the passenger seat of the loaded van eating a sandwich. He waves and, through a mouthful of bread, says, 'Thanks for all the tea, Mr W.'

'Pleasure,' Warlow says and turns to Bryn. 'Good to see those etiquette lessons are coming good with young Alwyn, too.'

The builder chuckles and shakes Warlow's offered hand. 'Final invoice will be in the post.'

'You sure you don't want cash?'

Bryn tuts and gives Warlow a wry smile. 'And you an ex-copper and all.'

Warlow shrugs. 'I'm happy to—'

'No, we'll stick with what we agreed. Bank transfer

whenever you're ready. Best I put most of it through the books. But the offer is much appreciated.'

They both agree that VAT – come to that, all tax – is the work of the devil; having discussed the world over a pint in the local pub when they met to agree the work.

Warlow watches the men drive away for the last time before retracing his steps. He stands outside the green oak extension at the rear running his hand over the thick wooden frame, enjoying its solid feel. He turns to study the view. Another grey day but dry and the cool air clears his head and washes away some of the fug that's plagued him since speaking with Buchannan.

He goes back inside to stare out at the same view, only this time from the warmth and comfort of an armchair. But there's nothing restful about today because he's decided. It's an uncomfortable decision. Still, the Buccaneer will have to manage without him.

He's got walks to do with Cadi. Some minor planting to do in the garden, too. Sod it, he might even try and grow something edible this year in bags. His dad was a dab-hand at onions and carrots.

And then there's a choir, or starting a blog, or dance classes.

Jesus.

He puts down the coffee cup, his teeth grinding in his head just as his phone rings. He doesn't recognise the number but answers, prepared to give anyone offering him a deal on his mobile phone account short shrift.

'Hello?' His voice is gruff.

'Hello? DCI Warlow?' A woman's voice. Apprehensive. Not a cold caller then.

'Ex DCI, but yes, this is Warlow.'

After a moment's pause, the call resumes. 'This is Tanya Ogilvie. Tanya Pickering as was.'

Warlow puts his coffee down. He plucks the voice from his memory, compares the two and marks them a match.

'Tanya. How are you?'

'I'm well, thank you. Frazzled, I suppose, but well.'

'What can I—'

She cuts across him. 'I had a call from a Superintendent Buchannan this morning. About Mum and Dad.'

Warlow doesn't answer immediately. He squeezes his eyes shut. He's not with the police anymore. He could say that and end the call. But he doesn't. Certain things will always haunt you despite handing back the warrant card. Deep in his core he's still a copper.

'I'm so sorry, Tanya.'

'So it's true? I wanted to hear it from—' A sob breaks the sentence and then she continues, 'I wanted to hear it from you.'

He senses no accusation in her words, only facts. Warlow had been in charge of the case. He'd spoken regularly to Tanya during the investigation. Weekly at first, then monthly, and then once every three or four months until he retired.

'When you stopped contacting me, I sort of knew.'

'Tanya, I stopped phoning because I left the force.'

'Oh.' Her disappointment is evident even in one syllable. 'I assumed that … I'm sorry to bother you.'

'You're not bothering me. You'll never be bothering me. I got a call last night too.'

'They found Dad's bus pass.'

Warlow stays silent.

'I've seen photos. Drone shots. The two of them in that hole …' Her words quiver with pain and horror. 'Who would do something like that to my mum and dad?'

'I don't know, Tanya. But there are good people who are going to do their utmost to find out.'

No reply for a while. Only soft crying. When the words

do come, they're like sharp needles in his brain. 'I wish it was you.'

'Tanya, I–'

'I realise I'm being selfish. I always got the impression that you truly cared about them. That you did your best. Now we know why you couldn't find them. Because they were stuffed into a crack in a cliff.' Another sob.

Warlow inhales deeply. 'Anybody with you, Tanya?'

'My husband. The kids are out at friends.'

He searches for something to give this woman. 'There'll be a funeral now. There'll be a chance to say goodbye.'

'Will you be there?'

'I will. I promise you that.'

'Thank you.' Her voice has become progressively smaller. Now it's tiny. Cowering under a canopy of grief. There's more talk. Warlow steers it around to her children. He remembers their names from his calls, and she relaxes. He promises that if he finds out more, he'll let her know.

'Ring me any time. I mean that,' Warlow says five minutes later, when he's sure she's stopped crying.

He ends the call. For a fleeting moment he wonders if Buchannan has put her up to that.

Why don't you give old Evan a ring? Pull a few guilt strings.

But that's nonsense. Tanya hadn't known he'd retired. Her call was genuine. But he's been able to give her nothing back except platitudes. And hearing her voice has driven a stake through his self-conscious heart.

Buchannan rang him knowing what the answer would be. Warlow has withdrawn from work and society under the notion that it would be safer for everyone if he did so. And there are other equally capable police officers that could do Warlow's job right enough. He doesn't flatter himself by believing he's special, that he can do it better than anyone else. It's not that. He's only popular because he has knowledge about the Pickerings. But what he also has is a promise made to Tanya Pickering that he would find her parents.

He couldn't do that, and it eats at him.

Now all he can hear is her tiny voice saying, 'I wish it was you.'

He can't hide from the fact that it's the Pickerings who need his help. The dead have no voice other than those who speak up for them.

The cold and brittle fire in his gut flickers afresh.

And Warlow knows that despite the wall he's built to keep himself and everyone else free from harm, he cannot, in all conscience, say no to the Pickerings now. Alive or dead.

CHAPTER SIX

THE NEWS IS on in Limehouse Cottage as Izzy Ramsden carries two glasses through the remodelled living room. Outside it's still a lime-washed igneous rock wall and Welsh slate, but inside it's a Country Living centre spread. Nothing twee though. The lines are clean with no frippery. A little bit of north London embedded in this West Coast experiment of theirs.

One glass, hers, contains ice and water, the other for her partner, Marcus, is half full of Chianti. His second glass. She's not refilled it to the brim because he'll down it without thinking as he so often does when he's distracted.

'Why don't we watch something on Netflix, Marky. *Life in Pieces* or *Schitt's Creek*. I've had enough of this now.'

He waves the channel changer at the TV. 'This is Sky, Izzy, not the local rubbish. They're saying it's the Pickerings.'

'Even more reason to switch over.' Her mouth twitches into a pleading grin.

They'd heard the helicopter in the distance all that morning. Just as they had yesterday and the day before. It had faded away mid-afternoon, thank God.

'Here we go.' Izzy hands over the glass.

Marcus hunches forward on the seat, staring intently at the screen. He accepts the glass with a smile and a muttered, 'Thanks, darling.'

He's always polite. Always caring. His big smile was one of the first things she noticed about him. He held nothing back in that smile. The way it had faded to almost nothing made the decision to move so easy for her.

'He's too nice to be a trader,' her friends had said.

'Too nice' may have been an oversimplification. It wouldn't hold water as a diagnosis. And labelling other traders laddish and sociopathic by implication may have been too simplistic and clichéd. But in Marcus's case, there was no denying the fact that losing any semblance of work-life balance had taken its toll.

The hours and the stress were enough to wear anyone down. He'd be up at 5am and at his desk by 5.30am. Most often back not much before 8pm. The money was good. Great, in fact. And London prices were so silly. But what is the point of all those zeroes if you don't live long enough to spend it? The weekend drinking, she realised, was compensation. He'd always been someone who threw himself into things. Binge watch box sets. Splash out on the most expensive holidays. Delayed gratification was a foreign concept to Marcus Dexter.

And Izzy went along with it because he was still Marcus underneath all the glitz. The shy boy she'd met at a crap party neither of them wanted to be at a dozen years ago.

They'd both gravitated to London for work after university. Marcus to a dead-end cold calling financial firm, Izzy as a sales assistant in a Chelsea clothes shop. They were both ambitious. Both good at what they did. Progress and promotion were swift. And as they moved up, the London lifestyle sucked them in. She hated to admit it, but the benefits blindsided her for far too long. So what if Marcus sometimes drank himself into oblivion on a Friday and Saturday night? He'd bounce back from a hangover after an afternoon sleep and be up for it all over again. Not that she ever drank that much. Too many calories in wine and beer. Gin and slimline was Izzy's tipple. And after two or three she always somehow lost track of what Marcus was drinking, telling herself not to call the kettle black when she was doing a great impersonation of the pot.

Until he stopped smiling and she found out he was leaving the flat on Monday mornings and going to a drinking club instead of FMWealth's City office. That was when the klaxon sounded. That was the day she realised she would not be his enabler anymore.

She refused to call it an intervention. But there'd been little discussion. No argument from Marcus. He was delighted when she suggested (demanded) a complete change. Leave London. Sell the flat. Find somewhere with a sea view where they might keep chickens, rent out a field to a donkey sanctuary and work from home. And though he couldn't trade from home, between them they earned good money. He as a freelance analyst, she as a freelance designer for a variety of manufacturers.

It astonished Izzy when he didn't argue. Horrified her when he broke down and told her he'd been frightened of suggesting the same thing because he thought she'd say no.

He keeps telling her she's saved him.

But Izzy knows he is a work in progress.

A drone shot of the collapsed path appears for the tenth time on-screen. Beneath it, the rolling lines of news repeats.

. . .

'POLICE HAVE NOT RULED out the possibility that remains found on coastal path in Wales are those of couple missing for seven years.'

'AT LEAST WE know the axeman didn't bury them in the ravine now.' She raises an eyebrow.

'No.' Marcus laughs, but his eyes don't leave the TV.

The bodies in the ravine is a running joke they've shared since they bought the place. They'd gone down the weekend the house had gone on sale. Not deliberately house hunting. A jolly with coasteering on the Pembrokeshire coast had been their aim – well Marky's at any rate. A flash hotel in St Bride's as compensation for the wet and the wind had convinced her. They'd walked past the estate agent's as the details were being posted in the window by chance. They went to see Limehouse the next day and bought it then and there. Some might have called it impulsive, but Izzy's argument was that they'd already decided on a move and it was fate.

Of course they knew about the Pickerings. It was almost part of the sales pitch. She'd found it a little macabre, but Marcus lapped it up. Just as he is lapping up the news now.

'Did you see that man looking at our place today?' Izzy asks.

'No.' At last his eyes break contact with the screen to engage hers.

'Chap with a dog. He'd come up into one of Gower's fields. I hope it isn't the start of something.'

'People are naturally curious.'

'Like you, you mean?'

'We're a part of it, living here.' Marcus takes a sip of wine, his eyes shining like an excited child's as he turns back to the screen. 'Aren't you even the slightest bit curious?'

'Of course I am. But we don't know it's them, do we? And what would finding them on the path miles away from here have to do with this place?'

He turns to her with a disparaging look. 'Oh come on, Izzy. It's a genuine mystery, admit it. Like being in a film. Secrets and lies. Just up your street I'd have thought.'

'Give me the *Railway Children* over *Nightmare on Elm Street*.' Izzy reaches for a magazine.

'Says she whose favourite film is a Korean zombie flick called *Train to Busan*.'

Izzy ignores him and thumbs through pages she doesn't look at. 'I'm surprised you didn't see him. Weren't you working on the captain's cabin?'

'I was sorting out materials for the base. Sand, cement, plasticiser. I'll be barrowing it all up there tomorrow.'

The 'captain's cabin' is Marcus's project. They have sea views from their living room, but he wants a summer house on the edge of their property with a view down through the ravine to the rocky inlet below. Somewhere solid where they can sit and watch the storms come in. It's a tough spot. The land there is uneven and needs levelling. Someone, the Pickerings maybe, had built a small wooden base on a platform on the exact spot. Probably with the same idea in mind, but never finished. Marcus's plans are grander. He's hiring a mini digger and a cement mixer, laying a base within the granite outcroppings so that they can construct a proper building, using the stones jutting out of the earth as their anchor. Above, they'll have an enclosed viewing platform.

Izzy is all for it because it's keeping Marcus busy.

The drone shot now shows a forensic team in white Tyvek overalls, but there's a screen covering much of the path. No way of seeing what they're doing under there; what secrets are being unearthed.

She's resentful of all the hoo-ha. Marcus has been doing well. Almost back to the man she used to know. It hasn't been easy for her either, so far away from her friends, most of whom have been angling for a visit for months. But she and Marcus agreed on an entertainment moratorium until the summer, citing refurbishment as their valid reasons. And she's missed her friends. But Marcus is her soul mate. His recuperation from the sapping burn-out he's suffered is her priority. To do that, they need tranquillity and projects to keep him busy.

Marcus gulps down another inch of wine without even thinking about it.

That's why she hates the press circus over the bodies on the path and the effect it's having on him. Why she's so curious about the man and the dog.

It's also why she hasn't told Marcus about what she thinks she's seen in the dense thicket of scrub and gorse at the edge of the ravine. Three times now. Always at dusk when there's not enough light to be sure.

But she is sure.

Someone, or something, is watching them.

———

IT ISN'T easy living on the very edge of a country.

Izzy knew that getting anything done to the cottage would be a challenge. They were miles from the nearest town, offering serious retail or design services. London, even Cardiff-based companies, took one look at their postcode and said they would not travel that distance. But then they'd asked around and dug under the surface of the local communities to find individuals and bespoke companies that catered for needs such as theirs.

Plumbers, carpenters and upholsterers' ads were peeled off notice boards in the local Post Office and culled from an advertising magazine called the *Pembrokeshire Gazette*. All offered services and goods at much cheaper rates than the big stores could offer. Some were local firms, some, like Izzy and Marcus, were skilled incomers seeking a different life and bringing their work with them.

But it all takes time and effort.

And then there are the animals. They got a dozen chickens and lost all but two of them in one night to something that got in under the wire of the run and tore their heads off. They sourced a company in Powys that made walk-in runs from recycled building materials that were fox proof. Since installation, there'd been no foul casualties. They'd let a field to the Donkey Sanctuary, and the charity brought up three animals rescued from miserable existences in Spain.

All Izzy has to do is feed them.

There are wild rabbits, too. And huge gulls that sweep in from the Atlantic. So when the small pile of vegetables she'd left out one night by mistake are missing the following morning, she'd blamed rabbits or birds as the most likely culprits. But the carrots, turnips, old bananas and swedes that she keeps as treats for the donkeys had been in a bag and off the ground in a barrow. She normally locked them away in an outhouse but became distracted by Marcus needing her help with carrying building materials in from his SUV. The following morning all the bananas and carrots and swedes were gone. Only turnips and some unripe pears remained.

It is possible, of course, that she's made a mistake and forgotten that she'd given the rest to the donkeys, but she couldn't remember doing so. Thinking back, it was the first time she got the feeling that there might be something odd about Limehouse Cottage.

Two weeks later, at dusk, she'd been out to feed the chickens when a movement at the edge of their lower paddock caught her eye. Nothing much. More a suggestion of a pale shape within the deeper shadows of the trees shifting in the stiff onshore breeze beyond the fence where their land abutted the woods of the ravine.

Monty, their blue-eyed Weimaraner, more used to walks in London parks than the wild outdoors, looked up but then went back to worrying an old football, his mud-spattered toy of choice. The dog's lack of interest made Izzy doubt she'd seen anything. With Monty in tow, she'd walked through the paddock to stand ten yards back from the fence, peering into the undergrowth just a dozen yards away. The stunted trees, bent by years of wind screaming in from the southwest, leaned away from her as if they wanted to run. The land fell away down towards the gorge where the trees petered out. There, erosion had left nothing but rock for their roots to cling to. Izzy stared, anxious that a dog or a sheep had got lost, but in the five minutes that she stood there, nothing else caught her attention.

Nothing concrete.

There would be living creatures in the copse, of course there would. Rabbits, birds, perhaps rats. She hated rats, and when they'd lived in London, Marcus happily trotted out the adage that you were never more than six feet away from one. Urban myth twaddle, of course. And she'd done some reading. Since they border a farm, and agricultural properties are a favoured environment, she'd reasoned that there could be some. But what she's seen was not a rat. Too big and too pale.

'What's there, Monty, eh?' she'd asked the dog.

He'd glanced at her, wagged his stumpy tail and turned back to stare across towards the trees.

But when she turned away, Monty didn't move. He'd

trotted forward to stand right next to the wire fencing marking the border of their land, looking down into the trees.

'What is it, boy?' she'd urged.

Monty didn't respond. He didn't bark, nor turn around. He kept staring. As if he was seeing something that Izzy couldn't. His hackles weren't raised, but his nose was up.

She'd shivered then. The wind and the oncoming dark were chilling. Both reasons enough to hurry back to the cottage. She'd called the dog, but Monty stayed staring into the copse, only returning to her side when she was a few yards from the cottage's back door.

She'd toyed with telling Marcus, but something held her back. Night was approaching. The last thing she wanted was for Marcus to worry about some stray and start tramping around with a torch.

At least, that was what she told herself.

Now, with the finding of the bodies on the path and the shock of seeing the man looking at the cottage, the memory of that little episode with Monty comes back to her like an ache in an old wound. The real reason for not telling Marcus is that she has not wanted to overexcite him. She shakes her head. Thinking that makes him sound like a toddler. He isn't. But he is also a worrier. Someone with no barometer when it comes to reacting to things.

It's why she wants him to break off from the news.

Telling him about seeing something in the woods would distract him. But it might also trigger a worse reaction when there was nothing to react to.

Marcus loves mystery. Once, when they were on holiday in New Hampshire, they'd stumbled across a store selling Americana and T-shirts and she'd almost bought him one with the words, 'Mountains from Molehills' splashed over the chest. But she'd thought better of it, worried he might not see the funny side, even if they did both know how spot on it was.

And so she keeps the pale movement in the woods and the missing vegetables to herself, and watches, with concern, as Marcus's excitement grows over the palaver surrounding the bodies on the path.

For now, it'll be her secret.

And she's good at keeping those from Marcus.

CHAPTER SEVEN

INSTEAD OF THE familiar Davies and Clough van, when Warlow gets back from his walk with Cadi next morning, parked on his drive is a grey Ford Focus with unmarked car written all over it. As soon as he pulls up in his Jeep, the driver's side opens and a woman gets out. She's small, at around five three and when Warlow and she stood outside Nando's confronting an addict on her first day as a DC, she was blonde. Today her hair is shorter, chopped below her ears, a natural red that complements her pale skin. She still looks impossibly young to Warlow, but there's something different about her. The way she stands, her bearing. Somehow taller, more confident. The look that comes with experience, he surmises.

Warlow leaves Cadi dozing in the car. When he gets out, Catrin Richards' face breaks into a wide grin. 'Sir. Good to see you.'

Warlow smiles in return and goes for mock formality. 'Detective Constable Richards. This is a surprise.'

'Nice, I hope. Oh, and it's sergeant now.'

Warlow raises his eyebrows. 'Christ. they must give

those stripes out like sweets these days. Either that or I'm getting old.'

'You don't look it, sir.'

'Compliments too? Now I am worried.'

The passenger door of the Focus opens. A woman, mid-forties, taller than Richards and holding a phone to her ear gets out with athletic ease. Warlow hears her say, '… talk about it later,' before she puts the phone away and turns towards him. Hair, eyes, clothes all dark, she stands with a straight back and glances from the cottage to Warlow, trying to fit the two together.

Richards makes the introductions. 'Evan Warlow, this is DI Jessica Allanby.'

'Nice place.' The DI scans the cottage.

Her accent is not local. Somewhere North of Chester, he guesses. 'Will be once its finished,' he replies. 'Either of you have problems with dogs?'

Allanby shakes her head. Catrin says, 'No.'

'Good. The beast needs water.' Warlow lets Cadi out. The dog trots enthusiastically towards the women. Richards pats Cadi's head with a wary greeting.

'You're a big girl,' she says, a nervous edge to her voice.

Cadi wags her tail and turns to Allanby who squats to be on the dog's level and ruffles her ears and head. 'Hello gorgeous.' She's all smiles. Cadi enjoys the attention. It goes on for longer than it needs to be for politeness sake.

'You've got a friend there,' Warlow says.

'Did Superintendent Buchannan speak to you?' Catrin asks.

Warlow nods. 'I know why you're here.'

Allanby stands. Cadi trots off to a silver bowl near the front door and drinks. The wind is freshening and worries at the collar of the Inspector's white blouse. She's not wearing a coat over her suit jacket and she crosses her arms against the cold. It pulls the jacket tight, making it bow forward over her breasts. Tight enough for Warlow to notice.

Steady boy.

But they are only thoughts. Ethereal. Harmless. And he can forgive himself the transgression because the only human company he's had for months in this place has been Bryn and Alwyn. Nothing to look at there. Jess Allanby, by contrast, is a breath of fresh air. 'Things aren't moving that quickly. I thought it'd be easier if I introduced myself.'

No one moves. Warlow knows he's in great danger of coming across as more of a misanthrope than he is. At least what his reputation used to be. A bit dry, fools not welcome, allergic to criminals in all their guises. He's tried his best to move on from the force. Too many people retire but don't really leave, turning up to social gatherings and hovering like ghosts in the corners, reliving jaded anecdotes, unable to quite let go. But this is different. This is real. Tanya Pickering's call has kept him awake for half the night. A circular argument raging in his restless brain. A common-sense angel on one shoulder telling him to walk away, a red-eyed devil on the other telling him this was his one remaining chance to nail the bastards.

His memories of working with Catrin Richards are all positive. She's efficient and a stickler when it comes to the dregs she has to deal with. But that side of her is tempered with warmth, the kind that people talk to. An invaluable trait in dealing with victims. He's seen her mascara run at crime scenes and briefings. Others might have read that as a weakness. He never did. Cold logic is one thing, but this job needs some heart as well. He doesn't know Allanby yet, but she's passed the Cadi test with distinction. The two police officers regard him. He regards them back.

He walks to the front door, puts a key in the Yale lock and glances back over his shoulder. 'Coffee or tea?'

It's warm inside from the wood stove. They sit around the table to keep it business-like. Allanby cups her hands around the mug, but she's got some colour back into her cheeks as she looks around, nodding.

'This is—'

'If you say cosy, I'm going to ask you to leave.' Warlow slits his eyes.

She's quick to smile. White teeth. All even. He wonders if they're natural. Warlow had his done about ten years ago at Denise's insistence. Before shelling out for crowns his were a little wonky and vulpine. Now they're straight and since his consumption of red wine has plummeted, no longer stained.

'I was going to go with understated and charming.'

Warlow rotates an open hand back and forth in a weighing-up gesture. 'Okay. You can stay.'

Catrin has a file open on the tabletop and begins pulling out photographs of the Pickerings and the path's post-landslip revelations.

'I know about the bus pass.' Warlow forestalls her.

Catrin nods. 'Awaiting confirmation obviously. No phone or wallet, but the clothing fits according to reports of what they were wearing.'

The Pickerings had called into a garage for petrol. The woman behind the counter described their fleeces and coats accurately.

'We've had a geologist from Swansea uni look at the landslip. He says there's a crevice. He can tell from the rock next to where the bodies were. And from weathering, exposure, lichen growth. A natural fault line for when the rock face fell.'

Warlow turns back to the photographs. 'What's the thinking? Did they fall in? Did they climb in?'

Allanby shakes her head. 'We have photographs of the path before the slip. Photographs of the cliffs too.'

Warlow frowns.

'The internet is a wonderful thing.' Catrin looks up. 'We've contacted the RAF. They have a sackful of reconnaissance images of the coast in all seasons and weather.'

It doesn't surprise Warlow. Central Wales, including the border, form part of the RAF's Tactical Training Areas for low flying jets and Hercules Transports. Sometimes, on clear days, the planes scream by only five hundred feet above. Enough to make the uninitiated jump. It's never bothered him nor Cadi.

'Our pet geologist thinks he can see the crevice on several of these photographs. It's at least twenty feet below the level of the path and you'd need ropes to get to it,' Allanby explains.

'I don't remember the Pickerings being into egg collecting,' Warlow says.

'Is that a thing?'

'Oh, yes. At least one thieving twitcher falls off the path every year.' Warlow pauses, thinking. 'So if they didn't climb down, someone must have put them in there?'

'Crime scene bods say there's evidence of multiple fractures.' Allanby lifts her mug and uses a manicured finger to wipe away a ring of moisture. 'Looks like the bones were broken so that they could push the bodies deep inside the crevice.'

Warlow contemplates this, his discomfort growing. 'We searched the path with dogs. Searched the cliff bases too. Over fifty miles.' The little fire within him crackles. They'd have needed dogs with crampons to have found them in this hole. 'Cause of death?'

Catrin shuffles some papers and pulls one out. 'Provisionally, blunt trauma. Both bodies have skull fractures. Same weapon we think. Nothing official yet, but a hammer has been proposed.'

Warlow can't help shutting his eyes. Not a wince,

merely confirmation of the worst-case scenario he'd imagined but didn't want to believe. These two people had been attacked and brutally murdered on the path because there was no conceivable way it had happened anywhere else and the bodies carried there. A whispered 'Shit' escapes his lips.

Allanby sips her tea and puts the mug down. 'This case was never closed, as you know.'

He does. He'd insisted on it. Silence. Warlow waits.

Allanby continues. 'It's a cold case and I'm playing catch-up here. I also know that not finding the Pickerings was one of your biggest regrets.'

He shoots Catrin a raised eyebrow glance. It's theatrical, mock accusatory, implying she's been telling tales. The DS comes back with a so-what stare. But Allanby is dead right. This case is still the non-healing sore that wakes him at night. Common sense still tells him he should stay out of it. But something else tells him that closure would take away that niggling pain.

'What exactly do you want from me?'

Allanby seizes the initiative. 'You know the area. You know the people involved. I've been given the green light to get you back on board. I'm here to show you I'm on side with that.'

I've hung up my red nose, Tom.

Warlow wants to say, 'Can I think about it?' again. It would be the smart thing. Mull it over, tease out the pros and cons, end up with the negatives inevitably outweighing the positives. Then he could sit and ponder the decision to say no while it ate at him. Like it had throughout the night since Tanya's call. Instead, he says, 'I'd be working with you two?'

Allanby smiles. It's calculated. For a moment Warlow can't read it, but then he does.

'Buchannan showed you my email, didn't he?'

'Superintendent Buchannan felt it was only fair. Quid pro quo and all that.'

Warlow nods. His email to Buchannan before breakfast that morning had requested certain assurances. Not working with Caldwell was the main one. Buchannan hadn't replied. He'd sent Allanby instead. And it's a two-way street, he realises. As much as he's wanted to ensure Allanby is someone he can work with, she too has needed to know he's not a complete control freak, or worse, a has been.

Catrin watches this exchange with bewilderment. She, clearly, has not received the memo.

'Not Caldwell then?' Warlow wants to add, *'effing wonderboy'* but holds back. Allanby might be his work bestie for all he knows.

'Not Caldwell,' Allanby confirms.

'Am I missing something?' Catrin asks.

'I'll explain later,' Allanby replies.

'Will there be paperwork?' Warlow's mouth puckers.

'Always. But minimal.' Catrin is back on familiar ground.

'Good. Not a fan of paperwork.'

'The Buccaneer has warned me I'll be doing most of that,' Allanby reassures him with a deadpan delivery.

SIO training involves all kinds of crossed t's and dotted i's. Policy documents need to be written and budget spends justified. Warlow is glad he's not starting that all over again.

Catrin hands him an envelope. 'Temporary contract. It only needs a signature. You're exempted an interview.'

'Shame,' he quips and everyone in the room knows he doesn't mean it.

'We're setting up an Incident Room in Haverfordwest, and you're going to be more valuable to us on the ground. But there is the small matter of the original case files.' The

DI lays this out with a hopeful upward inflection at the end of her sentence.

Warlow nods. 'Yes. I get that I'm the world expert on those.'

Allanby answers him with a smile. It's a great one.

'Should I call you ma'am, now?' Warlow asks.

'Jess is fine.'

They shake on it.

She stands, signalling an end to the visit. 'I thought we could go out to the site tomorrow and then visit the Pickerings' property. Get my bearings.'

'Okay,' Warlow agrees.

And, for the first time in many months, so help him, he feels that it is.

CHAPTER EIGHT

Kieron 'Ket' Thomas looks up from his pint of Stella at the two people sitting at the corner table. A girl in her early twenties with too many piercings to count and an older man with a receding hairline, ponytail and a large tattoo of a fork-tailed bird on his neck. From what he can see, they have maybe seven teeth between them. But that's none of his business. They are regular paying customers. Who gives a shit what they look like?

He raises his chin questioningly.

The girl holds up two fingers. It's not a defiant gesture. It's an order.

Ket nods and turns back to his pint.

The King and Queen in Pembroke Dock is a traditional red-brick pub with mullioned white windows. The landlord lives on the premises on the top floor and puts hanging baskets up every spring. The owner, a drinks wholesaler, has kept the original decor. It has guest rooms and serves food from a menu written in chalk on a slate board. Ket sits in the public bar with his pint in front of him, one eye on a streamed football game playing on all three of the bar's screens. The other on the clientele that come and go.

He's only half interested in the game.

This is his office.

Ket, the name he is not so affectionately known by, is only partly down to his initials. Mostly it's related to the stuff he peddles. Special K or, to give it its real name, Ketamine. A widely used dissociative anaesthetic in animals and a psychedelic hallucinogenic in humans.

The couple are fidgety. Ket smiles, he knows the signs. They want to do business. Have to do business. But he doesn't hurry. He's been here all afternoon and dealing is thirsty work. He has a pint to finish. And telly to watch.

But the couple are antsy so Ket takes a healthy swallow of beer, stands, fishes out a pack of Marlboro Gold from his camo jacket and heads for the exit.

It's a miserable, gusty, drizzly afternoon so he stands to one side of the pub's porch out of the wind. It's a side entrance. One not covered by CCTV cameras. One minute later he's joined by the girl who takes out a pack of Bensons. She's crouched in on herself, shoulders hunched, shivering in the wind.

The girl takes out a packet of cigarettes and removes one but drops the packet. Ket stoops to pick it up and glances inside. No cigarettes. Instead he sees three rolled-up twenty-pound notes. Sixty quid for two baggies.

Bargain.

Ket pockets the Bensons.

In his hand is a lighter that he offers up to the woman's face. They stand close as she accepts and out of his fist he drops two plastic baggies into her conveniently cupped and ready hand. Inside the baggies are four K bombs, doses of ketamine wrapped in cigarette paper ready for swallowing.

He blows the girl a silent kiss. Close up he sees she has ravaged skin and dark-rimmed eyes.

The girl sends him a venomous glare. She may be his customer, but that doesn't mean that she likes him. Why should she? She's a slave to his wares.

She turns away and smokes on but walks around to the other side of the porch into the wind. The front door of the pub opens, and the ponytailed man emerges, turns left and he and the girl hurry off. That's it for Ket. He's sold his stash. Another day another six hundred quid. He finishes the Marlboro, goes back in and picks up his pint.

By now it's almost six. One screen above the bar switches to the news. Football stays on the other two. The volume is down so he sits through twenty minutes of bull-shit, reading the subtitles until he sees the images he's been waiting for.

Men in white suits on the coastal path.

He smiles. When he first saw these images he almost shat himself. No way. No fucking way after all this time. The first thing he wanted to do was ring Neil Morris, but the poor bastard was still doing time. It was then that the idea came to him.

This was on the news. So other people will have seen it. Everyone will have seen it.

Ket's life is all about trying to take advantage of situa-tions. Preying on those less fortunate than he is. Like the idiot with the ponytail and the girl with the piercings who paid a fiver more than they paid yesterday for the crap they can't live without.

Naturally, he sees the horror on the path as not a fail-ure, but something he should take advantage of. A chance to make a little coin out of a crap situation.

Outside, night has arrived.

He has a burner in his hand. A number he can contact if he needs to. Mainly about the product. There's never anyone there and he's meant to leave a message and wait until they get back to him. There is only one number in this phone's contacts on auto dial. He presses the button, waits, and then speaks.

'Yeah, uh, it's Ket. I seen the news and like, I think we need to chat. That job I done for you, the one I helped Morris with? Them two wasn't supposed to be found, was they? But it's all over the fucking news, man. We sealed the entrance and stuff but it's a real shit show now after that landslide. Thing is, if plod come asking, what am I supposed to say? I know what I should say, like, but, you now, with Morris in the nick and all, it's only me that knows. Thing is I reckon I should be compensated for the stress of it, like. Compensated so that I say the right thing if plod calls. I know we was paid but this is different, isn't it? This is some weird shit. Anyway, you got my number and I'm always in town. Best place is the King and Queen in the afternoons.'

Ket kills the call, waits, feels a ripple of excitement at knowing that soon things will happen. He smiles and takes a slug of lager.

Fuck yeah.

CHAPTER NINE

THERE IS no easy way to get to the cordoned-off section of path where the bodies are. To walk from normal access points like Moylgrove or Newport would take hours. Instead, the police have asked permission to park their vehicles along a farm lane that leads to and from stock sheds, a little to the east of a property called Castell Y Gaer. There isn't much room to turn vehicles around and Warlow parks a hundred yards further away in a barnyard, between Jess's black Golf and a crime scene van.

His name is on the crime scene manager's list, and so he has no trouble with access.

He nods to a couple of techies whose names he can't remember, but who obviously know him. Mud squelches as he walks northeast along a rutted dirt lane, its tracks churned up by the unusual volume of traffic. His boots will need a damn good clean when he gets home, but he's dressed in walking gear for the occasion. Brushed and sponged clean of the mud he's accumulated on his walks with Cadi. Now that he's off the bench, he has to make an effort.

The lane climbs gently before it falls away. When he

crests the rise, the view opens up with the iron-grey sky separated from a choppy green sea by a tantalising strip of gold on the horizon. A brisk wind picks up as he crosses a field, following a path marked by plastic triangles on temporary stakes.

When he reaches the stock fence, he climbs over a splayed ladder guarded by a uniformed officer in a high-vis tabard.

'Rob Owens.' Warlow greets him. 'Still doing all the glamorous jobs I see.'

Owens, a twenty-year veteran, grins through a grey-flecked beard. 'Mr Warlow, sir. A sight for sore eyes.'

'It's not sir anymore, Rob. It's Evan.'

Owens's grin doesn't slip. 'They're over by the tent, sir.'

Warlow thinks about objecting, but old habits die hard in this job and it would be churlish to push the point. Thirty yards along the narrow path, the stock fence has been redirected and a space in the field cleared. In it sits a white Tyvek tent.

Outside it, a figure glances in his direction and raises a hand. Though there is now a black puffer jacket above the suit trousers, he knows it's Jess because of the posture and the dark hair fighting a losing battle against the wind. The tent has its sides open to both the sea and the field. The remaining walls waft in and out like sails in the breeze. He walks to the rear, field side of the tent and sees two masked, white-suited figures. Warlow picks some gloves from a box on the table and slips them on. Where the tent is open to the sea, a safety net has been rigged next to the raw cleaved earth.

He raises a hand to a woman who introduces herself as, 'Jo Tannard, crime scene tech.'

'Hi, Jo.' She must be new because Warlow does not recall her face.

'Oh, and Alison sends her regards. She's caught up with the oil refinery fire otherwise she'd be here.'

Alison Povey runs the crime scene investigation team and she and Warlow go way back. It would have been good to have her on board. Ah well. The trouble with cold cases is that they're often not the highest priority on anyone's list.

'And this is Dr Chris Reddy, our forensic anthropologist from Cardiff.' Tannard holds out an open palm. The taller of the two white suits waves. Jess joins them from the cliff side where she's been waiting. 'Shall we?'

Tannard moves first, Reddy goes next and Warlow follows towards a ladder surrounded by scaffolding and boards, all inside the rigged safety netting. They step down onto a platform that runs across the face of the cliff. Below, the sound of the sea crashing against the rocks comes through the gaps in the boards. There is no path visible, just the sheer rocks and there, not three yards away and at knee height, a body.

Warlow stands where he is and stares at the macabre sight. One torso already removed, leaving the remains of one leg still in the crevice. But the second body is yet to be exhumed. Just shy of the crevice opening sits a skull with some skin still attached, wispy hair wafting in the breeze, slightly bent forward in contemplation. Next to it an arm thrusts upwards as if in an attempt at escape.

'There's been some disarticulation, and we had to remove the outermost remains because of the risk of it falling. But I can confirm that the removed body is male,' Reddy says.

Dark earth has spilled onto the boards at Warlow's feet. A thin odour of decay, like a damp forest floor, wafts out from the dark maw of the crevice entrance, which cannot be much more than a ragged three feet at its widest point.

Reddy points towards the skeleton and the pale bones

of the arm. 'The scapula and clavicle here are broken. Smashed almost.'

'So someone must have forced the body in?'

Reddy nods. 'I can't see any way that the person could climb with that sort of injury. Unless they were contortionists.'

Gallows humour. Warlow's no prude but there's a time and a place. This isn't it. He'd have said so in the old days. Now he turns away so they don't notice him grinding his teeth and studies the raw surface of the cliff. 'Quite the landslip.'

'Yes,' agrees Tannard. 'It's sheered a good ten feet off the old face. We got some help from the army engineers to rig up this examination platform.'

'And there's no possibility that they'd climbed up from below?'

'It's deadly down there. Jagged rocks. Big swells.' Tannard points up. 'My guess is that someone must have come down on ropes from above.'

'And stuffed them into this hole like a turkey at Christmas,' mutters Warlow. He feels a pain in the ball of his thumb. It's the nail of his own middle finger that's gouging the flesh. He relaxes his tight fist before he draws blood.

'I wanted you to see,' Jess says.

'Thanks.' It comes out wrong. Too harsh, too sardonic. He exhales and turns to her. 'Sorry. It's just—'

'You can't help wondering if you missed something?'

Warlow snorts. She's good. 'I must have walked over this spot a dozen times with no bloody idea …' His words trail off.

'I wanted you to be sure. They were dead long before they were reported missing.'

Cold comfort, he thinks. But already his mind is rejigging. Assessing. 'If they were brought down from the path, looks like at least a two-man job.'

Tannard nods. She has dark shaped eyebrows now frowning at this sordid discussion. 'Two at least.'

'And whoever it was knew about this spot, too,' Warlow adds.

'I'd say that was likely,' agrees Tannard.

Warlow notices other cracks in the rocks. One has a black cable snaking into it. He's seen these before. There'll be a tiny camera on the end of that cable. 'What are you looking for?' Warlow asks Reddy. 'Ark of the Covenant?'

'In a way. Making sure that this isn't a collapsed gravesite. It's happened.'

'Are there more?'

Reddy shakes his head. 'We'll be removing the other body today.'

'And then what?'

Tannard answers. 'Shipped to Cardiff for post-mortem exam by the HOP along with the other one.'

They're assuming he doesn't know. Or that he's forgotten. But he hasn't. A Home Office Pathologist will do the post-mortem as per protocol.

'Once it's out, we can sift the site,' Reddy adds.

Warlow hears but doesn't lift his eyes from Mrs Pickering's remains. Because he's convinced that's who she is.

Hello Marjorie.

'Anything else I need to see?' he asks Jess.

'Not here.'

He follows her up the ladder to a second, smaller exhibit tent and a table laden with bagged up items. Tannard picks one up.

'Clothing from the first body has already gone for assessment, but this scrap came away when we removed the remains. It's a piece of the shirt the second body was wearing.' Warlow leans in. The dirty material is bleached, but there is still enough colour to make out a blue check.

The same as Mrs Pickering wore the morning she went missing.

'I'd put money on this being Marjorie Pickering's,' Warlow says.

'Thought so.' Tannard nods.

Outside, the wind rattles the tent's ropes like some kind of elemental affirmation. As if the Pickerings were making their presence felt. Jess was right. He'd needed to see this. Needed certainty.

'Where's Catrin today?' he asks.

'Softening the blow for our next port of call,' Jess explains.

'Which is?'

'Limehouse Cottage.'

THEY GO in separate cars to Mwnt. Warlow parks and gets into the Golf with Jess. It smells nicer than his own car. Much nicer than the mouth of the cave on the path. He thinks about saying so but then checks himself because he suspects it isn't the aroma of a dangly air freshener he detects. It's a subtle perfume. Could be Catrin's but she isn't here. Most likely it's Jess's. He could say something, but he doesn't know her well enough to gauge how she'd take that yet.

Compliment or misguided flirting? Best to stay quiet.

He's glad when she opens up a conversation.

'I know we said you'd be in the field, but there is a daily PM debrief and we may ask you to attend.'

Warlow opts for silence to signal his disapproval.

'I'll do what I can,' Jess continues, reading it. 'Sion Buchannan may insist.'

She's right. But at this stage of the investigation there will not be much to report on other than to reopen the old investigation. It's fact finding. 'And the Incident Room will definitely be in Haverfordwest?'

The station there has HOLMES facilities despite the force's HQ being in Carmarthen.

'Haverfordwest, yes. Reddy and Tannard think they've seen skull injuries on both bodies. We'll get the rest of body one out today and then the second. There'll be a PM tomorrow. I'm going across. So is Buchannan.'

Warlow nods. The SIO is duty bound to attend the PM in murder enquiries. And he'd expect his lead investigator to be there. Warlow seizes on this as his get out clause. 'Let's wait and see what that throws up. I'll be more useful once we know.'

'It'll mean a second trip once we get the other body out,' she adds.

'I'm warning you now, The Heath is a bugger to park in.'

Jess pulls in to let a Tesco delivery van drive by. 'Heath?'

'What everyone calls the University Hospital in Cardiff. I'd suggest parking off site and walking a couple of hundred yards. I'll draw you a map.'

'Thanks.' Her smile is quick.

They've had to head inland to get to the shared narrow lane that leads both to Penmor Farm and to Limehouse Cottage. But finally, Jess turns off.

'Nothing much has changed in seven years,' Warlow says, bouncing in his seat as the Golf hits a pothole.

'Is that good or bad?'

Warlow shrugs. 'Bad for the Pickerings. Perhaps good for us. After this length of time, people believe they've got away with it. Sometimes they get sloppy.'

Catrin is in the cottage yard as they pull up. She's with a man. Tall, lean, hipster beard. The same man Warlow saw a few days ago when he ventured on the path. He towers over the detective sergeant, but their body language is non-confrontational. The yard is neat apart from a pile of building materials in one corner: sacks of cement, some rough stone, lengths of four-by-four pine. The flower beds Warlow remembers have been replaced with gravel for hard standing.

When they've parked and got out, Catrin introduces Warlow and Jess to Marcus Dexter.

'You've done a great job with the place,' Warlow says. The last time he was here, the stone walls had been in dire need of repointing. But now the whole of the building has undergone re-rendering, keeping the shape and uneven-ness of the rubble construction beneath. 'Couldn't have been a straightforward job.'

Dexter nods. 'Not me, I'm afraid. It's called bag rubbing. A specialist job.' His jovial accent isn't local. More at home in a leafy suburb somewhere South of London, Warlow decides. Dexter expands on the method. 'They hang damp hessian sacks over the render for five days until it goes off. Too hot or too cold and it doesn't work.' It's not a boast, but Warlow senses that he's proud of the natural approach. It would have been easier and quicker to use cement. But the Atlantic weather has a way of testing most modern materials, putting them to the climatic sword and finding them sorely lacking. Modern was not what this building needed. 'We've done the same inside,' adds Dexter.

But that's not all they've done. They've repainted the windows in the muted green that Warlow has seen on National Trust buildings. To the side is a new extension that's wood and glass under a slate roof. There are bay trees in stone pots either side of the door and the outbuild-ings, too, have new roofs.

'I like it,' says Warlow. He could engage Dexter in a discussion about renovation techniques seeing as how he's had to immerse himself in a similar project. Talk that would have everyone else comatose within a minute. But lime work is out of his sphere of knowledge and an almost arcane art. No accident that ancient lime mixes have been used for thousands of years in construction for breathability, water repellence, water proofing, you name it.

But now is not the time.

It's Jess who takes the lead. 'DS Richards has explained we're here for my benefit.'

'Yes. And a nice detective constable called yesterday to warn us.'

'That would be DC Harries. He'll be acting as a liaison.'

'Yeah, so he said. Izzy and I are more than happy to help any way we can.'

Jess nods and turns to Warlow. 'Mr Warlow was the investigating officer when Mr and Mrs Pickering went missing. The nature of the investigation has changed and so I'm familiarising myself with the details.'

'I've explained to Mr Dexter that it's likely there'll be renewed press interest. And that means they may have some callers.' Catrin flicks her gaze from Jess to Dexter.

Jess elaborates. 'You can deal with them as you see fit. But they can be intrusive. Sometimes they ask to take photographs of the property so that they can run a then and now piece.'

'They'll be looking for quotes. Anything to stir up interest,' Warlow says. 'My advice would be to say nothing and refer them back to the force press officer.' His real advice would be to buy a shotgun and pepper the sods with buckshot if they come anywhere near, but he keeps the lid on that one. For now.

'Okay. We'll take that on board.' Dexter says.

'Mind if we walk around the property?' Jess asks.

'Be my guest. Would you like some tea?'

'White, one sugar,' says Warlow. Jess declines, Catrin orders hers with milk but no sugar.

When Dexter leaves for the kitchen, the DS whispers, 'He's been very nice.'

'Seems pleasant enough.'

'He's getting a kick out of it,' Warlow says. 'Come on. He'll let us know when the tea is brewed. Let's get on with it.'

CHAPTER TEN

THE LAYOUT IS JUST as Warlow remembers. He starts off
with the nearest of the two fields that come with the property, the one now occupied by donkeys, and works his way
back towards where a walled garden abuts on to the
closed-off section of the coastal path. A low stone wall
gives on to a wire fence. The path beyond looks overgrown,
but when he steps up on the wall, he can look out over a
narrow strip of grazing to the sea beyond.

Jess joins him and frowns. 'So they could access the
path here, yet on the morning they went missing drove to
Newport. Have I got that right?'

'This part of the path doesn't join up with anything.
Ownership dispute. The local council has been to the High
Court more than once. But so far, the Retreat has won,'
Warlow explains.

'Retreat?'

'Yes. Craig y Môr. Huge place on the cliff.' Recall
brings an image to Warlow's mind. A clutch of low stone
buildings with a chapel and a cross perched on a stone
cairn. Smiling people who couldn't do enough for them
whenever they'd called. Keen to cooperate with the police

and steadfast in their opposition to intrusive tourism. 'It's an international prayer centre owned by the Light of the Apostles Church. People come from all over. They claim that opening up the path would be detrimental to the atmosphere of sanctuary and peace needed to get closer to God.'

'Doesn't sound very Christian to me,' Jess mutters.

Warlow can't argue with that. 'Like a lot of these organisations, they're not short of money, that's for sure. That gets them good lawyers. And the people in their employment have the added incentive of getting a leg up on the stairway to heaven – according to them. For now, they own the land and the island just off the coast and don't want nosy walkers tramping all over it.'

'Do you think that was a cause of friction between the Pickerings and them?' Jess asks.

They'd considered it of course. But nothing had come of it. 'I don't think the Pickerings liked it, but the dispute existed before they bought Limestone Cottage. And as far as we could tell, they got on well with the Gowers.'

'Is that the farmer next door?'

'Yes. They own the surrounding land.' Warlow turns back to complete the circuit of the property. They climb up the slope. Opposite the house, he pauses and points across the ravine to the Engine House. An improbable building for such a location, perched on the edge of a promontory. The main structure is narrow with a round tapering chimney, blackened by the weather, roofless and crumbling. The dark dolerite walls rise three storeys, and rows of empty windows gaze back at them.

'Ooh, brooding,' Jess says.

Warlow agrees. 'It is. Derelict for years. Even the local kids won't go near.'

'Don't tell me, it's haunted.'

'The locals think it is.' Warlow grins. 'And just as well,

because it's a death trap. The south wall has all but crumbled to dust. There are caves and tunnels beneath it. Who knows what it's like now.'

'Doesn't someone want to preserve it?' Catrin asks. 'Isn't it listed?'

Warlow walks forward a few steps to get to higher ground. 'It is. And there's been talk over the years. One or two societies raised money, but the business with the path put a stop to all of that. My guess is that neither the council nor the government want to spend money on a lost cause.'

He'd visited it three times. Never on his own. Something about the place made it cold and damp even on a sizzling July afternoon. The kind of dankness that seeped into your bones. The men who worked here managing the engine a hundred and some years ago earned their money.

He takes them up to the property's highest point. A corner angling ever closer to the dark trees of the ravine. The spot where Dexter is constructing their captain's cabin. He stops and reviews the building work. 'Looks like our bearded friend has been busy. The Gower's land curves around the property here. They've fenced this off because they lost an animal in the ravine once. I see they've made this a proper cow track now.' A gravelled five-yard-wide path dotted with cow pats is visible on the other side of a wooden post and rail fence with the same sort of fence on the far side. Down the track, the field balloons out into a strip of grazing between the cottage and the ravine as it falls steeply away towards the sea.

'Hardly think they'd bother grazing animals here.' A dubious Catrin studies the narrow patch of grass.

Warlow shrugs. 'You know what farmers are like. Land is their currency.'

There's a shout from the house. Tea is ready.

They walk back and tea is brought out by the woman

Warlow saw in the yard a few days before. She's introduced by Dexter as Izzy Ramsden, his partner. Close up she's bright-eyed, blonde hair pulled back from a pale face with spots of colour that may be from the cold but could of course have been painted on. He does not know about cosmetics. Doesn't even know if people still use compacts. Despite her thin frame, there's a steeliness about her. The words that spring to Warlow's mind are 'capable looking'.

The tea is hot and sweet. Izzy has also baked some Welsh cakes. Warlow only ever eats these in other people's houses. He takes one now.

'You're building up in the top corner.' Warlow sips his tea.

'Yes, finishing a project someone else started,' Izzy answers. Another accent. Still not local.

'It was just a base when I was here last,' Warlow muses.

'Still is. But we want to make it a little more substantial. Summer house and an observation platform. Like the bridge of a ship.' Izzy's voice is bright and enthusiastic.

'The Pickerings must have had the same idea,' Catrin says.

Izzy nods with enthusiasm. 'It wouldn't surprise me. It's a glorious spot. You can look down the ravine to the inlet.'

'What about the cows?'

Izzy laughs. 'We don't mind cows. That's why we're here. To lay in bed and count the sheep and cows.'

'And I'm working on our neighbour to sell me that strip beyond. It would make things a lot easier.' Dexter strokes his beard.

'How are negotiations going on that?' Warlow asks between munches of cake.

Dexter's turn to laugh with eyebrows raised. 'They're nice people. Stubborn but nice.'

Izzy puts a hand on his arm. 'It doesn't matter. It'll be

fine. We'll be high enough above the cows. We'll have the telescope, and we'll look at the stars and the sea.'

Warlow hears the reassuring tone and wonders if that's her default with Dexter. He knows little about them but surmises there must be a story. Why else would a thirty-something couple buy a place like this? They're getting away from something, if not everything. Trying to rebuild their lives, perhaps. But it's a distraction he doesn't need, and he puts the idea from his mind.

They finish their tea and Jess hands back the mug. 'We'll be in touch if there's anything else. And feel free to call us if the press become a nuisance. You have a contact number?'

Izzy smiles. 'DC Harries explained all that.' She turns to Warlow. 'But you were involved with the original case, am I right?'

Warlow, for a moment, is wrong-footed. 'I was.'

There's something approaching amusement in the little glint that appears in her eye. 'Your photo is the one that appears on all the search engines.'

He gives her a cool smile. 'I've weathered a bit since then.'

Izzy cocks her head. 'A bit. But not so bad.' She smiles and puts the mugs on a tray. Jess thanks them both and they take their leave.

Warlow suggests they leave the cars where they are and walk up the lane to the farm.

Halfway up Catrin voices what they're all thinking. 'What was that thing with the search engine all about?'

'Perhaps Ms Ramsden has taken a shine to Mr Warlow,' Jess says.

But Warlow doesn't rise to the bait. Izzy Ramsden has probably looked him up. And why not? Might be simple curiosity. Might be something else. Either way, she'll have her reasons. He'll wait to find out what they are.

But he doesn't dwell on the current occupant. His mind is with the Pickerings and their last day on earth. It doesn't take much effort because he's thought about it almost every day since the first time he drove down the track to Lime-house Cottage. When he opens his eyes and speaks, it's not the fields and sea he's seeing. It's someone else's journey. One that he'd pieced together from detailed enquiries.

'The Pickerings drove out of here at 8.30am on 7th of September 2014. None of the Gowers saw them leave, but then the farm is busy. However, a postman recognised their car as he pulled out of a junction half a mile away at eight thirty-five. He did not see another car in front or behind them. They were not pursued. They headed southeast and stopped at the Murco garage in Penparc on the A487. Both Pickerings went into the shop. Ken filled up, Marjorie bought *The Times*, some crisps for their lunch and paid with cash once Ken had finished with the petrol. The shop assistant, a woman called Phyllis Roberts, gave a detailed description and an exact time because it was stamped on the till receipt. When they left the garage, the Pickerings drove southwest on the A487, bypassing Cardigan and crossing the river Teifi. At the Ridgeway roundabout, they took the B4546 north to Poppit Sands. A woman walking her dog saw them arrive at the car park. If you like, we can do that journey and time it. The last time I tried it, it took twenty-nine minutes.'

It's only now that Warlow realises they've all stopped walking. Catrin is looking at him openly with a kind of dull horror. Jess wears an expression of mild shock. The sudden silence is deafening.

'Yeah, okay,' says Jess, eventually. 'We ought to do that. And we will. But first, let's see if the Gowers are around.'

CHAPTER ELEVEN

RYLAN GOWER LOOKS like a farmer straight out of central casting as he leans on the gate to the yard of Penmor farm. He's in uniform. Wellies and mud-spattered olive work trousers held up by green braces over a Viyella shirt under an open coat, equally filthy. One arm rests on the top rail of the gate, the other reaches up to scratch an itch at his temple under a tweed flat cap. He stands and waits while the police get out of the car.

'Rylan, it's been a long time,' Warlow says.

'A long time right enough.' Gower's accent sounds, to the uninitiated, more suggestive of Devon than this stretch of Welsh coast and Warlow notes Jess's quizzical frown. She's got a bit to learn about colonisation. Pembrokeshire has always been split in two by a thousand-year-old border running from Newgale in the west to Amroth in the east. Norman allocated lands lie to the south of a demarcation once fortified by castles. The Landsker Line created a twelfth century land-grab. Little Flanders beyond Wales. An area that morphed over the years into Little England. To the north, the native Welsh speakers from whom the lands were taken a thousand years before still congregate.

And though Penmor is north of the line it is from the south that Gower came in the 1990s when the family farm was split up and money found for the younger son, Rylan, to buy his own land. He brought the accent with him.

'Never thought I'd see you again at this gate.' Gower's mouth is oddly lopsided.

'Thought, or hoped?' Warlow grins. He remembers the old man suffered a facial palsy in his forties. Almost thirty years have passed since then, but the damage makes him inscrutable.

'Both,' says Gower.

Catrin steps forward and holds up her warrant card, introduces herself and Allanby.

'Courtesy call,' the DI explains. 'No doubt you've heard about the two bodies on the coastal path?'

Gower nods. His eyes, used to shielding from the sun, muddy grey slits in a ruddy face. 'It's them then, is it?'

No one needs to ask who he's referring to.

'We're not sure yet,' Jess says. 'But we wanted to warn you and your neighbours about press and nosy visitors. They'll come as the story breaks.'

Gower smiles, but only one half of his mouth responds and what comes across is a grotesque grimace. 'Don't you worry about visitors.'

A tractor trundles into the yard and two dogs bound out from the cab barking and snarling through the bars of the gate. 'Hush now,' Gower hisses. The dogs slink to lie behind him. Jess and Catrin eye the collies nervously, but Warlow's gaze has already shifted to the tractor and the man who jumps off it with practised ease. Ben Gower isn't as tall as his father but has the same gait and barrel chest. He takes one look at Warlow and walks off into an open shed without acknowledgement.

'Ben's grown.' Warlow follows the younger Gower's progress.

'That's what hard graft'll do for you.'

'That and keeping his nose clean,' Warlow adds. The insinuation isn't lost on Rylan Gower, who sends the ex DCI a venomous glance.

Two new Land Rovers with Pen 1 and Pen 2 as part of their registrations stand outside a square whitewashed farmhouse. To the left of the gate that Gower still guards runs a tarmac lane that ends in gravel hardstanding in front of two well-tended stone bed and breakfast cottages. Both buildings have shiny, freshly painted front doors and woodpiles in a neat stack on both open porches.

'Bookings okay?' Warlow asks.

'Can't complain. Keeps Mrs Gower busy doing the B and Bs.'

'We've told your neighbours to contact us if they're hassled by press,' Richards says. 'Feel free to do the same.'

Warlow notes that Jess doesn't offer a card this time. Evidently, she's decided that Gower can look after himself.

'They seem nice enough, your new neighbours,' Warlow observes.

'They do.'

'Says he's trying to buy that old strip of land near the ravine.'

Gower's lopsided smile widens. 'He's mentioned it.'

'Nice little garden for his summer house.'

'Bloody stupid idea if you ask me. When it rains hard, there'll be slurry in that corner he's building in. Runs in off the fields. I've told him. He's not inclined to listen, though.' Gower shrugs.

'He's young,' says Warlow, knowing it excuses a multi-tude of sins. Both men are aware that the Gowers know that only too well.

They retrace their steps to the cars. On the way, Catrin speaks her mind. 'Not exactly chatty, the young Gower, was he?'

Warlow grunts. 'That was one of his better days.'

'Did they and the Pickerings get on?' Jess asks.

'We found no evidence of arguments or disputes. The land was not really a thing.'

'What about the son?'

Warlow smiles. She had not missed the moment that sparked between the young farmer and the DCI.

'I never make Ben Gower's Christmas card list. Neither of you are likely to get on it either. He's allergic to the force. Ben was a little shit as a teenager. Bored, had a car, thought he was Colin Macrae–'

Catrin frowns. .

'Really? You don't know who Colin Macrae is?'

Catrin shakes her head.

'A rally driver,' explains Warlow, feeling old. 'Ben drove like a maniac around the lanes and got into all sorts of minor trouble with a wild crowd in Haverfordwest. Ended up with an arrest for possession with intent to supply and narrowly avoided going to Parc.'

'Parc?' Jess asks.

'A category B Young Offender's prison in Bridgend.'

'How avoid?'

'Strings were pulled. The right puppets twitched. It's a small community here. I remember it because there was a girl involved.'

Catrin sends him another questioning glance.

Warlow elaborates. 'Before your time. A year or two before the Pickering case even. Ben Gower was seventeen and, as I say, a right little thug. I'm convinced he was getting roped into a county lines operation but he denied all that. The girl took the fall and went to prison. Ben did not. But it curtailed his activities.' Warlow's gaze shifts to the passing fields. 'He didn't like that. He was jumpy and reticent throughout the Pickering investigation. Resented our presence mightily. Mine anyway.'

'Sounds like a charmer,' Catrin replies.

They reach the cars. Catrin heads back to the Incident Room in the Focus. Jess drives Warlow to his car in Mwnt.

'Thanks for the walkthrough,' Jess says when Warlow gets out.

'My pleasure.'

She looks up through the open passenger side window. 'The debrief is at four. I'll ring you as soon as it's done.'

'That gives me time to get the dog walked and fed.'

Warlow watches the Golf drive away. He'd stood in this car park alone, just as he's doing now, dozens of times during the Pickering investigation. He'd stood and wondered what it was he was missing. What little bit of the puzzle had he seen and not picked up on. Living with not knowing had been one of the most difficult things he'd had to cope with during his career. Until Dr Emmerson had turned her earnest gaze upon him.

When he'd finally put the case to rest knowing that other officers would review it from that point on, he'd done so with huge regret, never for one moment believing he'd be involved in investigating it again.

But here he is, part of a new team. No longer top dog, but a part of the pack. He's rusty. Hasn't had to think like a police officer for months. But it's a groove, and he's the stylus. It's a question of cranking up the turntable and letting the familiar tune play because he knows the words to the song they're singing well enough.

He lifts his face and sniffs the air. No scent. Not yet. But it's there. All he has to do is catch it on the wind.

CHAPTER TWELVE

At Limehouse Cottage it's avocado and sauerkraut for lunch. After the police left, they each went back to their chores. Izzy pensively, Marcus with a jaunty whistle. This is the first opportunity they've had to chat.

'What do you think they talked about when they walked around the place?' Marcus asks between munches.

'Warlow was reacquainting himself.'

'Yeah. He's kind of Poirot to Allanby's Marcella.'

Izzy snorts. 'Oh, Marky. It isn't TV.'

'You have to admit it's interesting though. Seeing them up close like that. Watching them work.'

'Suppose,' she says to appease him. But secretly, she has no idea why the police needed to visit at all. The Pickerings and all trace of them have long gone. She's concluded that it's not the house they're interested in, it's where it is and what surrounds it. Warlow struck her as someone experienced and so did Allanby, whereas the sergeant was so young she looked like someone on work experience from sixth form.

'What have you got planned for this afternoon?' She

mashes avocado with her fork before ladling it onto a rice cake.

'Transporting stuff to the site, oh, and there's a scaffolder calling. Remember when we went to Cornwall last year and saw that house where a tree had fallen on a garage?'

'Remind me.'

'On the way back it had scaffolding surrounded it and they were doing repairs under a plastic membrane. To keep the weather at bay.'

Izzy's face lights up. 'Oh, I remember.'

'Well, since the weather here is vicious, I thought we could do the same. It'd mean being able to press on throughout winter.'

'What a great idea.'

'How about you?'

Izzy shoots him a nervous look. 'I need to get my artwork over to the temperance hall in Cwmarth.'

'Shit. The exhibition.'

Izzy nods. 'Starts Saturday.'

'Need a hand?'

'No. It's only ten pieces. I have a small table in one corner.'

'Ding, ding,' says Marcus, grinning.

It's a silly in joke. The ding-ding alludes to a London bus. The implication is that her hobby, her artwork, is nothing but a busman's holiday for someone who works in design and fabric all day. It is as long-winded a joke as it is unfunny, yet she smiles, albeit with a shake of her head. Point is she loves working with fabrics and messing with collages and shapes is a natural extension. A chance to exhibit her little indulgences in a village hall is all the encouragement she's needed to get the pieces framed and finished.

'Want me to run you over there?'

'No need,' Izzy says. 'Stay here for your scaffolder.' But then she frowns. 'Have you talked to the Gowers about it? We don't want anything that'll scare the cows.'

'If he'd sell me the bloody field, there'd be no cows to scare.'

Izzy presses her lips together. 'It isn't going to happen, you know that. They're not interested.'

'We live in hope.'

'No, we live in Pembrokeshire in a dreamy cottage by the sea.'

Marcus raises his tea mug. Izzy does the same. They clink.

Later, with Marcus dressed in coat and boots and loading a wheelbarrow, Izzy unpins Allanby's card from the corkboard. She punches in the number and name into her phone contacts before flipping the card over and reading Warlow's number. She adds that too, muttering, 'Poirot it is then.'

Then she goes to her studio to collect up the box of framed fabric pieces for the exhibition.

———

CWMARTH HALL IS an early 19th century faux Tudor construction with a magnificent clock tower, sadly devoid of clock. The windows once had leaded lights featuring flower motifs. But a price-matched lottery renovation means that an aesthetically challenged hall committee have opted for double glazing over tradition. Inside, trestle tables are herring boned down the middle of the sizeable room while three of the four bays on each side are split into two to accommodate paintings, sculptures, pottery and items of handcrafted furniture. At the very back, three tables are laid end-to-end to span the entire width of the room and partitioned off into four booths. It's in one of these spaces, shared with a potter specialising in animal figurines, that Izzy displays her artwork.

She's arranged her pieces according to colour: darker pieces above on the two-by-one metre board with her lighter pieces on the flat surface of the table.

It's mid-afternoon quiet. The exhibition doesn't start until Saturday, and the only people in the space are fellow artists. What disturbs the peace is a woman in dungarees, far too much makeup and with little or no concept of what an inside voice is, conversing with the organiser. Or rather berating her about the poor light on the eastern side of the building. And of how a dull day affects the saturation of her colour palette.

'You could swear it was the sodding Tate,' says a disembodied voice from behind a partition on Izzy's section.

She's been so absorbed she's failed to notice someone else at this end of the room. Startled and intrigued, she creeps across to that last partitioned off area. A waft of something aromatic reaches her nose before she peeks around the wall to find a thirty-something woman with an elfin haircut and big hoop earrings looking up at her. The little table she's seated at has a magnifying lamp on a stand and various jewellery making tools scattered on the surface.

'Weather's a big talking point here though, isn't it?' Izzy replies.

'Sod all you can do about it,' says Hoop Earrings. 'Keep some wellies in the car and always have a cagoule.' She has a lot of dark makeup around her eyes and matching aubergine lipstick.

'I've learned that already.'

'First time?'

Izzy nods.

The woman stands and says, 'Angharad Brunton. As you can see, I'm into mythological exotica.' She waves a hand with black painted nails over her wares. 'That's why I'm down here in the naughty corner.'

'Is that what this is?'

Angharad nods. 'Newbies and nuisances.'

Izzy grins and takes in what's on show. It's an eclectic collection of jewellery made up of sickle moons and stars and Celtic knots and crosses. There are chunky bangles, fine earrings and charms on leather necklaces. And packs of cards. 'Wow, there's a lot of stuff here. I only have ten pieces.'

'The winters are dark and wet here.'

Izzy blinks. It's an odd explanation. Angharad reads her nonplussed expression and adds in a whisper, 'We don't have a TV.'

'Now I'm intrigued.'

'What more can an artist ask for?' Angharad's accent isn't local. It's lilting enough to be Welsh, but not the rapid rolling vowels of the Welsh speaker. More valleys, Izzy thinks. She's wearing a striped knitted jumper, a denim maxi skirt, socks and shoes that Izzy is willing to bet are not leather. It's topped off by a black stone set in the piercing through one side of her nose.

'Right, I've shown you mine. Now let's see yours.'

Angharad follows Izzy to her stand and her framed pieces. There are two series. One is geometric using the same dyes and original materials, and one more structural with emphasis on texture.

'These are amazing,' says Angharad. 'They remind me of buildings and maps.'

Izzy smiles. 'I am influenced by architecture I suppose.'

There are five minutes of silence while Angharad gives the work her attention.

'Fantastic colours. Lena would love these,' she says eventually.

The loud painter has gone, as has the organiser.

There's a hatchway near the entrance. Izzy's seen people going in and out with mugs.

'Fancy some tea?' she asks Angharad.

'Yes. But not that shit. I've got a flask of hot water and some fair-trade rooibos tea bags. You want?'

They go back to Angharad's spot and, while the tea is steeping, Izzy and her new unconventional friend chat. Or rather, Angharad chats and Izzy listens. Something she is good at, according to Marcus.

Angharad is as open as the sea. Within five minutes Izzy has learned that she and her partner, Lena, are both refugees from disastrous relationships. Men who'd found both women's alternative approaches to the everyday too irritating.

But, in each other, the women have found the perfect match.

'The final straw was when he called me a bloody witch. So I thought okay, yeah, why not?'

'Is that what you are?'

Angharad nods. 'I'm into Wicca. Lena is more the healer.'

'So Wicca … Spells and potions?' Izzy can't help her raised eyebrows.

'My expertise is more as a seer. A reader of the cards.'

Izzy nods, checking for any sign of self-consciousness, or the tic that might give away a piss-take. There isn't one so she goes with it. 'Then I'll come for a reading. Who doesn't want to know what's in store? Especially now that they've found the bodies on the path.'

Angharad raises her eyebrows.

'I live in Limehouse Cottage. Where the couple were from.'

'Wow,' Angharad says.

Izzy explains about Marky's excitement and about the police coming around.

'Oh my God, that's so random.'

'Not really. We knew they lived there when they went missing.'

'Still.'

The tea is excellent. Almost exotic. As is Angharad. There are packs of hand-finished cards dotted over the table. Each pack with a hand-printed descriptor. Izzy zeroes in on one label that reads: 'Local Myths and Legends'.

'Can I see?'

'You touch, you buy,' warns Angharad.

'Oh,' Izzy pulls her hands back.

Angharad giggles. 'Joke. I have all the cards on my iPad if you'd like to see them in close up?'

'That one caught my eye.' Izzy points.

'Ah, the Follower.' Angharad moves her fingers over the iPad's screen and the card appears in x2 magnification. It's a winding road under a lowering sky. A cowled figure, one hand clutching a staff, the other with a white and skeletal grasping hand. Through perspective, the card gets darker towards the centre, as does the figure's features so that the face is merely the suggestion of eyes in the cowl's shadow.

'Like it?' Angharad asks.

For a second, Izzy finds it difficult to drag her eyes away. The figure draws her in. She notices that the path is narrow and to the left there is sea and to the right, mountains.

'You're really talented,' Izzy says when she looks up.

'I've done a series of twenty-two trump cards. But everyone likes the Follower. I say likes; I mean it's the one everyone stops to stare at.'

'What does it signify?'

Angharad smiles. 'Maybe we should have another cup of tea?'

CHAPTER THIRTEEN

It takes an hour and a half and another two cups of rooibos before Izzy gets away from Angharad. She makes a run to Tesco and does a weekly shop. On the way home, she gets a text from Marcus.

> MARCUS: Come up to the captain's cabin. The scaffolding is peng.

She laughs when she reads this.

Who still uses peng?

No one over the age of twenty-four, that's for sure. And no one in Pembrokeshire, she suspects.

But then Marcus knows that. It's precisely why he's used it.

She parks the hybrid Lexus and heads up the little track that winds around the back of the cottage towards what looks like a two-storey polythene greenhouse. A hexagonal shape reflecting captain's cabin that Marcus is hoping to build inside it. This exoskeleton is much bigger though and the blue opaque plastic lends it an alien appearance. A doorway – nothing more than a split in the plastic weighed down with some stapled-on wood – marks an entrance. Izzy pulls back the polythene and peers in at the metal scaffolding poles that make up the bones of this skeleton and shouts, 'Hello?'

Marcus replies from somewhere above her.

'What do you think?'

Izzy cranes her neck. He's above where she's standing on a two-foot-wide platform. One of two that runs around the circumference of the scaffolding at two and four metres off the ground. Marcus is on the highest.

'What time is lift-off?' Izzy asks.

'Hah, I know. Bloody Apollo Eighteen, right?'

'Peng.'

'I thought you'd like that.'

Izzy inspects the works. 'Looks like it'll do the job.'

'Bloody right it will.' Marcus climbs down a fixed ladder tied securely with rope.

It's a cavernous space. In the middle, the base is a perfect circle, but a framework of studs in a hexagonal shape has already been nailed up. They both know it's going to be nothing more than a glorified shed, but one with insulation, double glazing and a wood burner. And, of course, on the top deck, big windows with a view of the ravine and the little rocky inlet right at its base.

Marcus reaches the bottom of the ladder and turns, grinning like a kid with candy floss. Izzy's so missed that grin.

'The boys were really efficient. Had it up in no time.'

'Expensive?'

'We'll only need it until the roof's on and the windows are in. All the inside stuff can be done once it's weatherproofed. And this' – Marcus waves an arm – 'means we can get the outside finished rain or shine.'

'Great.'

Marcus puts hands on hips, surveying this new Meccano set he's going to get to play with, a grin still plastered in place. But then a stray thought intrudes and his face falls. 'What about you? How did your thing at the Hall go?'

'Fine. I met a witch.'

'A what?'

There's a workbench to her left nestling in a pile of offcuts and sawdust. Izzy clears away a few bits of wood and takes out a pack of Angharad's Tarot trumps and lays the top five out.

'What are these?' Marcus's interest is piqued.

'Amazing, aren't they? The woman who made them, my new BFF Angharad, is also exhibiting. We got chatting, and she told me all about this chap.' She points at a card.

'Does he have a name?'

'The Follower.' Out of her bag she takes a leaflet, ornately decorated around its edge with alchemical symbols. Imprinted upon it is the Follower image and beneath is the legend that Izzy reads.

'The Follower has been the subject of many scholarly articles interpreting its origins. Most agree to the mythology pre-dating written history. Many pagan references document a fateful auger. Kings, shamans and druids sought wisdom in quiet isolated places only to find themselves no longer alone. The presence of the Follower, who never makes contact but remains in the background, symbolises imminent change. Perhaps an end to things. But the Follower is not always a harbinger of doom. Often there is also enlightenment. A life altered – perhaps for good, perhaps for bad – as opposed to the finality of death. Yet achieving said transformation comes at a cost. A price paid. A forfeit given. As a result, the Follower is a powerful but feared entity. If ever confronted, chaos follows with its attendant destruction.

'Beware the Follower.'

'Jolly sort of chap, then,' Marcus retorts.

'When the Pickerings went missing, some people blamed the Follower for their disappearance.'

Marcus trumps out a laugh. 'Really?'

'Oh, yes. Some people still think it might be him.'

He sends her a sideways glance. 'We ought to tell Poirot and Marcella, then.'

Izzy wrinkles her nose. 'They probably know already.'

Marcus gives her back the card. 'Mind if I crack on here. I need to measure the drop from the roof apex to the floor.'

Izzy scoops the cards up and uses the elasticated string supplied with the pack to bundle them together. 'I've got some salmon for supper.'

'I'll be up in in a couple of hours.'

'Ok. I'll make it for seven. Please don't be late. I can't stand overcooked fish.' It's a warning.

Marcus gives her a cursory peck on the cheek before clattering back up the ladder. Monty, sensing more chance of a treat with Izzy than with Marcus, trots after her as she leaves the build.

CHAPTER FOURTEEN

WARLOW IS at home wondering what he'll have for supper. He's walked and fed Cadi and she's happy in her basket, though she keeps one eye open because she instinctively knows it's that time when food prep might get her the odd morsel. And it is the odd morsel because Warlow is strict on titbits.

He likes to think he's organised, but the events of the last few days have thrown him off his 'always from fresh' course. But tonight he's thinking sardines on toast with a few fresh tomatoes. It's a go-to standby that ticks the right boxes what with oily fish and seeded bread – just the one slice.

He looks at Cadi and knows she'll be disappointed. Hardly any prep with sardines on toast. And therefore no morsels.

'Sorry girl,' he says.

Cadi pricks up her ears but then lays her head back down with a mournful look.

Warlow has the fridge door open when the phone rings. He looks at the caller ID. Jess Allanby.

He swings the fridge door shut.

'Evening,' Warlow says.

'Went on a bit too long. We finished about ten minutes ago.' He can hear her footsteps and the odd outdoor noise. On her way to the car, he suspects. No wasted effort here.

'Sorry I missed it then.'

'I bet. But we missed you. Got mentioned in despatches. Sion Buchannan no less.'

'I bet everyone cheered.'

'Not quite. It raised hackles in fact.'

'Oh?'

'It's great to know we have Evan on the team but isn't there a risk of contaminating the sterile corridor.' Jess delivers the words in an emotionless quote.

Warlow allows himself a wry smile. Of course they would be nervous having the DCI who'd investigated the original case in the middle of it all. Sterile corridor refers to contamination. Not with germs, but with ideas. The danger that Evan, the original investigator, would bring certain preconceptions, even misconceptions, to the party. The old injured lion still spoiling for a fight.

'Let me guess, DI Caldwell?'

'Yes.'

'Why was he even there?'

'He carried out the last review of the Pickerings' disappearance. That's why Buchannan wants fresh eyes. Why I'm the Acting Chief Investigating Officer for now.'

Warlow knows how this works. DCI's were the Senior Investigating Officers unless the case became a stranger attack. A bigger deal. Then a superintendent took over. But they weren't at that point yet. Not until they had the post-mortem results at least.

'Caldwell might have a point,' Warlow mutters.

Jess snorts. 'You know more about this case than anyone. It stands to reason you can help by reviewing the case files and providing me with a relevant summary.

Buchannan designated a Sergeant Mel Lewis to help you. I gather you know him well?'

'I do.'

Mel Lewis is one of the few colleagues besides Buchannan whom Warlow has spent some time with post retirement. A grafter and a hard drinker, Lewis is twice divorced with the scars to prove it and spends most of his leisure time crewing for one of the many boats harboured in Neyland Marina. His aspiration is to own his own fifty-footer. He's a sailor's sailor. A smoker and a drinker. Warlow found out early on that being at sea did not 'float his boat, pun very much intended' and his time spent with Lewis has usually revolved around watching the odd significant game – football or rugby internationals mainly – at a pub with a crowd of like-minded fans who put the party very much in partisan. Though anyone not in a red shirt is welcome at these gatherings, they better have thick skins and a sense of humour. Warlow inevitably leaves before Mel and while he's still capable of calling a cab. It's since devolved into a WhatsApp group and an open invitation.

More often than not, Warlow declines. Not because he doesn't enjoy these gatherings, but he doesn't like hangovers with attitude. He's far too old to spend Sunday mornings staring into a porcelain bowl. So it's been months since he and Sergeant Lewis shared a pint.

Jess's clicking heels stop and are replaced by the noise of a car door opening. 'He's tasked with retrieving the misper files. He'll make space in the Incident Room and meet you at Haverfordwest tomorrow morning. Will that be okay?'

Warlow answers in the affirmative and Jess kills the call.

He walks through to the living room and fetches his laptop. It's as light as air, a present from the boys last Christmas with a nice white fruit logo on the front. He has a Facebook account and dips in to NARPO – the National

Association of Retired Police Officers – now and again to see who else has hung up the Bat cape. But he's not on Twitter, nor Instagram. What he has is a couple of email accounts. Gmail for swapping stuff with the boys – 'Dad, can you send me a copy of my birth certificate?' – because it's dead easy to send attachments, and a BT account he uses for banking and any communication with officialdom.

He thinks the latter is safer, though Alun tells him that Google's security systems are second to none, what with two-factor authentication rolling out. And yes, 'it is a nuisance to have your mobile with you for the security code when you log on to the PC, but so what? Most of the time you do, right?'

He smiles as he remembers the exasperated tone his eldest son had used to deliver this IT lecture. Well, guess what? It is a nuisance because unlike millennials, Warlow does not have his mobile welded to his flesh twenty-four hours a sodding day. Still, Alun is right, because it's his BT account that gets all the spam. The emails informing him that there's a voice note message waiting for him from a total stranger and all he needs to do is 'click here'.

No thanks, Mr Phisherman. No phish today.

The BT account is also the address he uses for Denise-related stuff. And even he almost got caught out last year when she emailed to tell him she was stranded in Newcastle after having lost her purse and could he transfer a hundred quid to her PayPal account tout de suite.

He gives a little shake of his head as he remembers that. He can't believe it took him in for even a minute. But it made him pause because it would be the sort of thing Denise might do. Did when they were together. She'd lose keys or her phone and need picking up or dropping off because, for some inexplicable reason, she never learned to drive. He corrects himself. It was not inexplicable. Not once you knew Denise.

'Why would I learn to drive if it means I can't have a drink?'

Very savvy when it came to that kind of twisted logic was his ex. Now she has someone else to drive her. And that is something he is not sorry about.

He logs on to the BBC Wales news website. There's a drone shot of the path and the headline reads: 'Cave bodies found after path landslip may well be missing walkers.' He reads through the report, which is pure speculation. There's a rehash of the probable cause of the landslip and a photo of the walkers who made the 'horrific discovery'. But the only police source quote is bland: 'Every effort is being made to identify the bodies as quickly as possible.'

The lid, so far, remains screwed down.

He picks up his mobile and dials Mel's number. The DS picks up after four rings.

'Evan Warlow back in the saddle. Who'd have believed it?'

Mel sounds chuffed and a pang of guilt over his social reticence almost makes Warlow hesitate. But this is business.

'You've drawn the short straw, I hear.'

'Never. They call me lucky Lewis.'

'I heard it was lazy Lewis.'

'You need new batteries for that hearing aid then.'

Two men trading insults. The definition of a friendship.

'I've just come off the phone with Jess Allanby.' Warlow dangles the bait out there in the shallow water.

'What do you think?'

'She's the boss is what I think. I never discuss the boss.'

'Knows what she wants alright. So far.'

Warlow takes that as approval. 'Right. And she wants me to look through the Pickering file.'

'It's on the way from HQ as we speak. The indexers

will input it into HOLMES and I'll get them to copy it, too. So you'll end up with your own box of papers.'

'What time?'

'Eight-thirtyish?'

'Fine.' At least there'll be one old face he recognises in the Incident Room.

He eats his supper with relish and has an early night, though sleep does not come quickly.

It takes half an hour of tossing and turning before he realises why that is. And when the penny drops, he's shocked. It's something he hasn't experienced in a long while.

He's restless because he's excited to feel that old horse beneath him.

———

OUTSIDE, dusk oozes up from the fields, squeezing the remaining light towards the western horizon. But Izzy doesn't take the path directly towards the house. Instead she follows the fence and walks along it, to where it's closest to the ravine and their view of the Engine House.

That will of course change with the captain's cabin. If Marcus's plans come to fruition, they'll be two metres higher on the upper floor and able to see both the brooding industrial relic and the inlet beneath. But from where she is now, all that is hidden. What she sees is the apex of the Engine House's topmost walls and its fractured chimney, dark against the dying light.

She has never been a great one for superstition and legends. But something about this place, its elemental energy so close to sky and sea, gives her a delicious thrill. The isolation, the sounds of the waves crashing, the wheeling and bugling of the gulls. No wonder so many stories are written about lighthouse keepers. Not that she lives in a lighthouse. But Limehouse Cottage has the same aura. There's no doubt it was once an outpost of sorts. When storms were raging, she doubts whoever lived here had many visitors in the days or nights before cars and electric lighting.

Easy to believe what you want to believe out here.

But she's sensible. Whatever it is she's seen across the way will have an obvious explanation. Kids, or a stray animal. She has not felt threatened. Not yet. And even if it is the Follower – *how can it be, you idiot?* – she now senses it's a herald of change, rather than an agent of ill will.

She laughs at these thoughts. Kids or a stray cat or dog are a far better answer. And then there's the other possibility. Someone finding shelter in the old abandoned building. One of the lost. And that idea brings with it a pang of recollected angst. She knows about that only too well. Her older brother, Austen, dropped out of university when he was twenty and disappeared from the family's life for ten months. She'd been sixteen at the time and remembers the whispered conversations between her parents she had not been meant to hear. They'd all feared drugs as the root cause and it had taken months to find out the truth. That he'd suffered a severe bout of depression with no warning signs and no hint of how badly it was affecting him.

At one point, with no phone calls and no sightings from his supposed friends, they even feared that he'd died. Her father took six months off work and found Austen living on the streets of Nottingham, sleeping rough, ashamed and confused by what had happened to him, unable and unwilling to seek help. But they got him back and, with treatment, Austen was rebuilding his life. The episode had a profound effect on Izzy. She now gave street people all her change. Sometimes, she would stop and talk to them. Every one of them had a story to tell. Under the unwashed clothes and the dirty skin, there were damaged people.

These thoughts go through her head as she stares across the ravine. There are no street people here. But there is no rule that says people get lost only in cities.

Tonight she will try an experiment. Tonight, she'll leave some food out at this point. See what becomes of it. Somehow, she feels it's unlikely that a supernatural being will have an interest in a few Jaffa cakes, bananas and a couple of apples. But a lost person might.

A light flicks on in the 'Spaceship' and catches her eye. She's already accepted the name they've given the poly-thene shelter. And Marcus has power set up from the house through an armoured extension cable.

When she turns back to look across the ravine, in the deepening gloom she thinks she sees something moving in one of the dark glassless windows. A lighter shadow. She peers, but when it happens again, she realises it is only a branch waving across the hollow window space, driven by the wind.

She smiles to herself. Too much Angharad in one afternoon?

Yet, when she turns and walks back to the house, Monty stays, staring across the space between the fence and the ravine.

The wind drops. The trees are still.

But whatever moves in the Engine House window, this time unseen by Izzy, is not.

CHAPTER FIFTEEN

WARLOW MEETS Mel Lewis in Haverfordwest police station car park.

Knowing what his lifestyle is like, Lewis has no right to be lean and trim, but that's what he is. Five years younger than Warlow, wiry haired and ruddy from the weather. Perhaps from booze too, Warlow suspects, but his weathered appearance is great camouflage. He wears thin knitted ties and a grey suit that could do with leather patches on the elbows. His shoes have rubber soles, designed for comfort over style. The first thing Lewis does is hand over a new key card on a lanyard.

'They still had your photo on file, so I nabbed that,' Lewis explains.

'Good. Makes me look younger.'

'Makes you look like one of Interpol's most bloody wanted more like.'

Warlow glances at the photo. Unsmiling, unflattering. Like a passport photo of someone with the norovirus. 'You're not wrong. Shall we?'

Lewis nods and leads the way.

Merlin as a name and theme runs through West Wales. Poetic legends of the Wild Men of the Woods with origins in 12th century poetry. Druids, paganism, Tintagel and Uther Pendragon. What's not to like? But not much magic takes place in the unprepossessing 60s building on top of a grassy mound between Merlin's Hill and Milford Road in Haverfordwest. This is Dyfed-Powys police's Pembrokeshire stronghold. A three-storeys-high, red-brick and white-panelled nonentity that suggests more student accommodation than bastion of law enforcement.

This isn't either of these men's territory. But there are one or two nods and waves as they walk through and up the stairs to the space assigned as the Incident Room. Half a dozen people are busy on phones or at monitors and laptops. To the left of the doorway are noticeboards. One white, one buff. Everyone refers to them as the Gallery and the Job Centre. Already there are dozens of notes, images, photos and lists. Actions that will progress as the operation develops.

Warlow picks out the photographs of the path and the two corpses taken from several angles. Not one of them fit for Tanya Pickering's family album. Nor is he likely to forget now that he's seen them. He's spent years of his life searching for these people. It's sobering to know that he'd been only feet from finding them on a dozen occasions. They'd used dogs, of course. As yet, no one can explain why they didn't pick up the scent, though there have been theories. One is to do with the guano from the gulls and sea birds that sits on almost every surface of the cliff face. Enough ammonia to put any self-respecting bloodhound off its paces.

'Tea?' Lewis asks.

'No need to ask,' Warlow replies, snapping out of his musings. It's a rule. Take refreshments when on offer.

There will be times, soon, when everyone is too busy to drink or eat. Against the back wall, on a desk made of pale wood, are three lidded cardboard boxes labelled 'Pickering'. It's towards these that Warlow heads and the files and papers that he is so terribly familiar with.

It's not a quiet room. People are speaking into phones. Computer keyboards click. But the two men at the back are absorbed by the reams of paper they pull out. It takes only half an hour for Warlow to tut for the sixth time and send Lewis a despairing look.

'Christ, what the hell happened here? These are all over the shop. No timeline, no attempt at even rudimentary filing.'

'There's been a couple of reviews since you were last involved,' Lewis says with a sigh.

'Who did the last one? A troop of chimpanzees?'

'DI Caldwell.'

Warlow shakes his head. Caldwell is an easy target and he has very sharp arrows. But he's determined not to let emotion cloud his judgement. 'This isn't like him. He's Mr Methodical, you know that.'

Lewis sits, pondering, until he comes up with a thought. 'We've had another trial of digitising records since you left. Abandoned because it was about as user friendly as Ancient Greek. An outside company. They had complete access to files. They're top of my culprit list.'

Warlow sighs. 'Sorting this out is going to take days.'

Lewis has his sleeves rolled up. He glances at his watch and pushes back from the desk. 'Not ideal.'

'No. Not ideal.'

'I'm supposed to be somewhere else at eleven with the Op Wonderland Task Force and they're meeting in Aber. I'll come back afterwards. We'll have another go.'

Initiatives and operations are the backbone of police work. Warlow knows the score only too well. Even so, the sergeant's impending absence is an unwelcome inconvenience. 'Fine,' he mutters.

Lewis is sliding on his jacket but pauses on hearing the lack of conviction in the ex-DCI's voice. 'You alright, Evan?'

'I have a lot of skin in this game, Mel. Seeing something like this' – he waves at the boxes – 'it's bloody upsetting.'

'Don't worry. We'll get it sorted.'

'We'll need Harry Potter's pointy bloody hat to get this lot sorted. Has there been much fresh evidence since I kicked this one to touch?'

'Sod all until that landslip on the path last week.'

Lewis leaves and Warlow is left alone with two unopened boxes and an idea forming in his head. He waits ten minutes, letting the juices marinate. When they finally penetrate the meat of his thoughts the plan that's revealed is a juicy one. He has options. Either he can sit here trying to find the necessary ingredients buried in the files to cobble together a dog's dinner of paperwork that may, or may not, be useful. Or he can be practical and use his time to everyone's advantage.

The key word is practical. Like efficient, and expeditious, it can hide a multitude of sins.

He talks to a DS by the name of Sandra Griffiths. She's the Receiver, the officer who deals with all the documentation coming in, who prioritises and IDs important developments. She's also acting up as Incident Room Office Manager today. He tells her about the state of the original misper files and asks if there is anyone spare who could at least put them in date order before anything else goes to the indexers. He explains he has a meeting with DI Allanby and that he'll be back later to help.

Griffiths agrees to get someone on to it. Warlow

narrows his eyes as recognition dawns. 'We've worked together before.'

'Twice. On the Geoghan fraud case and on Lilly Hooper.'

Warlow purses his lips. The Geoghan case is like a wartime wound that still aches when the weather is cold and damp. And as for Lilly Hooper … She went missing from a day out with her family at a petting zoo. The bus driver who took her, caught on CCTV hand-in-hand with the child, is still in prison. If he ever gets out, Warlow is pretty sure that if he puts one foot inside the county, it'll be lopped off along with various limbs and his genitals, such was the strength of feeling in the community when the case went to court. Lilly has never been found.

Neither Warlow nor Griffiths need to say anything about that. It's seared into their memories.

'How's that boy of yours, Bryn wasn't it? I saw he got his under eighteen cap,' Warlow asks.

Griffiths beams. 'He's with the Ospreys now.'

'Wow. He's a pro?'

'The coaches like him. But I daren't mention the O word in here. They're all Scarlets.'

Warlow grins. Rugby remained ingrained in the West Wales soul. Rivalries flowed down from regions like the Scarlets and Ospreys, through feeder towns and into villages. Local derbies were often vicious, but instantly forgotten in the clubhouse afterwards. Once the blood was washed away.

'I'll be looking out for him.'

Griffiths's smile widens. 'Good to have you back, sir.'

He leaves the station and gets into his car. Of course, he can see the sense of having him go through the files. He's the expert. It's the logical thing. But it's also going to tie him up for days. If he was a suspicious man, he might even wonder if having him chained to a desk was a deliberate ploy. Not on Sion Buchannan's part, nor Jess Allan-by's. But you never knew who'd put the idea into someone's head. He's probably way off the mark, but even if it is just a series of unfortunate cockups, he has better and more efficient ways to use his time.

CHAPTER SIXTEEN

DESPITE WHAT HE'S said to Sergeant Griffiths, there is no meeting with Jess Allanby. Not yet. Instead, Warlow goes home to his cottage at Nevern. Cadi greets him as if he's been off on a six-month voyage. When she settles down, he goes upstairs and pulls down a telescopic ladder folded under a trap door on the landing. He's converted the tiny attic space into a box room full of things he'll probably never need. Old bits of outdated IT, routers, computer mice, stacks of paperbacks and CDs, and the odd album of family photos he can't bring himself to look at because it brings back too many memories and the realisation of what he's lost.

He's not bitter, merely not fond of feeling maudlin. There's a time and a place. What he's after today is in a battered and locked brown leather briefcase. He fishes it out and takes it downstairs to the living room, then plonks it on the table next to the laptop. This is his police file. Letters of appointment, promotions, thank you notes from victims, retirement cards, a toy sheriff's badge he was made to wear at the leaving party. Underneath these are two thick black pocketbooks, known as PNBs, and three thumb drives.

He knows that by rights he shouldn't have any of these. But they're not his official PNBs – the notebooks issued to officers containing accurate entries of investigations, interviews and findings. Those he'd returned on retirement for secure storage and retention as required by law. What he has in the case are the unofficial books he'd used as his day-to-day activity lists. Things to do. His thought processes. These are personal. And yes, a sharp barrister might take issue with some of the things Warlow had written in them, but that was why he kept them under lock and key.

The thumb drives were something else altogether. Sensitive, probably illegal. Detailed and compressed case notes of all the investigations he'd led as an SIO. He'd made copies of documents on his phone while at work and then, in the hours at home when he probably should have been talking to his wife – according to her – he'd poured over those files and distilled them down into a usable, always changing, up-to-date and concise SID.

A State of Investigation Document.

Confidential information was not meant to be taken out of police premises.

But then politicians were not meant to lie. And money was not meant to buy happiness.

What was meant to happen and what truly took place were areas as grey as a collier's back, as his grandmother used to say. And she should know because she'd scrubbed enough of those in her time.

SIDs were Warlow's method while he was in the Force. And, given that Mel Lewis had told him that little or no new information had been brought to the Pickering investigation until their bodies popped up out of the earth, his

State of the Investigation doc from seven years ago is as valid now as it was then. He reads through it, changes a few things, adds today's date, saves it as a new document and puts it on a new thumb drive. Exactly what Jess and Buchannan had asked him to prepare.

He stays in the cottage for lunch, walks Cadi and by two o'clock is back in the Incident Room where he prints off the document. He has half a dozen copies ready by the time Lewis returns mid-afternoon.

'Been busy I see,' Lewis says, looking around theatrically for boxes no longer on the desk. 'Don't tell me, you got so pissed off you set fire to the lot.'

'Sandra Griffiths is getting someone to put them in order. But it's okay because I found what I was looking for. Look.' Warlow hands him three sheets stapled together. 'I knew there was a summary document in there somewhere. Just a matter of finding it.'

Lewis scans the sheets, looking impressed. 'Bit of luck then.'

'We all need a little of that. You're welcome to check everything.'

'Forget it. I trust you, Evan. Tea?'

But Lewis gets no chance to even boil a kettle. He's halfway across the Incident Room when Catrin Richards puts her head in.

'DI Allanby is back from Cardiff. She'd like a word.'

They meet in Jess's office. Strictly speaking it's the SIO's office for this investigation. So it's soulless. Used as something else under less pressing circumstances if the blue-tacked wall planner and the filing cabinet in one corner are anything to go by. But it has a desk, some chairs, a computer. All the essentials. The only thing that belongs to the DI is the body sitting behind the desk.

She looks tired. Four hours in the car there and back to Cardiff is bad enough. But interspersed with the joys of two hours in the University Hospital of Wales' pathology department with the Home Office pathologist does not make for a fun-filled morning.

Catrin and Warlow find seats. Lewis puts his head in only to apologise for ducking out. He's there only as a helping hand for Warlow and mutters something about a child abuse case he's neck deep in. So it's just the three of them in the room.

'How was it?' Warlow asks.

Jess wrinkles her nose. 'The smell wasn't too bad. The findings were worse.'

'Tiernon his usual charming self?'

Jess yields to a wry smile. 'I take it that his misery wasn't only for my benefit, then?'

'No. He's very generous in that sense. Not known for his wit and sparkling repartee. May even have podiumed in the miserable bastard Olympics. Not for us, of course. The Welsh don't have a team. We're far too happy go lucky.' He delivers all this with a stony expression that earns a stifled laugh from Catrin.

Jess switches to business. 'Both victims died from blunt trauma. Multiple blows to the skull with a round-ended weapon.'

'As in what, ma'am?' Catrin asks.

'As in a hammer, Catrin. Other injuries included broken arms and ankle. Probably from the same weapon.'

'So they couldn't fight back,' Warlow says. 'Or run.'

Jess nods. 'That's what Superintendent Buchannan thinks, too.'

It's grim. Worse than Warlow has bargained for.

'We've had confirmation of identity from dental records. DNA will take another day,' Catrin says.

Teeth. The old-fashioned way. Warlow hands over his summary. 'Not sure any of this will help. We looked hard at all the people who knew the Pickerings.'

Both female officers read it. Warlow doesn't have to.

Halfway through, Jess looks up. 'Is it worth us looking at any of these again? The farmers maybe?'

Warlow fends the question off. 'Every one of them had alibis. They were all working on the farm. All accounted for.'

'What about this business of a land purchase?'

'It's nothing. The Pickerings' daughter mentioned it as something her parents would have liked to do. If you remember, the current occupiers had the same thought. Extend their garden a bit. But it was never for sale. It was never contentious.'

Jess's gaze is unflinching. Forensic even. For the first time Warlow notices her eyes are grey in colour. Not the brown he was expecting to go with the dark hair. 'So not worth re-interviewing?'

'The Gower's farm spreads over 250 acres. A big patch with all kinds of dark corners. If it was they who wanted the Pickerings to disappear, there'd be at least three convenient slurry pits to throw them into, or a warm spot under a hole already dug for a dead cow. You saw the Gowers. Neither one of them gets much work on the standup circuit, but even Rylan could throw Ken and Marjorie into the sea with one arm tied behind his back.' Warlow shakes his head. 'Stuffing them into a crevice on the side of a cliff makes no sense whatsoever.'

Jess ponders his answer. 'Who else called up at the house with the Pickerings?'

Warlow reels this off without effort. 'In the days leading up to their death, the postman, and a woman from the WI delivering cakes.'

Jess inhales and exhales deeply. 'So it's looking more and more likely that it's a stranger attack.'

Warlow concedes with a question of his own. 'But a

stranger with local knowledge. Who else would even know that there was a hiding place in the cliff?'

Jess considers this. 'Okay. So it's possible that they were in the wrong place at the wrong time. What if they stumbled across someone doing something illicit? And I don't mean stealing eggs from a nest.'

'Hiding something?' Catrin asks.

Warlow considers this option, runs with it. 'Someone using the crevice as a hiding place and the Pickerings interrupted them.'

'That sounds more plausible. So what might whoever it is have been hiding?' Jess says.

'Money or drugs,' Catrin answers.

There's a knock on the door and a fresh-faced DC called Rhys Harries sticks his head in. He's a big lad and Warlow wouldn't bet against him being a rugby player. He gives Catrin a nod. 'Lab on the phone, Sarge.'

Catrin excuses herself. Jess lightens the mood. 'Is it strange being back at work?'

'Different words, same old tune.'

Jess smiles. 'I've lost count of the people who've said how lucky I am to be working with ex DCI Warlow.'

'Don't believe the hype,' Warlow answers in a rumble.

When Jess says nothing, he takes the hint. 'And in amongst the nostalgia, you're wondering how much of a poisoned chalice it's going to be, am I right?'

'I like to do things a certain way.'

'This is your case, Jessica.'

'It's Jess. And thanks for that. But I don't want to cramp your style. The Buccaneer is having me do plans and explaining actions by the book. Literally. Which means if you see anything, go for it. Don't wait for me to tick a box. And this' – she picks up the summary – 'this has saved us days. Miraculous considering the state those files were in.'

Warlow raises one eyebrow in acknowledgement.

'Catrin had a quick look through when they arrived yesterday,' Jess explains with a grin.

'I'm a quick worker.'

'Or you have your own records.'

'That's not allowed, Detective Inspector. As you well know.'

Jess smiles. Soft and toothless. 'I do. But it's what I would have done. What I do. A method.'

Something passes between them. An unspoken understanding. A contract drawn up and underlined. When Warlow speaks next, the conversation takes a right-angled turn.

'So, how are you finding things here in sleepy West Wales, Jess?'

'Not so sleepy, judging by this.' She waves the summary. 'Were you always this thinly spread?'

'It's a big patch.'

Jess nods. Warlow doesn't need to throw statistics at her. She knows that, covering fifty-two per cent of the country's landmass, Dyfed-Powys is the largest police area in the whole of England and Wales combined.

'You settling in?' Warlow asks.

'I'm enjoying it.'

'Renting?'

'For now, yes. In Cold Blow. We're on the lookout for somewhere on the coast. Molly – that's my daughter – she's a kayaker.' Jess's face becomes animated. 'We haven't done much of that for a while.'

Warlow knows a source of angst when he hears it. 'How old is she?'

'Sixteen going on twenty.'

'Difficult at that age. Upping sticks I mean.'

'It was a joint decision. Mine and hers. We couldn't stay where we were, that's for certain.' There's a sourness to the statement, but Jess doesn't offer more. Warlow doesn't probe. It's none of his business. The door opens and Catrin enters waving a printout. She looks flushed.

'Lab results on a jacket stuffed in with the bodies. Blood stains have a DNA match for the Pickerings. But there's another trace. One we have on record.'

Jess sits up.

Catrin reads from the sheet. 'A Kelly Scott. Sex worker from Swansea. Twenty-seven, two children in care. Known drug user.'

Warlow shoots her a glance. But this is Jess's show. 'So where is she now? Let's get her in.'

Catrin looks owl eyed as she hands over the sheet. 'That's the point, ma'am. We can't.'

'If she's in the nick we can still question her–'

'No. Catrin's right, we can't,' Warlow says.

Jess picks up on Warlow's tone. Realises he knows more than she does here and waits for him to explain.

'It was off our patch, but I know the history.' It's the truth. There are some cases in his long career that he is sketchy about. Names that he can't quite recall. Situations that he's forgotten the details of. But this is not an easy one to forget. 'We can't question Kelly Scott because she's dead. Murdered in a Swansea squat when she was two months pregnant.'

'Shit,' Jess says.

'Sorry, ma'am,' Catrin says.

'Don't be,' Warlow shakes his head. 'She was never going to be a suspect.'

'Why not?' Catrin asks.

Jess answers. She's looking at the sheet Catrin has handed her. 'Because the murder took place the year before the Pickerings went missing.'

'Then what's the link? How did her blood end up on that coat stuffed in with the Pickerings?'

Warlow shifts in his seat and takes the forensic report Jess hands to him. He fishes out glasses and reads, his eyes narrowing, his pulse ticking up a notch. After all these years, things, at last, are moving. 'That's an excellent question, Catrin,' he says. 'Exactly what we need to find out.'

CHAPTER SEVENTEEN

WARLOW AND CATRIN DIVVY the work up. The sergeant goes the official route. She'll dive into the hard facts of the Kelly Scott case, the coroner's report, what details there are on HOLMES.

Warlow, meanwhile, finds a phone and goes in a different direction.

DCI Wyn Davies is a couple of years younger than Warlow. He still has the same mobile number he had when he ran the Scott case. He's in a car when he answers Warlow's call.

'Wyn, It's Evan Warlow.'

'Jesus, the dead can speak.' Davies's voice is a bellow. At eighteen stone, it couldn't be anything else. 'I heard you'd been raised from the grave.'

Warlow isn't surprised. Word travels fast and Wales is a small country. 'Yes, they removed all the embalming fluid and shot me full of adrenaline.'

'The Pickerings' case, is it?'

'It is. Something's come up. A forensic link to Kelly Scott, would you believe.'

Warlow hears the tyres squeal in Davies's car. 'Jesus. Wait a minute. I'm pulling over.'

'On the way to the pub?'

'If by pub you mean a coma-inducing funding meeting at the Assembly, then yes. I'm so old now I'm even on a committee. Right, I've pulled into a lay-by and I'm all ears.'

Warlow fills him in. 'The lab threw up a DNA trace on some clothing found stuffed around the bodies on the path.'

'Christ, that's a strange one, Evan. Those poor buggers.'

'Can you remember Scott ever being linked to anyone up in Cardiganshire?'

Davies snorts. 'Not then. She'd never been further west than Llanelli. Classic case. Twenty-seven years old. Both of her kids taken from her just after birth. She was selling herself for drugs, though who would want to buy the state she was in is anyone's guess. Flirted with a really rough crowd and thought she had all the answers. You know the type.'

Warlow does. Only too well.

Davies continues. 'The rumour was she had the brilliant idea of splicing her stash with icing sugar and selling it on. Bad career move. She paid the price.'

Warlow sits up. 'You're convinced it was a drug related killing.'

'We were. No one saw or heard anything. They found her in an abandoned building on the High Street. Half of those places are still empty after two decades. Christ, some are still empty after the last war.'

'Remind me. Cause of death?'

'Blunt trauma. Someone took a hammer to her skull.'

Cogs whirr and shift in Warlow's head. 'You never found it?'

'The hammer? No.' Davies pauses a beat before asking, 'What is it you're not telling me, Evan?'

'The post-mortem report on the Pickerings reads the same.'

'You looking for a bloody carpenter too, then.'

'Looks like it. Was anyone in your cross hairs?'

'Oh yes. Kieron Thomas. Scum of the first water. He was her supplier and part-time pimp. Used her to provide favours for some of his clients. But he had half a dozen people swear he was fifty miles away at the time she was killed. Most of them paid in whatever injectable or sniffable currency took their fancy.'

'Is he still around?'

There's another beat while Davies thinks it through. 'Not on our patch. Last I heard he'd moved west. Better climate down there. Less competition for the bastards getting off the train from London with a suitcase full of crack.'

Warlow smiles grimly. 'I ought to look him up then.'

'Talk to Dai Vetch. He'll know where he is if anyone does.'

'Thanks, Wyn.'

'Fight the good fight, boy. Good to hear your voice.'

Warlow rings off. Makes notes in his book. Then he texts Catrin for DS Vetch's number. He's read the name in newspapers of late following successful joint operations with organised crime teams nationally. Operation Moose and Brenin targeting county line gangs have seen hefty sentences handed out over the last few months in Swansea crown court.

Catrin texts back within five minutes. Vetch is based in Aberystwyth. He doesn't answer his phone, and so Warlow leaves a message. At a little after four thirty, Jess walks over to his desk.

'Any joy with your South Wales Police connections?'

'A sniff. I'm waiting to follow up. What I know already is that Kelly Scott died from a hammer blow.'

'What?' Jess's big eyes get bigger.

Warlow lets the statement and all its implications hang.

Finally, Jess nods. Slow movements weighed down by thoughts. 'Right. I'm going to update the Buccaneer. I have to do all the SIO stuff by the book. I could be a while. I think it would be a good idea if we have a briefing tomorrow morning. Eight thirty suit you?'

'No problem.'

'Thanks, Evan. And thanks for the summary. It really saved us a lot of time.'

'You happy for me to borrow DS Richards if needs be?'

'Of course. Or there's this other reprobate.' She looks up and calls over to the DC who'd stuck his head around the door to beckon Sergeant Richards earlier. He sports dark stubble on a boyish face as he saunters over in tight shirt and skinny trousers. Warlow hasn't seen his jacket, but he knows it'll be too small for him. Which would not be difficult given his size. He thinks that the current fashion makes blokes look like they're all extras from Dickens' Dotheboys hall. But he doesn't say that. It wouldn't be polite. Maybe Jess has read Nicholas Nickleby, but he doubts many others in this room will have. Not snobbery, but he is one of the oldest here. He's had a lot more time.

'DC Rhys Harries, meet DCI Evan Warlow.'

Harries is taller than Warlow. Taller in fact than most. He has a bit too much hair to keep tidy and has a lanky frame with broad shoulders. A swimmer's frame, or, given the country they're in, a back row forward. 'Nice to meet you, sir. Heard a lot about you.'

'All good I hope.'

Warlow is glad to see that Harries doesn't balk as some

might at the challenge. Instead he offers a lopsided smile and offers a hand. It's taken and shaken.

'Mostly, sir.' Rhys delivers this with a straight face. Warlow nods. The boy does sarcasm. A good sign. As is the accent. It's local, with the round vowels of a Welsh speaker.

'Rhys is a whizz on everything social media,' Jess adds.

'Right. Good. I may need help with that new stuff. I still need to open an account.'

'What, Insta? TikTok?' Rhys sounds keen.

'No, you know, uh, what's it called … email.'

Rhys blinks, his face for a moment not quite registering what he's hearing before it splits into a grin. 'They said you were a bit of a joker, sir.'

Jess walks away. 'Just keep me in the loop, Evan.'

Rhys goes back to his desk with one sly glance back over his shoulder at Warlow. On the way to Buchannan's office, Jess stops to speak with half a dozen Incident Room staff. Warlow notes the way she has a word or two for them all. Making sure they know they're part of the team. Especially the junior, less experienced members manning phones or preparing briefing materials. She's a motivator, and that's a great sight to see.

SIO's do not get paid overtime. He remembers the long hours embroiled in a case and never begrudged the job one minute. He'd follow up leads brought to him by the other members of the team. Travel across the patch or even the whole country to visit other forces with information to share. Find specialists in all kinds of fields who might help advise a direction to take. Get to the Incident Room before everyone else and be the last to leave.

Denise never saw it that way. She begrudged every single minute. He hopes that Jess's daughter isn't the needy type.

Warlow reads some entries on the records system for a

while, but then sees no sense in hanging on. He's on the way out of the office when he gets a call from DS Vetch.

'Kieron Thomas?' asks Vetch after Warlow reiterates the request. 'What's that little shit done now?'

'That's what I need to find out.'

'Are you back in on this Pickering case?'

'I am.' Seems like everyone knows.

'Murder isn't Ket's – what Thomas is known as – style. He's more your low-level pusher. Some cannabis and keta-mine mainly. Easy to get stuff. They must have a pet vet somewhere.'

'You let him do that?'

'We do because, as yet we don't know where he gets the gear from. Steady supply, too. There are bigger fish to fry.'

Isn't there always, muses Warlow. 'So you won't mind if we ask him a few questions.'

'Be my guest. Spends most afternoons in a pub in Pembroke Dock. I'll text you the address.'

Warlow pockets his phone and looks back into the Incident Room. No sign of Jess or Catrin. He crosses to Rhys Harries's desk.

'Fancy a trip to the pub?'

Rhys frowns.

'Not a bonding session. To chat with a suspect.'

'You want me, sir?' He does an impression of Tigger and bounds out of his chair.

'Yes. Ever been to a pub in Pembroke Dock?'

'No, sir.'

'Okay. That means you'll be a fresh face. Consider it a part of your education. Oh, and see if you can dig up some photos of Kieron Thomas.'

Five minutes later, they're halfway out of the building when Warlow asks. 'Got everything?'

Rhys has a coat over his arm, Thomas's photo held in the other hand. His suit jacket, as expected, is a struggle to do up over a frame without a spare ounce of fat but plenty of muscle. 'Think so, sir.'

'You sure?'

Rhys looks at the coat and the keys before coming up blank.

Warlow puts him out of his misery. 'Next time you buy a suit, get one that's roomier. That way you won't rip the stitches when you pull it on over your stab vest.'

Warlow opens his coat to show the one he's wearing.

This time Rhys reddens. 'It's in my desk drawer, sir. The vest.'

'Good. Put it on and meet me in the car park.'

CHAPTER EIGHTEEN

WARLOW KEEPS HIS CAR CLEAN. The back seats are down and there's a dog guard behind his and Rhys's heads. Behind that is Cadi's German-designed car boot liner. Easy to let the car stink of wet dog. But Warlow won't stand for any of that.

It's one of his little rules, keeping the car clean. Like using the gym he's tacked on to the garage, though gym is stretching it a bit, he admits, in that it's an outhouse just big enough to lie down and do sit-ups in, swing a kettle bell and thump an old punchbag. He gets all the aerobic challenge he needs from walking the dog.

In the passenger seat, Rhys has shed his suit jacket. With the stab vest on, though it's white and could pass for a weird-looking pale jumper at first glance, the added bulk means the jacket is a no-no. Instead, the DC has his raincoat on his knees and Warlow, out of pity, has the heater on full blast.

'Did you do a degree, Rhys?' He flicks the DC a glance.

'Yes, sir. Criminology and psychology in Swansea.'

'Enjoy it?'

'I did.'

'How are you coping with all the glamour and excitement of the actual job?'

'Doing something like this makes up for the boring bits, sir.'

Warlow nods. Rhys is a copper after his own heart. Though their work involves having to outthink the criminal sods who kindly provide work for them, doing is what appeals to Warlow too. Perhaps because when he does find himself being forced into contemplating motivation, forced into becoming a tiny bit like the criminal in order to understand and get on with the job, he's always been a little shocked at how easy it's been for him to do so.

Doing is the Polyfilla in the crack he doesn't want to look into. In case he finds something really unpleasant has burrowed in and made a home in there.

The radio is on and some new romantic tripe is playing. He turns the volume down.

'Not a fan of the eighties vibe, sir?'

'Unlike you, detective constable, I was there. Couldn't be doing with all that ruffled sleeve and makeup bollocks. Thank God for Free and Foreigner and Floyd.'

Rhys is quiet for a moment. He has his phone in his hands and fidgets with it. Warlow senses he wants to say something. Eventually, he does.

'Sir, can I ask you a question?'

'Anything but politics.'

'Sergeant Lewis said they called you the wolf, sir.'

Warlow hasn't heard that in a while. Like all nicknames, and the police seem bloody obsessed with them in that predominantly male, blokey way of all teams, it's not something used face to face. But Warlow the Wolf he knows about.

'Some people did. And you're going to ask me why, am I right?'

'No, I–'

'Well, it's not because I howl at the moon.' He lets that one percolate before throwing Rhys a grin and adding, 'Not every month anyway. No, it's to do with the old cottage I've been renovating. Ffau'r Blaidd. Wolf's lair. That's what the shepherds who first used it called the place.'

Rhys half turns away with a knowing smile. 'Is it though?'

Warlow clasps the steering wheel a little tighter. 'Come on. Spit it out. What little gem did whoever you ask come up with?'

Harries turns back with an appropriately sheepish expression. 'Wolf because once it gets a scent it never gives up, no matter how long it takes to track its prey.'

Warlow shakes his head. 'Jesus. Did they tell you I can leap tall buildings at a single bound, too?'

'No. They said I could learn a lot from you, though.'

'Right. Lesson one, buy better-fitting suits. Lesson two, don't believe everything Sergeant Lewis, or anyone else tells you. Believe only what you can see and what you can prove is true.' Warlow sees Rhys nod. 'Now, when we get to the pub you go around the back because this little git is likely to fly as soon as he sees me.'

'Does he know you, sir?'

'No, but I suspect he'll have a sixth sense for DCIs. Whereas you look like someone on work experience.'

'None taken, sir.' Rhys grins. 'Y Blaidd.' He uses the Welsh for wolf. 'Great name.'

Warlow narrows his eyes and Rhys's grin fades away. 'Stay on your phone as we go in. Let's see if he's happy to see us.'

It's after five thirty and dark when they park up at the rear of the King and Queen. It's a big pub. The car park is poorly lit and pools of shadow line the edge of the space.

'Right, wait for my signal and then come in through the back door. If you see him coming out, don't do anything stupid.'

Rhys is a coiled spring. 'But do you want me to stop him?'

'Do your best. He's not under arrest. Not yet. We just need a chat. Remember that.'

Warlow leaves Rhys standing at the back entrance and walks around to the front. Before he opens the door, he calls the DC on WhatsApp.

'Okay, about to go in.'

Warlow pushes open the door and enters a big open space. He takes in the few customers, the faint smell of disinfectant with undertones of vomit, the three big screens. His eyes dart around the room. Three couples. The rest are blokes sitting with pints. Someone plays darts off to one side. A woman wearing an apron walks past with two plates laden with battered fish and chips. Warlow winces at the rancid aroma of grease that wafts off the food. But what he doesn't see is the face that Rhys has printed off and stuck on the car dashboard. One with an eyebrow ring, tattoos on the neck, a gingery scrawny beard and skin that looks like a meteorite crashed into it a thousand years ago.

'No sign yet,' Warlow says into the phone.

He walks in, heads to the bar, casually glances around as if he's meeting someone. Through the bar there's another room and steps going down to another lounge and the rear entrance.

'See anything?' Warlow asks.

'No.'

'Walk in slowly. Head for the bar.'

Footsteps and then Rhys again. 'I'm inside, but this place is huge.'

Warlow can't see the DC yet.

A barman saunters over. 'What can I get you?'

'Looking for a mate,' says Warlow.

The barman, young, bearded, hair tied back, looks vaguely interested but when Warlow slides over the mugshot of Ket, he stiffens, and his face turns to wood. It's that kind of pub.

'He's not here.'

'But you know him?'

'He comes in, yeah.'

'Not tonight?'

'He was in earlier.'

The barman studies the photograph without picking it up. Warlow swivels it back around as a door to his right opens. A woman walks through, dressed in a coat and stamping her feet from the cold. She pockets a pack of cigarettes.

'There's a side entrance.' Warlow speaks into the phone. 'A smoking spot. Don't approach. Wait until–'

'On it,' yells Rhys.

'No,' Warlow orders. But all he hears in reply are rapidly running steps.

He has time only to pick up the photograph and slide it into a pocket before the side door swings open again and in strides Kieron Thomas. It's twenty paces between the doorway and the bar. Warlow hasn't moved yet, but he's looking in that direction. And that's the problem. They lock eyes. And Ket, street wise from years of petty crime, reads hunter in the DCI's face.

Pure bad luck thinks Warlow. Or an elementary mistake from an old cop not quite on top of his game.

Ket turns and bolts.

Warlow runs across the room, phone still to his ear. He hears shouts, a phone clattering. Someone screams.

Warlow pushes out into the cold winter air. Three

people are standing around, two with cigarettes, all with hoods up. They're clustered around a figure on the floor.

'Rhys!' Warlow barks into his phone. 'Rhys.'

And then he sees it. A black iPhone on the floor. He picks it up, hears a strange echo of noise and knows it's still connected to his. He turns to the figure on the floor. Someone's kneeling over him. A woman dressed in jeans and a Parker.

'What happened?' Warlow barks out the question.

'A bloke ran from the pub and straight into this chap. Pushed him over. Then he … oh my God … I think he had a knife.'

Warlow hisses out air and kneels next to the woman. It's then he realises it's DC Harries. 'Rhys? Rhys?'

The DC groans. He's face-down. Warlow pulls him onto his back. Blood trickles from a head wound down over his neck.

'He hit the pavement pretty hard,' someone else says.

But Warlow is not listening. He's unzipping the DC's coat. Pulling it open, searching his torso for any signs of bleeding.

There are none.

Another groan and an expulsion of air from Rhys. 'Sorry, sir. Ran into me. Stupid, I …'

'Don't worry. Stay where you are.'

Rhys is as pale as a plastered wall. 'He hit my chest. I felt something …'

'You're fine. You hit your head.'

Rhys sits up. 'Sorry.'

'Don't apologise. We'd better get the head looked at, though.' Warlow calls it in.

'I'm only winded, sir.'

Warlow puts a hand on his shoulder. 'Hey, head injury rules apply. If you were playing rugby there'd be a mandatory assessment.'

Rhys shuts up after that.

Warlow turns to the crowd that's gathered. 'I'll need names and addresses. And don't think of disappearing because we've got body cams.' They haven't, but it seems to do the trick, and no one runs away.

It's a narrow escape. But later, when the people who know examine Rhys's vest, there are signs that tell them a knife was used. But the vest has done its job and kept it out of the DC's heart.

Warlow keeps the photo of Kieron Thomas as a reminder of what he's going to do to the little shit when he catches him.

CHAPTER NINETEEN

WARLOW TAKES RHYS TO A&E, flashes his warrant card and, as luck has it, knows the sister in charge who's been working at the hospital for as long as he can remember. The DC is seen and sutured in double quick time. Warlow takes him home to his parents' house, makes sure they know how well he did and has a cup of tea with them. Mrs Harries is a teacher of around Warlow's age and taught Tom English. The Harries's are proud of their only son. Proud that he's in the force. When the DCI apologises for the third time, Rhys's mother holds up a hand and throws a quote at him.

'People sleep peaceably in their beds only because rough men stand ready to do violence on their behalf.'

Sounds Churchillian but isn't.

'1984?' Warlow asks. Mrs Harries smiles in acknowledgement. There's pride in that smile.

He's home in Ffau'r Blaidd two hours after leaving the King and Queen in Pembroke.

'World bloody record,' he tells Cadi, as he ladles raw lamb mince into a bowl for her and puts it outside.

It's only once she's fed that he realises he's hardly eaten anything all day.

Saliva floods his mouth. How easy it would be to slip into the old ways of opening a packet or a can. Poor diets, lousy levels of exercise and a shit family life are the bane of the job. SIO's especially. But Jess strikes him as a woman who has strategies to deal with all that. The way she looks for a start. Whatever she does to keep herself fit, it's working. Can't be easy being a single parent in a new job in a new patch. He feels for her and her situation. The curse of the two-cop family.

But sometimes it's even worse for a civilian partner. Marry a copper and you marry the job. He's suffered the consequences of that. But he's grateful that he and Denise stayed together long enough for the boys to get through university. No need for them to suffer. They were the reason he'd stuck it for so long.

He's in the kitchen but pushes thoughts of eating aside for now because Ket's petrified face is all he sees. He'd looked scared. Genuinely scared, and not of Warlow. There was something else there that put him on edge.

He curses and sighs. Thomas was a lead, and the line has snapped before he's even had time to reel it in and take a peek at what was dangling on the end.

It's unusual for things to break this quickly. Especially in a case that's now almost seven and a half years old. Even more unusual for that new trail to run dry as quickly. That bothers him.

He makes himself some cheese on toast, leaves half of it and, a little after eight, makes a call.

'Jess,' he says, when she picks up.

'Hi.' She's intrigued more than bothered.

'It's late and you've left the office. But if it was my case, and I was SIO, I'd want to know.'

'Go on.'

'Kieron Thomas. I took Rhys with me to the pub he uses as an office to talk to the little shit. He spotted me and made a run for it. Knocked Rhys off his feet and he opened a cut after colliding with the pavement.'

'Is he okay?'

Warlow hesitates.

'Evan?'

Warlow opens the door to let Cadi back in. The blast of cold air is like a slap. 'He's fine. But Thomas tried to stab him. No damage, but it makes me think the bastard might have been expecting someone else.'

'Such as?'

'Someone he was prepared to attack before they attacked him.'

Silence from Jess.

He reads it as annoyance. 'Sorry to be a pain.'

'Don't apologise. And I'm glad you told me. It's not my first go on the roundabout, Evan.'

He's about to kill the call when Jess asks, 'Have you eaten?'

Warlow pokes a finger at his boring sandwich. 'No.'

'I've made a ton of moussaka and Molly never has seconds. It's either freezer or bin and I have a freezer full already.'

'No, that's nice of you but–'

Jess cuts across his objection with a low whisper. 'I could also do with a bit of adult conversation. Molly, God bless her, is driving me slightly mad.'

Warlow gives in without a fight. 'Okay. Forty-five minutes?'

'See you then. I'll text the address.' Jess kills the call.

———

NARBERTH IS AN OLD TOWN. Once an ancient prince's palace and a king's court, later a castle stronghold on the Landsker Line. Another military base for the Anglo-Norman suppression of the Welsh. Today people visit for the food, or the shopping, or to pay their last respects to the dead before they turn their loved ones to ash at the crematorium. Occasionally, people do all three things in one visit.

Life, as they say, is for the living. And death is bloody inconvenient.

Jess's rental is in the hamlet of Cold Blow, once a turn-pike on the old mail road, a couple of miles outside the town. It's a corner plot on a newish development. Built, Warlow suspects, as an investment vehicle by whoever owns it. Two floors, with the upper in a loft with skylight windows. It's a cheerful yellow colour and completely devoid of any character.

He parks next to a black Golf. He's brought Cadi in the Jeep and she sits up when he stops in front of the strange house. But he's brought her only by way of appeasement. Sometimes the trip in the car is as good as a walk; in terms of her thinking she's been out.

'Stay girl,' he orders and walks to the front door.

Jess is in jeans and a zip up sweatshirt, flat sandals on her sockless feet. The sandals are Birkenstock's with a flowery strap. He knows all this because his son had a girl-friend who had a pair stolen. The least he could do when he heard about it was look them up and gawp at how expensive they were, and at how bloody stupid anyone was to leave such items unattended on a beach in Corfu. Jess's toenails are dark blue. He absorbs all of this without directly looking. He's had years of practice.

Warlow holds up a bottle of wine. An appassimento from Majestic. Great with food.

Jess frowns. 'You know I can't take that.'

Warlow thrusts the wine towards her. 'If you're offering food it's the least I can do. Consider it barter.'

'Come in.' Jess steps back from the doorway with a sweep of her hand.

Inside it's open plan. A cream and mocha palette on the walls. Laminate wood flooring and leather sofas. There's a round table behind one sofa with two place settings at two and ten.

'What about your daughter?'

'She ate an hour ago.' Jess finds a corkscrew and hands it to Warlow. 'Please. Yours is bound to be nicer than mine. I haven't had time to restock so all I have is supermarket special offers.'

He opens the bottle and pours two glasses. Jess produces two bowls of moussaka and a green salad. He talks as they eat and tells her what he's found out about Kelly Scott and Kieron Thomas. The wine, as always, is good. He's recounting Dai Vetch's suggestion that they talk to Neil Morris when there's a drum beat of feet on the stairs and a girl in skinny jeans and a baggy T-shirt appears with an aluminium water bottle.

'Evan Warlow, this is Molly.'

She's not quite as tall as her mother and her jeans have frayed holes scattered over thighs and knees in the current fashion. She's piled her dark hair high on her head and the same almost-grey eyes as her mother's engage Warlow's.

'Hello,' she says with an apologetic smile. 'I just need a top up.'

She fills her bottle from a jug in the fridge.

'Evan is the Detective Chief Inspector involved in the original investigation of the Pickerings when they first went missing.' Jess motions for the jug from Molly and pours water for her guest.

Molly turns to Evan with an earnest expression. 'I hope you catch them.'

'So do I.'

Molly looks out of the window and shoots Warlow an over the shoulder glance. 'Is that a dog in your car?'

'It is. Cadi. She's a black lab.'

Molly's eyes light up. 'Is she a police dog?'

'If you mean is she trained in police work, then no.'

'Can she come in?'

Warlow holds his hands up. 'This isn't my house.'

Molly turns huge eyes towards her mother. 'Mum?'

Jess shrugs. 'Why not?'

Warlow gets Cadi out and the next ten minutes is all about dog meets woman, meets girl, rediscovers owner. It's a wag fest.

'She is gorgeous,' Molly repeats for the third time as Cadi does her best to get maximum contact. 'We so need a dog here.'

'One thing at a time, Mol.' Jess tries to be stern, but her expression has softened into admiration, too.

Warlow has some treats in his coat pocket and has brought in a ball, the mere mention of which makes Cadi's ears prick. He hands the ball to Molly. 'Tell her to sit and you hide the ball somewhere in the house. Then ask her to find it. It's one of her favourite things. Just remember to reward her afterwards or you'll never get it back.'

'Maybe not upst–' Jess warns, but Molly's already ordered a 'sit' and run up. Cadi watches and when Molly reappears and says the word find, she goes into tracker mode. Girl and dog disappear upstairs.

'Nicely done,' Jess says. 'You've just won over my daughter who normally treats everyone work-related like a leper.'

'Is that to do with her father?'

'Sion Buchannan's briefed you then.' Jess's toothless smile is tinged with bitterness.

'Can't be easy.'

'No. But she's a good kid.'

'Boyfriends?'

Jess makes eyes to the ceiling. 'Not here. Not yet. And the one she left behind wasn't serious.'

'I doubt she'll have any trouble on that score.'

'Hmm. She isn't driving yet, thank God. That's the next thing. She misses her kayaking though. I'm still working on that.'

Warlow sips his wine and plays with a few leaves of salad still on the plate. 'I made a mistake with Rhys tonight. I should have scoped the pub out. Realised there was another exit.'

'Sounds like sheer bad luck to me.'

Warlow shakes his head. 'I could have been sitting with his mother tonight explaining how her son was stabbed in the heart.'

Jess winces. 'We'll make finding Thomas our priority. He's attacked a copper. There's no excuse for that.'

But Warlow knows that if it ever came to court the little shit would wriggle free. They hadn't introduced themselves as police officers. Hadn't had the chance. Jess lifts the wine bottle and tilts the neck towards him. He puts a hand over the glass. 'Driving,' he says.

Jess replenishes her almost empty glass. 'Can I ask you a personal question. I've met burned out CID before and you do not strike me as one of them. You're still hungry. Why did you retire?' She keeps her eyes on the purple liquid as she asks.

For a moment Warlow thinks about telling her. The truth. The whole shebang. That she is asking reassures him that Buchannan has kept his promise on confidentiality. He opts instead for deflection. It works wonders. 'Well now, that's like asking a woman how old she is.'

Jess frowns. 'I'm forty-five. What century are you from?'

Warlow snorts. 'I needed time to take stock.'

'So personal reasons then?'

'Yeah. Something like that.' Warlow looks into Jess's grey eyes, trying not to make it a challenge and only half succeeding.

'Painful ones if I'm not mistaken.

Warlow plays with the stem of his glass. 'Not for polite conversation, that's for sure.'

Jess grabs up their plates. 'Mystery man it is then, Detective Chief Inspector.'

Warlow forces a smile, but he's spared more scrutiny by the sound of Molly and Cadi running downstairs.

'She's dead good at finding stuff,' Molly beams. Cadi has a ball in her mouth and looks ridiculously pleased with herself. 'I hid it at the bottom of your laundry basket, Mum.'

Jess looks pained as she castigates her daughter. 'Molly.'

'She found it in like, five minutes. When she pulled it out, she had your red knickers wrapped around it. You know, the nice ones,' Molly explains with glee.

Jess aims a wide-eyed glare at her daughter.

'Time we left,' Warlow says, grinning, but deciding this is a game he'd rather not be a part of. 'Thanks for the moussaka. See you bright and early tomorrow.'

'There's a big portion left. You're welcome to it.'

'No, honestly.'

'Go on, you'd be doing me a favour.' Jess is already snapping open a Tupperware container.

'Or we could cut out the middleman and throw it straight into the toilet,' Molly says, feigning innocence.

'Molly,' Jess chides her.

'I'll be happy to take what's left over.' Warlow accepts the food.

'You should try her lasagne if you like cholesterol

bombs.' Molly keeps her gaze firmly on Cadi as she delivers her one liner.

Jess sighs and shakes her head with a fixed smile. Warlow senses no malice in this interplay. It's merely banter between child and parent. And he remembers well enough how acerbic that can be in the teen years.

Cadi trots with him to the door. Molly kneels down for one last Labrador hug.

Warlow turns back. 'I know the chap who runs a canoeing club in Fishguard. Your mum said you were a bit of a canoer.'

'Used to be,' Molly says with exaggerated wistfulness.

'I had a word. He says they're doing the Cleddau estuary this Sunday and the weather looks good. If you're interested, give him a ring.'

Molly looks up from the dog. 'That would be amazing.'

Warlow reads out a number from his phone. Molly punches it into hers.

Girl and woman stand in the doorway to watch him leave. Jess has her arm around her daughter and mouths, 'Thank you' as he pulls away.

CHAPTER TWENTY

KET KNOWS HOW TO HIDE. It must have been the cops who came to the King and Queen. Must have been. Still, he isn't sure. He didn't recognise either of the scum. He's spent the evening lying low but now he needs to stash his money.

He's still in the Dock, as it's known to its denizens. Safer to stay here than try and get out for now. He knows the town like the back of his tattooed hand.

He heads for his grandmother's place, walking fast on expensive trainers that match his expensive skinny jeans. Best to be off the streets when you're carrying this kind of cash. People know him. Sometimes the wrong people. Ket reaches Hawksmere Road and the cut through along a back lane he always takes.

The alley is empty. Some of the houses backing onto it derelict. Most need some TLC. A third of the way along, Ket steps around a pile of wood that used to be a garage door and doesn't see the sucker punch that hits him on the side of the head.

The blow spins him into the opposite wall. He crunches an elbow into the bricks and his hearing dulls for a moment. There's a crackle and buzz, something stings in his chest and then the pain comes. A massive spasm surges through his body as the Taser fires. He collapses, unable to breathe and when he does, he sucks in air mixed with filthy puddle water from where he's lying. This triggers a coughing fit that brings a lot more pain. He offers no resistance as his hands and ankles are bound with ties. He's dragged out of the alley and down through a rubbish-strewn patch next to an old brick shed on the edge of the railway embankment and dumped onto a floor littered with abandoned syringes and little brown bottles.

He tries to shout, but it ends with a strip of gaffer tape over his mouth.

He moans and struggles until there's a shoe on his neck. He's quiet after that. He can hear traffic, the two-tone hoot of a train rumbling past on its way to the station, followed by the rhythmic clatter of wheels on rails. Something cold and sharp presses the skin over his Adam's apple. There's a ten second silence before he hears his own voice from a recorded message:

'Yeah, uh, it's Ket. I seen the news and like, I think we need to chat. That job I done for you, the one I helped Morris with? Them two wasn't supposed to be found, was they? But it's all over the fucking news, man. We sealed the entrance and stuff but it's a real shit show now after that landslide. Thing is, if plod come asking, what am I supposed to say? I know what I should say, like, but, you now, with Morris in the nick and all, it's only me that knows. Thing is I reckon I should be compensated for the stress of it, like. Compensated so that I say the right think if plod calls. I know we was paid at the time, but this is different, isn't it? This is some weird shit. Anyway, you got my number and I'm always in town. Best place is the King and Queen in the afternoons.'

A hard voice speaks from behind Ket. Out of sight. 'Use a burner for this?'

Ket moans a yes.

'You tell anyone?'

Ket's eyes are wide with fear. He shakes his head and a noise that might be 'no' comes through the tape. Cold steel with a razor edge kisses his throat.

'You're sure?'

Ket shakes again.

The knife moves away from his neck. Without warning, it's stabbed into his thigh.

Ket arches his back, the chords of muscle in his stringy neck tense in agony. A muffled scream rents the air.

'Mmammutha. Mmammtha,' moans Ket.

'Your grandmother? You told your grandmother?'

Ket nods. Many times to make sure.Tears of pain and fear course down his face.

'Good. Best to be a hundred per cent clear.'

Ket can't see his captor. He only hears noises from behind in the dark. Feels something cold and wet on his thigh. Smells the bright metallic aroma of lighter fluid.

Ket moans again, though there aren't any coherent words. He's crying, pleading. He begs in between the sobs. A hand searches his jacket pocket for cigarettes and lighter. Then he's thrown on his front, a knee in his back, his arm yanked back, something tight around his bicep. He struggles and bucks, then everything stops.

He waits for something worse. It comes as a searing pain in his other leg when the knife pierces designer jeans, skin, and muscle. It keeps going until it grinds to a stop against the bottom of the femur, just above the knee. 'Now keep still, you bastard. Or do you want more?'

Ket shakes his head. The knife shifts. The sounds he makes now are more like the mewling of a cat.

A tightness around his upper arm again. A stab of

brief pain and then ... and then no more pain. Nothing but the sweet oblivion of whatever has been injected into him. The struggles all stop. He's unaware of the ties being removed. The mewling ceases.

They only start up again when the flames take hold and start licking up over his thighs and chest. The fentanyl and ketamine dull the pain, but it doesn't take it away all together.

Neither does it remove the absolute certainty from Ket's awareness that he is about to die.

When he does, some minutes later, his captor is long gone.

CHAPTER TWENTY-ONE

A CERTAIN DYLAN THOMAS once called his hometown of Swansea, 'ugly, lovely, crawling, sprawling.' Three adjectives apply to HM prison on the Oystermouth Road with no prizes for guessing which of the four does not. Its grey Victorian facade is visible from the road, a handful of yards from the reclaimed Maritime Quarter. And unlike the towns' university that ranks in the country's top thirty, inspectors declared the jail unfit for purpose years ago. Its old-fashioned wings in a stacked cell design either side of a central atrium house remand and convicted prisoners. Designed to hold 220 inmates, it accommodates around 500.

Neil Morris shares a cell with a twenty-year-old burglar called Deakon who is no trouble except for his taste for Spice. It wasn't unusual to find Deakon zombied-out after a joint.

They eat in their cell, one metre from the toilet. Morris signed up for art courses when he got in. Even got paid to do it as part of his further 'education'. The other type of education that goes on involves self-discipline. How to stay away from the drugs that are rampant and for many the only way to survive. When he was on the outside, he'd seen documentaries about drones dropping drugs in the yards of prisons. Big joke in Swansea where you can sometimes spend twenty-three hours in your cell. Here, people bring in the goods wrapped in double condoms stuffed up their rectums – the body searches don't involve anal inspections. Though there are some inmates who would volunteer for one of those every day. Whatever melts your butter.

But he's stayed clean in prison. And anyway, he's a coke man outside. A recreational user. Although that could mean being recreational four days a week – and weekends. He misses it but trusts nothing he can get inside.

He's still resentful at being caught. It was a stupid thing to have done. But when a flash bastard in a Honda Civic Type R sticks his bonnet four feet from your boot, it's a challenge you don't back away from.

At least not in Morris's machismo-fuelled, petrol-head world.

He was on his way back from Merthyr in his Peugeot 405 on the heads of the valleys' road. Not the best route for a matchup. But he'd had a go. They pulled him over near Hirwaun and the pursuit vehicle had clocked him at 105. He already had twelve points, so that was his licence fucked. He'd only been back from a twelve month ban for five months. But it was the cocaine that did for him. Lucky he had just the one bag. That meant possession as opposed to intent to sell.

And now he's been told the cops want to talk to him again. The Kelly Scott case and Ket. Morris smiled when he heard that. What the fuck had the mad bastard done now? Despite asking, there's been no detail. Something about fresh evidence in an old case. He's agreed to it because at least it means a couple of hours out of his cell. If he can string them along, it might be more. He could even get a can or two of Pepsi out of it.

He's considering his manipulative options when a screw turns up at the door.

'Right, Morris, shower time.'

'What? Had one yesterday.' Every other day has been the rule since Morris arrived. Sometimes they stretched that to seventy-two hours.

'You've got visitors tomorrow. So you get special dispensation.'

'Wow, you lot want me smelling nice for the cops?' he grins, but his attempt at humour meets deaf ears.

'If you don't want to, just say the word,' the prison officer half turns away.

'Didn't say that, did I?' Morris grabs his towel. Another chance to break the boredom. Half an hour out of this shitty cell is not to be sniffed at.

'You lucky twat,' says his cellmate.

Morris grins and taps his nose. 'It's who you know Deakon. Who you know.' He follows the guard out into the corridor and heads for the shower block. Might as well enjoy this while it lasts.

CHAPTER TWENTY-TWO

EVERY MORNING, Izzy does her rounds of feeding the chickens and the donkeys. Today is no different. Except that today, once she'd done the feeding, she takes Monty to the spot at the fence where she left her offering.

It isn't there.

She's done her best to ensure a random fox hasn't taken it by tying the bag to the fence post and winding the plastic ears of the knot around a nail. She leans in to examine that now, reasoning that someone, or something, tearing at the bag might have left some evidence, some shreds or strands.

There are none.

She looks up and out at the ravine and the Engine House. It's a brisk, cool day. The ruins give nothing away. If she's hoping for a sign, there is none. And then she sees something on top of the fence post. It's five or six inches long and has a silvery yellow lustre. She stares, knowing that though razor clam shells are a common enough sight, it's not at all common to see one on top of a fence post.

Unless someone put it there.

As payment? The idea flicks into existence in a blink.

One half of a complete shell. But it's clean with no remnants of the flesh inside. She puts the shell into the pocket of her coat and turns away. She'll have something to tell Marcus over breakfast. And, as quickly as that thought occurs, she snuffs it out. She can hear his derisive laughter in her head. She'd have to suffer his waifs and strays' lecture. His conviction that she has a soft spot for all things lost. And of how the shell has ended up on the fencepost courtesy of luck and a rapacious seagull.

No. Not yet.

She'll do a little more digging first.

As she turns away, the buzz of a quad biker reaches her. A red Honda Fourtrax trundles through the cow-track gap between the ravine and the Spaceship. She raises her hand, being neighbourly, at the same time hoping, in a very un-neighbourly way, it isn't the younger Gower. The old man, Rylan, has been courteous, if a little dour. And Ben has been more than helpful with fixing a few fallen down fence posts when they needed to stock proof the paddock. But she's seen the way he'll sometimes watch her. Could simply be that he's young and full of testosterone. She's probably over-reacting. Perhaps she ought even to be flattered. After all, she's positively ancient compared to him. All she knows is she's happier not meeting him alone. But the ATV speeds up towards her and Izzy grits her teeth. She can't just ignore the thing as it pulls up and the driver pulls off the hood of his coat and unfurls the scarf around his face.

'Mornin', Izzy.'

'Morning, Ben.' Izzy smiles.

He's in work overalls with reinforced padding over the knees and shoulders. There's mud and worse spattered all over his legs and boots. The ATV is similarly decorated with cow dung. Ben's a farmer. What the hell should she expect? Still, it's all Izzy can do not to wrinkle her nose. He nods towards the Spaceship. 'Lot of plastic there.'

Izzy follows his gaze. 'A scaffold wrap. Means Marcus can get on and finish his lookout tower in any weather.'

Off the bike Ben is taller than Izzy. Taller and broader. But seated on the bike like this on the lower ground his side of the fence she stands above him. 'You know run off from the field can sometimes flood that corner,' he says.

'We know. That's why we're putting drainage in. A big soakaway to carry water down the slope.'

'And the wind here is wicked strong. Southwesterlies funnel through the ravine. Tell Marcus to be careful, right?'

'I will.'

Ben restarts the bike. The trailer, Izzy notices, is stacked with plastic bags full of cattle feed.

'Winter storms are coming,' Ben shouts over the noise of the engine.

'Thanks,' Izzy says. But as he turns away, she asks, 'Do you ever go to the Engine House?'

Ben stops and lets the ATV idle. 'No. Too dangerous. It's off limits. I used to go there when I was a kid, but not now. We've fenced it off. Why?'

'Curiosity. It's such a brooding structure. It has an amazing satanic mill vibe.'

'That a film is it?'

'No. It's from a poem.' She toys, for a second, with mentioning Blake's Jerusalem, but decides against it. A decision confirmed as wise by Ben's next comment.

'Not into that stuff.'

'No. Not everyone's cup of tea.'

Ben's face becomes stern. 'Like I say, it's dangerous. The walls are falling down and we've had a couple of tunnels collapse. Best to stay away if I was you.'

'Right.' She offers a smile.

Ben revs the bike and pulls away with a wave of his hand.

Full of the joys of spring as usual, Izzy muses. And then shakes her head. He was only being neighbourly in his own bluff way. She'll be glad when the cabin is finished and the Spaceship is gone. Hopefully it'll be summer and they can sit and enjoy the views and listen to the wind funnelling up through the ravine.

When she tells Marcus later, as he's lifting sandbags into a wheelbarrow, he shrugs it off.

'Take no notice. The scaffolding is solid steel and the wrap is indestructible and anchored with three-inch ties.'

'Good. Wouldn't want you flying off over the Irish Sea.'

'That would be something. A Phileas Fogg moment.'

'I prefer *UP* as a cinematic metaphor.'

'That's because you are soppy and a cartoon freak.' Marcus groans with effort as another bag enters the barrow.

'Oy. *UP* is a brilliant film.'

'One of your faves, yes I know.'

'But you will be careful, won't you?'

Marcus stops his labouring and wipes a trickle of sweat from his brow. 'My middle name.'

'The one after gung-ho, you mean?'

'I thought we agreed not to mention that branch of the family.'

'So droll. So very droll,' Izzy mutters and turns towards the house.

CHAPTER TWENTY-THREE

EIGHT THIRTY SHARP and the Incident Room is full.

The noticeboards have sprouted more notes: post-its with big question marks and even more photographs. Chief amongst the recent additions are the mugshots of Kieron Thomas. There are a dozen people in the room and Warlow, wearing a suit for maybe the third time since he retired, takes up a position at the rear where he leans against the wall. Mel Lewis is in there, seated at another desk and drinking coffee from a mug that has 'Good Morning Lover Boy' emblazoned across it.

The DS nods a greeting. There's a buzz of anticipation in the low whispers and a grim determination hovers in the air. Warlow's hands are icy. It's an adrenaline response. Most people in this room felt the same thing.

Jess is already leaning on a desk at the front in a dark-grey suit. She's striking, Warlow thinks. So do most of the other men. He can see it in the way their gazes linger. Probably some women, too. It's the 21st century and everything is up for grabs. But Warlow turns his mind away from that. Whatever 'everything' might mean, it's for other people. Not him.

Not anymore.

Notable for his absence is DC Rhys Harries. Warlow has phoned to check on him and, despite protestations, told him to stay home for today. Making sure he understands to contact him if he starts feeling sick or dizzy. Head injury protocol and all that.

The Buccaneer walks in and the room quietens. He summarises the situation regarding the Pickering corpses. Things Warlow already knows. But this is a catch-up for the team.

'Confirmation of a DNA match has come through for Marjorie and Kenneth.' He uses their first names. They are still people to the gathered investigators, not corpses, and Buchannan and Jess will want to keep it that way. Now there is no doubt who they are. No doubt either that the wounds are consistent with their heads being caved in with a hammer. The other injuries have the same MO as well.

'You will all have a summary of the original investigation into their disappearance provided by the senior officer in charge at the time. DCI Warlow has agreed to come back and assist us, and we are delighted to have him here. His summary is available on HOLMES.'

Half the people in the room turn. Warlow raises a hand in acknowledgement as Buchannan ploughs on. 'The two reviews into the case did not throw up any fresh evidence. However, as you will see and hear, things are now moving quickly.' He looks across at the Detective Inspector. 'Jess?'

Buchannan stands aside and Jess steps forward and summarises the DNA link to Kelly Scott.

'Scott had connections with a dealer called Kieron Thomas who is now on our patch.' Jess turns to the photo board. 'Last night, DCI Warlow and Rhys Harries tried to make contact. As a result, Rhys has five stitches in his head and is puncture free thanks only to a stab vest. The consensus is that Thomas is spooked. I would very much like to talk to him.

'Thomas was a suspect in the Kelly Scott killing and has a record peppered with arrests for threatening behaviour and a caution for possession of an offensive weapon in a public place. That weapon was a hammer.' She points to another image. 'I would like to ask him where he was on the day the Pickerings went missing. We need to get on to phone usage at the time of their disappearance, known associates, you know the drill. I want to know of anything that might link him either to the Pickerings directly, or any reason he might have had for being within five miles of the coastal path the day they disappeared. We have information on an associate of Thomas's. A Neil Morris, currently in Swansea prison. I intend to interview him as soon as I can. So, contacts, whereabouts, addresses please.'

Richards is writing on the board. Jess waves a finger in her direction. 'I've posted named assignments. You know how to get hold of me, DS Richards and DCI Warlow.' She nods at Sion Buchannan who takes over for the last few words. A pep talk for the team. Changing room motivation.

'Thanks, Jess. What we know is that the Pickerings were killed and their bodies hidden on the path. We doubt that could be done by one man working alone. What we do not know is whether the killers planned their attack so it happened at that point on the path, or whether the victims were in the wrong place at the wrong time. Perhaps the killers were using the cave as a depository. Whatever the situation, it seems likely they had local knowledge. That's why Kieron Thomas and his associates are of significant interest.' Buchannan turns to the photos of the Pickerings, smiling and happy.

'Marjorie and Ken died on that spot on the path. Their

killers have been wandering around free as a bird for years. Our task is to find them, prosecute them and get them off the path and the streets. That's my job and yours. Let's do it.'

The meeting ends, people turn back to screens and wander up to the boards to check on their assignments. Mel Lewis strolls over to Warlow.

'Bad luck with Thomas. Rhys okay?'

Warlow cocks one eyebrow. 'He's fine. I've told him to stay away.'

Lewis grins and tilts his mug in acknowledgement. 'Why they pay us the danger money, right?'

Catrin appears in front of them. 'DI Allanby wants us in her office.'

Lewis waves to Warlow. He's not part of the investigative team and so he's excused the meeting.

As they're threading their way through the office, Rhys Harries walks in with a raised bald patch on the back of his head where they'd shaved it for the suturing. On seeing Warlow, his face registers panic and he launches into an explanation.

'Sir, I know you said to stay home, but I was going crazy. My sister's boys are over with us and it's Uncle Rhys this and Uncle Rhys that. It's quieter here.'

Catrin stares at his head, grinning. 'Nice bump.'

Rhys shakes his head. 'What if I said something like that to you?'

'I'd thump you where it hurts the most.' Her grin widens.

'Not felt sick or anything?' Warlow asks.

'No. Nothing. I've had worse playing for Nant in the Cup.'

'I'd say you definitely need a CT scan if you're playing for Nant,' Catrin says.

'I'm known as the police interceptor, I'll have you–' Rhys catches Warlow's glower. 'Sorry, sir.'

'Let that be a lesson to you.' Catrin adopts a preachy tone.

'You live and learn,' Rhys responds, returning her cliché volley.

'I'd rather you learned and lived.' Warlow's growl puts a stop to their exchange. 'Now, let's see what DI Allanby wants.'

It's a brief meeting. Jess turns immediately to Catrin. 'Morris in Swansea nick. Where are we?'

Prison interviews were tricky. Prisoners had the same rights as non-prisoners, could either agree to a voluntary interview or could be made to answer if there were reasonable grounds though the governor would need to give permission. Catrin is up to the task.

'The Prison Liaison Officer has had a word with Morris, and he's agreed to speak to us about Kelly Scott. He was a part of Thomas's alibi.'

'Solicitor?'

'He's declined the offer.'

Jess shakes her head. Some people will never learn. 'Good. When can we do it?'

'They've set it up for three.'

'So let's find out what we can about what they got up to together before Morris was nicked.' Jess turns to Warlow. 'Evan, since you're up to speed with Thomas, any chance you can have a look at his flat?'

'No problem.'

'I'll find someone to go with you.'

Warlow turns to Rhys. 'I'll take this one since he's so keen to be here.'

'Is that wise, sir?' Catrin's eyebrows shoot up.

Warlow shrugs. 'You know what they say about falling off a horse, the sooner you get back on, the better.'

Rhys frowns, his eyes moving slowly from side to side. 'Sir, I've never ridden a horse.'

Catrin and Jess can only blink in speechless wonder.

'Well that's something you can work on for your CV.' Warlow keeps a straight face. 'But I wouldn't worry about it just for the moment. You up for another jaunt?'

The young detective constable sits up, chest out. 'Totally, sir. And I won't forget to bring my stab vest this time, promise.'

He reminds Warlow of Cadi when she's offered a bone.

CHAPTER TWENTY-FOUR

Izzy drives to the Hall. There's a queue outside. If she thought she could meander around inside surreptitiously, working out if anyone likes her stuff, she is wrong. She feels foolish and is about to get back into the car when someone toots a horn. She turns and sees Angharad in a mud-splashed Kia, smoking.

'No room at the inn, right?' Angharad says.

Izzy walks across. 'I had no idea there'd be so many people waiting.'

'Nor me. Can't be much on TV.'

'Maybe they've heard of the artistic treasures on show.'

'I hope that's just tobacco.' Izzy looks askance at the cigarette.

'Don't be silly.' Angharad blows some smoke in her direction. It's sweet and potent. 'Fancy a drink?'

'I'm driving and I need to get back.'

'So am I. One drink, not a sesh. We'll take both cars so you can shoot off.'

'Where?'

Angharad grins and starts to wind up her window. 'Follow me.'

Izzy does exactly that, along empty lanes to a hotel on the edge of the coast near Gwbert. A sprawling place with big lounges and an outside terrace where they sit in their coats under a patio heater. Only one other group braves the elements, but the girls are warm enough despite the unpromising weather. No rain at least. And the sky is grey enough to hint at snow. But there will be none as hardly any falls this far west.

'This is a nice place.' Izzy scans the surroundings.

Angharad nods. 'Great New Year's Eve parties. We usually book a room. You should come.'

'I'll tell Marcus. You never know.' She does, though. He won't come because he won't be able to drink. Well, not the amounts he usually guzzled at New Year's Eve parties. She doesn't blame him for that. What's the point of a sober 'Auld Lang Syne'?

Angharad is in a denim maxi skirt and a padded flowery jacket. She's bought a round of Prosecco. Her glass is already two thirds empty.

Izzy's sips hers slowly. 'I showed Marcus your cards. He's impressed.'

'Was he?'

'Yes, he was. They are amazing. Especially the Follower.'

Angharad offers a cheeky smile. 'You like him, don't you?'

'I do. It's as if you lifted him from our landscape. Like he's standing on the path at the bottom of our property. It's uncanny.'

Angharad sends Izzy a sceptical glance. 'You into that sort of thing? The uncanny?'

It's here, under normal circumstances, that Izzy would pull back – like a turtle retracting its head – to stay safe and avoid derision. But with Angharad, it's different. She's different. One peek at her feather earrings tells everyone that. 'Yes, I am. It's something I'd like to explore. The art, my textile stuff, that's fun. But like Marcus says, it's a ding dong. A busman's holiday. What I really want to do is write.'

'As in books?'

'Yes.' Izzy's heart is beating fast. She's told no one this. Not even Marcus. 'Fantasy stuff. Mythology.'

'Like *Game of Thrones*? Or more *Twilight*?'

'Neither. Not so gory and not so silly. More … contemporary maybe. A different world hidden within ours.' She drops her eyes. 'I'm still working on it.'

'But you've written stuff already?' Angharad is persistent.

Izzy thinks of the files on her laptop. A dozen ideas. Fifty thousand words. 'I always have a work in progress. But your Follower has given me new inspiration. There's an abandoned Engine House across the ravine from where we live. A crumbling old relic from the last but one century. I can stand at the fence in my garden and study its wonky tower and play the "what if" game.'

'Wow. Hidden depths, Izzy. You ought to meet Lena. She'd love you.'

'I'd like to. But you must feel it too. Your cards are amazing. Something must inspire you here.'

'Yeah.' Angharad angles her face and drops her voice. 'But I get just as much from a spliff.' She eases out a tobacco-roughened laugh. 'Just think what you could do if you smoked a joint.'

Izzy takes a sip of the Prosecco, pleased that Angharad hasn't laughed at her.

Angharad is persistent. 'So, come on, tell me what this story is about.'

'No. Some people say it's bad luck to speak of it before it's finished.'

'Bollocks. Pretend I'm the Big Publisher and there's a

storm and we're stuck in this hotel together. You've wandered out and found me sitting here, smoking. You need a light so you sit down and we get talking about the crap weather, the crap accommodation, the Netflix movie about vampire sheep I'm shooting.' She affects a bad American accent. 'So, Izzy, give me the pitch.'

Izzy doesn't. Not to start with. But Angharad just waits, eyebrows raised.

'Okay. What if there's a lost soul? Someone you were destined to meet but who was taken before you could. What if there's a door in an abandoned building on the edge of the world that they can come through? What if destiny takes our hero to that building to meet that soul? Only there is someone else, watching, who wants to stop them meeting. A malevolence who wants to keep them in misery. Our hero has to overcome that darkness. But it's a sly and vicious enemy.'

Izzy has said all of this while looking out at the grey sea, losing herself in her own words. When she flicks her gaze back, Angharad is staring at her, mouth open.

'Christ, you are a bloody writer.'

'If only.'

'Yeah, if only.' Angharad shakes her head. 'Do it.'

'I will. At least, I'm going to try. I may even call it the Follower. I'm going to stick your Tarot card on my desk and use it as inspiration.'

'Is he a hero or a villain?' The question takes Izzy by surprise.

'Who knows? The story isn't written yet.'

Angharad downs her drink. 'This calls for a celebration.'

'Not for me. Driving.'

'So am I. One more. And then a coffee.'

Izzy knows that won't cancel anything out. But she

gives in. It is a celebration. A cat out of the bag moment. They call the server over and order.

Angharad pins Izzy with her earnest gaze. 'What was the inspiration for that, Izzy? Or did that spring from out of nowhere in that hidden depths head of yours?'

Perhaps it's the Prosecco. Perhaps it's the belief she can trust this woman, that there's a bond between them. Whatever it is, Izzy throws caution to the wind and opens up. Pretty soon she can't stop because it is exhilarating to tell her the other part of her story. The part she's told no one else. Ever.

'Do you believe in spiritualism?'

Angharad leans forward. 'Are you kidding? Of course I believe.'

'Is it real, you think?'

'I'm not into the religious side of it, if that's what you're asking. But Lena is into it in a big way,' Angharad gushes. 'She even goes to services where mediums communicate with the dead.'

'Really?' Izzy blinks rapidly.

The server walks by with a smile. Angharad waits until she's passed.

'Ghosties and ghoulies are a load of old twaddle, but magical thinking is on the up. I sell loads of decks online. I can't make the damn things fast enough. Type in #witch on Insta and you see millions of posts. Clothes, potions, even bloody broomsticks if you fancy one of those between your legs.' Angharad giggles and then frowns. 'Do you want to go to one of Lena's services?'

'No, I ...' Another sigh. 'I don't know what I'm asking.'

'Okay, let me rephrase that. Do I believe that there's something after death? The answer is yes, I do.'

One thing she likes about Angharad is her directness, even if it is coloured by the sense that she's motivated more by finding a willing public ready to buy her cards than an all-consuming belief in the supernatural. Still, isn't that what art is? Izzy searches for any sign that she's being strung along. But Angharad seems genuine. Heartfelt, even.

'Why are you asking all this?' Angharad asks.

'Because I want to believe, too.'

'So you can write about it?'

'No,' says Izzy quickly, but then corrects herself. 'I … Something happened to me and … It's difficult to explain. Difficult to talk about. Seeing your Follower has made me wonder all over again and now that I have, I realise I hadn't processed it. I'm wondering if looking at it a different way, a more spiritual way, might help.'

'Try me,' Angharad says, as the waitress arrives with two fresh glasses of bubbly.

So Izzy does. 'Do you know what a chemical pregnancy is?'

———

HER GP HAD EXPLAINED it clearly enough. A positive pregnancy test that wasn't positive a few days later. You needed enough levels of HCG – human chorionic gonadotrophin – in your blood for a pregnancy test to be positive. And the only thing that could cause that was an implanted embryo in the womb. She'd missed her period by a week but had thought little about it. She'd always been erratic. Sometimes light, sometimes – especially when she was younger – heavy with sapping, aching pains that sent her to bed with a hot water bottle. But on the eighth day after her period date and with nothing showing, she'd taken the test and watched with eyebrows raised as the blue line formed.

It was bewildering. She hadn't felt any different. It wasn't as if she and Marcus had even been trying … She winced. Stopping the pill was only ever going to end up with one outcome in the long term.

But that had not been the plan.

She'd stopped the pill at Marky's suggestion after he'd read a click-bait headline that said being on it might cause an increased risk of blood clots. Admittedly, it was an *Express* headline, so a hefty pinch of salt was needed. Even so, it made for a stark warning:

'A million women at risk from killer pill. British GPs told to warn about threat from popular contraceptive.'

It was mad really. Yet another headline without the detail. And then, a week later, the BBC ran an interview with the head honcho of the College of GPs that tore the *Express's* scaremongering apart by delving into the detail. That perhaps one in a thousand women were at risk. And Izzy didn't smoke, was not obese and wasn't immobile, all of which added to the risks. So she'd waited out her cycle before restarting the pill.

Just the once.

She'd been touched by Marky's concern and the promise that he'd be careful and take responsibility if she came off it. A promise that had flown out of the window two weeks in after a Saturday night party. They'd both woken up on Sunday and stayed in bed. One thing led to another, as it sometimes did when they were a little hungover, and before she knew it, the lazy morning turned into slow easy sex and the deed was done. It was only afterwards she remembered about Marcus needing to take precautions. He hadn't of course. Hadn't even bought any condoms. But they'd both felt foolish at not remembering and spent most of that day wondering what they'd do if she fell pregnant. How they'd cope. It ended up being a fun day, coming up with names, where they might live eventually, all the things they'd never talked about before.

It was tongue in cheek. A laugh. Preparation for the

proper conversation they'd hopefully need to have one day. And she ended up assuring Marcus that nothing would happen. She had friends who'd been trying to get pregnant for months with zero luck, for crying out loud. And she and Marky had had unprotected sex just the once. Nothing was going to happen.

Famous last words.

After that first positive test, she had said nothing to anybody. Instead, she stoppered her excitement – well, her anxiety at least – and told herself to be sensible, wait two days and repeat the test.

The cramps came as she was walking home from the chemist where she'd bought a brand new First Response kit. She hadn't been that surprised or disappointed when she bled. Something, an instinct, had told her to be patient. And when the test showed negative, she put the first result down as a false positive.

Until she spoke to her doctor about it. Izzy had been fine on the combination pill for years, the one containing oestrogen and progesterone, but since the article and even after knowing it was a low risk, she'd looked into trying the progesterone-only pill. It was during that appointment that she explained about the positive pregnancy test, the cramping and the bleeding.

When she did, the GP frowned, put down her pen and asked for more detail. Izzy had never heard the term chemical pregnancy before that visit. But Dr Payne – Marky always grinned like a loon whenever Izzy mentioned her – seemed certain. She was kind and explained why the professionals used those terms. As a way of avoiding the emotional devastation that came with calling it a miscarriage.

A matter of semantics.

And in a way Izzy wished it hadn't been explained. Because now she thought of it as a miscarriage. Little consolation to know that they often associated it with a damaged embryo or an imperfect implantation. So she hadn't told Marcus. What was the point? It was a done deal and besides, it happened right after she discovered his visits to the drinking club. He was going through such a rough patch then. The last thing he needed was to worry about her. About them.

No point making a fuss about such a minor blip.

And yet she'd unburdened this hidden psychological bruise on a virtual stranger. Most surprising of all was that there'd been tears in that unburdening. Not Izzy's. All Angharad's.

'Poor you,' Angharad had said, by then on her second tissue.

'I'm fine.'

'But it's a life lost, isn't it? Is that what you're feeling? Is that what you want to write about?' Angharad insisted.

Izzy had never thought of it that way. All she could think of in response was to say, 'Maybe.'

'I would so read it if you wrote it, Izzy. You should. You should write about what you're feeling.'

She drives home with that conversation fresh in her mind. There's more to it, of course. Because what she hasn't told Angharad, what's stirring in her imagination, is that the story is big. About a woman who moves to an isolated cottage where an unborn spirit tries to contact her. It sounds mad. Hardly a story at all. But perhaps underneath it's a story about an exploration of grief. Something she hasn't at all considered until she saw Angharad's tears.

But now she wants to find out. About the Engine House. About the Follower. The inspiration for a story that is right on her doorstep. A story that may even be cathartic in the making.

CHAPTER TWENTY-FIVE

THE JEEP'S sat nav announces that they'll be at their destination in a hundred yards.

'Right, DC Harries, what do we know about this address of Thomas's?' Warlow parks on Queen Street, a good seventy yards from their target, Cask Street. No point giving Thomas advanced warning. They've driven around and there are back entrances to these houses. Easy for a nervous scrote to slip away.

Rhys has his notebook open. 'Thomas lives with his eighty-three-year-old grandmother and has done for the last five years. Previous to that, they were in Monkton. His grandmother went into hospital eighteen months ago and the council found her a single-storey property that was easier to manage.'

'So they've only been here a year and a half?'

'Yes.'

Warlow had driven past. A terraced row of tiny one-storey buildings with extensions at the rear. 'What was wrong with the grandmother?'

'Fractured hip that needed a pin and plate repair.

Chronic smoker and chest problems made the surgery difficult, apparently. She was also abusive to staff.'

'Yes, I read that, too. She's a fifty-a-day charmer. The
apple has not fallen far from the maternal tree it seems.'

'What?' Rhys eyebrows go up.

Warlow explains. 'German proverb. Like grandson, like
grandmother in the charm stakes.'

'Ah. Got you.'

Warlow somehow doubts that but puts a hand on the
car's door handle anyway. 'Okay. Remember, we only want
to speak to him. Not that I'm expecting him to be there,
but you never know. Follow my lead and do nothing stupid
to spook the little sod.'

It's an area of low rent flats and houses. A narrow road
with cars parked half on the pavement to give the traffic a
way through. The terrace runs the entire length of the
street, maybe two hundred yards, but the houses which all
started off as a row of fishermen's cottages have been
adapted in batches. Some extended upwards into dormers
with big ugly windows, most have gone backwards into
rear sunrooms and extensions. It's a street with no front
porches or gardens. You step out of your door onto
pavement.

It's not raining for once, but the day is grey and bitter.
Warlow has his coat done up. He's glad to see that Rhys has
learned a lesson from freezing on the pavement outside the
King and Queen. He's wearing a proper coat with a hood for
when the inevitable rain comes. Number Thirty-Three has
two white UPVC windows either side of a matching door.
The grey pebble dash exterior is a different shade to the one
next door. In fact, every house is pebble dashed in some shade
of grey or beige except for one or two where the owners have
splashed out on a tin of Sandtex in yellow or ochre.

Warlow drops his voice. 'Ready?'

'Go for it,' says Rhys.

It's a copper's knock. Three loud, firm, not-going-to-go-away raps. There's no answer. He raises his hand and repeats the sequence. The detectives stand, waiting, not speaking. After thirty seconds more of silence, Warlow steps to the side and cups his hands against the window, trying to see in through lace curtains.

'See anything, sir?'

'Too dim. But no TV on and no movement.'

'Perhaps there's no one at home, sir,' Rhys says and then suffers a look from Warlow which suggests he should review that statement. Given how they'd discussed Thomas's grandmother and her dodgy hip.

'Or maybe not home to us.' Warlow squints up and down the street. 'Walk up to the corner and observe. I'm going to go around the back. See what I can see. If someone comes out, do not engage, just follow, okay?'

Rhys nods.

'If you do follow, keep in touch at all times. Got your phone?'

The DC pulls it out of his pocket.

Warlow glances up at the chimney and the satellite dish and aerial pointing in opposite directions. The aerial is obsolete, but no one has bothered to take it down.

He strides back up Cask Street, takes a left and steps into a warren of lanes that form the rear entrances. He sees right away that they are unlit and says a silent thank you it isn't dark. He walks slowly along between breeze-blocked walls, discarded black bags and piles of rubble from aborted repairs. There are garage lockups and garden doors with little or no view into the rear of the houses. He studies the chimneys until he sees the dish and aerial going opposite ways. He makes a hill of broken concrete and bricks and stands on it to look over the breeze-block wall. Number Thirty-Three's 'garden' is an expanse of grey chippings. Some ancient garden furniture rusts near a low extension with a polycarbonate roof. There's a padlocked chain across the back gate in the wall, but no latch. Enough of a deterrent to stop vehicles. However, though limited by the play on the chain, by pushing one side forward there's a wide enough gap for a body to get through.

Warlow is agile enough.

He crunches across the gravel towards the door in the rear extension that runs the length of the building. There's a Yale lock but no handle. The lock cylinder is scuffed and dirty from use. Warlow pushes. Locked. He knocks again, this time adding, 'Mrs Thomas, it's the police. Can you open the door?'

No reply.

Warlow considers his options. Rhys is right, they may not be in. But there is also a chance that no reply could mean that something is wrong. He has no reason to believe that a crime is in progress, which would give him grounds for breaking in, but still. There's a vulnerable person inside, or there should be.

Beside the door next to a low brick wall is a black plastic bin. He lifts the lid and sees probably thirty empty cans of Foster's lager, greasy chip wrappers and a pizza box that's been in there long enough to feed twenty generations of flies. His phone buzzes. It's Rhys.

'Anything, sir?'

'Not yet. You?'

'No. Where are you?'

'At the back door. Stand by.'

He looks around again. The yard is empty of all attempts at making the space attractive. The patio set has a seat on its side and an upside-down table. Thrown there, he guesses, by someone in a fit of rage.

There is no shed. No need for gardening equipment.

After all, you can't mow chippings. The only concession to horticulture is a decorative bucket with the remnants of a plant long dead from dehydration against one wall. Warlow peers at it, lifts it and sees a single brass key underneath.

'Jesus,' he mutters.

He takes some blue nitrile gloves from his pocket, slips them on, slides the key into the door and turns it.

CHAPTER TWENTY-SIX

THE LEAN-TO SMELLS DAMP. More Foster's cans on a plastic table where someone has sat and contemplated the yard. He thinks of his own place and his view over the estuary. Each to his own, he supposes.

Another door leads into the main building. He opens this and enters an open plan kitchen: dirty surfaces, grease-stained walls and filthy lino. Despite that, the appliances look modern. A classic council retro fit, he assumes. The room beyond makes up the middle third of the house and the front door is only a few yards away. Nothing decorates the plain walls, but a huge TV sits against one, trailing wires to a games console and a DVD player next to it on a laminated floor littered with more pizza boxes and empty lager cans. The room reeks of stale food.

He calls out. 'Hello. It's the police. Is there anyone here?'

No answer.

Warlow walks across to the front door, opens it, looks up the street and motions to Rhys who trots down.

'How did you get in, sir?'

'Through the eaves. What I haven't told you yet is that I have the ability to turn into a bat.'

The look on Rhys's face is priceless for perhaps three seconds before his sardonic radar kicks in and a rueful smile appears. That'll all need work, thinks Warlow. Sarcasm is as vital for his police survival skills as the stab vest.

'Back door was open.' Warlow puts him out of his misery. He doesn't bother adding that he'd used the key to put the door into that state, nor that said key is now back under the bucket.

'No one here?' Rhys peers into the building.

'No. So where is Thomas's grandmother?'

'Maybe she went back into hospital.'

'Hmm.' Warlow pivots to study the tiny space. Three doors open off the living room, two right, one left. 'How many bedrooms in these places, you reckon?'

'Has to be two, sir. Some families live in these.'

Warlow nods. 'Right. Gloves on. You go left, I'll go right.'

The first door he tries opens into a bathroom. Whoever was there last has not pulled the chain and yellow fluid pools in the bowl. He's tempted to flush but thinks better of it in case this is a crime scene.

The second door leads to a small bedroom that smells of unwashed clothes and bedlinen, with piles of both on an unmade bed. Two drawers are open in a chest and piles of dark clothing are stuffed inside. On the floor next to the bed is an ash tray and the remnants of a couple of hand-rolled cigarettes. Warlow picks one up and smells the familiar sweetness of cannabis.

He's about to turn to an alcove where he's seen some discarded trainers and more clothes when Rhys shouts to him.

'Sir?'

Warlow retraces his steps and walks through the left-hand door off the living room. He enters a small atrium with two doors. One is open showing a bathroom with a walk-in shower in dire need of cleaning. The other shows a bedroom with a stripped bed and some photos on the wall hanging at untidy angles. There's a matching set of drawers, cheap looking with a scuffed varnish and a few more photos. But Warlow registers all this only in passing. Rhys is standing at the foot of the bed regarding what has been shoehorned into a corner. The thing is maybe a metre long and half a metre tall. All white, it hums gently with a white cable running from its base into a socket.

'It's a chest freezer, sir,' says Rhys in a thick voice.

'Top marks for observation, there, constable.'

The room is gloomy, curtains drawn. Warlow flicks on the light.

There is no sound apart from the hum of the freezer.

'Why would there be a freezer in this bedroom?' Rhys asks.

'Someone wants to stop something from spoiling is my guess.'

'Why not in the kitchen fridge?'

He sends the DC a grim look. Rhys is behind him, peering over his shoulder. The dial on the freezer is turned up to maximum. Condensation has pooled on the lid. Warlow puts his hand on the long handle and lifts it.

'Shit, shit, shit,' the DC hisses when he clocks what's inside.

'Looks like Mrs Thomas is in after all,' Warlow says, staring down into a pair of open, frost encrusted eyes. He turns to look at the DC. He's as pale as milk but not yet green. 'You okay, Rhys? If you're going to throw up, do it outside. These are new shoes I've got on.'

Rhys nods breathing through his mouth. 'No sir, I'm fine. Did someone put her in there?'

Warlow turns back to the freezer. 'I doubt she fell in chasing that one last Solero.' The woman has her legs bent up to her chest. Warlow somehow knows there will not be any sign of violence. Just a gut feeling but one he's inclined to go with.

'Do you think Thomas killed her?' Rhys asks.

'Don't know. Maybe, maybe not. We'll find out soon enough.' He shuts the lid.

'We going to leave her in there, sir?' Rhys sounds upset.

'We'll let Povey defrost her. When you're up to it, Rhys, better call it in.'

An hour later they're on the way back to Haverford-west in the car while the crime scene bods begin picking Number Thirty-Three apart. Rhys has been very quiet.

Warlow glances across. 'Need to get this all written up and into HOLMES as soon as you can, alright?'

Rhys nods, his expression contemplative.

'You okay?'

'Yes, sir. It's just … I've been in the police for four years and seen my share of accidents and the like. But it feels like more has happened in the three days I've worked with you than in those four years put together.'

Warlow snorts. 'Regretting it?'

'No, I just want to know if it's always like this. Working with you, I mean?'

'Not always like this. Sometimes there's more than one body in the freezer.'

Rhys's laugh is a nervous titter.

Warlow shakes his head. 'Nah. Sometimes it's donkey work. We man the phones and drink tea for days on end.'

The DC nods. 'Good. I think I'll have two sugars in mine.'

They get back to the Incident Room to find that Jess and Catrin are on their way to Swansea to interview

Morris. Warlow is on the cusp of ringing them when he takes a call.

'Evan, Wyn Davies. After our conversation last night about Thomas and Morris, you are not going to believe the call I just took from Swansea nick.'

'Surprise me.'

'I hope you're sitting down. They've just found Neil Morris in the showers with a length of twine around his neck.'

'What? Is he–'

'As a bloody Dodo.'

Warlow gets to his feet, mind buzzing. He's halfway out of the door when he almost bumps into Rhys carrying two mugs. 'As ordered, sir.'

Warlow looks at it longingly and then up into Rhys's face. 'Any chance you can find a paper cup? Looks like I'm going to have to drink this on the go.'

CHAPTER TWENTY-SEVEN

JESS IS on the M4 junction forty-five turn off to Swansea when Warlow reaches her. He's sitting in his car in the car park at Dyfed-Powys HQ when she answers.

'Oh, for f–,' is what he hears in reply before she corrects herself. 'What the hell is going on?'

'No idea. But there's a Costa at Cross Hands in the new retail park. Why don't I meet you both there?'

There's no point them going to Swansea prison now, and there's a muffled conversation between Jess and Catrin to that effect.

'Okay,' Jess says and kills the call.

It's the wrong direction for Warlow, but the sooner they can talk this through, the better. He knows Jess will feel the same. On the way, he rings Wyn Davies again for more details. It's his case, and he's already been to the prison. They've cordoned off the shower area but there's nothing to see, no sign of a struggle. And until the post-mortem, they won't know if this was a suicide, or a forced hanging. Bruises or any sign of a struggle might argue the latter. But that will be for the pathologist to decide.

'You're a bloody Jonah, Evan. I don't hear from you for

three years, then you ring me out of the blue about some sod in Swansea nick and the next thing you know, he's croaked,' Davies complains.

'Send me a wax effigy. I'll see what I can do.'

Davies let's out a rumbling laugh. 'My list of enemies is too long. But I'll keep you in the loop on this. We'll be interviewing other prisoners, obviously. Let's just say I don't expect a lot of noise when we do.'

Whatever has happened, even if this was not a suicide, informing on someone is a cardinal sin in prison. Anyone with a jot of survival instinct will say nothing.

Warlow gets to Costa first, texts Catrin for an order, buy coffees and finds a corner table out of earshot of other punters.

When they arrive, he repeats what Davies has told him.

Jess's mouth stays a thin white line. When he finishes, she says, 'I can see in your eyes that you don't think this is coincidental.'

She shakes her head slowly. 'I don't know what I think yet. But you're right. I smell fish.'

'You think he hanged himself because he got wind that we were coming?' Catrin asks.

'Either that or someone made that decision for him.' Warlow stirs his flat white.

'Makes it even more vital that we find Kieron Thomas, doesn't it?' Jess is staring at the table as she sips her coffee.

'About that,' Warlow says and explains about finding the Thomas's grandmother in the freezer.

'You're sure it's his grandmother?' Catrin asks.

'Not yet. But I doubt it's his Russian girlfriend.'

'Why would he kill his grandmother?'

'Who says he did?' Warlow throws the question back at her.

'How do you see it, Evan?' Jess asks.

He exhales slowly. 'Thomas's grandmother would get a pension. But that, of course, stops when you die.'

Catrin's expression is pained. 'So you think Thomas might have not wanted to report her death because of that?'

'It's a regular income. The pathologists might be able to tell us when she died but I suspect she may have started to pong a bit.'

'Hence the freezer.' Catrin nods.

'He sounds a real charmer,' Jess says. 'We've got people looking for him so it's only a matter of time. What the hell is going on here, Evan?' It's the second time she's appealed for an answer. The second time Warlow has none. All he can do at this stage is give a little headshake.

Jess looks at her watch. It's almost three. 'I'll get back to Haverfordwest. Get people looking at what Thomas and Morris got up to as a unit. We need to find out if Thomas visited Morris in prison, too. And who else visited him in the last few days. If we can get back by four at least we can make a start.'

'I need to get back for the dog,' Warlow says.

Jess smiles. 'Give her a cuddle from me.'

The women leave, but he stays to finish a second coffee.

What the hell is going on here, Evan?

Good question, Jess, he muses.

His brain is already teasing out the possibilities. Random ramblings to see where they end up. Eventually they come back around to Morris in Swansea prison. What was it one of his bosses once told him? Suicide argues strongly of guilt. Maybe it does. But it isn't the only reason. Depression, isolation, despair, fear. Which one of those discount deals did Morris go for?

If it was suicide. What if it wasn't? What if a couple of big bruisers slipped that noose around his neck and hoisted him, back-to-back, like a sack of coal? All they'd need to do was get Morris a foot off the ground. And then, once the deed was done, hang the corpse up to a pipe somewhere. He'd read of cases like that. Never seen it. But there is always a first time.

He mulls over these pleasant thoughts on the way back to Nevern. There, Cadi gives him a best-thing-since-sliced-liver greeting.

As promised, Jess rings him later. She has nothing new to add, but he can sense the frustration in her voice. The SIO's burden. It's likely she'll be working some if not all weekend. And if not in the Incident Room, then at home. He's promised himself not to interfere. His job is to be supportive. So he is.

'If there's anything I can do, all you need to do is ring. If Molly needs a ride or something. I'm around.'

'Thanks, Evan. I'll bear that in mind.'

He sits in the chair with a copy of the summary he printed out for the team and his notebooks. It's not the first time over the years that he's done exactly this. When he was still with Denise and with the boys already flown the nest, he'd go upstairs to one of their rooms. There he'd sit with his laptop at a teenager's desk to get away from the drone of the TV and the inane reality shows Denise was addicted to, vodka and tonic in hand if it was before seven, bowl of wine at the ready if it was after.

It's more comfortable here in the cottage though, in his newly completed extension. The late afternoon clings bravely on to daylight. He has a lamp on the table at the side of his chair and an empty glass on a coaster waiting for the wine he'll pour after six – 125mls, not a bowl. Next to it is a cup of fresh coffee. His third of the afternoon. Outside, a few twinkling lights are already visible through the window down towards the estuary.

But what he sees in his mind is a conjured image. The

Pickerings walking on the coastal path. Hale and hearty, greeting fellow walker or walkers, perhaps standing aside to let him or them pass. And then what? Was it Ken first? The bigger, stronger target. A hammer blow to the head. Immobilise him and then go for Marjorie. How many blows? One, two? A dozen? And then smash the ankles and wrists. If the Pickerings aren't already dead, that would incapacitate them. If there were screams or shouting, there'd be no one to hear.

No one but the gulls.

And then the part that he now has the most difficulty with. Somehow, their bodies are moved. Immediately? Or hidden until later and then lowered down to a cave in the cliff face someone must already have known about.

He replays the scenarios over and over in his head. He's seen some strange things in his career. Heard some ridiculous tales to explain away moments of destructive passion, madness even. But this isn't like anything he's heard before. And the more he thinks about it, the more it convinces him that there is little or nothing accidental about any of it. Whoever did this knew where to do it. Knew the path and the coast very well.

He glances down at Cadi curled up in her bed and takes a sip of coffee. Both the sight of the dog and the taste of the coffee please him. These are small things. Comforting things. Morsels of normality that everyone who has never had to examine violent deaths take for granted. But which Warlow appreciates and savours now as he lets the images fade from his mind.

But they don't fade completely.

His phone buzzes. DS Dai Vetch sounds miffed. 'Is this a bloody wind up?'

'Is what a bloody wind up?' Warlow replies.

'Your message about Kieron Thomas.'

'What about Kieron Thomas?'

'I took a call half an hour ago from an Acting DCI about the same Kieron Thomas.'

'What was the DCI's name?'

'Caldwell.'

Warlow can't help the jaw clamp that follows. 'What was it about?'

'It's about some kids finding what's left of a body in a burned out shed on the railways embankment in Pembroke Dock. Not much left of it, the shed nor the body, but they've just had the ID confirmed and Caldwell was asking if I knew of a reason he might have been barbecued, other than falling asleep on a fire.'

Warlow's gut twists, but he keeps his voice pretty even given the circumstances. 'Do you?'

'Not off-hand. I'm on the way to the crime scene now if you're around.'

'Haven't they moved the body?'

'They have. But I like to see these things for myself.'

'Good idea.' A man after his own heart, Warlow thinks. There's an hour of daylight left in the day when he gets into his car again and heads towards Pembroke Dock.

———

POLICE TAPE FLUTTERS across the cut through off Hawksmere Road. Warlow doesn't know this neck of the woods that well, but it looks predominantly residential. Terraced houses, the odd semi-detached. All relatively well kept. The patch of greenery the tape guards is next to a nursery. Warlow parks and waits in his car until a red Suzuki motorbike pulls up and the rider gets off. A man dismounts and removes his helmet. Dai Vetch hasn't shaved, but Warlow recognises him from the photo Catrin sent him.

He gets out of the car and introduces himself. Vetch is

tall, his leather jacket thick and padded. Preliminaries over, Vetch says, 'Shall we?'

He ducks under the tape and walks through the cut. The path winds towards the right and curves back on itself. But at the apex, the iron railings of the fence next to the embankment have been bent and hammered to leave a gap big enough for the men to walk through once Vetch has cut the tape away.

There's a lot more of it on the embankment and they can only get to within five yards of the place where the body was found. But the forensic team will have finished their voodoo by now. Vetch takes out his phone and flicks open some crime scene snaps. Warlow isn't squeamish, still he's glad he hasn't eaten yet. Kieron Thomas's charred remains show his arms bent up in a boxer's pose. Warlow knows this is all due to fire contracting the muscles and ligaments, but it makes it look as if the victim was fending someone off. Other shots show scattered drug paraphernalia and the remains of a lighter fluid tin. The ground, under the dead grass, shows discarded syringes and vials.

'Looks like a junky holiday venue.' Warlow looks around. It's a desolate spot.

'Must be, with the floor covered in DRL like this.'

Warlow has to think about that for a moment. Then it gels. Drug Related Litter. 'Tell me what Caldwell's thoughts were?' He turns to look at a train trundling by.

'That Kieron came here, shot up and somehow set fire to himself. Maybe while he was refuelling his lighter. They found his cigarettes and lighter fluid nearby.'

'Plausible?' Warlow asks.

'Ket – that's what he was known as – was a dealer. He has a flat he can use for injecting. He lets others use it; we know that.'

'You know?'

Vetch nods. 'There's a big drug project in Swansea. It

has an outreach here too. Better that we let the addicts inject somewhere inside than in the street. Because they will do it there if they can't find anywhere else.'

Drugs. Took a special kind of officer to deal with the problem. It's an unhappy marriage of chasing the big suppliers versus looking out for the users. The helpless addicts.

Vetch keeps talking. 'Swansea has the highest opioid overdose rate in Wales. Maybe even in the UK. It's spreading west. But this ...' He shakes his head. 'Something's not right here. This might look straightforward. Just another user making a terrible choice in a worse situation. But Ket was too smart for this sort of crap.'

Warlow waits.

'Don't get me wrong, he was a vicious little bastard. Capable of anything.'

'Let me stop you there.' Warlow walks a little way up the embankment to get his bearings. By his reckoning Cask Street is well within walking distance. 'We went to see Thomas this afternoon at his grandmother's house. No one there apart from the grandmother. And we found her inspecting the inside of a chest freezer.'

Vetch blinks. 'Not playing hide and seek, I assume?'

'Definitely not.'

'Anything suggestive of violence?'

Warlow shakes his head. 'Not that I could see and not that the crime scene lot could see on first viewing. I think maybe natural causes. Not reported because of the pension and benefits that would stop.'

'That sounds like Ket. If they gave degrees out for street smarts, he'd have a double first.'

'Are you going to tell Caldwell that?'

'Already have. He doesn't seem that interested.'

No. He wants it tidied away and filed under another junky tragedy #self-induced, thinks Warlow.

They walk back to their vehicles. Vetch pauses at his bike. 'I haven't asked why you're so interested in Thomas?'

He tells Vetch about Kelly Scott and the DNA related thread that links her to the Pickerings. And that DI Davies had interviewed Ket more than once over her death.

Vetch listens, head down. 'I wouldn't put it past him. He had anger problems. Not helped by cocaine, which was more his thing. And he'd be protective of anything that might undermine his client base like Kelly Scott cutting and selling on product. So I can see him as a candidate for the Scott killing. But I don't see it fitting in with killing two walkers on the coastal path. Unless he was high.'

'If he was high, how would he have got them into the crevice?' Warlow has already considered this scenario and thrown it out. 'And what the hell would someone like Thomas be doing on the path anyway? He doesn't strike me as an outdoors enthusiast.'

Vetch shakes his head.

'Looks like this is all a case of severe bad timing then,' Warlow says. 'Especially taking into consideration his partner, Neil Morris.'

Vetch looks momentarily confused. 'At least he's safe. The little sod got thirty months for dangerous driving and possession. He's halfway through his sentence. I'm sure he'd be delighted to see you. He's got bugger all else to—' Something in Warlow's expression dries up Vetch's words.

'Yes. About that.' The DCI explains to the detective sergeant about Morris being found dead. Vetch listens and asks some questions, but there's no denying the shock and bewilderment that registers on his face.

Later, Vetch forwards the crime scene photos as Warlow drives back to Nevern. The phone chimes a receipt, but he barely notices because his mind is churning. Drug associated deaths keep going up. A fifty per cent increase over the last ten years. He knows this because he reads the alerts or did while he was on the job. And he can't believe for one minute the trend has reversed in the eighteen months since he's been away. Drug misuse covers many eventualities. It isn't always an overdose that's the killer. People crash their cars when they're under the influence, inhale their own vomit, get septicaemia, fall asleep and drown in baths. A positive cornucopia of possibilities and every variation on a theme of the mind disconnecting from the body and allowing it to get in harm's way.

But Kieron Thomas's death is an especially harrowing example if it turns out to be the case.

If, indeed.

CHAPTER TWENTY-EIGHT

ON SATURDAY MORNING Warlow makes a call and by ten he's in the car with Cadi on the way to Newcastle Emlyn, a market town overlooking the river Teifi. Like a lot of Welsh towns, there's a ruined castle that tells of a long and fractious relationship between the Welsh and the English. And, as with most towns, and indeed villages this side of the Severn bridge, there's a rugby club.

Warlow parks in front of an impressive clubhouse on the meadows where several pitches are laid out and walks Cadi down to the river. One glimpse of the water and she's in. He has a Chuckit launcher and a ball and spends fifteen minutes putting her through her paces. When he gets a text, he calls the dog to him and walks to the two pitches where groups of kids aged from six to ten are getting mud-splattered with rugby balls that are almost bigger than they are.

Dai Vetch helps coach the under-nines. They play on half sized pitches. Warlow counts four games in progress. Vetch jogs over when Warlow raises a hand in greeting. It's officially winter, but that season has retreated, and the weather is mild. The swirling clouds and odd squalls remind Warlow of school matches on Saturday mornings when he was a youngster. When he was fit and a sprinter and his only worries were how he was going to sneak in to the rugby club dance without ID.

'Morning,' Vetch says.

'I thought Sunday was mini-rugby day.'

'It is. But we have a tournament today. Serious stuff.'

'And it means a lie in on Sunday for you.'

Vetch grins. 'That too.'

There's a hedge nearby. Warlow slips Cadi off her lead and she goes sniffing. 'I need to watch her. She'll eat anything, dead or alive. Labrador's curse.'

'She looks fit,' Vetch says. 'So do you.'

'That's the beauty of a dog. All-weather walking.' Warlow gets down to business. 'I've been cogitating about Morris and Thomas. I wanted to ask you about them. They were small beer, weren't they?'

'In a way. Morris was younger. He had links to the sixth form colleges. We suspected Thomas used him to sell a bit of weed. Some ecstasy occasionally, too. Thomas was Morris's dealer. They struck up a friendship. Got high together.'

'So nothing big?'

Vetch considers this with a slight jutting forward of his jaw. 'Only once when they were caught up in the Sorting Hat fiasco.'

'Remind me.'

'There was a spate of hospitalisations in the summer of 2017. We had a couple of small festivals. The kind that brings all the joys of MDMA with them. Chemists – the amateur type – have the bright idea of stamping tablets with logos to make them look pretty. Add some oomph. IKEA, Rolls Royce, the Sorting Hat. There often isn't much quality control on potency with E so you can end up with either very weak or very strong batches. Morris and Thomas were entrepreneurs. They'd buy a load and distribute. Not big numbers, say forty or fifty at a time. We were after the manufacturers, tailing Thomas to see where he got the product from. But when some festival goers ended up admitted with seizures, the shit hit the fan. We abandoned the operation and arrested Thomas and Morris. But the weird thing was that they got some really high-powered representation. No one local, some big cheese from Birmingham with an alligator briefcase. It all ended up a shit show. Someone messed up the search and all they got done for was possession.'

'You think someone else provided the legal muscle?'

'No doubt. Neither Thomas nor Morris had the resources for the sleaze bag that turned up in court.'

A cheer goes up as a girl in pigtails evades grasping hands and crosses the line for a try. She's the smallest on the field. But by far the quickest. Vetch looks over with an ear-to-ear grin and both arms raised high above his head.

'Da iawn, Medi.'

The girl makes a fist on hearing the praise in her mother tongue. Warlow sees the resemblance. Vetch grins.

'Yours?'

'My youngest. Spitting image of her mother.'

'I'll let you get back to it.'

But Vetch doesn't move yet. 'Ket's death smells all wrong. I was willing to let it go. Stranger things, right? But this business with Morris, too.' He shakes his head. 'I mean both dead within hours of each other.'

'It stinks.'

'It does. Any idea why?'

'Not yet. When I do, I'll let you know.'

'I'd appreciate that.'

A whistle blows. 'Half time,' says Vetch. 'They expect a pep talk.'

'Quartered oranges?'

Vetch half turns as he walks away. 'Way too old-fashioned. Haribo these days.' He taps his pocket.

Warlow takes Cadi back via the river to wash off the worst of the mud she's slid in while retrieving the ball. Denise would have had a fit. She wasn't a dog person. The boys had wanted one, but she'd been adamant in her refusal.

One more nail in the marital coffin.

Warlow believes most families should have a dog. It teaches the kids discipline and responsibility and how to deal with death. One of life's great cosmic jokes was giving dogs such a short lifespan. As he watches Cadi paddle about in the water, Warlow ponders Dai Vetch's words. Nothing he's learned has helped him understand how or why Thomas and Morris might be linked to the coastal path or to the Pickerings. They sounded like low grade pushers. Chancers out for a quick buck to buy a new Xbox game and to feed their own habits.

Jess's team needed something else to bite on. Something solid that might join two disparate dots. But needing and getting are two different things, as he knows only too well.

She rings him later that evening.

'That favour?' Jess asks.

'I'm listening.'

'I'm taking Molly up to the kayaking place tomorrow morning early. But I need to go into the office in the afternoon. The DCC wants to meet with Sion Buchannan. I'm expected to be there.'

'You want me to pick Molly up?'

'Can you?' She sings out the request.

'No problem. How's your day been?'

'Incident Room most of the afternoon. Molly went shopping.'

Warlow sucks air through his teeth. 'In Haverfordwest? How was that for her?'

'Not exactly the Trafford Centre is what she said. I'll make it up to her. Your day?'

'Went to watch some under-nines rugby.'

'Grandchildren?'

'God, no. An excuse to meet up with DS Vetch who has kids of that age. He knew Thomas and Morris.'

'Anything?'

'Something and nothing. Not enough to talk about yet. I'll let it simmer. Will Molly be okay with me picking her up?'

Jess laughs. 'You'll have Cadi with you?'

'I will.'

'Done deal then.'

CHAPTER TWENTY-NINE

WHEN IZZY GETS to the turn off for Limehouse Cottage after a half day at the Hall, instead of going home, she turns left through the gate of Penmawr Farm.

Both the Gower men are in the farmyard. She's met Mrs Gower only a handful of times, but she sees Rylan and Ben Gower out and about almost every day. Izzy knows little about farming but even she can see that the place is tidy. The machines all look new. Marcus has told her that farmers lease most of their tractors, bailers and hedge cutters. All business expensed. Either that or they contract out the work.

The dogs are yapping around Izzy's car. She waits for Rylan to call them to heel before she gets out. Rylan is closest. Ben, busy carrying a heavy sack, puts it down and waves a greeting.

'Hi,' Izzy says.

Rylan steps forward. 'Isabelle, to what do we owe the pleasure?'

'I wanted to call in and explain about the Spaceship.'

'Spaceship?'

'The scaffolding around Marcus's summer house project.'

Ben saunters over. He always seems to find his way into any conversation Izzy has with Rylan. Once again, she's aware of the way he looks at her. Hungry like the wolf, as Duran Duran liked to say.

'It's big,' Rylan says. 'Wind blows up something fierce through the ravine. Marcus needs to be careful.'

'Ben said that, too. I wanted to reassure you we'll only have it for as long as it takes Marcus to make the cabin weatherproof. We don't want to scare the cows.'

Rylan grunts. 'They're in the sheds for winter. Don't worry about them. You're still building it, then?'

'Marcus is determined.'

'You know about the runoff there. In winter it pours down from the field.'

'Yes, yes. Marcus has a plan.'

Ben chimes in. 'We don't want to be fishing you out of floodwater. Lost two cattle from that bit of pasture next to the cut after three days of storm. Washed right into the ravine they was. Both well over half a ton.'

Izzy shakes her head and wrinkles her nose. 'We won't be using it much in the dead of winter, that's for sure.'

'Just be careful, is all.' Rylan delivers this as a warning. 'But thanks for letting us know.'

'I wanted to ask one other thing.' She speaks quickly, emboldened by her conversation with Angharad. 'I'd really like a look at the Engine House. Not go inside. Go over and take some photos. Safe to cross the ravine, isn't it?'

Ben shakes his head and sniffs. 'It's a ruin, like I said. Owned by Natural Resources Wales. But since that section of path don't lead anywhere, we fenced it off for them.'

'I really do not want to go inside.' Izzy labours the point.

Rylan narrows his eyes into dark slits. 'Pretty overgrown. Hard going. Used to be a path down to the inlet but that's all eroded away.'

'But you wouldn't mind?'

Ben shrugs. 'It's not ours. We're just trying to stop kids vandalising it and doing themselves an injury.'

Rylan tilts his head. 'Why are you so interested?'

'It's research. For some writing ideas.'

'Writing? Like a book?'

Izzy bares her teeth in apology. 'I know. Sounds very grand. But a girl has to have a hobby.'

They don't laugh. The dour Gowers, Marcus calls them. 'So sometimes kids try and break in, do they?' Izzy asks because she can't stand the silence.

'Now and again. Used to anyway. On long summer nights. Why, you seen someone?' Ben's brow darkens.

'I thought I saw an animal of some sort. Pale in colour.'

The Gowers wait.

'I thought it might have been a stray dog or something.'

Still the Gowers say nothing.

Or it might be the Follower. Come to tell me something signifi-cant. She wonders what they'd say if she voiced those thoughts. She wonders if she would get a response.

'Well, if you do stroll over, make sure someone knows you're going. Or I could take you over there one day. Offer's still open.' Ben grins at her.

The voice in her head is loud and clear. *No thank you, brawny Ben.*

She snuffs it out. 'I may well take you up on that one day if I need a guide.' She has absolutely no intention, but his smile widens.

'Right, I'd better be getting home or Marcus'll think I've been kidnapped.'

She backs the car out while the dour Gowers watch. At

least she now knows that if she crosses the ravine she won't be trespassing on their land. That's another box ticked. Because she is going to go exploring. She's made up her mind even if her motives remain a little woolly. Okay, so Angharad thinks that writing about it – whatever the hell 'it' turns out to be – will help. Certainly won't do any harm. And she has to admit that talking things through has opened her eyes to the something lodged deep down in her psyche that needs a spring clean. Needs to be examined in the cold light of day.

Let Marky have his Spaceship. The Engine House and its mysteries, whether they be animal, human or … otherwise (she wants to add supernatural but shies away from the thought instantly) can be her new project.

CHAPTER THIRTY

On Sunday afternoon Warlow drives over to Fishguard to fetch Molly Allanby. Western Canoe Adventures have an industrial unit near the holiday park. They're unloading the kayaks off the trailer from their trip to the estuary when he arrives. Molly looks windswept but happy. Cadi makes straight for her when she's let out of the car.

'Enjoy it?' Warlow asks, getting out to help with Molly's kit.

'Brilliant. We went into some really spooky inlets.' She's on one knee, neck stretched up as the dog tries to lick her face.

'She's a natural. If she ever wants a job …' A man somewhere in his thirties with 70s hair to his shoulders and sun-taut skin chips in. His name is Tim Brody and his dad and Warlow are ex-colleagues. Tim's grin is infectious.

'Mum would throw a fit. There's no A-Level in kayaking.' Molly tries to stand and half-stumbles with Cadi wriggling between her legs.

'There's always the summer,' Warlow says.

Tim nods. 'We didn't do badly at all this last year. Everyone seemed to come west for their hols.'

'Fingers crossed it stays like that,' Warlow nods towards the Jeep. 'Throw your stuff in the boot, Molly.'

Molly hoists a backpack and gives Tim one of her dazzling smiles. 'Thanks Tim. It was dead awesome.'

'Any time. I mean that.'

While Molly packs her things in the boot, Warlow asks Tim how much he owes him.

'Nothing, Evan. I'm serious. She's brilliant. She's already got a couple of British canoeing certificates and could easily get Advanced Sea Kayaking. Probably a leadership award too. Then she'd be a real asset.'

Warlow is impressed. 'Well, don't count on it. Her mum has plans.'

Tim persists. 'But like you say, come the summer. These are two-day training courses with a day's assessment. Worth thinking about, I'd say.'

'You sound excited.' Warlow chortles.

'I am. good to see someone as jazzed as I am about the sport. In a couple of weeks we're doing an inshore tour. She's welcome to come to that.'

'I'll mention it to her mother. How's your dad?'

'Grumpy as always. Waiting on a hip op so can't stand on touchlines or at the bar for long. But he's still throwing stuff at the TV whenever he watches a game.' Tim's grin has not yet slipped. 'Molly tells me you're back working.'

'Helping with a case.'

Tim picks up a stray paddle. 'Those people on the path, right? I read about that. Dad was still working when that all happened, wasn't he?'

'He was.'

'And then that thing about Neil Morris on the news today.' Tim shakes his head.

'You knew him?

'Neil? Yeah. Wild child. Had a bit too much of a liking

for the wacky but a mean surfer in his day. Could have gone places but, you know, too fond of—'

'The wacky?'

Tim nods. 'But I used to see him about 'cos he worked with Rob Gamage at Venture Pembroke.'

Warlow tilts his head. 'That's a new one on me.'

'Worked with Rob for years and then got done for that silly thing with the car.'

'So Morris did what exactly? Kayaking?'

Tim stacks the paddle onto a trailer and begins securing the load with tension straps. 'Nah. Coasteering is their thing. Up and down cliffs.'

'You don't do that?'

Tim snorts. 'You need to be bit mad for that. Lovely in summer, but I've seen them out in gales. Some people like that. The wind and the rain. It can be an adrenaline rush. Mostly though it's bloody cold and wet.'

Cadi appears at Warlow's side followed by Molly. 'Any chance we can stop in a Greggs? I'm starving.'

They wave goodbye to Tim Brody. There's still a smell of wet dog in the car and Warlow apologises for it.'

'It'll be like that until the weather changes and we get dry dog. We can put up with it. But it's an acquired taste.'

Molly shrugs. 'It's not Cadi's fault. If you washed her properly, she wouldn't stink. Have you tried one of those mud pumps? A friend of mine in Alderly had one for their Golden Retriever that used to get totally filthy. You fill it up and it has a hand pump and squirts water out through a brush. She said it was brilliant.'

Warlow has never heard of it.

'I'll send you a link,' Molly says. She tries the radio, finds three stations that are not to her taste and then turns the thing off because it's 'so lame'. 'Do you have anything decent on your phone?' she asks.

'Define decent?'

'R&B? Soul?'

'You're into that?'

'Yeah. And other stuff, obviously.'

He can control his phone's music app from the steering column. He finds some Average White Band. Molly listens, taps her hand to 'If I Ever Lose This Heaven' and approves. 'Okay. This is cool.'

Warlow drives to the Greggs in Haverfordwest. Molly queues and buys a chicken bake and a Coke. The Coke is a zero. He hates to think how many calories are in the bake, but Molly looks like she can handle them. She hands him the coffee he's ordered and proceeds to demolish the bake in a snowdrift of crumbs.

'I see you're a faddy eater,' Warlow says.

'I am n–' she catches herself. 'Right, so you do sarcasm. Warn me next time.'

Warlow nods, keeps his eyes on the road.

'Mum thinks you're old school.'

'Fair comment.'

She nods. 'That's not a bad thing, though. She was worried you were going to be a prat. She says you are not a prat. She's dead chuffed at that.'

Warlow snorts. 'I'll take that as a positive then.'

Molly takes two gulps of Coke. 'Plus you look a bit like that bloke on the telly, him with the high forehead who does psychopaths and vicars. It's the hair and the secret smile that does it.'

Psychopaths and vicars. Warlow tries to think what actor falls into that category. Molly puts him out of his misery and shows him a photo of Tom Hollander on her phone. Warlow responds with a sceptical frown. He can't see it himself, but it's not the first time. Molly is on a roll. 'And you have Cadi and know a tune when you hear it. My guess is she's lucked out, professionally I mean.'

Warlow laughs softly.

'What?' Molly throws him a sideways glance. 'She was worried.'

'You and your mum share most things, do you?'

Molly takes another bite. 'Yeah. We do now. Since Dad did his thing with sergeant big tits, we made a deal with each other. Cards on the table.'

Warlow toys with exploring the sergeant big tits reference but decides quickly against it. 'Do you see your dad?'

'No. Not… at the moment.' She hurls a challenging glare in his direction. 'And before you say anything, yeah, I know he is still my dad, but he is a class A shit for doing that to Mum. He needs to be punished. I'll get over it. One day. Mum won't. Ever.'

Molly finishes eating and Warlow finds some Isley Brothers. 'Who's That Lady' segues into 'Summer Breeze'. She puts her head against the window and within five minutes is dozing.

Warlow doesn't mind. His brain is recalling the conversation he had with Tim the kayaker word for word. And all he can think about is that the recently deceased Morris was an expert on coasteering and climbing up and down cliffs.

CHAPTER THIRTY-ONE

MONDAY MORNING. Yawns and coffee cups abound in the Incident Room, but a lot has happened over the weekend. Some people are already logged on to computers or manning phones.

Mel Lewis is back today. He has years of experience in Incident Rooms and he's been tasked with tracking down records for Morris and Thomas, or at least supervising others and trawling through the old files to see if there was anything at all that put the men on the original investigation's radar. Even something incidental.

But that's work. And as always, the pre-briefing banter has nothing to do with that. Instead, it's about sailing and an upcoming regatta.

'You're still welcome to come, Evan boy. Any time. We're always looking for crew.' Mel perches his backside on a desk.

'Not my thing, Mel. I'll spend the whole sail throwing up or thinking about throwing up. Not my idea of fun.'

'Only way to get your sea legs is to stick with it.' As usual, Lewis is nursing a mug that steams gently. His eyes look puffy from lack of sleep or exposure to the wind. Probably both, thinks Warlow.

Warlow offers an impassive smile. 'I've already got legs, thanks. Ones that like walking on land. Preferably with the dog.'

'Don't know what you're missing, mun.'

'Oh, I do. Believe me.'

Lewis is the kind of sailor who thinks that crossing the Irish Sea in a thirty-knot wind is fun.

There's a different tempo in the room today. A sense of things moving. Maybe not as quickly as everyone would like, but moving, nevertheless. It's reflected in Sion Buchannan's demeanour when he marches in, this time with his chief investigating officer in tow.

Buchannan looks eye-bag tired, Jess much fresher. Up for the challenge. The Buccaneer asks for everyone's attention. He runs through Morris's apparent suicide and his link with Kieron Thomas. But there is icing on this stuff-we-already-know cake. Forensic assessment of the Picker-ings' clothing, bunched up and stuffed into the crypt-black space of that crevice, has yielded results. Everyone already knows about Kelly Scott, but now a second DNA surprise has emerged from a piece of chewing gum stuck to Mrs Pickering's waterproof trousers. From that gum, extracted DNA has thrown up another profile. Buchannan has been doing this too long to be dramatic, but there's a pin-drop hush before he says, 'That profile is already on the data-base and belonged to Neil Morris.'

There are mutterings of excitement. It means the investigation is on the right track. A win like this is better than any motivational speech.

Jess glances in Warlow's direction. He nods.

'What this tells us,' – she speaks loudly over the buzz but it takes only four words before she has everyone's attention and carries on in a normal voice – 'is that Morris was in proximity to Mrs Pickering for a period when she was wearing the clothes found with the body. It proves nothing else. Not yet. We also know Kieron Thomas liked hammers as his weapon of choice for intimidating people. What we don't have is where those two men were that day. For now, that's what we concentrate on.' Jess has sheets in her hand and calls people up for assignments. Catrin Richards is busy writing on a whiteboard.

Warlow waits for Buchannan to finish and then follows him out. He beckons Jess and Catrin to accompany them and waves to Rhys across the room to do the same.

'Sion. A word.'

They meet in the SIO's room. Strictly speaking, Sion Buchannan's room. But he's the regional BCU commander and has a much nicer office upstairs. So he isn't precious about this pokey space. He'd be mad if he was.

'That's a tremendous stroke of luck about the chewing gum,' Warlow says.

Buchannan however isn't happy. 'Too little too late.'

'Maybe. But I spoke to someone yesterday who knew Morris well. Before he was locked up for dangerous driving, he worked as a coasteering guide.'

Catrin's eyes, big already, seem to double in size.

Jess exhales. 'So he'd know the coast. All the coves and the cliffs.'

'He'd know exactly where to hide the Pickerings,' Buchannan spits. 'Two days. Two bloody days and we'd have had Morris and Thomas alive and in the interview room. Or one of them at least.' He runs a big hand around his broad neck. 'There's something we're not seeing here. Something barn door.' When he looks up. There's no smile, but genuine gratitude. 'Well done you two. But we press on. Try to find out what these two were up to.'

It doesn't take long. The most useful information comes from a sergeant in the drugs unit based in Pembroke

Dock. Someone who knew both Morris and Thomas even better than Dai Vetch. Again it's Jess who calls the team together.

Catrin gives Rhys the stage as it is he who spoke to the vice sergeant. He stands awkwardly in the small room, clutching a sheet of paper. Crib notes maybe. Or just a prop to keep his hands busy.

'Apparently both Thomas and Morris were trouble-makers, mostly low-grade stuff like affray and a couple of cases of assault for which neither of them were charged. They bought and sold drugs, too. But the drug squad officer also said that according to their activity logs around the time of the Pickerings' disappearance, both Morris and Thomas dropped off the radar.'

'Afterwards you mean?' Jess asks.

'Before and after.'

'Did they move away?' Catrin peers at the DC.

Rhys glances at his notes. 'I checked with Morris's employer. He worked for Venture the whole of that year with no gaps.'

'What about Thomas?' Jess presses.

'We're checking his benefit records and job centre interviews, etc.'

'It'll be as normal,' Warlow says. It earns him three inquisitive looks before he qualifies his statement. 'Vetch told me that the two of them were caught up in a rogue MDMA scandal during a music festival. I checked the dates and it all happened two months before the Pickerings went missing. Some kids ended up in hospital after ingesting bad Ecstasy tablets. Thomas and Morris sold them the drugs, but they got off with the help of an expensive lawyer neither of them could afford.'

'How does that fit in?' Catrin asks.

Warlow narrows his gaze and looks at the notice board, searching for an answer he knows isn't there. Not yet.

'Someone else had their back. Someone a lot more powerful and with money to spend.'

'Like who?' Harries asks.

'My guess would be whoever supplied them with drugs.' Jess pushes off the desk she's been perching on. 'We need phone records. See who it was they were in touch with around that time. If this pans out then at some point I'm going to need a conversation with organised crime.'

'Mel Lewis is already on to the phone records,' Catrin says.

Jess nods. 'Good. The sooner the better.'

———

In the eighteenth and nineteenth centuries, lime kilns dotted the coast of West Wales. Although lime was used as mortar for building, its primary use in Cardiganshire and Pembrokeshire was for agriculture. Inland soil was thin and acidic. The addition of slaked lime to farmland significantly increased its fertility. Before railways, lime was brought to the west coast by boat, often offloaded at high tide to be collected on beaches and inlets when the sea receded. To make lime, limestone was heated to high temperatures over 800 degrees to make calcium oxide or quicklime. The ruins of the kilns at Mwnt are unique in that the nearby winch or Engine House is an excellent example of how quickly businesses rose and fell. Stone for construction of the kilns came from a nearby coastal cliff quarry. As the seaborne lime industry fell away with railway transport, so the quarry found a new market as road stone. Metalled roads required hard stone and the local dolerite, a finer grained stone than granite, was ideal. The Engine House was used to transport stone in drams on a tramway from the quarry to the cliff top. From there it was crushed, and the winches lowered the drams to the base of the cliff through unusual curved tunnels, 125 metres to the narrow inlet below for loading on a jetty. Other tunnels were constructed as storage caverns for the crushed dolerite and, before that, the lime-

stone. The enclosed map from 1885 shows a narrow road climbing across the cliff face and winding through the ravine. That road and the jetty it led to have almost washed away with at least 40cms of cliff face being eroded per year. The Engine House held a horse driven whim, then a crab winch and finally a 12kW Roby engine. As rubber pneumatic tyres took over from iron wheels, the demand for stone for road fell away and when the Great Depression hit, the business, as with the bigger concern at Porthgain further up the coast, collapsed.

IZZY READS the online account from a Historical Society website. There are photos, too. From organised field trips and aerial shots of the land and sea. Her view, from the edge of Limehouse Cottage, is nowhere near as good as the website images.

The photographs reveal a narrow building, three storeys high, with the remains of its tall round chimney jutting up above the roofless sides. Crags abut the ground floor walls, giving the building the impression of having grown up from the earth itself. All the windows are small and square, bar the arched main entrance that reminds her somehow of a place of worship. Behind the building, the remains of a linear tramway, its rails long taken up and now grown over with grass and weeds, is just visible in the aerial shots, running off to the northwest where the gouged remnants of a small quarry scars the landscape. On the building's seaward side, the cliff edge looms impossibly close and she sees what the article means by erosion. The whole thing looks precarious and otherworldly. Dangerous even.

Ben Gower's words echo in her ears. In an ideal world the coastal path would have run right next to the Engine House. But health and safety, for once genuine, has diverted it away and around the ravine. Still, had someone gone missing all those years ago, she felt sure that it would have been one place the police must have searched.

It makes her wonder.

A memory intrudes, of visiting her brother, Austen, at a psychiatric hospital shortly after their father found him. He'd begun treatment, but the illness was clear in his sadness. Yet what she remembers most, what has triggered this recall, is the look in his eyes. There was one word she could use to describe it. Haunted. He'd hugged her and they'd both cried. He kept apologising and saying that 'he'd got a bit lost.' The doctor told them that there was a significantly higher rate of drug abuse amongst bipolar patients.

But the look in her brother's eye stayed with her because she'd seen it before. It came to her as she sat in her dad's car on the way home and later, alone in her room, she confirmed it with a Google search. Something she'd seen that had lodged in her brain. A plane crashing into the Potomac river in the eighties. The harrowing sight of people drowning under a bridge in the full view of camera crews. It wasn't so much the wreckage or the rescues that disturbed her. It was the look on the face of an almost drowning woman. Her wild and sunken eyes.

The same look she'd seen in her brother.

She does not know why these thoughts occur to her now. Her fixation on things lost perhaps. But it's all the incentive she needs to pick up her mobile and, from her purse, fish out a card the young sergeant had given her. The number she dials answers almost immediately.

'Detective Constable Harries.'

'Oh, hi. This is Izzy Ramsden.'

'Hello, Ms Ramsden.' Harries is chirpy. 'Sergeant Richards is away from her desk. Can I help?'

'Sorry to bother you. I don't even know why I'm ringing. I don't want to waste your time.'

'Not a problem. How can I help?'

'Just a question about the Engine House. Curiosity more than anything. I'm doing some research and ... this is going to sound a little mad.'

'No, go on, I'm listening.'

'Okay. I was wondering if maybe someone involved in the original investigation could give me a ring sometime? Not related to what's going on. I wanted to pick their brains about the Engine House.'

'That building opposite your cottage?'

'That's right. On the edge of the cliff near where we are. I would guess it formed part of the search area when the Pickerings first went missing.'

'And what was it you were interested in exactly?'

Izzy lets out an embarrassed laugh. 'I wanted their impression of it. Had they found anything there? Signs of recent occupation for example. Kids using it to drink illicit cider. Graffiti on the walls. That sort of thing. It's crumbling into the sea and I'm thinking of writing about it. A short story perhaps and I want to get a feel for it ... I don't want to waste your time.'

'You're not.' Harries remains polite, but his tone is a little stiffer. 'How are things there? Not too many curious callers, I hope?'

'We've had a few people taking photos. One newspaper wanting to come and do an interview. We've turned them all away.'

'Good. Glad to hear it. I'll pass this on and someone will be in touch. Not right away maybe.'

'No, no, of course not. You're all so busy.'

And the last thing you want to do is chat to a woman about scary houses and mythology.

'We will be in touch, though.'

She ends the call and instantly wishes she hadn't made it. What must Harries be thinking? They're investigating a murder and she is asking them about how scary the building is. Flaky doesn't come close.

She puts her hands in her hair and groans. It's quickly followed by a sigh and the realisation that it's unlikely anyone from the police will get back to her.

But there's a lot she can do online.

A lot more by going over there and seeing for herself.

CHAPTER THIRTY-TWO

MONDAY AFTERNOON, Tanya Ogilvie arrives at Haverfordwest police station. Jess settles on an interview room though she gets rid of the desks and there's no recording equipment running. She has Catrin and Rhys outside listening while she and Warlow do the hard part. Warlow agrees it will do the rest of the investigative team good to see the human side of this situation.

Tanya is what Warlow's ex, Denise, would term heavy-set. More so than before. It's been years since he saw her in the flesh and though her clothes are better and she now dresses to disguise her top-heavy features, there's no denying that she could do with a few less takeaways of a weekend. Not that he'd ever say that but his doctor son, Tom, having worked on both vascular and diabetic wards and having seen the unfit and overweight fall like flies, is now a zealot. Warlow sometimes fantasises about being a fly on the wall whenever Denise and Tom talk because Denise is no beanpole herself. Not anymore. The booze has given her the bloated belly and thin legs of an alcoholic. She hides it well with clever clothes, but not well enough.

'Thank you for seeing me,' Tanya says. It's a nonde-script accent from somewhere in Berkshire, if Warlow's memory is correct. Where the Pickerings had moved from once they had Tanya off their hands, safely married and settled.

'How are you, Tanya?' Warlow asks.

There's an attempt at a brave smile. 'I'm not sure. On the one hand, relieved that you found them, on the other …' She squeezes her eyes shut as if to banish the images of her mother and father jutting out of that crevice in the cliffs. 'The worst thing is that the kids have seen those photographs of their gran and grandad now. I can't change that.'

'Tanya,' Jess says in a low, even tone, 'you know ex DCI Warlow very well, but I'm new to this case and, though we have reams of interviews on record, now that we under-stand the situation better, would you mind if I asked you some questions and record the answers for my benefit?'

'No, I don't mind.'

Jess opens a recording app on her phone and places it on the desk. 'It's a long time since your parents went miss-ing. A long time to reflect. But since we found them, is there anything at all you can think of that might help? Something they might have said or done out of the ordinary?'

Tanya gives a tiny nod. 'I've been thinking about nothing else for days. There was nothing going on. They walked almost every day and they absolutely loved where they lived. They loved the coastal path. They'd been coming to this part of Wales for years. We always had holi-days here. Walking was a way of life for them. They'd get up, check the weather and in summer they'd be in the car and off by eight.'

'Always the path?'

'No. Sometimes they'd drive up to the Black Mountains

or the Preselis. Mum would pack sandwiches. They'd sometimes send me "guess where we are" photos.'

'And things were alright at home?'

Tanya doesn't know what to do with her hands. Since entering, she's wrung them together. Now she settles with folding them on her lap. 'They'd been married for forty-one years. They had their quirks, of course they did. Dad moaned about Mum's paints getting over everything. Mum said Dad preferred knocking nails in things to having a conversation. But they were happy.'

'So your mum painted?'

Tanya nods with a wistful smile. 'And Dad was a DIYer. They were both into local history. They'd researched the path. All about how Irish raiders came in the 4th century. Smugglers in the coves, the old lime kilns along the coast. They'd explore. They couldn't get enough of it. One of the main reasons they moved here. When they found the cottage within walking distance of a decrepit old Engine House, you'd swear they'd struck oil.'

'And they'd not said anything to you about seeing odd people or anything unusual?'

Tanya laughs. It's brief, like a flickering flame. 'They were always seeing odd people on the path. Eccentric people, I mean. Walkers in flip flops, or someone in arctic gear in mid-July. Mum painted. She loved local legends. So she'd paint moody landscapes. Sometimes with odd figures.'

'The Follower,' Warlow says. 'I remember she painted that.'

Tanya sighs. 'And somehow the press got hold of that and we had to endure weeks of that nonsense.'

'The Follower?' Jess's sharp gaze darts between Warlow and Tanya.

'A not-so-urban legend,' Warlow explains. 'Sometimes, if you're alone on the path, you get the sense of being followed. Some people even claim to see someone in the distance. But the figure never catches up. Never there if someone else approaches.'

'Was there talk between them of this Follower at around the time they went missing?' Jess is intrigued.

Tanya frowns. 'Not that I can recall. It was just Mum's imagination. Whereas Dad wanted to build a summer house to sit and look at the Engine House and watch for smugglers.' She smiles. 'They were both harmless. Worked hard all their lives to enjoy a few years of, I don't know, indulging themselves I suppose. Mum with her Follower sketches, and Dad with his sea lanterns and pirates.'

'Lanterns?'

'He used to say he saw lights out at sea at night. Probably fishing boats, or moonlight reflecting off rocks, but they both had great imaginations.'

'How far did they get with the summer house?' Jess asks.

'Ideally they'd wanted to build it at the highest point to get the best view. They even offered to buy some of the farmer's land.'

'And old Gower wouldn't sell them any land?' Jess knows the answer, but Tanya is free flowing now.

'No. And who can blame him. There were always cows in that tiny field they wanted to buy, even though it was steep and ran down into the ravine. So Dad began building their summerhouse in a little hollow at the top corner of their property. Somewhere that always got waterlogged. But Dad never gave up asking.'

Jess turns a page in her pocketbook. She's made a few notes prior to the interview. 'Were they on good terms with the Gowers would you say?'

'Oh, yeah. Used to get eggs from them and everything. The summerhouse became a running joke.' There's a pause and Tanya starts wringing her hands again. Slow, writhing movements. 'Have you any idea who could have done this?'

Though it's Jess's case she glances at Warlow for this one, letting him have the reins.

The DCI clears his throat. 'We have some suspects in mind. We think your mum and dad were killed on the path near to where they were hidden.'

'Why?'

The big question. Warlow opts for honesty. 'That we don't know. It's possible they stumbled across something illegal, or someone doing something illegal.'

'Like what?'

'That we don't know either. Not yet.'

Tanya's voice cracked. 'So the press is right. It wasn't an accident.'

Warlow leans forward. 'No. No accident could put them in that crevice in the cliff, Tanya.'

She slumps then, head down. There aren't any tears. Too many have flowed already. Words, too.

'As soon as we have something concrete we'll be in touch,' Jess says.

'Me,' says Warlow. 'I'll be in touch.'

Catrin comes back into the room and escorts Tanya out while Rhys makes sure of her contact details. Warlow and Jess stay in the interview room because the DI has questions.

'Why this fascination with the Engine House?'

'What it says on the tin.' Warlow explains about the lime industry, how they'd float it out to ships from the beach and then from a jetty for the stone from the quarry. 'It's just a big shed that housed an engine. With a roof that kept the rain off. It wasn't in good nick seven years ago. Probably worse now. But we searched it top to bottom more than once. No sign of the Pickerings of course, and now we know why. Fenced off soon afterwards. There are issues around landownership on the path further south and it would take a fortune to make the place safe. Mel Lewis had another look about four years ago at the last review. All a complete waste of time.'

'Because the Pickerings were in their tomb a dozen miles away.'

'Exactly.'

Jess shudders. 'I can't imagine what Tanya's gone through all these years. Never knowing. Always wondering. Probably harbouring a tiny spark of hope that they might turn up in a villa in Spain.'

'That's why I'd like this bloody thing sorted out before the press speculate all over again.'

Jess nods. Then her face softens. 'Thanks again for bringing Molly home.'

'It was fun.'

'Cordon bleu Greggs on the way home, I hear.'

'I know how to give a girl a good time.'

Jess shakes her head. 'I dread to think what she told you. Molly's filters are set on low at the best of times.'

Warlow grins. 'She's a credit to you.'

'She's given you a nickname by the way. Cadi's daddy, the silver fox.'

'Hmm.'

Jess smiles. 'Doesn't matter what you think of it, I'd take it if I were you. She only ever gives nicknames to people she likes.'

He files that away for future reference.

CHAPTER THIRTY-THREE

WHEN IZZY GOES out to the fencepost, the food she left out last night – half a loaf of bread, some fruit, a carton of juice – is gone. As have the other bags she's left out over the last couple of nights. This time, on the fence post, is a cockle shell. She looks out over the ravine and up towards the horizon. It's a grey morning, but the forecast is for the weather to dry up with a piercing wind coming in from the north west. A change from the blustery southwesterlies they've had for almost two weeks.

She pockets the shell and walks back to the house. Her phone chimes as she steps through the kitchen door.

'Hey babe.' Angharad's sing song voice drips with concern.

'Hey yourself.'

'How are you?'

'I'm fine.' Izzy's answer seeks to reassure. She's already explained that there is no need for Angharad to worry. Several times.

'I've had a word with Lena. She thinks you ought to come over. No pressure. But someone in your situation usually benefits from a session.'

There's a lot in Angharad's sentence. Izzy needs to peel it apart. 'My situation?'

'Yes. Someone who's lost something without ever having the chance to say goodbye.'

'Okaaaay.' Izzy knows she sounds sceptical. After all, ten days of a possible pregnancy may not even constitute an embryo, let alone a sentient being.

'When does a soul become a soul, Izzy?'

'No idea.'

'No. No one does. But it's a part of you and Marcus that's been lost. And that part needs to be acknowledged.'

'What are you saying?'

'That perhaps it wants a chance to say goodbye.'

Though derision threatens to mount a giggly response, Izzy holds back. 'So by session, what do you mean, exactly?'

'Communication. If you're a believer that is.'

'I don't know what to believe.'

Angharad lets a few heavy seconds pass before she poses the question. 'Something is communicating with you though, isn't it?'

'If by communicating you mean taking my offered food, then yes.'

'Then why not try and find out what's going on?'

Izzy winces. 'I am trying. Only, I'm not sure I want to try your way. Not yet.'

'But it isn't good to wait, Izzy. Restless spirits are not patient.' Angharad adopts a wheedling tone.

Izzy wants to laugh at that. Restless spirits my foot. But something stops her. As always with the Angharads of this world – one of their neighbours in London was a reiki therapist – it's easy to scoff. But there's no doubting her well-meaning offer of friendship. And Izzy is not an unkind person.

'Look, I have a few things I need to do. Blow away some cobwebs. Let me do that and I'll get back to you. And be sure to thank Lena for me.'

There's a stretch of silence before Angharad says, 'Alright. If that's what you want. But the Follower doesn't follow without reason. You know that, right?'

Izzy does laugh this time. A nervous little chortle because she isn't sure if Angharad is being serious. When she feels the urge to ask, it's too late. The line is dead.

The call preys on her mind throughout the morning and throughout a lunch she eats in the kitchen alone because Marcus has texted to say he's caught up, 'battening'. She takes him a sandwich and a flask of tea. But he's up in the scaffolding with a drill when she calls to him. He shouts down a thanks but she can hardly hear him for the flapping of the plastic wrap in the wind that is now almost a gale. She wants to ask him to leave it for the day, but when she texts the request, he comes back with:

'Another hour and the vapour membrane is finished on two sides.'

She's not sure what a vapour membrane is, but she knows that Marcus's two hours have the knack of expanding into four. Einstein would need to rewrite his general theory if he worked on the captain's cabin.

But at least Marcus is busy. It gives her time to ponder. And now what she ponders about is Angharad's call. Forget the offer of a 'session' with Lena. Though she likes Angharad, her doom-laden warnings are less than inspiring. She's well-meaning, Izzy appreciates that. But she also knows what Marky would say if she told him about Lena's spiritual sessions. She can almost hear him say it.

'Communicating with the dead? Great. While you're there ask my gran where her premium bond certificates are?'

But there is one thing that Angharad has said that strikes a chord. *It isn't good to wait, Izzy.*

She's right there. And Izzy's patience was never her strongest suit.

Mid-afternoon, she decides. She dresses warmly, walking boots, three layers under her windproof coat, hat, gloves and Monty as her guide. Woman and dog set off through the garden to the gate that leads out into the Gower's field and a track down into the ravine.

There are no cows in the field today. None for a good week. They're inside, safe from the weather and the damp fields that can rot their hooves.

Monty's ears flap like crazy and Izzy has to lean into the wind to make progress. It isn't until she drops through the stunted tree line on her side of the ravine that its power eases. She takes her time, looking for a path. There isn't one so she hugs the contour and is careful to stay away from the edge as much as she can. The drop here is not as steep, but a wrong foot and a tumble does not look appealing. She works her way inland, the descent easing until she reaches a narrow gap, maybe a dozen feet across, where the stream pouring down off the field over bare rock flattens off. A couple of rotten posts suggest that there might have been a bridge here once. But the stones are big and Monty skips across with ease. Izzy follows, slipping just the once and getting a wet foot for her trouble. Her boots are waterproof, but her misstep takes her in over her ankle.

She curses.

Monty gives her a look with a tilt of his head. He's up for it, bounding up the slope in front of her through the trees. It's a steeper ascent this side and Izzy stops to catch her breath on an outcrop. Down to her left the ravine funnels to the narrow V-shaped shingle beach a hundred feet below. There is no way down to it and, thirty yards out, the water surges around the rocks at the cliff base. She can't imagine there ever being a way for ships to tie up there but there must have been.

Back over her shoulder is where the cottage sits but it isn't visible from where she is now. She can see the top half of the Spaceship, though. By definition, were he to look, Marcus could see her. And she realises that when it's finished and they sit in their observation deck they'll be able to admire the same view that she now has of the cleft in the earth and the sea that caresses it.

Good old Marcus, she thinks.

As she climbs and crests the steepest part of the ravine, she steps out from the shelter of the land and is whipped by the wind. The remains of the Engine House tower are just visible above her eighty yards away. Izzy pushes her way through thick gorse and grasses, climbs until she gets to a more open patch of land where she stands, wind-buffeted, but with an unobstructed view of the derelict remains of the building below her. It's guarded by a fence topped with barbed wire running from the edge of the ravine further down, across the promontory on which the Engine House sits, to curve around, hiding it off from nosy visitors. Though how anyone would get to this point without crossing the Gower's or her land is a mystery since the coastal path diverts walkers well inland from here.

The building has a haunting beauty. Something so permanent and industrial seems alien in this rugged land-scape. Monty stands next to her, as if awaiting permission. But all Izzy does is stand and, with her phone, takes photographs. She will get closer but seeing the building set against the background of sea and sky stirs her imagination enough to capture it in the moment. As she frames the photos, a movement catches her eye. Something on the edge of the building near steps that lead in through the main doorless arch.

Something caught in the wind?

For a moment she thinks it's a bird, but the fluttering is too erratic and violent. The wind thunders at her, threatening to blow off her hat. She puts a clamping hand up and realises that the fluttering thing must be light. Paper or plastic of some sort.

She curses. Damned plastic is everywhere these days.

She's taken three steps towards the fence when she hears it. An alteration in the background sound that's been in her ears ever since cresting the ravine. A flapping reverberation from the Spaceship's coverings which suddenly changes in tone, if anything, diminishing in volume.

She turns and her stomach pitches.

Across the ravine, the Spaceship is moving, tilting up on one side, precarious, monstrous, until it topples with a juddering crunch. There's a two second delay before the accompanying clatter and clang of collapsing scaffolding meets her ears. Izzy lets out a noise that's half shout, half scream. Then she's running, back down the slope she's just crested, across the stream, Monty with her, barking at this new game.

Izzy scrambles, falls twice, scrambles some more until she's back up on the other side. The bottom half of the Spaceship, now on its side, is sagging. But the top half remains a vague square, held together by bolted metal poles. Izzy runs up the field, screaming Marcus's name.

Further up, towards the track that leads to the distant farm, she sees a tractor next to stacked black silage bales. She waves her arms as she runs.

'Help! Help!'

She's closer to the tractor than she is to the Spaceship. The driver hasn't seen what's happened. But the machine stops loading when Izzy's desperate pointing arm shows where she's going.

The machine reverses, turns and starts trundling towards her.

Then she's at the Spaceship.

'Marcus! Marcus!' She bellows his name. Roars it out three more times above the keening wind.

'Here,' he answers. 'Here.' It's a feeble response. Desperate.

She follows his voice. He's lying on the ground under the intact end of the crumpled scaffold exoskeleton, swaddled in the blue plastic wrapping. He looks pale and frightened.

'Marcus, oh my God. What happened?'

'The wind must have …' He stops, then makes a strange face and shudders.

'Are you okay?'

'No, my leg.'

Izzy peels away the plastic. Marcus's left leg is trapped under a twenty-foot length of scaffold pole that's still attached to the framework. There's blood seeping through his trousers.

Izzy's hand flies to her mouth. 'Oh, Marky.'

The tractor is getting louder. Izzy stands. Waves to the driver. It's Ben Gower. He parks on the other side of the fence and jumps down.

'What's happened?' he yells above the wind.

'The Spaceship … the scaffolding, the wind must have caught it. Marcus is hurt.'

Ben follows her around and looks down at the scene and then the trapped man. 'Hey, Marcus.'

'Hi Ben,' Marcus says. But he's shivering and the words come out through chattering teeth.

Ben kneels to study the injury. 'It's being crushed,' he says.

'What does …what …' Izzy can't find the words.

'Ring for an ambulance. We ought to get him out from under there.'

'But they say not to move people.'

Ben takes charge. 'I've seen it with animals. It's a crush injury. We need to get the weight off there. We can put a tourniquet on higher up.'

'Okay.' Izzy's response is full of doubt, but she doesn't argue because there isn't anything else to say. She rings for the ambulance with one hand over her ear to block out the wind and stands back as Ben goes back to the tractor, lifts the fence with the big bucket, flattens it and drives through.

Ben is good on the machine. He slides the bucket under the scaffolding with careful, astonishing accuracy. Izzy doesn't have to do anything, neither does Marcus. He's too busy groaning through a clenched jaw at the pain. The tractor lifts the entire structure and pushes it slowly six feet away. Then Ben jumps down. He has a loop of twine in his hands as he kneels next to Marcus.

'This might hurt a bit.'

He pushes twine under Marcus's knee and ties it tight two inches below the joint.

The cords in Marcus's neck tighten as he lifts his head and huffs out breaths. Ben fetches an old coat from the tractor cab and wraps it, and his own, around the injured man.

'I'll shoot back and guide the ambulance in,' Ben says.

Izzy nods and watches him go, the tractor speeding off along the field to the track. She holds Marcus's hand. It's cold. His lips are bloodless, the whole of his lower jaw fluttering. 'It's going to be okay, Marky. It's going to be okay. The ambulance is on its way.'

'Mmm … my l-l-leg hu-hurts.'

Shock, thinks Izzy. 'I know, darling. I know. I wish I could make it go away.'

Marcus makes a noise, deep in his throat. A constant moan. But Izzy doesn't mind. While he's moaning, he's alive.

The ambulance takes twenty minutes to come.

When it does, Izzy leans in and tells Marcus. He doesn't answer with words. But he moans a little louder. It's the best sound Izzy has ever heard.

CHAPTER THIRTY-FOUR

WARLOW HAS HAD two boxes back from Sergeant Griffiths, the Incident Room office manager. Both now sorted in date order, labelled and colour coded. He works through these at a snail's pace, checking to see if anything has been missed. It's hardly enthralling, but a necessary evil. He's not expecting to find anything, and so far, so good. It's reassuring to know his State of Investigation file has no gaps.

As with most police work, there are lulls. Days where legwork, or fielding calls, or staring at screens make up the working day. In the middle of this slow patch, a couple of days after Tanya Ogilvie's visit, Catrin and Jess approach Warlow's file-strewn desk.

'Welcome to the South Pole,' he says. 'I was wondering when they'd send in a rescue team.'

Jess stands before him. A woman on a mission. 'Catrin has just been in touch with Venture Pembroke. It's been a job to get the owners in the same building but they're there now. I wondered if you fancied a trip out? I'd go but …'

Warlow stands. He doesn't need to be asked twice.

'Delighted. You drive, sergeant. I'll provide entertainment in the form of amusing anecdotes.'

They pick up coffees on the way out and take a pool car. It's the grey Focus. On their way through the entrance gates they pass a blue BMW with the number plate J999 KC coming in through the gates. Driving it is DI Kelvin Caldwell.

Catrin raises her hand in a polite wave.

Warlow stares and shakes his head.

———

KELVIN WAS DI Caldwell's first name. KC were his initials. It hadn't taken long for the wags in the department to come up with an appropriate nickname. On hearing one sergeant cursing under his breath and railing against being given some useless task to do by muttering, 'Kelvin Fucking Caldwell', one of the quicker PC's had morphed the initials into KFC. Caldwell was thus less than affectionately known to almost all junior colleagues by those initials, or all varieties of meals pertaining to a certain establishment that shared those initials. Such as 'bargain bucket', or 'finger licking …', with an added epithet of choice. And some of them were extremely choice.

Of course, being a fellow senior officer, junior officers did not use such terms in Warlow's presence. But you had to be stone deaf not to hear them.

Seeing the J999 private number plate is the icing on the cake for Warlow.

He'd always called Caldwell by his last name. And though he has enough personal cause to despise the man, Warlow's disrespect is multifaceted. Caldwell's more a manager than a copper. He has no instinct for the job, is happy to see things remain unresolved and filed away under 'pending'. The man is a lazy thinker, preferring to direct from his office than be with his team. And that, in Warlow's book, should be a crime in a category all of its own. There are many examples of sloppiness that he can recall, but the most recent irked him especially.

He'd read about the case in the local news. Heard from Mel Lewis that Caldwell had caught it. Unlike the Pickerings, this hadn't made the nationals. As sickening as it sounded, in these days of God knows how many immigrants drowning every week from capsizing plastic boats off Mediterranean islands, a body washing up on a West Wales beach was small fry.

So, though he shouldn't, he probes. It isn't fair to put a junior colleague on the spot, but the number plate has lit a fuse and he's buggered if he's going to stamp it out. Better to let it fizz.

'Worked with Kelvin Caldwell much, Sergeant?'

'A bit,' Catrin replies.

'Were you involved with the floater, I don't know, maybe two years ago?'

Early morning fishermen found a body in the water at an inlet near Trwyn Crou, about four miles from New Quay in Cardiganshire. That meant whoever it was must have drowned at least a week before. It takes that long for enough carbon dioxide, methane and ammonia from putrefaction to pump up the cavities for buoyancy. A self-inflating buffet for the lucky gulls and mackerel. The body was naked. No jewellery. A male, 175cms tall. Catrin throws him a wary glance. 'You think that's a part of this?'

Warlow laughs. 'No. Intrigued is all.'

Catrin nods. 'I worked on it with DI Caldwell. I did some liaison with the ferry companies.'

'What was the outcome?' Warlow asks.

Catrin keeps her eyes front and gives a non-committal shrug. 'DI Caldwell seems pretty much on top of it.'

Warlow gives a brief nod. Catrin is being diplomatic

but doesn't seem uncomfortable discussing it, so he presses on. 'What were your thoughts, though?'

Catrin obliges. 'All the big tankers that use Milford Haven have crew. But none of the shipping lines reported any ratings missing. The Fishguard-Rosslare ferry had no missing passengers. DI Caldwell thinks the drowned man might have committed suicide. Or that he'd stowed away on the ferry or a tanker.'

Warlow is sceptical but not totally dismissive. He's seen such things before.

'And no ID at all? How does DI Caldwell explain that?' He was trying to read Catrin's body language and expression. What came over was a kind of strained neutrality.

'He thinks the man jumped into the water after getting rid of his clothes and all links to his previous existence. The post-mortem suggested a Mediterranean or Middle Eastern ethnicity. Minimal dental work. Poor nutrition.'

'DNA?' Warlow asks.

'Nothing on the database. And dental records sent to a variety of embassies including Greek, Turkish and all the Gulf states drew a blank.'

'Doesn't sound right. There are easier ways to top yourself. And clothes can float off if they're loose fitting.'

'DI Caldwell seems happy that it's a self-inflicted cause of death, given the lack of ID.' And there's something in the way her mouth tightens that tells Warlow that she isn't happy either. Yes, it's the simplest and tidiest answer. The quickest, too. But they both knew that you accepted 'simple' and 'tidy' only after eliminating the elaborate and complicated. But Warlow says nothing else because, from the way the little muscles at the side of Catrin's jaw is clenching and unclenching, she hasn't finished.

Warlow puts the sergeant at a little over thirty. The way she holds herself adds to her height. She takes no prisoners with the more boisterous young men with testosterone issues. He's delighted she's on the team. He's also seen her dab her eyes at the most poignant scenes of crime and believes that she trusts him.

It's a belief that's justified when she abruptly ends the taut silence that's grown between them. Though he's seen it coming. She's almost got the copper's deadpan look sorted out but not quite. And a dull anger is showing up in the narrowing of her eyes.

'I went to the post-mortem. The pathologist was chatty. Experienced, like you.'

'Old, you mean?'

Catrin lets out a tiny laugh that fades as soon as it forms. 'He was a locum who'd been involved with Yorkshire Police's task force investigating the death of the cockle pickers in Morecambe Bay in 2004.'

She doesn't need to elaborate. Warlow knows it well. All illegal, undocumented immigrants under the cosh of a gang master trafficker. A container had shipped them to Liverpool and hired them out like ponies through agents linked to the Triads.

In Yorkshire.

Even when the truth emerged, it seemed hardly plausible. It sounded fantastical, like the plot of some overblown novel. But the deaths of twenty-one people, mainly men in their twenties and thirties, drowned in the incoming tide, was no fiction. It became a national scandal.

'What are you saying, Sergeant?'

'Don't know, sir. It's just … I mean, all three of our counties in the patch have coastal borders. We're too far west and the waters are too treacherous for attempts at illegal crossings from desperate asylum seekers in Calais. They'd need to come all the way around the south coast for that. But Border Force make big drug seizures off the Welsh coast. There are loads of inlets and jetties. It's a smuggler's dream. And Ireland is not that far away. Only twenty-seven miles from the edge of the Llŷn Peninsula in the north to Wicklow Head.'

'You think there's more to it, then?' Warlow demands.

'DI Caldwell seems happy with it as it is.'

But you aren't. Nor would I be.

He doesn't say these words. He doesn't need to. It sounds like Caldwell has ignored the bigger picture and let the case lie. And so the corpse remains unidentified. Someone's son, brother, father, uncle, forever lost to those who cared. Warlow knows he would beaver away until he had some sort of answer. Caldwell had filed and forgotten.

Warlow sips his coffee. It's still hot but tastes of sod all.

Caldwell had done the last review on the Pickering case. The thought of him short-cutting his way through the unsolved murder makes his gut roll over. Warlow had maintained a professional relationship with the man on the job, but there has been no love lost between them and both men knew the score.

Catrin looks across at him, her expression softening. There are no more words about the floater or Caldwell. Instead, she says, 'It's good to have you back, sir.'

CHAPTER THIRTY-FIVE

CATRIN IS an excellent driver and she follows the sat nav instructions over the Cleddau Bridge to an Innovation Centre in Pembroke next to the estuary. The car park is virtually empty.

'It's quiet,' Warlow says.

'It's a Tuesday in winter.' Catrin slides the car into a spot and kills the engine.

Venture Pembroke, Morris's old employer, rent an office at the end of a line of office units next to a charter company. The two units next to that are empty.

As with most of these outdoor pursuits companies that totally depend on the weather, it's a small operation driven by someone who is mad for the open air but managed by someone who'd prefer a log fire and a good book. The Gamages fit the bill perfectly. Rob Gamage braves the sea and the elements, while his wife does the books.

Vikki Gamage is mid-forties, fit-looking in jeans and a fisherman's jumper. She has everything ready for them when they call. The office is small: two desks facing one another, with two PCs, a printer, filing cabinet and shelves with brochures for sending out to those few luddites who can't be bothered to access a website, Warlow guesses.

Vikki keeps excellent records.

'Yes, um, Neil Morris was in our employ in 2013.' She holds out a piece of paper that looks like an employment contract. Her husband, the outdoorsman, is sitting at the opposite desk. Wiry Rob Gamage shaves his head to avoid a comb-over, Warlow guesses. It's he who explains why they remember so well.

'It was the storms. Those specific dates might have been difficult to pin down had it not been for an Atlantic monster blowing for two days. It was petering out on the day you flagged up, but still too strong for us. Okay for a walk on the path, but too windy for coasteering.'

'Does that happen often?' Warlow's gaze sharpens.

'Not too often, but if the coastguard tells us to, we shut up shop.'

'So you sent Morris home?'

Gamage shakes his head with a little laugh. 'Not exactly. We sent him on an away day.'

'Away day?'

'Yes. An exploration day. Finding unknown places where we can access the coast in not too dangerous a fashion. No point him hanging around here since we had to cancel bookings.'

Catrin makes a note. 'So he was out and about. On the coastal path even?'

'Well, he would not have been on a boat, that's for certain.'

Warlow and Catrin exchange glances. Vikki Gamage misinterprets this as frustration. 'I'm sorry we can't be more specific. It doesn't look like we've been much help.'

Warlow grins. 'Oh, no. You've been very helpful indeed.'

They now know that if Morris had been alive to answer their question, he would have no alibi.

'And when he was on these away days, would he go prepared?' Warlow looks around at the sparse office.

Rob Gamage responds. 'If you mean, would he have had kit, then yes.'

'And what exactly does kit entail?' Richards asks.

Rob Gamage shrugs. 'The usual. Helmet, wetsuit, and since he was exploring, ropes.'

———

THEY HOLD a quick debrief when Warlow gets back to the Incident Room and Catrin tells the team about Morris's whereabouts on the day the Pickerings went missing.

When she's finished, Rhys looks worried. 'So you think the Pickerings might have stumbled on Morris and maybe Thomas that day?'

'Possibly. It's one theory. But it would be useful to know what they were up to.' Jess walks to the notice boards.

The one outstanding action yet to be completed is getting phone records for the two of them. Rhys has been trying all afternoon to get a hold of Mel Lewis to check on progress, only to be told Lewis is in court in Aberystwyth. The bane of not having enough officers to cover such a huge patch is that people are thinly spread with other ongoing cases.

Jess turns back to face the team. 'Any news on Kieron Thomas's death?'

Catrin shakes her head. 'It's DI Caldwell's case, ma'am.'

'We ought to get his thoughts. Both suspects dead within days. Does Caldwell think Thomas's death is suspicious?'

Catrin and Rhys exchange glances.

'Neither of you have asked?' Jess can't hide her annoyance.

'I'll see him,' says Warlow.

There's something in the way he says it that raises Jess's eyebrows. 'That's not a problem, is it?'

'No.'

But of course it is. Caldwell is the problem. At least he's a problem for Warlow. But he's here to do a job for the Buccaneer and Jess. Caldwell is merely a bump in the road. But the trouble with bumps is that you can't see how much damage they cause until you've run over the bastards.

'Good.' Jess glances at her watch. 'I'll give him a heads up. Tell him you're on the way.'

Warlow knows the A40 only too well. It's a pain. A rural artery furred up with tractors and road works. He can't remember more than a dozen occasions when he's been on it and some improvement or other has not been taking place. Some of the hills are three lane death traps where itchy drivers ignore white lines. There's been talk, over the years, of making the whole thing a dual carriageway. A fast continuation of the M4 from Cross Hands all the way to Fishguard for the ferry traffic. Warlow doubts it'll ever happen. The further west you go in Wales, the sparser the population. The easier to kick a political can down the road.

But it has its compensations, this journey. As he travels east, a vista of rolling knolls and hedged fields opens up to the north. Green pastures and farmland, the odd Iron Age fort, the blue Preseli hills in the distance. Great walking country. That brings Cadi to mind. He's left her at home and will need to go back lunchtime or soon after to let her out. But first, there's Caldwell.

Warlow parks at the force HQ in Llangunnor.

Pencadlys Yr Heddlu.

This is a Welsh speaking county and it's the Welsh

language that appears first on the sign in front of a sprawling red-brick complex surrounded by green fields. He's stopped and greeted by three people on his way to meet Caldwell. All three interactions involve a double-take and a surprised, 'I thought you'd finished' before a quick catch-up.

His key card has no credit here and so he's taken up to Caldwell's office by a secretary. He walks along quiet corridors. None of the frenetic energy that's so palpable in the Haverfordwest Incident Room here. He passes no one he knows. He's glad of that. Caldwell's office door is shut. The label is new. It reads: Acting DCI K Caldwell. The secretary knocks and waits before entering. It's a long five seconds before they hear, 'Come in.'

The secretary speaks in a hushed tone. 'Mr Warlow to see you, Chief Inspector.'

'Acting,' mutters Warlow. The secretary does a double-take. The 'Acting' DCI, if he hears, doesn't show it.

Caldwell's office is like the man. Organised, orderly and unadorned.

'Evan, take a seat.' Caldwell is a short-sleeved shirt guy. Always white with a plain tie knotted tight to the top button. The jacket of his grey suit is on a hanger behind the door. 'I've spoken with Jessica Allanby already. You're here about the Thomas case?'

Straight to the point avoiding all niceties. Caldwell hasn't changed a bit. But then glaciers hardly ever do.

Warlow nods. 'Then you'll know Dai Vetch and I went down to where Kieron Thomas's body was found. We wanted your thoughts on the matter.'

Caldwell sits forward, elbows on the desk. He has a saucer-shaped face, with a jutting chin and large poppy eyes behind his myopic glasses. 'Thomas was a dealer and a known user. Most of the upper torso and head severely burned but the lower limbs preserved. Toxicology showed alcohol and opiates, the latter at concentrations consistent with an overdose.'

'What about the fire?' Warlow keeps his tone level but he can feel the spring coiling inside him.

'He was a smoker. There was a can of lighter fluid. He was found in an area where addicts are known to self-administer.'

'But he was only half a mile from his grandmother's flat. Don't you find that odd?'

'Sometimes, as you well know, cravings can overtake reason.'

Thanks for the lecture, you … Warlow allows himself an inward growl but perseveres. He's not here for a fight. 'So, as far as you're concerned, you say he was trying to refuel his lighter and then what, exactly?'

Caldwell's smile is small but highly patronising. 'May have attempted refuelling his lighter in a drugged state. Attempted to and spilled some lighter fluid. He lights a cigarette and is too intoxicated to respond to being set alight. It's a viable scenario.'

'So out of it that all he can do is lie there and watch himself turn into Guy bloody Fawkes instead of getting up and running out of the building with his arse on fire screaming like a banshee, is that it?'

Caldwell offers nothing but a raised eyebrow blankness in return.

'Jesus Christ, man. What was he intoxicated with, a general sodding anaesthetic?'

KFC picks up a sheet of paper from his desk and scans it. 'Ketamine. He hit a vein while injecting. It's usually intramuscular, as you know. And you must know it is used sometimes as an anaesthetic.'

'Yes, I do. So according to you, he knocks himself out with this powerful drug and then, in a trance-like state decides to refuel his lighter. Have I got that right, Kelvin?'

'More or less.'

Warlow breathes in through his nose to compose himself, bites back the urge to yell into Caldwell's face and tries reason again. 'Vetch doesn't have Thomas down as a ketamine addict. He sold the stuff, yes, but cocaine was more his thing.'

'Perhaps he mixed and matched.'

Warlow searches in vain for any sign of humour and fails. Caldwell is a mannequin when it comes to emotions. 'What about his prior movements?'

'We have CCTV of him entering the King and Queen in Pembroke Dock at 1.30pm. He leaves at a little after 6pm.'

'Was he selling drugs?'

'He was of course known to the drug squad as a user and petty thief.'

'Have you traced the people he spoke to?'

At this Caldwell looks a tad uncomfortable. 'Not yet. The landlord of the King and Queen told us he spent most afternoons drinking with other people.'

'He used the pub as his sales office.'

Caldwell hesitates before answering but then smiles. It's the kind that never reaches his eyes. 'You already know that, Evan, since you tried to visit him there.'

'But you feel his death is not suspicious?' Warlow presses for an answer.

'If you're asking if I think it involved a third party, then there is no evidence to support that.' Caldwell sits back in his chair.

'You're right. Except for the fact that Thomas is linked to a dead girl in Swansea whose DNA they found at the Pickerings' murder site.'

Caldwell shrugs and tries to bat that inconvenient fact away. 'He also stored his dead grandmother in a freezer in her bedroom. But the post-mortem on her reveals no evidence of foul play. It seems she died of a stroke.'

Warlow snorts. 'That was just Thomas playing fast and loose with the pensions agency. I'm talking about his fondness for a hammer when he was playing the heavy.'

Caldwell puffs out his cheeks, drops his eyes and then looks back into Warlow's. 'I can see that requires some explanation. But these are tenuous links, Evan.'

Tenuous links are sometimes all there are in murders. Thin lines you reel in to find a big wriggling fish on the other end.

'If your team has a list of people from the pub, we'd like to have it.' Warlow flexes his fingers. They've been bunched into fists for the last two minutes and he needs to get some circulation back into them.

'Anything I can do to help.' Caldwell smiles. At least he does something with his mouth and lips, but his eyes remain completely cold still. 'And how is the return to work going?'

'Like I've never been away. How is Acting DCI working out for you?'

'More administration and supervision than I am used to, but I will adapt.'

I bet you will.

'And you're working with DI Allanby,' Caldwell adds. 'I expect she is glad to have your experience to hand?'

'She doesn't need me. She's managing fine on her own. I'm on board because of my knowledge of the case.'

Caldwell's mouth turns down at the edges and he nods sagely. 'You were thorough, though in my review I wondered about the logistics of the Pickerings ever leaving the path. I would have concentrated my search there instead of the ferry ports at Pembroke and Fishguard.'

You twat. State the bloody obvious why don't you.

The fact was that they'd had to consider all eventualities.

That somehow the Pickerings had left their car at Poppit Sands and then taken off. Either under their own free will for reasons unknown, or at the behest of someone else for all kinds of nefarious reasons. And the nearest places for dropping off the radar in another country were the ferry ports. But hearing Caldwell criticise him changes nothing other than making Warlow even more grateful that this is the only direct involvement with the case KFC is likely to have.

'Well you were right on that score,' Warlow says with a slight smile. The one he likes to think is wolfish. 'Did you go back and search the path as part of your review?'

'I saw no point. What evidence there might have been would've degraded—'

'It would have degraded within days. Another low came in the day after the Pickerings went missing. We had to abandon searching the path because the weather was atrocious.'

But Caldwell hasn't finished. 'It's a big area to search, I'll admit. Sergeant Lewis coordinated the physical review of the site. There was nothing new to add. He tells me you've already discussed that with him. Still, it can't be easy knowing you were so close to finding them on so many occasions. A matter of inches in reality.'

Warlow hopes there is nothing malicious in this. That it's Caldwell's thick-skinned, insensitive, dispassionate nature and nothing else.

'Frustrating, yes,' Warlow says, surprised by how low his voice has dropped. He stares at KFC with the same caring expression he uses for all the special ones. The thieves and rapists and things other dog owners have left uncollected in steaming piles on his walks with Cadi.

The Acting DCI puts his hands on the desk as if to push back. 'Let me get you some coffee while I organise that list. Shame you didn't have it when you visited the

King and Queen. It might have saved young DC Harries a nasty head injury.'

Warlow bristles. 'Come on Kelvin, spit it out.'

KFC shrugs. 'Okay. I've always found you headstrong when it came to the thrust of an investigation. And, after a such a long period of inactivity, it's fair to question whether your judgement might be a little … rusty?'

Warlow nods and smiles. Or at least bares his teeth in what barely passes as one. There's a pen on Caldwell's desk. He toys with picking it up and stabbing the bastard in his podgy hand with it. 'Okay, Kelvin. Your candid thoughts on my behaviour are, as always, unasked for and crass but freely given. Believe me, as welcome as your comments always are, we'll let others be the judge of that, eh?'

Caldwell frowns. It might be an act, but Warlow has seen it too many times to believe that it is. He doesn't do sarcasm. And the fact he can't see what he's just said as being in any way blundering speaks volumes for his emotional sensitivity, too. But this time, Warlow doesn't feel like playing.

'I'm simply being–'

'A twat. And you can't help that. Just like a rattler can't help being a snake. So why don't you get me that list and I'll be on my way, okay?'

Caldwell leaves the room, but not until logging out of his computer. Just as the book says you ought to.

He comes back a few minutes later and hands over a typed sheet. Warlow glances at the list of names and stands up. 'I'll get this back to Jess.'

On his way to the door, Caldwell fires off one last salvo. 'I could have emailed you this. Why did you come in person?'

'Because the SIO in a murder case asked me to,' says

Warlow. 'She thought it might be valuable. And I thought I might bump into some old friends.'

'Did you?'

'No. Just you. So, wrong on both counts. Still, you can't win them all.'

Caldwell's face hardens. 'There is nothing in the Thomas case that suggests anyone else's involvement. I can't change that.'

'No, but he's the second of two suspects to die. That should ring alarm bells.'

'It doesn't alter the facts. The crime scene is a classic case of drug induced accidental death.'

Warlow puts a hand to his ear and cocks his head. 'And yet I still hear those bells ringing.'

'Well I do not.'

'Then I suggest you hurry the fuck up and get your ears syringed, Kelvin.'

And for a moment, there is only one DCI and one DI in that room, despite what the label on Caldwell's door might say.

CHAPTER THIRTY-SIX

THE DRIVE back to Haverfordwest is uncomfortable. Same road, same scenery, same weather as when he'd driven down. But his mind is buzzing from the encounter.

Shame you didn't have it when you visited the King and Queen. It might have saved young DC Harries a nasty head injury.

Jesus H Christ. Even if he thought that of a fellow officer, he would never say it. But Caldwell is known for it. For speaking his mind. No, that isn't strictly true because that would make him a straight talker, something one might even admire. That isn't Caldwell. What he does is get everyone riled. Gets under your skin; like one of those burrowing worms that gives you a horrible disease.

He's certainly a worm alright. Hiding under a rock, wriggling out of the daylight.

But he's wrong about Kieron Thomas. His death is far too convenient. A ketamine overdose by inadvertent administration into a vein is entirely possible. But, though he dealt the stuff, Vetch was adamant that Ket did not partake of the Special K himself. And yes, some addicts get desperate. Knowing you were going back to a house containing your frozen grandmother's body was enough to make anyone crave distraction. But in a piss-stained old shed on the edge of a railway embankment?

It didn't add up.

None of it did.

Warlow is still trying to do the maths when he gets back to the office. Rhys intercepts him on the way in. He has some good news and some bad.

'Give me the good stuff first.'

'The search of Thirty-Three Cask Street came up with nothing useful.'

'Apart from the grandmother.'

'Apart from Doris Thomas, yes. Oh, and £1700 in cash. The rough estimate is that she's been dead for three months. Her pension is paid into her bank account directly. Withdrawals from said account have been continuing to last week.'

'As we thought,' Warlow says.

'But the drug squad also raided a second property in Milford, Thomas's girlfriend's place. They found a toolbox Thomas used to put together a TV cabinet to hold games and his fifty-five-inch flat screen. The hammer inside had suspicious markings around the head. It's with the forensic team now.'

'Good,' says Warlow. 'And the bad news?'

'Superintendent Buchannan asked me to send you straight up to him as soon as you arrived.'

Warlow nods. But Rhys hovers.

'And?' prompts the DCI.

'It's just … he didn't look thrilled, sir.'

They meet in the upstairs office away from the constant toing and froing of the Incident Room. Two old colleagues from the trenches up for a chat about how things are going.

'So,' Buchannan says, leaning sideways in his chair

with one long leg stretched out, 'what do you think of Jess?'

'Very competent. Doesn't let whatever happened before get in her way. She can run a team. Delegates well. She's doing fine. But then you're aware of all that.'

Buchannan drops his head. Warlow reads the signals. 'What's this about, Sion?'

Buchannan's eyes come up. 'Kelvin Caldwell's been on the blower. He isn't happy.'

'Tell me something we both don't know.'

'He resents the thought of you interfering in his investigation and badgering Mel Lewis.'

Warlow sighs inwardly and attempts a plastered-on smile. 'First, Kieron Thomas is not exclusively his case anymore. And as for Mel, he's a grown up. And he has pertinent information from the review of the Pickerings' case that Caldwell oversaw three years ago. I'd hardly call that badgering.'

'No.'

Warlow sits forward. 'Christ, Sion. My bet is that Thomas was drugged and then set alight. Caldwell is happy to go along with a lighter fuel accident. Still is. Tell me you're not suggesting we should accept that without looking at every angle?'

The Buccaneer shifts in his chair. 'In his defence, in the early stages of the investigation there were no grounds for the sort of suspicion–'

'Agreed.' Warlow's response is barely short of seething. 'But you still go looking. You still scratch the surface. Kelvin doesn't like scratched surfaces. He enjoys polishing them until he can see his smug face smirking back at him. But we all know what happens when you try polishing a turd. It smells bad and it isn't pretty.'

Buchannan sighs. 'He's written to the DCC. Questioning your suitability, competence and fitness for this role.'

Warlow's smile freezes on his lips when he hears fitness. 'What does he mean by that?'

'I don't think he means anyth–'

'Does he know?'

Buchannan frowns. 'About you? No, of course he doesn't.'

'I wouldn't put it past him.' And he wouldn't. Because Caldwell is a pain, a cold fish and a prat. But a methodical prat. And Warlow's retirement would have intrigued him. He'd have been the last person to shed a tear but seeing a DCI at the top of his game walk away from a job he was bloody good at would intrigue a bloke like Caldwell. And there'd be ways a very determined detective might dig. A glitch in the system, a colleague in HR – the type that gives you a funny handshake when handshakes were a thing. By rights HR should be none the wiser. But you never knew. Was there an errant email from the hospital on the system? A letter from Dr Emmerson that got misplaced? There should not be. He was careful. He's kept everything away from work. He doesn't even think he told Emmerson what he did.

'I'm aware you and Kelvin don't see eye to eye,' Buchannan says.

Warlow holds back the hysterical laugh with difficulty. 'You could say that.'

'But I'm still bewildered by that. Kelvin clears cases. He mentors. Takes the job seriously.'

All that was true. One hundred per cent true. But he was also a disapprover. Of detectives like Warlow who'd learned through experience. Warlow often wondered if it was a defence mechanism, maybe even a sign of insecurity from someone who'd come in through the accelerated appointment scheme and dropped from a great height into a world that could be full of cronies, macho posturing and long-standing professional friendships. But there'd been little or no resentment at Caldwell's appointment from the established workforce. They'd accepted him at face value. And his initial reluctance to get his hands dirty was understandable given his lack of street experience. But that reluctance never seemed to truly go away. Caldwell was a delegator par excellence. Maybe that came from his admin background in industry. But the rumour also began circulating that it came from a yellow streak a foot wide running down his back.

And none of that would have mattered because there was enough testosterone floating around a CID unit to make up for a lack in Caldwell. Big DSs and uniformed PCs more than willing to be the first in any confrontation. The trouble was Caldwell was indiscriminate in his disregard for the donkey work. And Warlow, relentless, someone who liked to get his hands dirty, paid the price for that disregard.

Sion Buchannan, newly promoted when Warlow decided to leave, knows why he left. It's their professional secret at Warlow's request. But he doesn't know all of it. He doesn't know how Caldwell fits into the picture. And even though he's asking, there'll be no explanation today.

'Does it really matter?' Warlow replies.

'No. And the DCC will tell Caldwell that we will take his concerns into consideration, but that the decision to involve you is mine. The way this case is playing out is more than enough justification.'

Warlow glowers at the superintendent. 'If it hadn't been for the fact he'd picked up the Thomas case I would have stayed well away.'

'Probably best. If you need to talk to him about anything, use Jess or Catrin.'

It's not exactly a bollocking, but Warlow takes the hint. 'With pleasure.'

Job done, Buchannan shifts gears. 'What do you make of this link to Thomas and Morris?'

'There'll be drugs involved somewhere.'

'Agreed. And how is the Pickerings' daughter taking it all?'

'Much as you'd expect if your missing parents have been murdered and stuffed into a pothole.' About as much fun as having a fingernail extracted, Warlow suspects. But deep down she's known this outcome was on the cards.

Buchannan exhales and massages the skin around his eyes. 'I'd like to get this one squared away, Evan.'

'You and me both, Sion.'

CHAPTER THIRTY-SEVEN

When he leaves Buchannan's office, Warlow does not go back to the Incident Room. Instead he heads for the loo, finds an empty cubicle and sits there with the door locked, inhaling the pungent aroma of urine and bleach. Since his mind is full of thoughts of Kelvin Caldwell, it's a highly appropriate aroma. It's a male toilet, but it still amazes him how many of his colleagues seem incapable of lifting a toilet seat before they spray the porcelain.

Buchannan's question about his dislike for Caldwell had been direct. He probably deserved an answer. Yet it's one that Warlow isn't particularly proud of because he does his best every day to bury that resentment. Dig a big hole, throw the grudge in and cover it all back up.

And every day it crawls back out again, barely alive and rotten to the core.

He takes his phone out and scrolls to his calendar. He has an appointment at the hospital in four weeks. They're six monthly now. But it's with the same doctor that broke the news to him that first time.

Dr Emmerson.

There was one hundred per cent eye contact when she

explained it all to him and he appreciated that. He remembers, too, the way his head filled with a buzzing noise and the world went out of focus. But he'd squeezed his eyes shut and said nothing. Letting it sink in. Eventually he'd asked, 'Does anyone else need to know? My employer?'

'No. It's no one's business but yours.'

'Fine,' he'd said. 'We'll keep it like that.'

'I'm not sure how wise that is. It's a lot to carry alone.'

'I'll manage.'

And so he had. He'd told no one except for Sion Buchannan. So taking a rebuke, no matter how small it was, from him, holds a certain gravitas. Shared knowledge that adds extra weight. But worse is knowing that Caldwell may be right. He should never have let Rhys get into that situation. Should never have allowed Kieron Thomas to clock him. Perhaps he was off his game. Perhaps the boots he'd once hung up would never fit quite as well ever again.

He heads back to the Incident Room to pick up his coat. There is no sign of Jess and Catrin, nor Mel Lewis, but he bumps into Rhys on his way from the kitchenette with a mug of tea. There must be something in Warlow's expression, a shadow of his dark introspection in the loo because it triggers a response.

'You alright, sir?'

'I'm fine.'

'I can get you a cup of tea if you like?'

Tempting though it is, Warlow declines the offer. 'No, I need to get home. Feed the dog.'

Rhys breaks into a grin. 'What do you have?'

'A black lab.'

'My mum has a Dachshund. Obsessed with tennis balls, he is. Honestly, show him a tennis ball and he'll play for hours on his own.'

Warlow slides on his coat. 'No sign of Mel Lewis yet?'

'Nah. He'll be in tomorrow I daresay. He's a busy man.'

'Like all of us,' Warlow tells him.

Rhys's gaze darts to the little pile of paperwork on his own desk. 'But then, as my gran used to say, Dyfal donc …'

Warlow knows the saying. Dyfal donc a dyr y garreg. Keep tapping and the stone will eventually break. A proverb about the merits of perseverance. A corner of his mouth sneaks up in a smile as he regards Rhys, the philosopher, in a new light. 'There's hope for you yet, DC Harries.'

There's a pause. Rhys doesn't yield to many silences and so Warlow lets this one linger. It takes only ten seconds for it to end as the DC drops his voice into a whisper. 'I know this case is unusual, sir. Mental to be honest. But DS Mertens says I won't see another one like it. Is that true?'

'Probably.' Warlow fishes out his car keys, hoping that Rhys will take the hint.

The DC shakes his head. 'I feel sorry for Mrs Ogilvie. She must have suspected they were dead though, right?'

'Until it's confirmed, there's always a spark of hope.'

'So weird though. I read the newspaper reports from the files. I mean seagull attacks, and serial killers. The Follower?' He tuts. 'All that rubbish must have been horrible for her.'

Warlow doesn't argue. 'It was.'

'And that Engine House place. Funny that the new owners and the Pickerings were so interested in it. I suppose if you live across the way from a spooky old building you'd want to know all about it in case something goes bump in the night.'

'Why? It's an old industrial ruin that's all. No fables attached. It's weird-free.'

A puzzling look crosses Rhys's face as he ponders Warlow's attempt at a pun. But he can't quite put it together and carries on regardless. 'Mrs Ramsden was asking about it. I couldn't answer her questions so I passed them on. Oh, and I think I've found an address for Kieron Thomas for when the attack took place. The day the Pickerings went missing, I mean.'

Warlow nods. The kid is enthusiastic and diligent. 'Excellent work, Rhys. Find out if he was living there alone. If he wasn't, we should try to trace whoever he lived with.'

'I will, sir.'

Warlow tosses his car keys up and catches them. At last, Rhys takes the hint and goes back to his desk. Warlow, his mind still mulling over the 'talk' with Sion Buchannan and the rattling skeletons it has uncovered heads home to feed Cadi, trying to ignore the little itch that has started bothering him about this case. It's barely there, but experience had taught him to ignore these things at his peril.

Warlow breaks most of the rules he's set for himself that night. He calls in for fish and chips at a place he's never been to before and leaves two thirds of the greasy, disappointing mess on his plate. Then he opens a new bottle of red and watches three hours of TV that pours in through his eyes and ears but makes no connection at all with his preoccupied brain.

He sits and re-runs what Sion Buchannan said. Caldwell's opinion of him – which he would normally brush off – stings like a mosquito bite. Enough to wonder if it's exactly what others might think too. He's been walking around, trying not to tread on toes, still not sure of how he'll best fit in to an organisation he's already said his goodbyes to. Trying to be a part of a team. But it's not his team. That should not be a problem. Not for him because he knows what hubris means, and he's pretty sure he's avoided it so far. Unlike Caldwell, who has a reputation as a quick closer of cases to protect.

Warlow swears the man's hair seems to get darker every time he sees him. Probably gets Just for Men delivered by the crate load.

Despising Caldwell doesn't shake the feeling Warlow has that he's a fish out of water in the Incident Room though. But worse is the knowledge that by putting himself back in the thick of it, he's asking for trouble. That he's a danger to others.

He goes out to the new extension, to the photograph he's hung behind the door. It's there for him to look at, not a trophy for others. Three figures in a harbour scene, a little fishing boat behind, two grown men and a boy of seventeen. The boy is him, the snap taken after a fishing trip in 1985. The resemblance between the men is obvious. Rhodri Warlow, Evan's father, the older of the two brothers stands one side, Uncle Gron, almost nine years younger than his brother, stands on the other. Both men have an arm across the young Evan's shoulder. Everyone is grinning. Sun-bronzed and happy.

Warlow remembers the day. They caught mackerel and sea bass. Told jokes, listened to Gron's stories, most of which were inappropriate, all of which were irreverent. That same summer Gron bought the shepherd's hut while on holiday from his job in the Nigerian oil fields.

He returned from that job in January of the following year with a nagging chest infection. Eight months later he was dead. He spent the last five months in a bed in the Warlow family home. A three-up three-down ex council house at the top end of a coal-scarred valley.

At first the doctors had no idea what was wrong with him. And Warlow spent many a wet weekend listening to his uncle's adventures and planning what they might do when he got better. But that never happened.

Eventually, they found the problem. A virus. Probably

caught on one of his uncle's wild nights out in Nigeria. A virus with no cure and a devastating syndrome.

No one knew much about AIDS then. But they would soon. Not the 'gay virus' as some had termed it. But one that was ripping through Africa's sex workers paying no heed to orientation. Ironic to think that he has profited from that virus. That he's living in the house that was his uncle's dream. He shakes his head and does his best to bury these destructive thoughts.

But Caldwell's accusation of him being a liability keeps resurfacing. The implication that he's past it. That his judgement is off. Then he realises he's more concerned by what Jess and Catrin and the impressionable Rhys Harries might say. And it matters to him because they've let him in. They've trusted him. But he hasn't been completely honest with them.

'What a mess, eh Cadi?'

He folds and unfolds the dog's ear with his fingers. She sits at the side of his chair, enjoying the fondle, while Warlow takes another sip of vino siciliano. The trouble is that people believe in him. What a curse that is. Yet, it's one he's taken on willingly. Didn't he say in the interview room that very morning to Tanya Ogilvie that he'd be in touch if they found out anything solid?

He'd be in touch.

Well, perhaps someone else could do that. He couldn't find her parents when they went missing. Making empty promises about finding out why two pieces of dirt like Thomas and Morris beat them to death and hid the bodies is just as empty. He might have been the man to do it seven years ago, but now he's not so sure.

He toys with ringing Jess there and then. He's not too bothered about Buchannan because he knows the score. But Jess doesn't know anything about his demons. About him. He dares not wonder what Molly might say.

'Cadi's daddy the saddy,' or something along those lines, he suspects. Not that it's a big deal, he's only met the kid twice. But he likes her. And he likes Jess. Helping them both is a pleasure, but if he cuts the professional cord regarding the investigation, maintaining a unique relationship might seem a little odd.

A little desperate.

No, Jess deserves to be told face to face. Not the whole truth, but enough for her to realise that getting embroiled in the case isn't working out for him. Thanks but no thanks. I've given it a go, and it isn't for me.

All the doubts he's shrink-wrapped into little pocket-sized packages and squeezed into a locked drawer in his head now spring open and expand. Like a trick foam snake darting out of a fake can of crisps. Great fun for everyone except the poor bugger terrified of snakes. And his thoughts are a nest of vipers once more writhing and hissing in front of him.

What if he gets injured somehow? The job will bring him into contact with violence. Goes with the territory, what if he falls, or gets stabbed? What then?

He squeezes his eyes shut. These last few days have been fulfilling. He's enjoyed them more than he thought he ever would. And if he gives it all up again, then what?

It'll be back to Plan B. Walks with Cadi. Long evenings alone. Maybe not see anyone for weeks on end now that the builders have gone.

Perhaps he should take Mel Lewis up on his sailing offer again. Start crewing on his new boat. He might find some sea legs, eventually. He snorts. No he won't. He's a landlubber. At sea he's a serial vomiter.

All that's left are solitary pursuits. And at least this whole episode has made him dig out old notes and relive his past. There's enough there to sit down with his laptop and start scribbling. He's even played with a title. *The Bodies Under the Path.*

Cringe making. But not after three glasses of red.

He could self-publish. Memoirs of a has-been.

At eleven, he turns off the TV, settles Cadi with a night-time biscuit and heads to bed, feeling crappy for knowing what he is going to do the next day.

CHAPTER THIRTY-EIGHT

Marcus is in hospital for two days. They put a pin and plate in his lower leg. On the third day, Izzy takes him home to Limehouse Cottage.

'Like Lazarus,' Marcus says with a forced grin.

Izzy has a supporting hand under his elbow. 'That was the fourth day.'

'So picky,' Marcus says, only it comes out as a kind of groan as he hobbles to the car. It's more a swing and hop since he must not bear weight for several weeks.

She's set up a bed in his study on the ground floor. He'll still have to go upstairs to shower – but that's a long way off. Not until the plaster comes off. In the meantime he'll have to do the best he can with the downstairs sink and loo. Marcus is on pain killers and that means he shouldn't drink.

They discuss it. He agrees. The good news is that in his current state, there'll be no way of hiding anything. She sits with him for the first few hours, but then he tells her there's no need. He's happy with Sky Sports and Netflix boxsets.

The scaffolders come and scratch their heads. They've

never seen or heard of anything like it. The foreman visits Marcus and brings him a bottle of whisky.

Nice of them.

Izzy puts it upstairs. At the back of her shoe cupboard.

The foreman's men dismantle the Spaceship and put a much smaller, tighter framework around the skeleton of the cabin, anchor the foot plates with big bags of sand, and say that Marcus and Izzy can keep the scaffolding for as long as it takes for no charge.

Izzy doesn't like to leave Marcus for too long. But she has to make a run to Tesco in Cardigan the next day and slips to a bakery that doubles as a café. Their sourdough is to die for. But she's also arranged to meet Angharad for a quick coffee. Gwraidd, meaning root, is modern and spacious in a souped-up ex-car showroom unit with enormous windows. They bake everything from scratch and source local produce. It's the sort of place Izzy's London friends would swoon over.

Angharad waves to her as soon as she walks through the door. Izzy mouths 'want something?' and gets a shake of the head in reply. She picks up an oat milk cappuccino and joins her friend, noting the crumb-dusted plate on the table.

Angharad holds both hands up admitting guilt. 'Doughnut. Two actually. I can't resist them when I come here.'

'You've left some crumbs.'

'They are for picking at while I sip my Americano.' Angharad demonstrates with the press of an index finger. 'How are you? How's the patient?'

Izzy sighs. 'We're both fine. Lucky escape though.'

'Sounds horrible. What the hell happened?'

It's all the invite Izzy needs to recount the story. The high wind. The fractured tibia and fibula that needs a pin and plate. Marcus's recovery nest in the lounge. She finishes up with a trite, 'but it could have been so much worse.'

Angharad's face is a picture of concern. 'And how are you holding up?'

'Fine. I'm ... we're fine.'

Angharad nods, waits a beat. 'The offer still stands, you know that?'

'Offer?'

'To come and visit us. Lena and me. Have you had any more connection?'

Izzy has to think. Connection? 'You mean my food-accepting visitor?'

'Yes.'

'I haven't even thought about it. Since Marcus's accident it's ... I haven't thought about it.'

Angharad shoots a hand out to grab Izzy's arm. 'But you should. Think about it I mean.'

'In what way?'

'It's an omen.'

Once more she feels she ought to laugh. But Angharad's earnestness dispels that and it only takes a second for meaning to solidify. Does she mean foretelling disaster? She knows the Follower is depicted as a harbinger of change. And, she supposes, Marcus's accident has been a pretty big change.

Yes, it has. And it would be an omen if the Follower was real. Which it isn't, Izzy. How can it be?

She heeds the voice of reason that forces out a stifled guffaw. 'Oh, I don't know about that.'

Angharad keeps going, head down in a persistent whisper. 'All I'm saying is that there are more things in heaven and earth ...'

She nods. Her dad used to add the next line. Or rather complete the line and add the next sentence: '... Horatio, than are dreamt of in your philosophy.' Bit of a pedant is Izzy's dad.

But she doesn't want to fall out with Angharad. So she steers the subject back to the Hall and the fact that she missed the last two days of the exhibition. Angharad has some gossip about the whining landscape painter and the next ten minutes is amiable enough. But twenty minutes after arriving, Izzy makes her excuses, using Marcus unashamedly.

Angharad nods. 'Is he being the helpless male?'

Izzy spits out a laugh. 'He can't walk yet, so I am fetching and carrying. But it's a genuine need.'

'Send him my love,' Angharad says.

She's never met Marcus, but the sentiment is heartfelt.

CHAPTER THIRTY-NINE

NEXT MORNING WARLOW is up early and out with Cadi before the sun is up. But he takes a longer walk than usual. He's texted Jess and explained that he's going to miss the briefing. This he must do one to one.

Warlow showers and breakfasts and arrives in Haverfordwest mid-morning. The Incident Room is busy. Hardly surprising. More people to look into Kieron Thomas's and Neil Morris's contacts and acquaintances, more information coming in. Warlow speaks to an indexer and asks if she's seen Jess.

'In a meeting.' She nods towards the SIO office.

He can wait. He wanders to the desk at the back and a vacant desktop. He logs on and checks his emails. Nothing inspiring. Despite Catrin's reassurances, HR want him to come and sign some sort of formal contract. There's mandatory training that needs to be done online, too. He closes them all down. None of that will be necessary.

He notices now that three of the boxes of original files and papers from the Pickerings' misper case are back. He opens the lid of box three. Inside, the papers are stacked neatly, attached together by little paper clips, tidily confined to plastic folders. This is the way they should have been when they came from storage. The way he thinks that Caldwell would have wanted to leave them. Tight-arsed control freak that he is.

Perhaps their disarray is all down to those pesky data handlers tasked with making everything electronic. Warlow ponders this for a while as he waits for Jess to become free.

There's a new face on the desk next to his. A round-faced woman with the name Bethan Carter on her lanyard. Warlow leans over.

'Has Mel Lewis been in today?'

'Uh, no. Someone said he'd phoned in sick.'

'Ah.' He nods a thank you. At the top end of the room, both Rhys and Catrin have entered. Warlow intuits that perhaps they were a part of the meeting and their appearance signals its end. Worth a shout, he thinks.

Jess is in the office when he knocks. She looks busy but lights up when she sees him.

'Oh good, you're here. I've got the post-mortem back from Morris. Definitely strangulation. But bruises on his arms might indicate someone holding him—'

He holds up a hand to stop her. 'Jess, we need to talk.'

'A shut door talk?'

'Yep.' Warlow closes the door behind him and turns to address her earnestly. 'You're a good detective, Jess.'

'This already sounds like a breakup conversation.' She laughs, frowning.

'What is there to break up? I haven't done much.'

Jess sits back in her chair and fiddles with a pen. 'This isn't about Caldwell's petty complaint, is it?'

'He's got a point.'

'He's got piece of red tape stuck up his arse is the point.'

Warlow sighs. 'As you know, I said I'd give it a go here—'

Jess pushes forward so her hands are on the desk, the

pen still a prop. 'And we both know you're still at the top of your game. We probably would have got to Kieron Thomas at some point, but you got us there in half the time. Because you knew where to look.'

Warlow shakes his head. 'But I looked too bloody late.'

Jess isn't having any of it. 'Someone didn't want him found, Evan.'

'Look, it's not just Caldwell.'

Jess puts the pen down and folds her arms. 'Then what is it? Don't you like the team?'

'This is not about you or Rhys, or Catrin, or Sion Buchannan. This is about me.' He gazes directly into Jess's grey eyes. If he was hoping for sympathy, there is none in her expression. Instead, there's a dull annoyance.

She holds up a finger and tilts her chin up. 'So, let me get this straight. You burned out. You left the job early because you lost your mojo as Molly would say. And now you've seen your arse because you still haven't found it.'

'Seen my arse?'

'Mithered. Annoyed. Have I got that about right?'

Warlow shrugs. She isn't going to make this easy. But loss of mojo is as good a lie as any. 'Yeah. Something like that.'

Jess's expression hardens. 'Crap, Evan. It's something else, I know it is. And it's none of my business, I know that too. But it's week two of a complex investigation. You want to quit? Fine. But give us until the end of the week. Let me handle Caldwell.'

Warlow puffs out his cheeks.

Jess persists. 'You know this case better than anyone else. And I don't buy the mojo malarkey. I've watched you helping Catrin and involving Rhys and I'm grateful for you helping me. I know you're good at this. So whatever's drilling into you, it's none of my business. But end of the week is surely not going to make much difference.'

Warlow wants to say no. He should just get up and walk out. It would be the best thing to do.

'Please?' Jess asks, slitting her eyes. 'I mean, what are you rushing home to?'

Warlow blinks at her. It's harsh, but true. Of course it's true. Being here makes him feel alive. And alone in the cottage all he has are Cadi, his thoughts and his fears. And they are a slow poison eating into his heart and his head.

Despite himself and all the justifications he's layered on for walking away, now that he's sitting in front of Jess, faced with the reality of what he's contemplating, he can't let her down.

He nods. 'Two days then.'

She holds his gaze until she finally nods.

Warlow picks up where they left off. 'You were talking about Morris?'

Jess inhales deeply and then lets it out quickly. 'There were bruises on his upper arms.'

'Was he held down?'

'Possibly. But it's not enough.'

'And no one is saying anything?'

'Swansea's like any other nick. You keep your mouth shut if you want to survive.'

Warlow nods.

Jess unfolds her arms and leans forward, all business again. 'Catrin's off out interviewing an ex-partner of Thomas's. Rhys is chasing up phone records for Thomas and Morris. Both recent and around the time of the Pickerings' disappearance.'

Warlow's surprised. This should have been sorted by now. 'What's Mel been doing?'

Jess does a mini eye-roll. A pared-down version of an expression he's seen Molly already do half a dozen times. 'Good question. Busy, I expect. Back in court today, I heard.'

Warlow frowns. Phone records shouldn't take this long. All the major carriers have dedicated personnel whose job it is to respond to police requests.

'Let me do some badgering. See if I can rattle some cages.'

'Thanks.' Jess's smile reaches her eyes. 'I appreciate this, Evan. We all do.'

If anything, her words make him feel even worse.

Warlow leaves Jess to it. Deputy SIO comes with a ton of paperwork and she looked busy.

Instead, he goes in search of Rhys. Something about the phone records is niggling him. And it adds to the little itch that the previous night's conversation with the DC had triggered. He's been so preoccupied with his angst that he'd forgotten about it until now. It'll do no harm to scratch it. He crosses the Incident Room to where Rhys is staring at a screen.

'How far did Mel get on with the phone record request?' he asks.

Rhys swivels in his chair and pushes a half-empty packet of crisps to the edge of his desk. He swallows quickly. 'Uh, yeah, that's the weird thing. It's Vodafone for Thomas and EE for Morris. I've rung them again and they say they've received no request from us. I've given them all the details again. Dates and such.'

'Good.' Warlow sits on the edge of the desk. 'Last night, as I was leaving, you mentioned something about the Engine House.'

'Did I?' Rhys's eyes go wide as he tries to remember. 'Oh yeah, I said it was a weird coincidence that both sets of owners of Limehouse Cottage were so interested. The Pickerings first and then Ms Ramsden phoned to ask about it.'

Warlow feels a little tingle in his scalp. 'What did she ask?'

Rhys shrugs. 'She was doing some research for a story, I think. She said she'd like to pick someone's brains.'

'What did you tell her?'

'I didn't. I left a note for someone else.'

'Who?'

'Sergeant Lewis. He knows all about the Engine House. I reckoned he'd be able to answer all her questions.'

Warlow pushes off the desk, mind racing. 'Okay. Good. Chase those records.'

He goes back to his desk and the boxes of old files. He sits and stares at them, thinking, his antennae twitching.

He's given in to Jess but at least he's set out his stall. That could explain his restlessness. Yet, underneath there's something else. It's an unpleasant feeling. Like the one you get when you're about to board a plane and you just aren't sure you locked the car. Which is now at the mercy of whatever chancer walks past in the gigantic sodding multi-storey carpark. It's a vague and unsettling niggle. Familiar because he's felt it before on cases. When he's near to understanding something but hasn't quite got all the ducks in a row.

But he knows what to do. He jiggles the mouse and the screen comes back to life. The trick, in his experience, is to not overthink things. To let his thoughts run with all the brakes off.

The first thing he does is pull up crown court hearings for yesterday afternoon in Swansea. Three courts were sitting. Three trials. Warlow scans the brief details and learns what he needs to know in seconds. There are no crown courts in the Dyfed-Powys patch anymore. Everything takes place in Swansea and it's a court that caters for a big swathe of South Wales Police's area too. There are other courts. Magistrates sit in Aberystwyth and Llanelli. But on the whole they don't require a police presence for evidence. Whereas anything involving a jury, as in Swansea, would.

But every case heard yesterday came from the South Wales Police's patch. An aggravated assault in Neath. A potential murder in Swansea. A big drug operation in Port Talbot.

Warlow glances at the misper boxes again, his gut twisting, thoughts narrowing down to a focus. He wishes he didn't have this feeling, but it's there. A little fire that either needs to be fed or put out.

Checking on the Swansea courts has fanned the embers.

He searches for Kieron Thomas's arrest records. It's long and depressing. Thomas was a serial offender. He'd been in prison more than once. But Warlow isn't interested in the offences he was done for. He's more interested in the one he got away with.

He texts Vetch, half hoping the drug squad officer will not remember the name he's after and that all this will fizzle out. But Vetch texts back within two minutes with that name. Huw Ibbotson. The chap that Thomas once threatened with a hammer.

Warlow finds what he's looking for by cross-referencing the victim's name. The police were called to an altercation. Both men arrested. Ibbotson ended up in hospital for stitches, Thomas in custody. The latter, in his statement, said that he was on the way to help Ibbotson put up some shelves.

Warlow re-reads the statement. It's a first. He's never heard of GBH being passed off as a DIY accident before.

The subtext of this story is that Ibbotson, too, has an arrest record. Possession and burglary. But the notes show he was likely selling on. Much like Kelly Scott had been doing. Something Kieron Thomas frowned upon. Ibbotson's initial statement to the first on scene officers is that

Thomas was trying to kill him and hit him with a hammer. But when he gets out of hospital, he changes his mind. His new statement suggests a tit-for-tat fight. He does not want to press charges. There's still possession of a deadly weapon facing Kieron Thomas, but then Ibbotson says that Thomas had a hammer because he was going to help him put up some shelves.

Pity the poor shelves.

It sounds likely that Ibbotson had time to reflect while in hospital awaiting treatment. Time to get real. Warlow has seen it all before. It doesn't surprise him. But that isn't what he's after here. What he wants to know is who brought him in from the hospital to the station to make a statement.

When he finds out, his gut twists a little more.

CHAPTER FORTY

Izzy's brought soup with crusty sourdough rolls fresh from Gwraidd for lunch. Marcus falls asleep on the settee afterwards. It's been four days since the accident and he's still on pain killers. They work well enough, but his nights are restless.

'This plaster is like trying to turn over a log,' he explains when she asks. 'Plus it takes ten minutes to go to the loo.'

'I could give you a bottle.'

His eyebrows go up.

'One with a really wide neck,' she teases.

'Don't make me laugh, Izzy. That's cruel.'

Izzy washes up the lunch plates and wanders into her workroom with a chai latte tea. It's the first time she's been in since the Spaceship blew over. What with visiting Marcus in hospital and then nursing him at home, she hasn't found the time. Hasn't even looked at the photos of the Engine House she took that day.

But now she fires up her laptop, opens the photo app and studies the snaps that her iPhone has already sent to her cloud storage and linked to her other devices. Since talking to Angharad, there's been something she's wanted to check.

She pulls up the photographs – she managed only four before that terrible sound of the scaffolding tipping reached her – and enlarges them. She's looking for whatever fluttered near the base of the entrance to the building that day.

She finds it quickly, zooms in and sees that it's a plastic bag. The thin, candy-striped insubstantial type that the local garage has. The type she stuffs in a drawer, meaning to take some with her next time she goes so that she doesn't have to accept yet another from the sales assistant. She wants to do her bit for the planet. She forgets more times than she remembers.

But of late she's found some use for them. They came in handy when she'd left food out near the fencepost. Offerings for which she'd received shells as payment.

They're common, these bags.

It's too much of a coincidence for Izzy. Surely this must be the bag she'd left out for the Follower?

But why would a mythological entity need food, Izzy?

Perhaps it's accepting her offerings as a token of belief, duh.

She laughs at herself and holds the thought up to look at it a different way.

A mythological entity doesn't need food. But a living one does. But what sort of a living being would hide out in an abandoned Engine House?

And what harm would it do to inspect?

Waifs and strays, Izzy. Waifs and strays. The carping comment in her head comes in Marcus's voice.

She looks again at the text she's received that morning and the offer it contains. One that she hasn't hesitated to take up.

When another text comes through advising her that

her visitor has arrived, rather than wake Marcus, Izzy writes him an old-fashioned note and leaves it on his coffee cup: 'Out exploring the Engine House with guide. Bizzy + Izzy! Text if need anything urgent.'

The walk is unfinished business and so she dresses just as she did before for her expedition across the ravine. It's mid-afternoon, plenty of light for the quick trip over and back. There's still a stiffish breeze but it's dry and nowhere near as blustery as last time. She looks in on Marcus just before she leaves. Monty gives her a quizzical tilt of his head.

'You stay here, boy,' she whispers, turns and lets herself out of the back door to join the man waiting for her at the end of the garden.

CHAPTER FORTY-ONE

THERE IS one more call Warlow needs to make. To one of the gang that he meets up with for international matches in the pub. Barry Roberts runs a boatyard in Neyland. He's a man of the sea. A man who knows all there is to know about the buying and selling of yachts in the area. Their conversation is short and sharp. Full of banter to start with but Warlow steers it around quickly enough. He chats about the forthcoming regatta. Roberts is happy to oblige. After all, he's on a committee. Warlow listens but takes no notes and turns the conversation casually around to the familiar. To shared acquaintances and friends. He knows how to do so subtly, hiding what he wants to know in a partial truth.

The regatta he could not care less about.

It's the mutual friends he's after.

When he gets off the phone, Warlow doesn't move, letting his conclusions slosh around in his brain until the murky waters settle. He sits with his elbows on the table, head down with his thumbs massaging the inner ends of both his eyebrows, eyes closed. A couple of people glance his way. He might be praying. He might be feeling unwell.

In truth, it's a bit of both.

Finally, when he's teased apart his thinking, mentally argued against his reasoning and still can find no other explanation, he lifts his head and whispers one word to himself. 'Shit.'

His late morning efforts have concertinaed time and lunch has come and gone. But he isn't hungry. He finds Rhys and asks after Jess. She's in with Buchannan. He reaches for his mobile and texts her. Upper case all the way.

WARLOW: IMPERATIVE YOU MAKE YOUR EXCUSES
AND MEET ME IN THE OFFICE

Two SECONDS later he gets a reply. A single thumbs up.

Warlow waits in the SIO office. Jess arrives five minutes later.

She's grinning. 'Imperative? That's a big word, Evan. Why the cloak and dagger?'

Warlow doesn't smile. 'Have a seat. Close the door.'

Jess's eyebrows go up, but she does both. 'Getting to be a habit,' she mutters.

Warlow doesn't wait for the door to shut. 'Who brought Mel Lewis in on the case?'

Jess tilts her head in thought. 'I think he contacted Sion. He volunteered because he'd done the last Pickerings' case review. Had history with it.'

'So before I was on board?'

'Yes. What's going on, Evan?'

'Mel's a busy boy. Tail end of Op Wonderland. Neck deep in Operation Compass, too.' Another big residential care home investigation had resulted in a region wide operation into a chain of Nursing Homes owned by the same company. And for company read money grabbing shyster. Warlow had seen some reports. It made for grim reading.

'He's putting in the miles between here and Carmarthen.' Jess nods in agreement. 'And the court cases in Swansea.'

Warlow sits. He's calm despite the pulse pounding in his head. 'Yeah, the court cases. I checked. No cases from our patch were heard in Crown Court yesterday.'

Jess's confusion is evident.

Warlow presses on. 'What if we've got this all wrong? What if the Pickerings weren't in the wrong place at the wrong time. But the right place at exactly the right time.'

Jess blinks. 'I'm listening.'

'Mel wasn't with me on the Pickerings' case but we go back years. How well do you know him?'

'I don't. I've been here six months and worked with him only on this.'

Warlow summarises. 'Mel has two ex-wives, four kids and a couple of grandchildren. He'll be working until he's seventy. We drink together occasionally. But he's broke. Always has been.'

'Not the only copper—'

'Hear me out. Kieron Thomas dies the day after the Pickerings are found. Morris kills himself – supposedly – the night before we go to see him. It's possible he did that to escape retribution. But there is another possibility. If they were both involved in killing the Pickerings, then the discovery of the bodies would not come as a big surprise to them. A shock, yes. But a surprise, no, since they put them there. But what if someone had paid them to do a job? Someone who assumed that they'd done it properly and got rid of the bodies, not hidden them. Those employers would not be thrilled.'

'So you're saying that Thomas was silenced before he could speak to us?'

'Thomas and Morris both.'

Jess spots the flaw in Warlow's argument and smiles. 'Ah, but no one knew we were on to Morris.'

'Not true. No one outside this Incident Room.'

Jess stares at Warlow, a smile trying to fight through her confusion. Trying and faltering. 'Oh, come on, Evan.'

'Hear me out. When we got the misper files back they were in a state of disarray. Mel told me he thought it was the data transfer firm that left them that way. But these people were looking for a contract. They'd have been squeaky clean. It was in their interest to put all the files and notes back properly.'

Jess stares back at Warlow. He sees the flicker of suspicion in her eyes, but he carries on. 'I hate saying this, but the one person to have access to those boxes of files before I got here was Mel.'

'Are you saying he deliberately messed them up? Why would he do that?'

'Rhys hasn't told you because he's a good kid and doesn't want to get a gnarly old sergeant into trouble. But when I spoke to him three hours ago, he told me Mel hadn't contacted the providers for the Thomas and Morris phone records.'

Jess's face fills with dawning horror.

Warlow has to see this through, though the words that come out of his mouth taste as sour as vomit on his tongue. 'I don't know where Mel was yesterday, but he was not in Swansea Crown Court. And he's not there today because no scheduled cases there involve him. And when Thomas was arrested for possession of a deadly weapon – namely a hammer – eight years ago, the victim withdrew the complaint. Mel was the one who brought that victim in for his statement. And Mel was in the Incident Room when you told us you were going to see Morris in Swansea nick.'

'But so were a dozen other people.' Jess's objection is vehement, but it sounds hollow to both of them.

'Agreed. But I've just found out that Mel is also the new co-owner of a forty foot Beneteau yacht worth 50k. Recently bought. When I say co-owner, I mean he bought a seventy-five per cent share. My guess is he brought the other guy in to allay suspicion. That's over thirty-five grand. A lot of cash for a non-saver like Mel. No way would he have had that kind of cash in his piggy bank.'

'Why would Mel want the Pickerings dead?' Jess speaks in an almost whisper.

'He didn't. But whoever pays him did.'

Jess's mouth is open. She shuts it now. 'I'm struggling with this, Evan.'

Warlow sees she needs more convincing. 'What if the answer has to do with where the Pickerings lived rather than where they ended up on the path?'

'You searched the house and the grounds.'

'POLSA did. Found nothing.' He remembers it all like yesterday. 'The inlet, the abandoned Engine House, every sodding shell and pebble. And the Gowers have fenced off the place to keep it safe since then. But Rhys told me that Izzy Ramsden was interested in the old Engine House. And he passed that message on to Mel as someone who might answer her queries. I haven't seen him since.'

Jess gets up and leaves the room. Warlow sits, wondering if she's gone to call for an ambulance and a straitjacket for him. But she comes back in with Catrin and Rhys.

She sits them down and quizzes them about Lewis. Finds out they have involved him much more than she was aware of. He's been offering to help, fingers in almost every aspect of the investigation. But also not completing the tasks he's been given. Both the young detectives appear uncomfortable and anxious with this new suspicion over a colleague.

Jess reads their confusion. 'Nothing of what we've just talked about leaves this office, are we clear?'

Separate 'yes ma'ams' from the both of them. Jess addresses Catrin. 'Get a secretary to find Mel. Ask him to come in for a chat with me. Apologise and say it's something to do with Caldwell's review of the misper file. Something we need clearing up. And let's contact Limehouse Cottage. I want to go back out there.'

Rhys and Catrin leave with tense unhappy expressions.

'I must talk to Sion about this, Evan.' Jess gets up from her desk again.

Warlow nods. 'I know. But we need to be sure. A hundred per cent sure.'

Jess lifts her chin and says to the ceiling, 'Shit.'

Rhys comes back before Jess can leave the room, cheeks flushed. 'No joy with DS Lewis, but I've just spoken to Marcus Dexter at Limehouse Cottage. You will not believe this. He's in plaster with a broken leg. The scaffolding he was working on collapsed.'

Jess throws Warlow a loaded look. The calculator in both of their heads has two deaths and now a serious accident to tally up.

'Thanks, Rhys. Keep on at the mobile companies for those records. Make it your top priority.'

Rhys gives her a flurry of brief nods and leaves. Jess grabs her coat.

'Are we going somewhere?' Warlow asks.

'You know we are.' Jess is halfway through the door when she says it. 'Catrin, you're with us.'

CHAPTER FORTY-TWO

CATRIN DRIVES. When they get to their destination, Warlow is pleased to see only Ramsden's and Dexter's cars in the yard.

'Come in, the door is open. Don't mind the dog. He doesn't bite.' Marcus Dexter's disembodied words reach the three detectives' ears as they stand on the threshold of Limehouse Cottage. Warlow opens the door to be met with Monty's black nose.

'Hello boy,' Warlow says.

Monty's rear end sashays back and forth in greeting.

'I'm in here.' Marcus's shout draws them in.

Jess leads the way. Marcus is on the sofa. He's wearing shorts and Warlow suspects they're the only thing he can get over the plaster on his broken leg, which is propped up on the settee, the other resting on the floor. It's not flip-flop weather but that's what he has on his one foot.

'As you can see, I wasn't expecting company. But if you want to make yourselves some tea, feel free. Kitchen is through there.' Marcus points over his shoulder.

'That would be great.' Jess follows his finger. 'Never say no to a cuppa.'

Catrin is already on her way.

'What happened to your leg, Marcus?' Warlow asks.

'Freak accident last week. Remember the wind?'

Warlow does. They'd given it a name. Something banal like Gordon. He's been too busy with the Pickerings to take much notice. As far as he's concerned, the best forecast involves looking out of the window. Rain or shine, Cadi gets a walk.

'We'd built this wicked external skeleton with scaffolding and wrap so that I could work on the captain's cabin in the foul weather. And it was going really well until that storm.' Marcus shifts his position. The movement brings on a wince.

'Were you blown off?' Jess asks.

'Not quite. The wind caught the structure and tipped the whole thing over with me inside.' He laughs a little. 'It could have been a damn sight worse. As it was, some boards fell on my leg. Big long things with reinforced metal edging. I got a juicy tib and fib fracture and the surgeons fixed it with plates and screws. No more swimming for me for a while. I might rust.'

He's making a good show of it and Warlow wonders if his joviality is his nature or the result of the pain killers he's on. He's happy to talk, so they listen to a blow-by-blow account of his time in hospital while Catrin brings the tea in matching mugs.

'Lucky Izzy heard the crash and came running. Ben Gower came up with his tractor and pushed the thing off me and put a tourniquet around my leg. He was fantastic. Not sure what we would have done without him.'

Warlow sips the brown liquid. It's hot. Richards has remembered the one sugar.

'And Ms Ramsden? She wasn't hurt at all?' Jess asks.

Marcus holds his mug in both hands, propped up on a pillow. 'No. She wasn't anywhere near. She was out walking. Lucky for me she hadn't gone far. She was over the other side of the ravine looking at the Engine House.'

'Yes, the Engine House. What's the attraction?' Warlow asks.

'It's this place, isn't it?' Marcus grins. 'Izzy always had a bit of an imagination. And she's got this thing about the Follower and—'

'Follower?' Jess asks.

It's Catrin who explains. 'Local legend, ma'am. Some people claim that when they're out on the path they sometimes see someone following them. But no one ever catches up with them. And if they back-track to look, there's no one ever there.'

Jess's brief smile tells Warlow she's not impressed with old wives' tales.

'I know,' Marcus says. 'It's BS. But Izzy's into omens and stuff. At one point she thought she'd seen something over there. A stray animal or … whatever. I even caught her leaving food out for it. Bloody stupid if you ask me, I mean, if it is a fox; we have chickens. Not a good idea to encourage the wild.'

'And where is Ms Ramsden today?' Jess blows on her tea and takes a sip.

'Out again. But then you already know that.'

'Do we?' Jess asks.

Marcus snorts. 'Well unless you lot don't talk to each other. I thought that's why you've turned up. Though why it needs four of you to show her a ruin, I do not understand. Nice and all that, but someone could argue it's not the best use of police time.'

Warlow puts down his mug, an unpleasant swooping sensation growing in his gut. 'What do you mean, four of us?'

'Izzy's out exploring. I assumed it was with one of your lot. It's in her note.' Marcus waves the paper.

Warlow reads it.

'Out exploring the Engine House with guide. Bizzy +
Izzy!'

Marcus grins. 'Her grandmother's from Liverpool.
She's always called the police, bizzies. Sometimes Izzy does
too in a very bad Scouse accent. I expect they're already at
the Engine House by—'

Warlow is on his feet in a second. Jess and Catrin follow
him to the door. The afternoon is sliding into January
gloom, the low sun close to setting and blanketed in thick
cloud. Across the ravine, silhouetted against the grey sky,
the chimney of the Engine House rises over the hillocks
like a beacon. Or perhaps a warning to the curious.

'Bad idea to go over there alone, Evan,' Jess warns.

'Of course it is.' Warlow continues walking.

'But two idiots are better than one, right?' She turns to
Catrin. 'Get some bodies out here ASAP.'

Catrin already has her phone out. 'Ma'am.'

Jess hurries out to the car. 'Give me one minute to
change these sodding shoes. I've got a goody bag, too.' It's
not a request.

Warlow complies. She's the SIO.

There are other names for a goody bag. Some forces
called it a grab bag. He used to have one ready for when
and if he ever got a call to a case. Things like a policy
book, a spare charger for the phone, a police radio, a torch
and spare batteries, a Tyvek suit and mask, the SIO's
handbook and maybe a baton and whatever else was essen-
tial for protection and field work. Like waterproof clothing
and footwear.

While he waits, Warlow turns his face impatiently away
from the onshore breeze slapping the collar of his coat
against his flesh. The wind reminds him of one of his boys

when they were young. An irritating child craving attention from a dozing parent.

As metaphors go it's an appropriate one. Because he realises that he's been sleepwalking into this case from the very beginning.

It's about time that he bloody well woke up before the nightmare becomes a reality.

Unless they're already too late.

CHAPTER FORTY-THREE

Izzy follows Lewis along the familiar path across the ravine and the broken bridge. She stays close behind to listen to what he says because the wind is fresh off the Irish Sea and steals his words away if she doesn't concentrate. And he's worth listening to, chatty and knowledgeable about the local history.

'They've used lime on this land for centuries. Way before they built the kilns. Now they've become, what's that word, iconic? You can even do a kiln tour up the coast.' Lewis lets out a derisory laugh.

Izzy knows you can. She'd looked up a couple. But there are local societies that meet for guided walks. She plans to do that one day. More personal, she's decided.

'Always a two-man job, the lime kiln. A quarryman and a burner. More an art than a science, it was. The burners were like alchemists, knowing what size to break up the limestone, disperse heat, how to stack the stones for the fill. If they overdid the burn, they'd glaze the quicklime, and it wouldn't slake to make mortar. The burner would have to watch the fires. Sometimes all night.'

They arrive at the point where Izzy got to the day of

Marcus's accident and once again she stops to survey the view.

'So how do we get across?'

Lewis smiles. 'There is a gate. Right at the far end where no one sees, so no one's tempted to break the lock. Luckily I have the key. Since the bodies were found we've been over once or twice. Just in case.'

Izzy is surprised because she's seen no activity.

'In case of what? What would you be looking for?'

'Good question. Not much at this stage. But this place is a box that needs ticking and a good copper does as he's told.'

Lewis turns and grins at her. He's wearing waterproof trousers and walking shoes with heavy treads. He's come prepared. When they reach the chain-link fence topped with barbed wire, he takes a left and they follow the fence as the terrain descends. Fifty yards along, Izzy stops to examine the bottom of the fence where the ground beneath looks disturbed. As if it's been dug to form a dip.

'Rabbits probably. Foxes possibly,' Lewis says. 'They put the gate in the fence immediately before angling down at forty-five degrees to a point where the ravine becomes sheer. Canny buggers those Gowers.'

When they get there, half a dozen steps away the ravine dips sharply a good ninety feet above the boulders below. Lewis puts the key into the padlock and opens the gate; a section of reinforced fence hinged between two metal posts.

'Good of you to do this, Sergeant,' Izzy says, as she steps through.

'Pleasure. Just as well I check things over for you. It's not part of a crime scene but we don't want just anyone clambering about here. The buildings are precarious and the path leading down to the cliff edge is not in too good a state. In fact, I'd suggest we take a big loop around the site and approach it from the front. You get a much better view looking back at it from there.'

He doesn't bother locking the gate. The path now runs parallel to the ravine towards the end of the promontory atop which the Engine House sits. It's more exposed here and they both lean into the gusting wind as they walk on. Conversation is difficult. Their words need to be half shouts to be heard.

'What sort of story are you going to write?' Lewis asks. 'Historical fiction?'

'No. You'll laugh if I tell you.'

'Try me.'

'I'm thinking more in terms of fantasy. Mythology. Perhaps work something around the Follower.'

'The Follower?' Lewis turns a grinning face towards her. 'That old cobblers.'

'I know, but I might give it a new twist.'

The path takes them past the arched entrance of the Engine House, the full height of its chimney now visible some thirty yards to their right. But Lewis keeps walking. Past a scattering of crumbling outbuildings and piles of fallen stones.

'I've often thought this is an impressive setting for a good crime novel.' Lewis is still grinning.

Izzy laughs. 'I suppose you would. But look at this place. It has Gothic written all over it.'

They reach the western tip of the headland. There is a path of sorts but Lewis is right, it's faint and narrow. He stands, looking out to the Irish Sea. 'I had something darker in mind. A murder mystery. Troubled wife murders invalid husband and then throws herself off the rocks in anguish. You know the sort of thing.'

Izzy nods. 'A pot boiler. Don't know if I have a dark enough imagination.'

Lewis turns to face her. 'I could help you with the details.'

He's smiling, but there's something off in his expression. A wildness in his eyes. Izzy glances back. They're out of sight of the fence. Of any habitation. A sudden surge of apprehension grips her. But she dials it down. He's a police officer who's giving up his time to help her. She shivers. He sees.

'It's an eerie spot,' she says and her shiver is only partly from the cold.

'And dangerous, too. You can see why we don't want people wandering about here.'

'Yes.' She takes a couple of steps back from the edge.

'And this is the best view of the Engine House.'

She turns and looks. From this angle the whole of what's left of the chimney is visible, its diameter much wider at the base, tapering upwards. Despite the wind's icy blast, all she can think of is how remarkable it is that it's still standing. She can't imagine the conditions the men who worked there had to put up with. And she's only been out in this weather for half an hour.

The Engine House's walls, constantly exposed to wind and spray, are a different colour from this side. Something to do with the light, she thinks. The apex of the gable end is the only intact wall, all the rest are diminished, stepped where the stones have broken away. Truly an awe-inspiring site. And, though she knows the reason this building exists where it does, near to the sea atop a cliff, she can't help but feel she's looking into an alien world.

She's not sure what makes her glance back towards the sergeant. Perhaps her heightened nervousness and imagination. Perhaps the creeping movement that registers in her peripheral vision. But, when she does, she sees he has stepped closer. Within a couple of metres and closing. A sudden apprehension grips her and she dances away just as he lunges. His hand makes a swooshing noise as his fingers brush against the slick material of her alpine anorak.

'What are you doing?' Izzy's voice is thin and shrill in the wind.

But she gets no response. Lewis's features are set. His expression distorted and angry and wild looking.

Izzy takes some more hurried steps. They're matched by Lewis who suddenly runs towards her. She knows then that she is in trouble. Real trouble. Adrenaline bursts into her system. She can hear him, hear his breathing. She bounds back up the slope but he is only feet behind her. At any moment she expects his hand to close on her leg or her back, spinning her around, or thrusting her sideways over the edge of the cliff.

The nearest outbuilding is fifteen feet away now. Instinct takes over in Izzy and she screams out the word, 'Help!'

No one answers.

And then his hand catches her ankle and she trips. Her right knee breaks the fall and she feels something give. She turns, wincing. Lewis, too, has lost his footing in reaching for her. But he recovers quickly, five yards down the slope. Izzy tries to get up but her knee feels strange and dizziness threatens.

Lewis is on his feet. His features aren't those of the kind sergeant anymore.

Izzy screams.

The noise galvanises Lewis. But it also galvanises something else.

Izzy sees it first. Something dark shoots up from the outbuilding. It has a small upright shape, its body swathed in a black shiny material, head covered in a mass of dark hair. But Izzy only has a second to register this before it launches something at Lewis. It isn't a big stone, but it is accurate and finds a target in Lewis's head. The sergeant stumbles, clutching his face. The dark shape moves, running towards the Engine House.

Lewis roars and moves to run after it but then he stops and turns a bloody head back to Izzy.

'You first.'

'No, please, no.'

But he ignores her and picks his way over the stony ground, pausing only to pick up a rock that can fit easily into his gloved hand.

CHAPTER FORTY-FOUR

IT'S Jess who finds the gate in the fence. She calls to Warlow and they inspect the padlock hanging open on the latch together.

'Would Lewis have a key to this?' Allanby asks.

'If he did, I don't know why.'

They walk through along a faded path.

'God, that's like something out of Dickens.' Jess stops to stare at the bleak Engine House.

'He'd have had a field day here. Someone with his social conscience. Kids were working in the quarry at thirteen.'

Jess doesn't hide her shiver. 'Should we go there first or—'

Her question is rear-ended by a woman's voice reaching them on the wind. A high-pitched plea, raw with terror. 'Help!'

'Over the ridge.' Warlow is already moving, tearing up the small incline to where the path dips and curves towards the tip of the headland. When he gets to the top he stops, taking in the scene. Izzy Ramsden on her back on the path. Lewis looming over her. Izzy screams again. Warlow is too far away to prevent the blow that is threatened. All he can to do is announce his presence.

'Mel!'

Lewis hesitates and looks up. There is no wave of acknowledgement. Instead, he stares first at Warlow, then at the rock in his hand and finally down at the woman on the floor.

'Fuck!' Lewis shouts and hurls the stone he's holding into the grass. He aims two vicious kicks at the woman who's curled up into a ball. They're more in frustration than any attempt at being lethal. He looks up once more, turns and hurries away along the path.

Warlow and Jess scramble down to Izzy. They kneel and ask if she's okay.

Izzy moans and clutches at her leg. 'My knee.'

Jess examines it, feels the kneecap not quite where it should be and draws back her lips. 'Dislocated.'

'You okay, here?' asks Warlow.

'Go,' says Jess.

Warlow hurries after Lewis. He turns a corner and sees the sergeant thirty yards ahead. Lewis stops, pivots, and steps forward off the path to the very edge of the cliff.

'Mel, what are you doing?' Warlow slows his approach, hands held out.

'What does it look like?'

'Christ man, what's going on?'

'You'll work it out, Evan. You always do. That's why I messed up the misper files. Give you something to distract you. Didn't happen though, did it?' The smile on Lewis's face is fixed.

'You've got to come back with me, Mel. Sort all this out.'

Lewis's smile drops to sub-zero. 'If only you'd stayed in your little cottage, eh, Evan.'

Warlow is out of breath from his exertions. 'Mel …
come on.'

Lewis shakes his head. 'How long in the water this time
of year, you reckon?'

'For Christ's sake–' Warlow sends a quick glance down
to the sea below.

Lewis answers his own question, shifts from one foot to
the other. 'Couple of hours perhaps? Maybe longer. Less if
I exhaust myself. Better I hit the rocks then.'

'The Pickerings, Mel? Was that you?'

'I subcontracted. Big mistake. Thomas and Morris
owed me favours. I should have known those two idiots
couldn't fucking hack it.'

'Jesus, Mel–'

Lewis shakes his head. 'Fucking amateurs. But we'd
run out of time.'

'Whatever this is, Mel, it isn't worth it.'

Lewis lets out a noise that might be a laugh, or a moan.
'I can't go to prison, Evan. Not with the lot I'm dealing
with. I'm too much of a risk.'

Warlow won't give up. 'Give evidence then. Witness
protection.'

'For conspiracy to murder?'

Warlow doesn't reply immediately. When he does, it's a
question. 'Kieron Thomas. Was that you, too?'

'One less turd floating in the cesspool, eh, Evan?
Remember who used to say that?'

The words are tantamount to an admission. And
Warlow does indeed remember the reference. An old DI
they worked with whose take on inclusivity was to treat
everyone brought in for charging like the filth he considered them to be. He was long gone and would not have
survived in the brave new world of transparent policing
and body cams the uniformed officers lived with today.

Lewis has a haunted look when next he speaks. 'Next time the boys play, raise a glass for me, eh?'

'Mel, I–'

Warlow doesn't finish because Lewis moves. Three quick steps, the last one with his hands crossed over his chest, a stride out into open air and the rocks and sea below. Warlow stumbles forward, teetering on the lip of the cliff to stare down, unsteady against the buffeting wind. But Lewis disappears under the churning waves and big sharp rocks. Warlow's breath heaves in and out of his chest. He turns away, reaching for his phone, his fingers trembling on the keyboard. They'll need an ambulance and the coastguard.

It takes three attempts before he can find the right sequence to speed dial.

He hurries back to the women and helps Jess half carry Izzy Ramsden up the slope. Catrin is running through the fence when they arrive.

'Thank you,' Izzy mutters.

'Can you tell us what happened?' Jess asks.

She does. Disjointed words because of the shock, but stark in horrific content. He'd offered to show her the Engine House. Izzy thinks he was planning to throw her off and then go back and deal with Marcus. She isn't sure how but thinks he would somehow implicate her in that. There's nothing in her story that explains any of it. But when she finishes and wipes away the tears, she's shivering, and her last words emerge strange and jittery. 'Did you see it?'

'See what?'

'The Follower.'

Jess slides her wary eyes up to Warlow.

'I'm not delirious if that's what you're thinking,' Izzy insists. She's pale, slit-eyed with pain. 'There was some-thing hiding in those outbuildings. Something small, all black with long hair. Really long hair. It threw a stone at Sergeant … at him. It saved my life.'

'Is that why he had blood on his face?' Warlow asks.

Izzy nods.

'You think it's the Follower?' Jess asks.

'I don't know what it is, but it went into the Engine House.'

Warlow looks up towards the derelict building.

'Right, Catrin, look after Izzy.' Jess says. 'Since everyone else seems so bloody interested, we'd better look at what's in this sodding Engine House.'

CHAPTER FORTY-FIVE

THE LIGHT IS FADING, turning the green and brown of the gorse, bracken and heather into muted blues and purples, but still the sea moves beyond the land, grey and constant. Warlow tries not to think of Lewis. Whether he's dead or injured and in pain as the heat leeches from his broken body in the icy waters. He pushes the thought away because he needs to concentrate. But it's hard because etched onto his retinas is the image of Lewis stepping off that cliff edge with that haunted, lost expression.

When they get to the arched entry, reached by crumbling steps, Warlow has his phone out and uses it as a torch. But Jess, like the excellent, organised police officer she is, has a Maglite with an adjustable beam. Small but powerful, it lights up the shadowy interior of the Engine House.

'Save your battery,' she says, as she waves the beam around the vast space. It's quieter out of the wind, and the packed earth of the floor has dark puddles of stagnant water from the recent rains. There's a musky ammoniacal smell, too. There could be rats here, or rabbits or, according to Izzy Ramsden, something else.

They cover the floor methodically, picking out old scraps of paper and plastic in the torch's beam, as well as discarded cans and a torn tent, all of which speak of previous occupation. Before the fence went up, Warlow assumes.

The apex of the far wall has half collapsed and the tumbled stones form a rough pyramid on the floor. If there is anything hiding in here, the stones provide the only cover. When they're within a few feet, Warlow calls a halt and points to something on the floor. Something pale and irregular, about the size of half a tennis ball. He kneels down and moves it with a pen.

'Orange peel,' he says. 'Recent.'

Jess throws Warlow a bewildered glance. 'What the hell is going on here, Evan?'

He holds up the orange peel. 'Could be an OrangUtan sanctuary.'

She sends him a scathing look.

Warlow shrugs and stands up. 'I have no id–'

He doesn't get to finish. From behind the pile of stones, something moves. Explodes out and away. Something much larger than a rat. Allanby slides the beam up and catches a shape scuttling towards the far corner of the Engine House where the base of the chimney abuts. A blur of dark movement that disappears in an instant.

'Where the hell did it go?' Jess shouts.

Warlow keeps his eyes trained on the spot. 'It went low. There must be a gap.'

They approach slowly, zig-zagging their way over the scattered stones. 'I saw it turn. I saw two eyes,' Jess says.

Warlow nods. 'I saw a body covered in what looked like bin bags. If I have to put money on it, I'd say it was a kid.'

Jess utters a low groan. 'I was afraid you'd say that.'

When they reach the corner, the darkness deepens. The base of the wall and the adjacent curve of the chimney have fallen out leaving a space. A waft of cold sea air greets them as they near this maw.

'Please don't tell me we're going down there?' Jess says.

'We could wait for uniforms,' Warlow answers in a flat tone. It would be the sensible thing to do.

'What if it is a kid, though?' Jess's words echo around the space.

Warlow goes first. Jess provides illumination from behind with the torch. The gap is about two foot by three with the odd stone jutting out like a broken tooth. But Warlow gets through by rotating his trunk. His foot finds a stone, then another, until he stands on the floor of a small chamber with blackened, sooty walls. Fires have been lit here.

'Well?' Jess calls from above.

'It's cosy. Come down.'

Jess hands him the torch, but just as her leg appears, Warlow feels a sharp pain in his lower back. As if he's been struck. He turns with the torch and takes an involuntary step back unable to prevent the oath from rushing out.

'Christ almighty.'

There, just yards away and lit up in the torchlight, is something from a nightmare.

His sons have recommended a few films over the years. Blair Witch, Cloverfield, Paranormal; low-light mockumentaries designed to suggest rather than show. A good way to cure your constipation if you're able to suspend belief. But there is little left to the imagination here. And this isn't a film. What stands in front of him with hand raised against the glare of the light is no mythological beast.

It's a child, he knows that. He can't tell whether it's male or female because the hair reaching almost to its waist hangs over its dirt smeared face like a curtain. The arms and legs are caked with dirt and he was right about the layers of bin bags wrapped around the body. In its other hand it holds a rock ready for launching. Warlow guesses that the only reason it hasn't been thrown is the torch acting as a deterrent.

'Oy,' yells Warlow. It's the second time he's used his voice to warn. Second time it's worked.

The child jerks in fright, drops the rock, turns and scampers away towards another even darker gap in the wall.

'What happened?' Jess steps down, wiping cobwebs from her coat.

Warlow is already moving. 'Our rat is a kid. He, or she, looks almost feral. It went that way.'

'Great. Another hole.'

Once again Warlow goes first. This time the gap is wider and the space he enters seems familiar. He says as much to Jess as he points to the rough walls. 'These are tunnels from the Engine House down to the inlet. I've been in these before. Not all of them. But you can smell the sea.'

'So is it down or up?'

Warlow points the torch beam behind them. The tunnel ends in a tumble of stones. He swings it back to the space ahead that curves into nothingness. 'I'd say down.'

Jess replies with a moan.

———

THEY KEEP their eyes down because the floor is strewn with stones that could turn an ankle in a trice. The walls either side are rough, the ceiling low. The light picks out blue water-pipes and corrugated plastic lines tight against one wall at floor level.

'Careful,' Warlow warns. 'They built these just high enough for a small horse. The men used to have to stoop.'

Jess grunts as she ducks to avoid a protruding rock. 'You're sure what you saw was a child?'

'As sure as I can be. And not some bloody troglodyte, I know that.'

The tunnel winds down and around. When he'd been here there'd been a whole POLSA team with lights and dogs. And then he remembers something else. 'Lewis said he'd been down here as part of the Pickerings' misper review.'

'The one run by Caldwell?'

'Yes.'

'The "C" word again,' mutters Jess.

Warlow doesn't query that. He doesn't like words that begin with C either. Such as coincidence, or Caldwell, or another word with just the four letters that he wouldn't use even though it springs to mind unbidden whenever he thinks of the DI. Polite company and all that.

The going is slow and they pick their way around larger stones fallen from the roof. A different smell too. More industrial; oil or petrol.

'I don't like this place. I don't like it with a vengeance,' Jess says.

'No. I can think of better ways to spend an evening.'

'Molly's going home to an empty house again.'

Warlow sends an over the shoulder glance at Jess. 'She's a copper's daughter. She's used to it, isn't she?'

'Not something a kid should have to get used to,' Jess says and Warlow hears regret and concern in her voice.

'I don't think you need to worry.' He continues his crouched advance. 'She has her head on straight.'

'Do you think so?'

'I do.'

'Thank you. I appreciate that.'

'Yes, well—'

Jess's hand on Warlow's arm shuts him up. They stop

and listen. Warlow hears it now, too. Faint whimpering noises. As they creep closer towards a bend in the tunnel, other noises come through. A whispering voice. Words that they can't make out and, most incongruous of all, the faint suggestion of tinny music.

Warlow inches his way forward, back against the curve, angling Jess's torch beam down to the floor with the DI on his shoulder. He knows that the child – if it is a child – isn't armed, but he doesn't want a rock bouncing off his head or risk getting one in the eye.

But there is no rock. When he pushes his head around to peer and the torch beam lights up the space, what he sees stops him dead. The tunnel ends twenty yards further on. Another collapse, this time with a massive stone completely blocking the way. But ten yards before that there is an offshoot, an alcove of sorts. It too looks blocked, with smaller stones in a cone shaped heap. And lying on that heap with its hand reaching forward through the gap at the very top is the child.

Its whimpering is pitiful.

In response, the whispering comes from the other side of the stones. Reassuring, cajoling. And beyond that, somewhere, the music.

'Hello,' Jess whispers.

The child stops whimpering, pulls its hand back and stares at them.

'It's okay,' says Warlow. 'It's okay.'

But the child doesn't answer. It scurries back and retreats down the tunnel towards the rock collapse to wriggle in amongst the stones, only the head and eyes remaining visible.

'What the hell is going on here?' Warlow whispers.

Jess walks forward in the torch light towards the child, hand held out. 'It's alright. You're alright.'

But her reassuring words only make the child push further back around the rocks, deeper into shadow.

Jess stops opposite the alcove.

'There's a gap at the top here. Not much of a gap but–'

'Please.'

The voice, desperate and broken and barely a whisper comes through that gap. 'Please. No hurt.'

Warlow joins Jess. He shines the torch through the gap but all they see is the same dark rock roof. Higher than the tunnel's but just as rough.

'Hello? Who are you?' Warlow asks.

'Please, please, no hurt.' It's not a British accent. The 'r's roll too much. Warlow can't pinpoint it but it suggests an eastern origin. Middle eastern perhaps.

'We're not going to hurt anyone,' Jess says. 'We are the police. Who are you?'

'Please, please.'

Warlow grabs the topmost stone and pulls it away. Jess helps. Between them they shift a dozen. When they do and the space enlarges, a face appears. The whisperer's face, female, wearing a besmirched headscarf. It takes Warlow a moment to realise it's a hijab. He and Jess continue to widen the space to reveal more of the whispering woman because there is a light on in the other side. She's wearing a sweat shirt and pants. Both hang off her frame. Either the clothes are too big, or she is too small.

'Please.'

'Okay,' says Jess. 'We hear you. Let's clear more of this stuff away.'

The stones halfway down are bigger, the pile broader. Most require both Jess's and Warlow's strength to shift. Ten minutes later, they've made a gap big enough to wriggle through. Warlow goes first. He steps down on a spilled pile of more rock into a bigger space with a taller, curved roof and precarious footing. Some of the collapsed rock has formed a spillway to a flatter floor. And it's what is arranged against the walls on this floor that Warlow stares at under ceiling-strung bulb lights. There are camp beds and strewn clothes and a smell of unwashed bodies and stale food. The music is louder, from somewhere further off under a shut but makeshift door.

Jess follows Warlow through the gap and they stand in a room that now looks like a dormitory.

'I count eight beds,' Warlow says.

Behind them they hear more whispers and then a cry. Not desperate anymore, now full of relief. The woman in the hijab has scrambled up the stones and has reached through into the tunnel. And now her arms are full of black bin bag and hair as she pulls the child through into a hug.

'Samir. Samir.'

'Umma. Umma.'

Both police officers stand and don't interfere. The woman cries, the child sobs. But eventually Jess turns to the door on the other side of the room. 'Whatever this is, I do not like it one tiny bit.' She removes an extendable baton out of her fanny pack and flicks it open. 'We need to open that door.'

Warlow goes first. It's a simple enough affair. Wooden, the type found on a thousand sheds in gardens everywhere, hung from a rough frame of two-by-two wood fitted into the stone space. There's no lock. Just a latch which clicks as he lifts and pulls the door open.

The music is louder here. Not very loud, but it is the only noise. Bright LED strip lights hang from the ceiling. The room is the mirror image of the dormitory, only three times as big. And here no one is sleeping. Three trestle tables are set up. On both sides of these tables stand people, four women in hijabs and two heavily bearded men. All wearing dust-stained clothing, sweatpants and tops. Grey, blue, green. The cheap type, with dirty grey or white socks and black slides on their feet. All of them wear paper hats and masks and they all stand in silence to watch as Jess and Warlow enter.

It's oppressively warm and it doesn't take a genius to work out why.

Behind the tables, row upon row of green plants in large pots stretch away. Cannabis in full bud. Enough to keep Glasto in orbit for a week. Above, banks of 600-watt lights attached to reflective canopies dangle from the ceiling. A tangle of wiring leads to a bank of transformers and a socket board that sits suspended from two wooden beams running the width of the space.

Against the other walls, plastic containers next to bags of fertiliser sit next to blue water-butts. Huge corrugated plastic ducting pipes run across to another linking passage. From what Warlow can recall, there were four storage tunnels down here.

Above the tables, harvested plants are drying on plastic lines of yellow nylon cord.

Warlow turns to the people at the tables. He knows the answer before he asks the question, but he asks it anyway. 'Are you here of your own accord?'

Four of them look bewildered. One just stares. The other, a woman, shakes her head.

Something shifts in Warlow then. Something seismic. He feels the heat of a flush spreading up his neck as fresh sharp anger comes to the boil. 'Who is responsible for all this?'

No one answers. But the music suddenly stops.

'We are the police.' Jess holds out her warrant card. 'You have nothing to fear.'

'No, they don't. But you do.'

The voice comes from the lit passageway leading to the

next storage tunnel. Jess and Warlow wheel around together. Ben Gower stands there, glowering.

But neither police officer dwells on his face. Their eyes are drawn instantly to the shotgun Gower holds in his hands.

CHAPTER FORTY-SIX

GOWER GRINS at Jess's silence. 'What? Think we'd skimp on CCTV when we've spent all this cash on equipment? I saw you two fuckers come in.'

Warlow doesn't take his eyes off the weapon. 'Ben, put the gun down. There is only one way out of this for you.'

'Oh yeah? And what is that, Mr Warlow?' Gower puts extra emphasis on the mister. He walks in, keeping the gun up and trained on them both.

'Come on, Ben. We aren't alone. Mel Lewis is dead.' Warlow's words sound harsh in his own ears.

Gower sneers. 'Waste of space anyway. Piss artist that he was.'

'Put the gun down, Ben,' Jess says.

'Shut up. And you, throw that bloody thing on the floor.' Gower jerks the gun forward.

Jess lets the baton go. It clatters to the floor.

'Big operation. You've been busy.' Warlow shifts his weight.

Gower sees it. 'Uh-uh. Move back into the rat hole. Where the beds are.'

'Why?'

'Move now or I put one barrel into your girlfriend's leg. Take off the whole thing below the knee from here.'

Warlow moves as instructed, Jess follows. From behind them, Gower says, 'And you fuckers get on with it.'

The people at the table get back to trimming the buds.

Gower follows them into the dormitory. It's a squalid place and now Warlow senses another smell. Human waste.

'Shithole, right?' Gower grins. 'Old school bogs. Goes straight into the sea. Wouldn't eat the lobsters from this bay if I were you.'

'You didn't do this yourself, did you, Ben?' Warlow poses this as a statement more than a question.

'No shit, Sherlock. And it's all down to your lot, thank you very much. When I was nabbed all those years ago? You wanted me to suffer for it. But Laura admitted it, remember? She went to jail for intent to sell. Four years she got. But the deal was I got off if the big guys could use the farm. My dad thought of this place. Fucking genius.' Gower is enjoying himself.

'Did Pickering know what you were up to?' Warlow asks.

Gower hisses out a disdainful exhalation. 'No. But he was going to find out once he built his shitty little summerhouse.'

'The inlet.' Warlow nods. He can see it now. The answer.

It's epitomised by Ben Gower's mocking disdain; knowing the cop he has in his double-barrelled sights can do sod all about it. 'Got it in one. We float the goods out. Stick them on the pebbles at low tide on a buoyed rope. It's fucking sweet. Boat comes in and scoops them up once a week without even needing to dock. Like the lime workers in reverse.'

Without warning, the woman in the hijab that whispered to them emerges from the shadows in the room. Gower shifts his gaze to her and snarls. 'What the fuck are you doing here? I swear you are a pain in the arse. Always wanting shitty toilet breaks. Get back in there.'

She shakes her head.

Gower steps forward and thrusts the gun into her chest. 'Get back to work.'

Warlow inches forward.

'Don't,' warns Gower. 'Unless you want to talk to me through a hole in this bitch's chest.'

The whispering woman does as she's told but throws two desperate glances behind her before she gets to the door. Gower pushes her through and shuts it with his foot. The latch clicks home.

Warlow looks around. The Follower – who is not a man at all but a child called Samir – is nowhere in sight. Jess is trembling but not through fear. It's pure adrenaline. Warlow knows this because when he looks at his own hand, he sees he is too. But it is Jess who speaks.

'So what now, Ben? Like DCI Warlow says, we're not alone. You shoot us, it's murder and there are witnesses.'

The smirk on Gower's face is nauseating. 'Are there? Your witnesses are on the other side of that door. And they can't give evidence if they're dead, right? Slash and burn, that's what I've been told to do if the shit hits the fan. So guess what? I can smell the shit and so can you. We've rigged this whole place with nitrate.' He shakes his head as if he can hardly believe his own words. 'That's the thing with working on a farm. We can get nitrogen fertiliser by the ton. After I've shot you two, there'll be a big fucking bang. Tunnels collapsing, the lot. Even the Engine House will disappear.'

'There's no way–' Warlow begins.

'There is if everyone thinks I was with you. Take years to excavate this place. The pot farms been a winner and

I've got money stashed. A lot of money. You turning up is my ticket out of this shit-hole. As long as I leave no witnesses, the supplier doesn't care. I've got a place on the Black Sea. Dad can do what he likes. But I've done my bit for them.'

'Them?'

Gower snorts. 'You never know their names. There are only handlers who come and set you up, fix up the arrangement and piss off. They supply the workers, too. This is the third lot.'

Something cold rolls over Warlow like slick tainted mud. 'What happened to the last–'

'You don't want to know.' Gower's grin, plastered over his face, is that of a spoiled child. 'The mackerel are well fed here, that's all I'm saying.'

'I have a daughter,' says Jess.

'Great. I'll get a mate to look her up. She classy in black? What's her name?'

Jess shakes her head. Gower angles the gun six inches higher towards her head.

Jess squeezes her eyes shut. When she speaks it's barely audible. 'Molly. Her name is Molly.'

'Well, if she's anything like you, it'll be worth a shufti. Get over against the wall. I've got work to do.' He pulls the gun to his shoulder.

Behind him, the door latch clicks open.

Gower doesn't move. 'Shut that fucking door or you're next.'

But Warlow sees the whispering woman. Sees the same desperate determination in her face. She shouts something.

'Samir! Samir!'

'Jesus,' Gower hisses. But his eyes never waver from Jess and Warlow. Never waver and therefore do not see the dark shape emerge from its hiding place until it runs across the space towards its mother. Only then does he swivel his eyes, though the gun stays resolutely pointed at the police officers.

But when Samir sees the man look at him, he reacts the same way he did with Lewis. From only six yards away he throws a stone. Warlow doesn't know what this child's life has been like. But he can throw. And throw accurately.

A stone the size of a hen's egg hits Gower square on the cheek. His head jerks and so do his fingers. The gun fires. It misses its target because Warlow has pulled Jess down and Gower's arm angles upwards as a reflex to the jerk of his head. It's then that Warlow moves.

He grabs Allanby's baton from the floor, takes three steps so he is inside the reach of the gun and hits the staggering Gower on the wrist. Metal clashes with bone and the gun clatters away. Gower stumbles with a yell. But he is younger and stronger than Warlow. With a roar he gets to his knees, his face a mask of murderous anger.

But looking up is his undoing. His eyes and mouth are wide open when a blast from Jess's PAVA spray hits him in the eyes and nose from three feet. He splutters, screams, clutches his face and rolls away.

It ends there. With three puffs of an aerosol can that contains a synthetic capsaicinoid derived from chilli peppers. Standard issue for British Police since they banned CS gas sprays. All uniformed officers carry it in their utility vests. Plain-clothed officers carry it at their discretion. Warlow has never bothered, but he says a silent prayer of thanks that Jess is better organised than he is.

She has handcuffs, too. Between them, they manhandle Gower. It isn't easy, hindered as they are by his reluctance to move his hands from his face. By his agonised protests. By his farmworker's strength. But they get help from the two pot factory men who are more than willing to lend a hand to incapacitate their erstwhile captor.

They take four minutes, but they finally secure Gower,

his face red and his eyes half shut and streaming. Throughout the whole thing, he screams he is going blind. When it's done and he's handcuffed and his legs trussed with cable ties, Warlow looks up at the whispering woman and her son standing against the rough-hewn stone walls, and, doing his utmost to give her a reassuring smile asks her one question.

'His name, say it again?'

'Samir,' she says.

Warlow looks at the boy and holds his thumb up. 'Samir, you are a very good shot. Thank you.'

The boy, matted and filthy and clinging to his mother's waist, peeps from behind her leg. He studies Warlow's hand gravely until slowly, carefully, he raises his thumb in return.

CHAPTER FORTY-SEVEN

Izzy is taken to hospital in Haverfordwest. By the time she's seen, her kneecap has spontaneously relocated. Though her physical injuries are minima, she is badly shaken and in shock. Marcus texts her to say that he's been evacuated with Monty to a dog-friendly hotel in Swansea, but that they're both okay.

The doctor sutures a cut on Izzy's forearm. She gets a brace for her knee and is told to rest it. The bruise on her head where she fell and the neuro obs she has to undergo through the night disrupts what little sleep she gets. The next morning, a CT scan is reported as normal and late that afternoon Catrin arrives to pick her up.

'Bomb squad have just given us the all-clear, so I can take you home.'

Marcus is already there. So are the swarming police who set up checkpoints on the turnoff to the farm, at the farm gates and the lane leading to Limehouse Cottage. When Izzy gets out of the car, she stares across at the pointing finger of the Engine House's chimney. Just a day ago it was looming over her as Lewis chased her down.

Catrin puts a hand on her upper arm. 'Okay, Izzy?'

'Yes … yes, I'm fine.'

'Let's go in. I'll sort you out a cup of tea.'

'No. Look, Catrin, is it alright if you don't? Marcus is having kittens. He's texted me about a thousand times. I think we'd rather be alone.'

Catrin nods. 'No problem. You have my number. There will be a lot more questions and DI Allanby and former DCI Warlow will want to talk to you. As you can see, we're not far away.'

Two vans and a marked police car are parked in the field next to the cottage garden. The breeze has stiffened and has a bite to it this afternoon. Izzy shivers in her coat.

'Will you thank them for me? If it wasn't for them I …'

'You did well, Izzy. Really well.'

Izzy looks at Catrin and suddenly fights back the tears. She hasn't told them of the fear she'd felt. The terror that gripped as she saw Lewis's expression change into something cold and inhuman. She will tell them in more than one of her many statements. But now, with the Engine House so close and visible, she can't because the memory of it all is visceral and raw.

'I need to go in. Thanks for picking me up.'

Catrin waits while Izzy opens the cottage door.

'Izzy, is that you?' Marcus's voice reaches her from the living room. And then a bounding, leggy Monty hurtles around the door, and almost knocks her over.

'Hello, boy. Hello, my boy.' Izzy bends at the waist and fondles the dog.

'Has Monty poleaxed you?'

'Almost.'

Izzy placates the dog and limps into the living room. Marcus is on the sofa, one leg raised, arms outstretched. She goes to him. It's an awkward embrace because his plaster and her brace get in the way. But it is an embrace. They hug one another and there are mutual tears.

'I've been so scared,' says Marcus. 'When they told me—'

Izzy holds his face in her hands. 'I'm sorry. Sorry to scare you. Sorry to be such an idiot.'

'I thought I'd lost you.'

She pulls back, wipes tears away with a finger. 'I'm indestructible, you know that.'

Marcus shakes his head. 'I've been thinking. All this, everything that's happened, it's because of me. My stupid ideas of escaping. But I've decided. We'll move. Go wherever you want us to. A beach house in Goa. A flat in Richmond. Whatever.'

Izzy looks at him. This fragile man she's made her life partner.

'I don't want to go anywhere. I want us to finish the captain's cabin. And I want to walk the path.'

Marcus searches her face. 'Are you sure?'

'I am. It's a second chance, don't you see?' She looks down at his plaster. 'We make ourselves cosy. Batten down the hatches. Let the storm come. You can binge watch Netflix, I can write.'

'More fantasy?'

'Perhaps. Or a crime novel.'

'Wow. Have you been inspired?'

'I know what being frightened is like, let's put it that way.'

Monty pushes his nose between them. Marcus laughs. 'Okay, boy, we know you're here.'

The dog's wet nose is cold on her hand. For the first time since yesterday, she feels safe. At home with the familiar. Yet, nothing is as it was. And Monty's touch presses a button.

'When I was on the path and Lewis was after me, all sorts of thoughts ran through my head. But the one that bothered me the most was what I hadn't told you.'

Marcus doesn't speak, but his brow creases. 'Is this where you tell me about the affair you've been having?'

Izzy dips her chin. 'I wish.'

Marcus's face falls.

She looks up, grinning. 'I'm kidding, you twit.' The smile softens and becomes serious. 'It's something I should have told you a long time ago. It didn't seem that important at the time. But what's happened has changed all that and I've realised how wrong I was and that I should have shared it with you.'

Marcus pushes himself up. 'Now I'm really on edge.'

'Don't be.' She takes a deep breath. 'Have you ever heard the term chemical pregnancy?'

CHAPTER FORTY-EIGHT

THE AFTERMATH of the Engine Room discovery is a circus.

An army of police invade Penmor farm and its surroundings. Bomb squad officers find and remove the bags of Hiaman fertiliser full of ammonium nitrate stashed in crude stacks along the tunnels under the house, linked by petrol-soaked rags in corrugated drainage pipes. Ben Gower was not bluffing.

It takes twenty-four hours to make the place safe.

When drug squad officers and the forensic investigators gain access to the illegal underground cannabis farm, they estimate it has a street value of over four million.

They arrest the Gower family en masse. Ben says nothing under interrogation, but the old man, Rylan, is less of a clam. He wants assurances that they leave his wife out of it. She knows nothing of what went on, he protests. Jess is disinclined to believe him, but Warlow thinks there is a possibility that it's true.

'Gower is old-fashioned. He gave his wife the Airbnb business and ran the farm with Ben. She may have been unaware of comings and goings. Especially if it all took place from the sea.'

'That's hard to believe in a setup as sophisticated as that.' Jess has a point.

'I'm not defending anyone,' Warlow protests.

'Good, because Rylan Gower is going to find out PDQ that there's such a thing as the Proceeds of Crime act. He could lose everything. As for his wife, we'll find out what she knows when she's questioned.'

Warlow's spared sitting in on interviews and isn't sorry. Jess doesn't need any help with that. She doesn't need any help, full stop, he thinks, but he doesn't say so because he enjoys her company.

They're sitting in his cottage five days after finding the pot farm. Warlow's been in a couple of afternoons to give statements and write up his reports. But this catch-up away from work is at Jess's insistence.

'Rylan Gower has not given us any names. Setting up these farms is a slick operation and I agree, Ben Gower had sod all to do with that, either. My colleagues in organised crime tell me they source the electricians and plumbers from Romania or Bulgaria, and all they then need is power, which, since it's on a farm, is easy enough to get.'

Warlow remembers the professional-looking wiring and the lights in the storage tunnels. 'And the workers?'

Jess's expression darkens. 'Immigration and social services are working on that, but they're Syrian. Shipped to Kent on a raft and then stuck in a lorry and brought by another boat at night to those tunnels. They've been kept as prisoners there with no prospect of escape because there was nowhere else to go.'

'How long ago?'

'Some have been there for years.'

Warlow drops his head. 'Jesus.'

Jess keeps talking. 'The pot farm is bad enough. But this is out and out slavery and human trafficking. I hope the Gowers get thirty years and that the old man dies in there. He knew what was going on alright.'

Warlow has been thinking about this. How organised crime gets its claws into people. 'I wasn't directly involved with Ben Gower but he knew how I felt about him getting off with possession that time we caught him with a car full of drugs. He'd always make himself scarce when I was around. As if he had something to hide.'

'Which he sodding well did.' Jess has a glass of water in front of her. She takes a sip now. 'They call it cuckooing. Whoever is behind this operation might even have set Ben up with the girl and the drugs to entrap the family. A promise to get Ben off so long as he cooperated with them afterwards. They made the girl admit she was the owner of the drugs with intent to sell. No doubt they'll have made it worth her while, too. Or coerced her, who knows. Either way she exonerated Ben Gower in what was clearly an organised county lines operation. In return, they force the Gowers into letting them use their property to set up their own illicit drug factory.'

Warlow grunts. 'And they co-opted Mel Lewis to monitor police operations.'

'That's what it looks like.'

Drugs, human trafficking, modern slavery. One begets another.

Warlow has wondered about what might happen if they made marijuana legal. He's listened to the arguments. Seen the experiments in Canada and parts of the USA. He's no expert on the medical side of things, but he is an expert in substance abuse. Because he's an ex-police officer and knows what it does to people. He can't see how anyone can argue the difference. If alcohol was discovered today, it would be a banned substance. And yet anyone can go out and get legless on a Saturday night and assault someone else, a cop or a paramedic, drive while under the influence, cause an accident, get a dozen diseases and drain the NHS. So something in the argument that cannabis is worse than booze doesn't quite add up.

Hypocrisy, thy name is vodka.

'What's going to happen to them?'

'The workers?'

Warlow nods. They all needed medical treatment and a few are still in hospital. 'They're asylum seekers, I presume?'

'Yes,' Jess says.

'Anything we can do to help them out?'

'Who knows? Letters of support can't do any harm.'

'Letters of support, my arse. They should give that kid and his mother a medal.'

Jess grins. 'Say that in a testimonial. I'm sure it'll help coming from a senior officer like you.'

'Less of the senior, please.'

Jess stands. Time to go. 'Samir's mother is called Dalila Alsous. They've both been in hospital. She has a chest infection, and the poor kid has worms. I'm going to interview her once we get a translator set up. Sion Buchannan wants us all in on for a Friday debrief. Oh and Molly's asking if you and Cadi would like to come around to ours for supper Thursday night?'

'Is Molly cooking?'

Jess grins. 'I love a comedian.'

'What's on the menu?'

'Surprise.'

'Only asking for the sake of the wine, you know, white or red?'

Jess raises both eyebrows.

Warlow nods. 'You're right. Stupid question. One of each it is.'

CHAPTER FORTY-NINE

They find Mel Lewis's body the following morning. Sion Buchannan rings him to break the news. The tides and strong currents have carried it up the coast to Cwmtydu Bay. A bell rings in Warlow's head and he checks the map. It's within two miles of where they found the unidentified body that Caldwell assumed was a deckhand off one of the ships three years before.

A fact worth noting. Though he says nothing to Buchannan. Not yet. He doubts KFC will pick up on it either.

But, on Thursday evening, before they sit down to eat – while Molly and Cadi are off playing in another room having had a warning from Jess that the laundry basket is definitely off limits – Warlow brings up the link between the two drowned bodies.

'So you don't think that's happened by chance?' Jess asks.

'We'd need to check with someone who knows the currents, but you saw that hell-hole of a dormitory. As unsanitary a place as I've seen or smelled. I doubt Ben Gower had them on a health plan.'

Jess doesn't respond but her expression is full of pained recollection.

'You heard what he said about not eating the lobsters,' Warlow adds.

'Yes, but he was referring to the waste disposal, surely.'

Warlow says nothing in reply. His silence speaks harrowing volumes.

'Oh, God.' Jess puts down her wine. 'I'll talk to Sion tomorrow. See what the coastguards think.'

'Good idea. I know one unidentified body washed up just before I left the force. Sure to be under one of Caldwell's closed case files.'

Jess looks like she wants to say something but then Molly comes back in to join the adults with Cadi in tow and the talk turns to other things. Normal things. Sometimes frivolous things. But it's okay because both Jess and Warlow welcome the distraction. No shop talk in front of Molly. And sometimes you need an injection of frivolity to balance out the darkness and the horror. So Warlow is a willing participant in discussions about kayaking, school, where the Allanbys would like to travel to. And he has to answer and discuss New Zealand and South America. Maybe a trip to Patagonia. Neither of them believe there's a Welsh speaking colony in the Chubut Valley. Warlow is happy to give them a history lesson.

He also recounts a trip to Chicago when he was a sergeant in the Met in pursuit of a suspected murderer who'd absconded to the USA. He'd gone in early February when Lake Michigan was frozen over. He'd never been so cold and cannot understand how anyone functions in that sort of weather.

'I could barely speak. My mouth seized up.' He does an impression and Jess jets wine all over her plate.

Molly pretends to be horrified. 'Mum, oh my God, you're worse than a four-year-old.'

When the laughter dies, Molly asks if they caught the 'perp.'

That triggers another smile from Warlow and a giggle from Jess.

'What's wrong with perp?' Molly demands.

'Nothing, Mol,' Jess says. 'We use that all the time.'

Molly's eyes flash but she's half laughing. Warlow grounds everyone by saying, without irony, that they caught the 'perp', but he was tried in the States and is still in jail there.

Molly has a feistiness about her that comes with her age and a determination not to be overawed by him, the male. She isn't hostile, but she goads. Persistently. Warlow doesn't mind. She's lost her father. He's still alive but lost to her. And Molly has ideas. Most of them are good, some not so. She has an idealism that some might easily dismiss as naïve, but which Warlow sees as invigorating.

So they discuss climate change, child poverty, human trafficking, Welsh independence and the breaking up of the union. He tells them a little about this place that they've come to. A country where a language is inextricably linked to nationalism, struggling to restructure its economy in its centres of population after the closure of the mines, where the old stereotypes persist in the minds of outsiders. And for that read the rest of Britain.

'And then there's rugby,' Molly says with jazz hands.

'There is,' Warlow agrees.

'Why is everyone so obsessed here?'

'Because it's classless. The Welsh are proud of that.'

Jess tells him, coyly, that her great grandfather was Welsh.

'Oh, so there's a bit in you, Molly,' Warlow says.

'Probably the bit that makes me sing in the shower then.'

'Is that what the noise is?' Jess teases.

'You have a voice?' Warlow asks.

It's a segue into music. They discuss what they like, what they don't. It's common ground and Molly is happy to illustrate it with snippets from her phone.

When it comes time to leave around ten, Warlow is shocked to find that he's reluctant to go. But it's a school night and both he and Jess have the big debrief in the morning.

Supposedly.

Molly sees Cadi to the car and then disappears inside the house.

'So long, Cadi's daddy. See you next time.'

Jess watches her go, a surprised look on her face. 'My my. Next time isn't something you hear a lot of from Mol.'

'She hasn't finished pummelling me into submission about being equivocal about Bowie.'

'I know.' Jess shakes her head. 'It's as if this lot have just discovered him.'

Warlow smiles. 'Thanks for this, I needed it.'

'Any time.' She's standing close. Warlow wonders if it's polite to kiss her on the cheek. But he doesn't. He has his reasons.

Jess senses an awkwardness and shifts gears. 'You're a good man, Evan Warlow. But next time someone is pointing a shotgun at us, please don't stand in front of me. We should have been trying to get further apart.'

'Next time I'll stand behind you. Promise.'

Jess shivers. 'God forbid there's a next time.' She regards him with a narrowed gaze. 'I haven't quite worked it out yet, DCI Warlow, but I will.'

'Worked what out?'

'Whatever's eating you from the inside out.'

Warlow bats it away. 'Psychoanalysis your specialist subject, is it?'

'No.' She raises her eyebrows in warning. 'But there is

something. And you don't want to tell me and I respect that. But I will find out. I'm good at my job.'

'I can't argue with that.'

'See. Sodding deflection again. You're a slippery eel, DCI Warlow.' She gives him a lopsided grin. 'See you tomorrow.'

Warlow sighs. 'I don't think so, Jess.'

Her face falls. 'But people will be expecting–'

'Yeah. People. They're always expecting. That's their trouble.'

She looks disappointed.

He shakes his head. 'You don't need me to be there for the back slapping, Jess.'

'God, you can be hard work.'

'You been speaking to my ex?'

'Poor beggar,' Jess says, but she delivers it with a smile that takes the sting out of her words.

Warlow gets into the car and guns the engine, aware that he's enjoyed himself. He's about to drive away when she waves frantically for him to stop. He winds down the window. 'Wait, one minute.'

She runs back into the house while he sits with the engine idling. Cadi looks out of the back window wistfully at the house.

'I know, girl. I know. Molly likes you too.'

He knows that he has to be bloody careful. But knowing that does not take away how much he despises not having the backbone to be truthful with Jess.

She comes back out and leans down to talk through the window.

'You asked about the asylum seekers. I taped Dalila Alsous's statement. I've listened to it three times. I thought you'd like to. Ought to.'

Warlow takes the offered USB stick and puts it in his pocket.

When he drives away, he sees her standing in the drive, waving. Cadi gives a little whine.

'It's okay, girl. Come on, let's go home.'

CHAPTER FIFTY

THE ATMOSPHERE in the Incident Room is different. There have been big wins and significant losses. But everyone knows the wins outweigh the losses even when that loss is one of their own. At the front, Superintendent Sion Buchannan is the master of ceremonies once again. At his side, DI Jess Allanby, looking smart and capable in a grey suit. She must use something expensive on her skin because a summer glow shines against the starchy white of her blouse whereas the men around her are all as pasty as is appropriate for a British winter. Of course, nothing stops men from using cosmetic products. But they're still men. And this is West Wales.

Buchannan speaks.

'First of all I want to thank each and every person in this room for their hard work over the last couple of weeks. Eventful doesn't even come close. Both Ben and Rylan Gower are in custody. What we need to concentrate on is establishing links between the Gowers, Kieron Thomas and Morris. In addition, and I realise this is not going to be palatable to some of you, we must investigate Mel Lewis too. His bank records show separate accounts, two using only his middle name of Tudor. Both contain six figure sums. Most of the deposits come from the Gowers' business account so there's plenty of work to do. We need to trace any other contacts Ben Gower had locally. If he's travelled outside the area, I want to know where to and when. Same for Rylan Gower.

'We're going through Mel Lewis's emails and his computer logs. We already have CCTV of his car in Pembroke the night Kieron Thomas died. That in itself would not raise any suspicions but we need to consider that it is relevant to events. Jess, do you want to bring us up to speed on the cannabis farm?'

Jess does that. On the one hand she's keen to keep up the momentum. Closing down the cannabis lab will hurt whoever is behind the operation. But she and the Chief Constable want more. She has a meeting set up with the regional task force in organised crime and underlines what Buchannan has said already. But her main thrust is with the harvesters. The imprisoned foreign nationals who were held against their will and forced to pick and package the drugs.

'We're tracing names. Trying to get information back to relatives who must, by now, have assumed their loved ones were missing or dead. Ben Gower admits to the farm being operational for upwards of six years. Prior to that, they used the tunnels to smuggle in drugs. Presumably, the Pickerings were getting too nosy. Seeing things they should not have seen. '

She lets that sink in, gratified to see the look of distaste on everyone's face. 'Prelim interviews on the immigrants at the farm indicate that the longest some of them have been there is five years. We have no idea what happened to the people there before that. Suffice to say we're getting a cadaver dog team over to the farm.'

A hard, dead silence follows this pronouncement.

'We've been allocated extra funding from Border Control and Immigration and we'll need to liaise with them. Catrin will be allocating tasks as soon as we finish here. But I also want to echo what Mr Buchannan has said. There's a way to go but great job everyone.'

The room erupts in applause. When it dies down, Jess asks for questions. Rhys is the first to put his hand up but looks around nervously before speaking.

'One thing that's been niggling me about the scaffolding. It's supposed to have blown over and fallen on Marcus. But I checked with the scaffolders. A new scaffolding board weighs nearly twenty kilos. A six and half metre pole almost thirty.'

'What are you thinking, Rhys?'

'A mate of mine does engineering. He did some calculations for the size and weight of the scaffolding. There was wind that day, but not enough to lift that kind of structure. But, he said that if the thing got a nudge so that wind could get underneath …'

'A nudge?' Jess frowns. 'From what?'

'From Ben Gower's tractor.'

'But he rescued Marcus,' Catrin says.

Rhys nods. 'Yeah, but he wasn't expecting Isabelle Ramsden to turn up as quickly as she did. He'd have no choice but to help. Marcus broke his leg but it could easily have been a lot worse. If he'd died then Izzy Ramsden would've lost interest in the Engine House.'

A hush falls as they all consider this. No one speaks until another DS whispers, 'Jesus.'

It's not meant as a prayer but to Jess's ears sounds very much like one in light of yet another example of how far Ben Gower has fallen. Not so much from grace, but into the darkness.

No one in this room doubts the existence of evil and its many guises.

Buchannan speaks. 'I can't see Gower admitting to that. He's not said anything other than "no comment" so far. But worth flagging up to forensics. See if they can pick anything up from the tractor.'

He exhales and takes a deep breath in before finishing. 'This started out as an investigation into the deaths of Marjorie and Kenneth Pickering, but it's blown up into something much bigger. I'd like to echo DI Allanby's words of congratulations. When circumstances allow, I can assure you that we will celebrate this. And you'll all need taxis home.'

Everyone knows the circumstances are Mel Lewis. Even so, Buchannan's words are greeted with smiles and laughs and murmurs of approval. It's a good day.

The superintendent turns to Jess. 'Once you're done here, I'd like to see you and the rest of the team in my office.'

'Of course, sir.'

'Where's Evan?'

'He's not here. I ... he's having second thoughts.'

Buchannan drops his head. 'I thought for one minute that we'd got him back.'

'Sir, is there something I should know?'

Buchannan quells her with a look. It tells Jess two things, that there is something and that she does not as yet have the right to know.

'Shall we say ten minutes.' It's a statement rather than a request from Buchannan.

Jess watches him go and hides her disappointment. 'Oh, Evan,' she mutters to herself.

DS Richards is within earshot. 'Isn't DCI Warlow coming in, ma'am?'

Jess shakes her head.

'Such a shame. I know he can be a bit ...'

'Uncompromising?' Jess offers the word with a grin

knowing it's a euphemism for an obstinate, undemonstrative cynic.

Catrin nods. 'He helped me a lot when I was a newbie. Not many people would have done that.'

'No, they wouldn't,' agrees Jess with such feeling that it earns a sideways look from the sergeant. But suddenly Jess is all business. 'Come on, fetch Rhys. Superintendent Buchannan wants a word.'

CHAPTER FIFTY-ONE

WARLOW TAKES a volley of calls over the next few days. All are congratulatory. Those from the press he doesn't answer. But one from the Deputy Chief Constable he does.

'I don't need to tell you all how huge this is. TARIAN almost wet themselves over it.'

Warlow has to think for a moment because if there's one thing the police like doing, it's giving teams and ops code names. This one is particularly appropriate. Tarian means shield in Welsh and is a multi-force Regional Organised Crime Unit, part funded by the Home Office, staffed by Dyfed-Powys, Gwent and South Wales Police.

'And since I am the regional coordinator for modern slavery, it's a feather in my cap, too. You lot are shining examples of multi-disciplinary working. The downside is that there will be a press conference and you are all expected to be there.'

Warlow doesn't hesitate in replying. 'I don't think so, ma'am.'

'But you were in on this case from the outset, Evan. You deserve it.'

'There are others much more deserving than me.'

'So you prefer to be our man in the shadows. The puppet master.'

'Not sure if I like that either,' Warlow mutters.

The DCC snorts. 'No, perhaps not. But the offer still stands. The Chief Constable will also be ringing you. Perhaps he can convince you if I can't.'

'I doubt it.'

He can't. And neither can Sion Buchannan. The one person who doesn't ring is Jess Allanby. But then why should she? He's said his piece. But that doesn't blunt his disappointment.

On the morning of Mel Lewis's funeral, Warlow wears his most sober suit but can't find his wallet. Most of the time he keeps a credit card hidden in the car for fuel and gets by with this for days at a time. The policeman in him knows it's mad to do such a thing, but he still does it. Accepts it as part of his moral decline. The wallet only comes out on special occasions. The last time he had it was when he went to the Allanby's. He goes to his wardrobe and fishes it out of the pocket of his good jeans and what comes with it is the thumb drive Jess gave him.

Outside, it's a bright, bitter day, the sky a washed-out blue with scudding high clouds. Cadi has been walked and she's content in her basket. The funeral is at ten thirty. He's showered and on his second cup of coffee with half an hour to spare when he fires up his laptop and slides in the USB stick.

It's a sound-only file, dictated for a secretary to type up and add on to HOLMES, Warlow concludes. She could have sent him that typed note, but she wants him to listen instead. He opens the file presses play and listens to Jess's voice.

. . .

STATEMENT OF DALILA ALSOUS, read and confirmed as correct by DI Jess Allanby, DS Catrin Richards, Tarej Allanham, translator.

My name is Dalila Alsous. I am from Idlib in Syria. Before the war came in 2015, we had a good life. My husband was a teacher and we had a pleasant apartment. Samir was five when the war started. When the bombs dropped in our neighbourhood, we knew we had to leave. My husband took us to Lebanon, to the refugee camp there. It was not a very nice place. We were always insulted. No respect shown to my husband or me. There were fights and robberies and rapes. We could not stay there.

We had some money and my husband got us on a ferry to Turkey. We stayed there for two months. Yusuf found work in a clothing factory, but they paid him only half what they paid the Turkish workers. It was very hard. In the end Yusuf paid a smuggler $2000 to get us to Greece. It was not a good journey. Forty of us in a lorry with no windows for four hours, then a boat that held twenty people only. It was dark and cold, the smuggler took the boat out into the sea and then got off onto another boat. He made one passenger drive our boat but he did not know the way. We were in that boat for six hours. Just a blow-up boat. We were sinking when we saw the island. It was called Lesbos. People came to help us. Two refugees drowned.

In Greece, we stayed only two weeks because Samir was not well. He had a cough and we needed medicine. But we got help from a doctor there who was kind. But Yusuf wanted us to come west. We took many boats and trains and buses but also walked. So far we walked on the Ant road like so many others. Always away from towns so that the police would not see us. Up through Hungary until we got a bus to Budapest and then a train that took us to France.

In the Calais jungle, it was the worst. Only one meal a day. It was early in the year and freezing. Much colder than Idlib. We found some other people who had tried to come across to England on lorries but they had all failed. Then Yusuf met the Afghan Pavir. He said he could get us to England for 7000 dollars each. It was all the money we had. It took a long time to arrange. Three months before the weather was good enough. When it was time, they drove us to a beach where there was grass out into the sea. We had to walk to a small boat. But it was good weather and we got across the sea to Folkestone.

When we got to the other side I was so happy. We were all happy. But there were other men there who told us we had to go with them to be safe. It was a big lorry with only canvas sides. Very uncomfortable. No food or water. Yusuf was angry. When he argued with the men, one of them hit him and broke his nose. I knew then that this was not a good deal. We arrived somewhere in the dark. Again by the sea. But it smelled not the same as Folkestone. Another boat. Better than those from Calais. When the boat stopped, we were made to climb up a ladder into a big space in the side of a mountain in the sea. Inside was the farm.

It was not like a farm where there is sky and sun. This was in the caves. Bright lights and many plants. All needed to be watered and tended. At first, Samir stayed with us every day, but it was not a place for him. Never hot food. And never enough. The farmer – that was what we called him – had a gun. He would sometimes shoot seagulls to show us what he could do and that the gun was real.

Once when Samir was playing he knocked over some plants. The farmer got very angry. He said he would throw Samir into the sea from the cave if we could not control him. But he was only a little boy. My husband decided we would need to get away. In the sleeping room, there was a hole in the wall. A small hole. One night, Yusuf, cleared away some stones. He was going to get us out. He found the way to make the hole bigger and said there were tunnels on the other side. He put Samir through first, but then the stones fell and blocked the way, leaving only a small hole through which we could hold Samir's hand. Yusuf decided he must find Samir by the other way. But no one had ever tried to leave that way because we were many feet above the sea and the rocks beneath. A hundred feet below the top of the cliff. In the third cave of plants, there was a way through to the outside, but only to a ledge above the water.

One night, two years ago, Yusuf left. I have not seen him since. Samir had to live outside the sleeping room in the tunnel. I could give him food and we could talk, but he was alone. I was alone. It broke my heart. He used to tell me of the big house above us. The ruin. He said there were other houses too. And lately one where a kind woman would leave food out for him. Before that he would steal food from the farmer or those who came to the houses. What they threw away. He would do that at night when it was quiet.

When the police came, the man and the woman, I knew we would be saved. If I had my chance again, I would have picked up the farmer's gun and shot him. He treated us like animals. Worse than animals. When some others were too weak, they took them away. I don't want to think about what happened to them. But I know nothing of guns. The police were brave. So was Samir. He can throw stones. His father, when we find him, will be very proud of him.'

There's a noise like papers being put down and then Jess again. 'Will you ask Mrs Alsous one question. Why didn't she tell Samir to find help? Find someone, the authorities.'

A voice repeats the question in a language Warlow does not understand. There's an exchange, and then, a heavily accented male voice comes back in English.

'She says that in Idlib you could not go to the police. It was not safe. There were no authorities. The same in the camps. If you spoke, said the wrong words, it could be very bad for you. Safer to tell Samir to hide in the tunnels.'

WARLOW DOESN'T WANT to listen to it again. But he does. Three times. By the time he powers down his computer something has shifted inside him. The child, Samir, the Follower, might still be in that tunnel with both a dead mother and father if it had not been for him. This isn't hubris. It isn't ego. It's the simple truth. The realisation pierces him like a needle. How many Yusufs might there have been? How many more Samirs? And if even one of them suffered because he was too worried about himself, what sort of a man did that make him?

When Cadi comes to him the second time to nudge him, he buries his face in her fur for a long minute.

Then he gets dressed to help bury the dead.

CHAPTER FIFTY-TWO

IT'S A QUIET FUNERAL. Warlow counts sixty people. Half of those are police officers.

He gets to the crematorium late, his careful arrangements torpedoed by what Jess made him listen to. The last one in, he's pleased that it's a humanist service and that there are no hymns. Mel Lewis was not a hymn kind of guy.

The officiator says some good things about the younger Lewis. Not the murderer, or the slaver, or the man accepting money from organised crime. The one who laughed a lot, made crappy jokes and sent thieves and violent criminals away. The one that everyone prefers to remember.

There's one ex-wife Warlow recognises in the chapel. One younger man that has enough similarity to be Lewis's son. After ten minutes of talking, the coffin disappears behind the curtains, accompanied by Bread of Heaven. And yes, it's a hymn, but it's also a rugby anthem which Warlow has heard Lewis sing a dozen times both sober and drunk. He seems to remember he was more in tune when he was drunk.

Outside, there's a posse awaiting him. Buchannan, Jess, Catrin and Rhys, soberly dressed and huddled in the damp winter air.

Jess smiles on seeing him. 'Hi, Evan.'

'Jess.'

Buchannan nods a greeting. 'Good of you to come.'

'Mel and I, we go back a long way.'

'My place is the closest,' Jess says. 'We're going back for a cuppa, or something stronger.'

'We should have one for his memory. The old Lewis,' Buchannan says.

The others look uncertain. But they're unlikely to object since both their bosses are keen. Warlow could. But Lewis was once a man he considered his friend. Before greed or envy or burn-out poisoned him and made him into what he became.

'Okay,' he says.

Jess's house is only a few minutes' drive. It's a school day for Molly so the house is empty. They all have tea in mugs and Warlow brings in a bottle of Lagavulin from his car and holds it up.

'Mel used to have one of these towards the end of a night. Brought his own in a flask usually as it's too expensive for pubs to stock. I thought about pouring a little out on the grounds of the cemetery, but he'd call me a dozen names, none with over four letters, if he ever found out.'

Jess has some shot glasses. Warlow pours half a thimble full for himself. He sees Catrin isn't happy and Rhys won't look at him. It needs words. He obliges.

'I know that this might not sit right with some of you. I understand that he's implicated in drug smuggling, trafficking, even murder. I'm not mourning that man that he became. If we lived in a different century he'd be hung, drawn and quartered. But I remember a different Lewis. Before the rot set in. Before the job kept him away from his wife and kids for too many nights so that when he got home, he ended up being a stranger. I'm not asking you to forgive him. That can't happen. There is no excuse. But there is a lesson to be learned. So I'll drink to a memory. You prosecute the monster. And let's not have any hard feelings about it either way.'

He offers the bottle again. Catrin puts a hand over her glass and so does Rhys. But Buchannan and Jess do not and Warlow feels a rush of gratitude for that. He pours them both a tiny amount and speaks no more words when he upends the glass. The malt is pure smoke and peat in his throat.

'Thank you,' Warlow says. He screws the top back on the bottle. He will not mourn Lewis anymore.

Catrin has a wistful smile on her lips. 'Funny thing is, Sergeant Lewis was responsible for us first working together, sir.'

He's given up trying to ask her to call him Evan. 'How so?'

'You must remember the junky, McLean. That day we went to Eastgate in Llanelli and she went completely ape-sh … wild. The day she flew at me and you stopped her–'

'You should never have been sent to meet McLean on your own. Caldwell …' Warlow interrupts but puts the brakes on the words he wants to speak. Instead he says, 'He should have known that.'

Catrin looks perplexed. She shrugs. 'DI Caldwell asked Mel Lewis to go and I was supposed to go with him, but he cried off at the last minute. Said it would do me good to go it alone for once.'

Warlow stares at her, his pulse thrumming in his head. Catrin's words prick a balloon that's been swollen tight in his chest for more months that he dares to count. 'But it was Caldwell's case.'

'Yes, but DS Lewis was the one who said he knew

where McLean would be. And then he took a phone call and said he had to leave, that I'd be okay on my own. That's when you offered to go with me.' Catrin's eyes are shining. Whether it's with gratitude or sadness, Warlow can't tell.

He forces a smile but has to turn away. She doesn't need to elaborate because he remembers every second of that encounter. And now he has someone else to blame besides Caldwell. *Mel Lewis. The bent copper. The sloppy police officer.* He stares at a photograph of Jess and Molly on the wall by way of distraction but it doesn't rid him of the memory, so he squeezes his eyes shut and clenches the fist that isn't holding the tea and hopes that no one notices.

Buchannan puts his mug down and clears his throat. 'This is the first time I've had you all in the same room. I've said my thanks and congratulations to you all as individuals. But I'd like to add that congratulations to you as a team.'

Jess raises her mug. Catrin and Rhys do the same, as eventually does Warlow.

Buchannan hasn't finished. 'Now that Evan is here, once the wrinkles are shaken out of this one, I'd like to keep you as a team. We don't have Major Investigation Units as you know, but I've chatted with the Chief Superintendent and he's on board with the idea of establishing rapid response teams for major crime support across the patch. Jess has told me how well you work together, and she would be happy to have you two' – he nods to the two younger officers – 'whenever she catches a case.' He looks up at Warlow. 'So that leaves only you, Evan. Jess needs another few cases as a deputy SIO under her belt. Having you along would be a great asset. As a mentor.'

It's an ambush. And on the way over in the car he's thought hard about it, wondering if he'd have time to say what he ought to.

Here it is. On a bloody plate.

'I had reservations about coming back. The spare wheel. The old codger. The interfering old DCI who would better spend his time walking the dog. I was right. I hated it. Hated finding out that a colleague who I thought of as my friend led me up the garden path. But we none of us are perfect. And you three are great. Dedicated, smart, a credit to the force. Even Rhys, when he remembers to bring his equipment.'

'Never forget again, sir,' says the young DC with feeling.

Warlow snorts a smile. 'I don't think I can teach any of you very much. So I made my mind up that I didn't want to be a hanger-on.'

Jess's eyes fall to her mug.

'But then I listened to Dalila Alsous's story.' He stops and holds Jess's gaze as she looks back up, a little furrow in the space between her eyebrows. What he says next is directed at her. 'You've tested, haven't you?'

Jess knows what he's talking about. Her resigned smile tells him that. 'DNA confirms a paternal match between the body found washed up on Trwyn Crou beach two years ago and Samir Alsous. The floater was Yusuf Alsous, Samir's father. From Dalila's statement, we suspect he fell trying to climb up the cliff face.'

Warlow has run it through his own mind a dozen times since hearing Dalila's statement that morning. He's tried to imagine it, the horror of it. Your six-year-old son, the son you've just pushed through a hole in the bloody wall is lost to you. He's on his own. You can't get to him. But you have to try. Would you climb down to the sea, or up to the clifftop? Either way, it's dark and slippery and who knows what the weather is like. Maybe he fell. Perhaps he jumped into the water. What did Lewis say, anything from an hour to four depending on the sea temperature? They'll check the date with Dalila. And the tides around the Welsh coast are fierce things. Easy to be carried out. Out and along to almost the same place Lewis ends up as fish fodder.

Mel sodding Lewis.

Warlow waits, reading the horror of it reflected in the surrounding faces. Friendly faces doing good things, putting criminals behind bars. Like he should be doing. He inhales some fresh air. 'In a way I wish I hadn't heard her statement. She didn't deserve what happened. Neither did her husband. Neither did her child.'

He stops there because there's more to say. He's rehearsed the caveat many times. The reason he can't. Deep breath, Evan.

But there's something I need to tell you all …

And though it runs through his head like black sand through an hourglass, he says nothing. One day he might tell someone other than Sion Buchannan what he keeps in the locked chamber of his heart. The reason he left the force. The secret he does battle with daily. From the reaction he sees in the others' faces, they have no idea. For the moment it's still his dark little secret.

The silence stretches to several seconds.

'The offer still stands, Evan.' Buchannan bounces the ball back into Warlow's court.

This time, the words that form in Warlow's head find their way out of his mouth. 'I don't know how long I'll be useful for, but if you want me to, I'm willing to help for a few months. Thanks to Dalila Alsous I don't think I could live with myself knowing that I can still make a bloody difference.'

Buchannan grins. Catrin smiles. Rhys makes a triumphant fist.

Jess is the last to look at him. All she does is nod slowly. And though her eyes are shining, she's holding something back. It's the cop in her, Warlow surmises. Suspicion is her stock in trade.

'Good,' says Buchannan. 'Back as DCI?'

'Fine by me,' says Warlow.

And, so help him, it is.

THE END

A FREE BOOK FOR YOU

Visit my website and join up to the Rhys Dylan VIP Reader's Club and get a FREE novella, *The Wolf Hunts Alone*, by visiting: **https://rhysdylan.com**

The Wolf Hunts Alone.

One man and his dog... will track you down.

DCI Evan Warlow is at a crossroads in his life. Living alone, contending with the bad hand fate has dealt him, he finds solace in simple things like walking his neighbour's dog.

But even that is not as safe as it was. Dogs are going missing from a country park. And not only one, now three have disappeared. When he takes it upon himself to root out the cause of the lost animals, Warlow faces ridicule and a thuggish enemy.

But are these simply dog thefts? Or is there a more sinister malevolence at work? One with its sights on bigger, two legged prey.

Only one thing is for certain; Warlow will not rest until he finds out.

———

By joining the club, you will also be the first to hear about new releases via the few but fun emails I'll send you. This includes a no spam promise from me, and you can unsubscribe at any time.

ACKNOWLEDGMENTS

As with all writing endeavours, the existence of this novel depends upon me, the author, and a small army of 'others' who turn an idea into a reality. My wife, Eleri, who gives me the space to indulge my imagination and picks out my stupid mistakes. Sian Phillips, Tim Barber and of course, Martin Davies. Thank you all for your help. Special mention goes to Ela the dog who drags me away from the writing cave and the computer for walks, rain or shine. Actually, she's a bit of a princess so the rain is a no-no. Good dog!

But my biggest thanks goes to you, lovely reader, for being there and actually reading this. It is great to have you along and I do appreciate you spending your time in joining me on this roller-caster ride with Evan and the rest of the team.

CAN YOU HELP?

With that in mind, and if you enjoyed it, I do have a favour to ask. Could you spare a moment to leave a review? A few words will do, but it's really the only way to help others like you discover the books. Probably the best way to help authors you like. Just visit my page on Amazon and leave a few words.

AUTHOR'S NOTE

The Engine House is very much a work of fiction, though the location is very real, perched on the western edge of the ancient kingdom of Dyfed in West Wales. Mwnt and its whitewashed church exist as does the chough walk. But I've taken artistic licence in borrowing the engine house, as depicted, from Cornwall, though lime was transported from west Wales all along the Pembrokeshire and Cardiganshire coasts. If you enjoyed this story there are more to come in the Black Beacons mystery crime series.

Why the Black Beacons?

Spread over 500 square miles, the Brecon Beacons mountain range sits like a giant doorstop at the heads of the South Wales valleys. To the north and west, they nestle in the crook of the ancient kingdoms of Powys and Dyfed, stretching from the eastern borderlands to the wild western coast. Many of the mountain peaks in the range have names. Others are simply referred to as black. It is in this timeless landscape that the books are set.

I'm lucky enough to live in this neck of the woods having moved here in the 1980s. It's an amazing part of the world, full of warm and wonderful people, wild coastlines, golden and craggy mountains. But like everywhere, even this little haven is not immune from the woes of the world. Those of you who've read The Wolf Hunts Alone will know exactly what I mean. And who knows what and who Warlow is going to come up against next! So once again, thank you for sparing your precious time on this new endeavour. I hope I'll get the chance to show you more of this part of the world and that it'll give you the urge to visit.

Not everyone here is a murderer. Not everyone... Cue tense music!

All the best, and see you all soon, Rhys.

READY FOR MORE?

DCI Evan Warlow and the team are back in... CAUTION DEATH AT WORK. You can read on for some sample chapters.

CAUTION DEATH AT WORK - PREVIEW

EVAN WARLOW IS BACK in the saddle as a DCI, though he isn't yet sure he deserves to be, and there are others who share his doubts.

When a brutal attack on two mountain bikers in the vast solitude of the Brechfa forest leaves one dead and the other badly injured, the hunt is on for the killer. And though the evidence points firmly in one direction, soon an open and shut case becomes murky and unclear.

It's not the first-time bad things have happened in these woods. Things that some have tried desperately to forget. But for the killer there's the small matter of unfinished business.

Unless Evan and the team can outwit a vengeful and clever murderer, someone else is sure to die.

Chapter 1 - Preview

'OH MY GOD, Dad, I swear we are going around in circles. I saw that sign to Peniel ten minutes ago.' From the back seat, Amelia Rewston extended her arm over her father's shoulder and pointed through the windscreen at the rusting post opposite.

They'd pulled up at a junction and, much as he hated to admit it, Chris Rewston thought she was probably right. The post leaned precariously to the left and a smear of bird droppings that all but wiped out the 'P' of Peniel helped contribute both to its unique appearance and uselessness as a sign.

Best to confess, Christopher. He gritted his teeth. 'It's the damned young farmers, I tell you. I swear they move the signs for fun.'

'Use the sat nav, Dad.' In the back seat next to his sister, twelve-year-old Benjamin muttered the suggestion without looking up from his Nintendo Switch.

'Can't. No signal up here.'

'You're telling me.' Amelia sat back, arms folded in a sulk, phone face down in her lap. 'Why did we have to come back through this stupid forest, anyway?'

In the passenger seat, Rachel Rewston half turned to contemplate her fourteen-going-on-twenty-year-old daughter. 'It's not a stupid forest. It's Brechfa Forest. And every time we visit your Uncle Peter in New Quay we've promised ourselves that we'd make this run on the way home so you could see it.'

'The trees all look the same,' Amelia muttered.

'It's getting dark, too, Mam,' Ben remarked.

'It wasn't an hour ago. But you wouldn't notice with your nose buried in that thing.' Rachel's comment was a groove in a stuck record.

Ben looked up, frowning. 'It's not a thing, it's Mario Kart.'

'This forest is a national treasure, you two,' Chris said. 'Amazing walking and biking trails. It's ancient. Part of our heritage.'

Amelia let out a long-suffering moan and squeezed her folded arms a little tighter. 'Not the H word again.'

'We're not that far from home now.' Rachel tried appeasement. Her specialist subject as a mother of two. 'We just have to hit the main road.'

'You said that twenty minutes ago.' Amelia sent her a poisonous glare.

'I reckon if we turn left here we should be okay,' Chris mused.

'I'm hungry,' Ben muttered without looking up.

'We all are, *cariad*. Once we get a signal, I'll ring for a pizza. It'll be there by the time we get home. How about that?' Rachel gave him a bright smile.

'Bribery will not work.' Amelia huffed air out through her nostrils.

'Yes it will.' Ben looked up with a perky smile, earning a withering glance from his sister.

The road curved sharply on Chris's right into a blind bend. He eased off the brakes, but slammed them back on with a jerk just as lights lit up the tops of the trimmed hedgerow. Seconds later a red hatchback hurtled around the corner and zoomed past at high revs.

'Wow.' Ben sat up. 'What was that?'

'A death-trap, that's what.' His mother looked across at her husband with alarm.

'They used to hold rallies up here,' Chris explained. 'Some people still think it's a circuit.'

'Can we just go home, please?' Amelia's sigh was deep and prolonged.

Chris turned off onto a lane as narrow and as unlit as all the others they'd navigated for the good part of thirty minutes. Grass had found a foothold and grew down the middle of the tarmac. The way was wide enough for one vehicle only. Ah well, the best laid plans. He had to admit he was hungry too. His brother and sister-in-law had only offered them twee sandwiches and crisps as a snack despite inviting them over for a meal.

Bloody cheapskates. Chris's stomach rumbled. The sandwiches had been hours ago and pizza suddenly sounded wonderful. Especially accompanied by a cold beer. Buoyed by the thought, he pressed on. The hedges were high on both sides, and when they petered out as they climbed and the fields gave way once more to forest, the trees encroached to the very edge of the road. They were what, ten miles from the county town of Carmarthen and major roads? Yet it seemed so remote, with no lights from buildings anywhere around them.

'It's spooky here,' Amelia said, echoing his thoughts.

'Isn't it great to know you can drive a dozen miles from home and find something like this?'

'Yeah, great.' Amelia rolled her eyes. 'Real Eden Lake territory.'

'Have you seen that?' Ben whispered; eyes wide.

Amelia shot her mother a glance. Probably best not to admit it, though she doubted her mum would know anything about horror films.

'Maybe,' Amelia whispered back.

'They say it's sick,' he hissed.

'Shut up, Ben.'

'They say some people actually threw up in the cine—'

He got no chance to finish. Though the road had flattened out ahead of them, well-lit by the SUV's twin beams, Chris held his speed at only twenty, praying that there'd be no more boy racers around. But what he hadn't bargained for was what stumbled out from the trees and staggered into the road thirty yards ahead, making him slam on the brakes for a second time in almost as many minutes.

Amelia screamed.

The car slid to a smooth stop and, for one moment, the only sound was the engine's idling hum.

'Dad, what is that?' Amelia broke the silence.

In the headlights, blinking into the lights, dressed in cycling shorts and a stained fleece that once may have been light blue, crouched a man. Mud caked his legs and smudged his wild, bewildered looking face.

'Stay here.' Chris opened the door.

'Where are you going?' Amelia protested, half a tone short of hysterical.

'That man looks hurt, love.' Rachel turned in her seat to address her daughter.

'He looks like a zombie,' Ben yelped in a voice that made him sound five years younger than he was.

'Shut up.' Amelia rounded on him and slapped him gently on the thigh.

'Just sit tight.' Chris ordered.

'Dad,' Amelia wailed, but by then Chris had both feet on the lane.

He reached into the door's side pocket and took out some gloves. 'Busman's holiday, it looks like.' He smiled weakly at Rachel.

'It's okay, Amelia.' Rachel squeezed Chris's hand. 'Your dad knows what he's doing.'

Chris walked toward the man who'd stood up on shaky legs, swaying with a hand up over his face to ward off the glare of the headlights.

'Hello? Are you okay?' Chris shouted.

The man staggered forward and fell to his knees with a grunt. Chris broke into a trot. Behind, from inside the car, Amelia let out a little squeal of fright.

As he got nearer Chris held a hand out and introduced himself quickly. 'Hi, my name's Chris. I'm a paramedic and I can see you're hurt.'

A pale face, streaked with blood from a matted wound on his scalp, looked up.

'Help,' he croaked.

Chris knelt and put a hand on the man's shoulder. 'What's your name?'

'Rob.'

'Okay, Rob. Have you been in an accident?'

A shivering Rob shook his head.

'So what—'

'I ran ... I ... got away.'

'From what?'

Rob's head dropped between his shoulders and he let out a sob. 'I couldn't do anything. I couldn't help ... It was dark ... I ...' Slowly, he turned his head to glare white-eyed over his shoulder into the dense blackness of the trees behind him. 'We need to get help.'

'Sure. But we need to get somewhere where there's a

signal. It's useless here. I know because we've been trying. We'll get an ambulance. As soon as—'

Rob sent Chris a desperate look and shook his head. 'Too late for an ambulance. We need the police. It's Andy. He's still in there.' He threw a rueful glance over his shoulder into the darkness of the forest.

Chris followed his gaze. 'Andy? Is he lost?'

Rob heaved in a ragged breath. 'Not lost. I think… I think he's dead.'

———

CAUTION DEATH AT WORK
Available now to buy.